EDGAR ALLAN POE was born in Boston on January 18, 1809, the son of theatrical parents. Orphaned at three, he was adopted by the wealthy Mr. and Mrs. John Allan of Richmond, Virginia, in whose family he lived until 1827. He received a good education, first in England, then in a private school at Richmond, and later for a year at the University of Virginia before he ran away to enlist in the army. Between 1827 and 1831, he published three volumes of poetry: *Tamerlane* (1827), *Al Aaraaf* (1829), *Poems* (1831). From 1831 to 1835, he lived in Baltimore, where he began a lifelong struggle with poverty, disappointments in love, and addiction to alcohol. This last defect made it impossible for him to retain the editorial positions he later secured on magazines in Richmond, Philadelphia, and New York—despite the fact that the tales and book reviews he contributed greatly increased circulation. In May, 1836, he married Virginia Clemm, a child of thirteen and the daughter of a paternal aunt. In April, 1844, he moved his family to New York and in January of the following year his literary fortunes turned when his poem "The Raven" appeared in the New York *Evening News*. Overnight, he became the most talked about man of letters in America. Early in 1847, his wife died and the year 1848 saw the end of two unhappy love affairs. He died on October 7, 1849.

THE FALL OF THE

Edgar Allan Poe

HOUSE OF USHER
And Other Tales

WITH AN AFTERWORD BY
R. P. Blackmur

(Revised and Updated
Bibliography)

A SIGNET CLASSIC

SIGNET CLASSIC
Published by the Penguin Group
Penguin Books USA Inc., 375 Hudson Street,
New York, New York 10014, U.S.A.
Penguin Books Ltd, 27 Wrights Lane,
London W8 5TZ, England
Penguin Books Australia Ltd, Ringwood,
Victoria, Australia
Penguin Books Canada Ltd, 10 Alcorn Avenue,
Toronto, Ontario, Canada M4V 3B2
Penguin Books (N.Z.) Ltd, 182–190 Wairau Road,
Auckland 10, New Zealand

Penguin Books Ltd, Registered Offices:
Harmondsworth, Middlesex, England

34 33 32 31 30 29 28 27

Printed in the United States of America

CONTENTS

The Balloon-Hoax

[Astounding News by Express, *viâ* Norfolk!—The Atlantic Crossed in Three Days! Signal Triumph of Mr. Monck Mason's Flying Machine!—Arrival at Sullivan's Island, near Charleston, S. C., of Mr. Mason, Mr. Robert Holland, Mr. Henson, Mr. Harrison Ainsworth, and four others, in the Steering Balloon, "Victoria," after a Passage of Seventy-five Hours from Land to Land! Full Particulars of the Voyage!

The subjoined *jeu d'esprit* with the preceding heading in magnificent capitals, well interspersed with notes of admiration, was originally published, as matter of fact, in the *New York Sun,* a daily newspaper, and therein fully subserved the purpose of creating indigestible aliment for the *quidnuncs* during the few hours intervening between a couple of the Charleston mails. The rush for the "sole paper which had the news," was something beyond even the prodigious; and, in fact, if (as some assert) the "Victoria" *did* not absolutely accomplish the voyage recorded, it will be difficult to assign a reason why she *should* not have accomplished it.]

T HE GREAT PROBLEM is at length solved! The air, as well as the earth and the ocean, has been subdued by science, and will become a common and convenient highway for mankind. *The Atlantic has been actually crossed in a Balloon!* and this too without difficulty—without any great apparent danger—with thorough control of the machine—and in the inconceivably brief period of seventy-five hours from shore to shore! By the energy of an agent at Charleston, S. C., we are enabled to be the first to

furnish the public with a detailed account of this most extraordinary voyage, which was performed between Saturday, the 6th instant, at 11 A.M. and 2 P.M., on Tuesday, the 9th instant, by Sir Everard Bringhurst; Mr. Osborne, a nephew of Lord Bentinck's; Mr. Monck Mason and Mr. Robert Holland, the well-known aëronauts; Mr. Harrison Ainsworth, author of "Jack Sheppard," etc.; and Mr. Henson, the projector of the late unsuccessful flying machine—with two seamen from Woolwich—in all, eight persons. The particulars furnished below may be relied on as authentic and accurate in every respect, as, with a slight exception, they are copied *verbatim* from the joint diaries of Mr. Monck Mason and Mr. Harrison Ainsworth, to whose politeness our agent is also indebted for much verbal information respecting the balloon itself, its construction, and other matters of interest. The only alteration in the MS. received, has been made for the purpose of throwing the hurried account of our Agent, Mr. Forsyth, into a connected and intelligible form.

"THE BALLOON

"Two very decided failures, of late,—those of Mr. Henson and Sir George Cayley,—had much weakened the public interest in the subject of aërial navigation. Mr. Henson's scheme (which at first was considered very feasible even by men of science) was founded upon the principle of an inclined plane, starting from an eminence by an extrinsic force, applied and continued by the revolution of impinging vanes, in form and number resembling the vanes of a windmill. But, in all the experiments made with models at the Adelaide Gallery, it was found that the operation of these fans not only did not propel the machine, but actually impeded its flight. The only propelling force it ever exhibited, was the mere *impetus* acquired from the descent of the inclined plane; and this *impetus* carried the machine farther when the vanes were at rest, than when they were in motion—a fact which sufficiently demonstrates their inutility; and in the absence of the propelling, which was also the *sustaining*, power, the whole fabric would necessarily descend. This consideration led Sir George Cayley to think only of adapting a propeller to some machine having of itself

an independent power of support—in a word, to a balloon; the idea, however, being novel, or original, with Sir George, only so far as regards the mode of its application to practice. He exhibited a model of his invention at the Polytechnic Institution. The propelling principle, or power, was here, also, applied to interrupted surfaces, or vanes, put in revolution. These vanes were four in number, but were found entirely ineffectual in moving the balloon, or in aiding its ascending power. The whole project was thus a complete failure.

"It was at this juncture that Mr. Monck Mason (whose voyage from Dover to Weilburg in the balloon, 'Nassau,' occasioned so much excitement in 1837) conceived the idea of employing the principle of the Archimedean screw for the purpose of propulsion through the air —rightly attributing the failure of Mr. Henson's scheme, and of Sir George Cayley's, to the interruption of surface in the independent vanes. He made the first public experiment at Willis's Rooms, but afterward removed his model to the Adelaide Gallery.

"Like Sir George Cayley's balloon, his own was an ellipsoid. Its length was thirteen feet six inches—height, six feet eight inches. It contained about three hundred and twenty cubic feet of gas, which, if pure hydrogen, would support twenty-one pounds upon its first inflation, before the gas has time to deteriorate or escape. The weight of the whole machine and apparatus was seventeen pounds—leaving about four pounds to spare. Beneath the centre of the balloon, was a frame of light wood, about nine feet long, and rigged on to the balloon itself with a network in the customary manner. From this framework was suspended a wicker basket or car.

"The screw consists of an axis of hollow brass tube, eighteen inches in length, through which, upon a semi-spiral inclined at fifteen degrees, pass a series of steel-wire radii, two feet long, and thus projecting a foot on either side. These radii are connected at the outer extremities by two bands of flattened wire—the whole in this manner forming the framework of the screw, which is completed by a covering of oiled silk cut into gores, and tightened so as to present a tolerably uniform surface. At each end of its axis this screw is supported by pillars of hollow brass tube descending from the hoop. In the lower ends of these tubes are holes in which the

pivots of the axis revolve. From the end of the axis which is next the car, proceeds a shaft of steel, connecting the screw with the pinion of a piece of spring machinery fixed in the car. By the operation of this spring, the screw is made to revolve with great rapidity, communicating a progressive motion to the whole. By means of the rudder, the machine was readily turned in any direction. The spring was of great power, compared with its dimensions, being capable of raising forty-five pounds upon a barrel of four inches diameter, after the first turn, and gradually increasing as it was wound up. It weighed, altogether, eight pounds six ounces. The rudder was a light frame of cane covered with silk, shaped somewhat like a battledore, and was about three feet long, and at the widest, one foot. Its weight was about two ounces. It could be turned *flat*, and directed upward or downward, as well as to the right or left; and thus enabled the aëronaut to transfer the resistance of the air which in an inclined position it must generate in its passage, to any side upon which he might desire to act; thus determining the balloon in the opposite direction.

"This model (which, through want of time, we have necessarily described in an imperfect manner) was put in action at the Adelaide Gallery, where it accomplished a velocity of five miles per hour; although, strange to say, it excited very little interest in comparison with the previous complex machine of Mr. Henson—so resolute is the world to despise any thing which carries with it an air of simplicity. To accomplish the great desideratum of aërial navigation, it was very generally supposed that some exceedingly complicated application must be made of some unusually profound principle in dynamics.

"So well satisfied, however, was Mr. Mason of the ultimate success of his invention, that he determined to construct immediately, if possible, a balloon of sufficient capacity to test the question by a voyage of some extent —the original design being to cross the British Channel, as before, in the Nassau balloon. To carry out his views, he solicited and obtained the patronage of Sir Everard Bringhurst and Mr. Osborne, two gentlemen well known for scientific acquirement, and especially for the interest they have exhibited in the progress of aërostation. The project, at the desire of Mr. Osborne, was kept a profound secret from the public—the only persons entrusted

with the design being those actually engaged in the construction of the machine, which was built (under the superintendence of Mr. Mason, Mr. Holland, Sir Everard Bringhurst, and Mr. Osborne) at the seat of the latter gentleman near Penstruthal, in Wales. Mr. Henson, accompanied by his friend Mr. Ainsworth, was admitted to a private view of the balloon, on Saturday last—when the two gentlemen made final arrangements to be included in the adventure. We are not informed for what reason the two seamen were also included in the party—but, in the course of a day or two, we shall put our readers in possession of the minutest particulars respecting this extraordinary voyage.

"The balloon is composed of silk, varnished with the liquid gum caoutchouc. It is of vast dimensions, containing more than 40,000 cubic feet of gas; but as coal-gas was employed in place of the more expensive and inconvenient hydrogen, the supporting power of the machine, when fully inflated, and immediately after inflation, is not more than about 2500 pounds. The coal-gas is not only much less costly, but is easily procured and managed.

"For its introduction into common use for purposes of aërostation, we are indebted to Mr. Charles Green. Up to his discovery, the process of inflation was not only exceedingly expensive, but uncertain. Two and even three days have frequently been wasted in futile attempts to procure a sufficiency of hydrogen to fill a balloon, from which it had great tendency to escape, owing to its extreme subtlety, and its affinity for the surrounding atmosphere. In a balloon sufficiently perfect to retain its contents of coal-gas unaltered, in quality or amount, for six months, an equal quantity of hydrogen could not be maintained in equal purity for six weeks.

"The supporting power being estimated at 2500 pounds, and the united weights of the party amounting only to about 1200, there was left a surplus of 1300, of which again 1200 was exhausted by ballast, arranged in bags of different sizes, with their respective weights marked upon them—by cordage, barometers, telescopes, barrels containing provision for a fortnight, water-casks, cloaks, carpet-bags, and various other indispensable matters, including a coffee-warmer, contrived for warming coffee by means of slack-lime, so as to dispense altogether with fire, if it should be judged prudent to do so.

All these articles, with the exception of the ballast, and a few trifles, were suspended from the hoop overhead. The car is much smaller and lighter, in proportion, than the one appended to the model. It is formed of a light wicker, and is wonderfully strong, for so frail-looking a machine. Its rim is about four feet deep. The rudder is also very much larger, in proportion, than that of the model; and the screw is considerably smaller. The balloon is furnished besides with a grapnel, and a guide-rope; which latter is of the most indispensable importance. A few words, in explanation, will here be necessary for such of our readers as are not conversant with the details of aërostation.

"As soon as the balloon quits the earth, it is subjected to the influence of many circumstances tending to create a difference in its weight; augmenting or diminishing its ascending power. For example, there may be a deposition of dew upon the silk, to the extent, even, of several hundred pounds; ballast has then to be thrown out, or the machine may descend. This ballast being discarded, and a clear sunshine evaporating the dew, and at the same time expanding the gas in the silk, the whole will again rapidly ascend. To check this ascent, the only resource is (or rather *was,* until Mr. Green's invention of the guide-rope) the permission of the escape of gas from the valve; but, in the loss of gas, is a proportionate general loss of ascending power; so that, in a comparatively brief period, the best-constructed balloon must necessarily exhaust all its resources, and come to the earth. This was the great obstacle to voyages of length.

"The guide-rope remedies the difficulty in the simplest manner conceivable. It is merely a very long rope which is suffered to trail from the car, and the effect of which is to prevent the balloon from changing its level in any material degree. If, for example, there should be a deposition of moisture upon the silk, and the machine begins to descend in consequence, there will be no necessity for discharging ballast to remedy the increase of weight, for it is remedied, or counteracted, in an exactly just proportion, by the deposit on the ground of just so much of the end of the rope as is necessary. If, on the other hand, any circumstances should cause undue levity, and consequent ascent, this levity is immediately counteracted by the additional weight of rope upraised from the earth.

Thus, the balloon can neither ascend nor descend, except within very narrow limits, and its resources, either in gas or ballast, remain comparatively unimpaired. When passing over an expanse of water, it becomes necessary to employ small kegs of copper or wood, filled with liquid ballast of a lighter nature than water. These float, and serve all the purposes of a mere rope on land. Another most important office of the guide-rope, is to point out the *direction* of the balloon. The rope *drags,* either on land or sea, while the balloon is free; the latter, consequently, is always in advance, when any progress whatever is made: a comparison, therefore, by means of the compass, of the relative positions of the two objects, will always indicate the *course*. In the same way, the angle formed by the rope with the vertical axis of the machine, indicates the *velocity*. When there is *no* angle—in other words, when the rope hangs perpendicularly, the whole apparatus is stationary; but the larger the angle, that is to say, the farther the balloon precedes the end of the rope, the greater the velocity; and the converse.

"As the original design was to cross the British Channel, and alight as near Paris as possible, the voyagers had taken the precaution to prepare themselves with passports directed to all parts of the Continent, specifying the nature of the expedition, as in the case of the 'Nassau' voyage, and entitling the adventurers to exemption from the usual formalities of office; unexpected events, however, rendered these passports superfluous.

"The inflation was commenced very quietly at daybreak, on Saturday morning, the 6th instant, in the courtyard of Wheal-Vor House, Mr. Osborne's seat, about a mile from Penstruthal, in North Wales; and at seven minutes past eleven, every thing being ready for departure, the balloon was set free, rising gently but steadily, in a direction nearly south; no use being made, for the first half hour, of either the screw or the rudder. We proceed now with the journal, as transcribed by Mr. Forsyth from the joint MSS. of Mr. Monck Mason and Mr. Ainsworth. The body of the journal, as given, is in the handwriting of Mr. Mason, and a P. S. is appended, each day, by Mr. Ainsworth, who has in preparation, and will shortly give the public a more minute and, no doubt, a thrillingly interesting account of the voyage.

"THE JOURNAL"

"Saturday, April the 6th.—Every preparation likely to
embarrass us having been made overnight, we com-
menced the inflation this morning at daybreak; but ow-
ing to a thick fog, which encumbered the folds of the silk
and rendered it unmanageable, we did not get through be-
fore nearly eleven o'clock. Cut loose, then, in high spirits,
and rose gently but steadily, with a light breeze at north,
which bore us in the direction of the British Channel.
Found the ascending force greater than we had expected;
and as we arose higher and so got clear of the cliffs, and
more in the sun's rays, our ascent became very rapid. I
did not wish, however, to lose gas at so early a period
of the adventure, and so concluded to ascend for the pres-
ent. We soon ran out our guide-rope; but even when we
had raised it clear of the earth, we still went up very
rapidly. The balloon was unusually steady, and looked
beautiful. In about ten minutes after starting, the barom-
eter indicated an altitude of 15,000 feet. The weather
was remarkably fine, and the view of the subjacent coun-
try—a most romantic one when seen from any point—
was now especially sublime. The numerous deep gorges
presented the appearance of lakes, on account of the
dense vapors with which they were filled, and the pin-
nacles and crags to the southeast, piled in inextricable
confusion, resembling nothing so much as the giant cities
of Eastern fable. We were rapidly approaching the moun-
tains in the south, but our elevation was more than suf-
ficient to enable us to pass them in safety. In a few min-
utes we soared over them in fine style; and Mr. Ains-
worth, with the seamen, was surprised at their apparent
want of altitude when viewed from the car, the tendency
of great elevation in a balloon being to reduce inequalities
of the surface below, to nearly a dead level. At half-past
eleven still proceeding nearly south, we obtained our first
view of the Bristol Channel; and, in fifteen minutes
afterward, the line of breakers on the coast appeared
immediately beneath us, and we were fairly out at sea.
We now resolved to let off enough gas to bring our guide-
rope, with the buoys affixed, into the water. This was
immediately done, and we commenced a gradual descent.
In about twenty minutes our first buoy dipped, and at

the touch of the second soon afterward, we remained stationary as to elevation. We were all now anxious to test the efficiency of the rudder and screw, and we put them both into requisition forthwith, for the purpose of altering our direction more to the eastward, and in a line for Paris. By means of the rudder we instantly effected the necessary change of direction, and our course was brought nearly at right angles to that of the wind; when we set in motion the spring of the screw, and were rejoiced to find it propel us readily as desired. Upon this we gave nine hearty cheers, and dropped in the sea a bottle, inclosing a slip of parchment with a brief account of the principle of the invention. Hardly, however, had we done with our rejoicings, when an unforeseen accident occurred which discouraged us in no little degree. The steel rod connecting the spring with the propeller was suddenly jerked out of place, at the car end, (by a swaying of the car through some movement of one of the two seamen we had taken up,) and in an instant hung dangling out of reach, from the pivot of the axis of the screw. While we were endeavoring to regain it, our attention being completely absorbed, we became involved in a strong current of wind from the east, which bore us, with rapidly increasing force, toward the Atlantic. We soon found ourselves driving out to sea at the rate of not less, certainly, than fifty or sixty miles an hour, so that we came up with Cape Clear, at some forty miles to our north, before we had secured the rod, and had time to think what we were about. It was now that Mr. Ainsworth made an extraordinary but, to my fancy, a by no means unreasonable or chimerical proposition, in which he was instantly seconded by Mr. Holland—viz.: that we should take advantage of the strong gale which bore us on, and in place of beating back to Paris, make an attempt to reach the coast of North America. After slight reflection I gave a willing assent to this bold proposition, which (strange to say) met with objection from the two seamen only. As the stronger party, however, we overruled their fears, and kept resolutely upon our course. We steered due west; but as the trailing of the buoys materially impeded our progress, and we had the balloon abundantly at command, either for ascent or descent, we first threw out fifty pounds of ballast, and then wound up (by means of a windlass) so much of the rope as

brought it quite clear of the sea. We perceived the effect of this manœuvre immediately, in a vastly increased rate of progress; and, as the gale freshened, we flew with a velocity nearly inconceivable; the guide-rope flying out behind the car, like a streamer from a vessel. It is needless to say that a very short time sufficed us to lose sight of the coast. We passed over innumerable vessels of all kinds, a few of which were endeavoring to beat up, but the most of them lying to. We occasioned the greatest excitement on board all—an excitement greatly relished by ourselves, and especially by our two men, who, now under the influence of a dram of Geneva, seemed resolved to give all scruple, or fear, to the wind. Many of the vessels fired signal guns; and in all we were saluted with loud cheers (which we heard with surprising distinctness) and the waving of caps and handkerchiefs. We kept on in this manner throughout the day with no material incident, and, as the shades of night closed around us, we made a rough estimate of the distance traversed. It could not have been less than five hundred miles, and was probably much more. The propeller was kept in constant operation, and, no doubt, aided our progress materially. As the sun went down, the gale freshened into an absolute hurricane, and the ocean beneath was clearly visible on account of its phosphorescence. The wind was from the east all night, and gave us the brightest omen of success. We suffered no little from cold, and the dampness of the atmosphere was most unpleasant; but the ample space in the car enabled us to lie down, and by means of cloaks and a few blankets we did sufficiently well.

"P. S. [by Mr. Ainsworth.] The last nine hours have been unquestionably the most exciting of my life. I can conceive nothing more sublimating than the strange peril and novelty of an adventure such as this. May God grant that we succeed! I ask not success for mere safety to my insignificant person, but for the sake of human knowledge and—for the vastness of the triumph. And yet the feat is only so evidently feasible that the sole wonder is why men have scrupled to attempt it before. One single gale such as now befriends us—let such a tempest whirl forward a balloon for four or five days (these gales often last longer) and the voyager will be easily borne, in that period, from coast to coast. In view

of such a gale the broad Atlantic becomes a mere lake. I am more struck, just now, with the supreme silence which reigns in the sea beneath us, notwithstanding its agitation, than with any other phenomenon presenting itself. The waters give up no voice to the heavens. The immense flaming ocean writhes and is tortured uncomplainingly. The mountainous surges suggest the idea of innumerable dumb gigantic fiends struggling in impotent agony. In a night such as is this to me, a man *lives*—lives a whole century of ordinary life—nor would I forego this rapturous delight for that of a whole century of ordinary existence.

"*Sunday, the 7th.* [Mr. Mason's MS.] This morning the gale, by ten, had subsided to an eight- or nine-knot breeze (for a vessel at sea), and bears us, perhaps, thirty miles per hour, or more. It has veered, however, very considerably to the north; and now, at sundown, we are holding our course due west, principally by the screw and rudder, which answer their purposes to admiration. I regard the project as thoroughly successful, and the easy navigation of the air in any direction (not exactly in the teeth of a gale) as no longer problematical. We could not have made head against the strong wind of yesterday; but, by ascending, we might have got out of its influence, if requisite. Against a pretty stiff breeze, I feel convinced, we can make our way with the propeller. At noon, to-day, ascended to an elevation of nearly 25,000 feet, by discharging ballast. Did this to search for a more direct current, but found none so favorable as the one we are now in. We have an abundance of gas to take us across this small pond, even should the voyage last three weeks. I have not the slightest fear for the result. The difficulty has been strangely exaggerated and misapprehended. I can choose my current, and should I find *all* currents against me, I can make very tolerable headway with the propeller. We have had no incidents worth recording. The night promises fair.

"P. S. [By Mr. Ainsworth.] I have little to record, except the fact (to me quite a surprising one) that, at an elevation equal to that of Cotopaxi, I experienced neither very intense cold, nor headache, nor difficulty of breathing; neither, I find, did Mr. Mason, nor Mr. Holland, nor Sir Everard. Mr. Osborne complained of constriction of the chest—but this soon wore off. We have

flown at a great rate during the day, and we must be
more than half way across the Atlantic. We have passed
over some twenty or thirty vessels of various kinds, and
all seem to be delightfully astonished. Crossing the
ocean in a balloon is not so difficult a feat after all.
Omne ignotum pro magnifico. Mem.: at 25,000 feet
elevation the sky appears nearly black, and the stars are
distinctly visible; while the sea does not seem convex
(as one might suppose) but absolutely and most un-
equivocally *concave.*[1]

 "*Monday, the 8th.* [Mr. Mason's MS.] This morn-
ing we had again some little trouble with the rod of the
propeller, which must be entirely remodelled, for fear
of serious accident—I mean the steel rod, not the vanes.
The latter could not be improved. The wind has been
blowing steadily and strongly from the northeast all day;
and so far fortune seems bent upon favoring us. Just be-
fore day, we were all somewhat alarmed at some odd
noises and concussions in the balloon, accompanied with
the apparent rapid subsidence of the whole machine.
These phenomena were occasioned by the expansion of
the gas, through increase of heat in the atmosphere, and
the consequent disruption of the minute particles of ice
with which the network had become encrusted during
the night. Threw down several bottles to the vessels below.
See one of them picked up by a large ship—seemingly

[1] "*Note*—Mr. Ainsworth has not attempted to account for this
phenomenon, which, however, is quite susceptible of explana-
tion. A line dropped from an elevation of 25,000 feet, per-
pendicularly to the surface of the earth (or sea), would form the
perpendicular of a right-angled triangle, of which the base would
extend from the right angle to the horizon, and the hy-
pothenuse from the horizon to the balloon. But the 25,000 feet
of altitude is little or nothing, in comparison with the extent
of the prospect. In other words, the base and hypothenuse of
the supposed triangle would be so long, when compared with
the perpendicular, that the two former may be regarded as
nearly parallel. In this manner the horizon of the aëronaut
would appear to be *on a level* with the car. But, as the point
immediately beneath him seems, and is, at a great distance be-
low him, it seems, of course, also, at a great distance below the
horizon. Hence the impression of *concavity;* and this impression
must remain, until the elevation shall bear so great a proportion
to the extent of prospect, that the apparent parallelism of the
base and hypothenuse disappears—when the earth's real convex-
ity must become apparent.

one of the New York line packets. Endeavored to make out her name, but could not be sure of it. Mr. Osborne's telescope made it out something like 'Atalanta.' It is now twelve at night, and we are still going nearly west, at a rapid pace. The sea is peculiarly phosphorescent.

"P. S. [By Mr. Ainsworth.] It is now two A.M., and nearly calm, as well as I can judge—but it is very difficult to determine this point, since we move *with* the air so completely. I have not slept since quitting Wheal-Vor, but can stand it no longer, and must take a nap. We cannot be far from the American coast.

"*Tuesday, the 9th.* [Mr. Ainsworth's MS.] *One* P.M. *We are in full view of the low coast of South Carolina.* The great problem is accomplished. We have crossed the Atlantic—fairly and *easily* crossed it in a balloon! God be praised! Who shall say that any thing is impossible hereafter?"

The Journal here ceases. Some particulars of the descent were communicated, however, by Mr. Ainsworth to Mr. Forsyth. It was nearly dead calm when the voyagers first came in view of the coast, which was immediately recognized by both the seamen, and by Mr. Osborne. The latter gentleman having acquaintances at Fort Moultrie, it was immediately resolved to descend in its vicinity. The balloon was brought over the beach (the tide being out and the sand hard, smooth, and admirably adapted for a descent), and the grapnel let go, which took firm hold at once. The inhabitants of the island, and of the fort, thronged out, of course, to see the balloon; but it was with the greatest difficulty that any one could be made to credit the actual voyage—*the crossing of the Atlantic.* The grapnel caught at two P.M. precisely; and thus the whole voyage was completed in seventy-five hours; or rather less, counting from shore to shore. No serious accident occurred. No real danger was at any time apprehended. The balloon was exhausted and secured without trouble; and when the MS. from which this narrative is compiled was despatched from Charleston, the party were still at Fort Moultrie. Their further intentions were not ascertained; but we can safely promise our readers some additional information

either on Monday or in the course of the next day, at furthest.

This is unquestionably the most stupendous, the most interesting, and the most important undertaking ever accomplished or even attempted by man. What magnificent events may ensue, it would be useless now to think of determining.

Ms. Found in a Bottle

Qui n'a plus qu'un moment à vivre
N'a plus rien à dissimuler. *Quinault—Atys*

O F MY COUNTRY and of my family I have little to say.
Ill usage and length of years have driven me from the
one, and estranged me from the other. Hereditary wealth
afforded me an education of no common order, and a
contemplative turn of mind enabled me to methodise the
stores which early study diligently garnered up. Beyond
all things, the works of the German moralists gave me
great delight; not from my ill-advised admiration of their
eloquent madness, but from the ease with which my
habits of rigid thoughts enabled me to detect their falsi-
ties. I have often been reproached with the aridity of my
genius; a deficiency of imagination has been imputed to
me as a crime; and the Pyrrhonism of my opinions has
at all times rendered me notorious. Indeed, a strong
relish for physical philosophy has, I fear, tinctured my
mind with a very common error of this age—I mean
the habit of referring occurrences, even the least sus-
ceptible of such reference, to the principles of that
science. Upon the whole, no person could be less liable
than myself to be led away from the severe precincts of
truth by the *ignes fatui* of superstition. I have thought
proper to premise this much, lest the incredible tale I
have to tell should be considered rather the raving of a
crude imagination, than the positive experience of a mind
to which the reveries of fancy have been a dead letter and
a nullity.

After many years spent in foreign travel, I sailed in
the year 18—, from the port of Batavia, in the rich and
populous island of Java, on a voyage to the Archipelago

Islands. I went as passenger—having no other induce-
ment than a kind of nervous restlessness which haunted
me as a fiend.

Our vessel was a beautiful ship of about four hundred
tons, copper-fastened, and built at Bombay of Malabar
teak. She was freighted with cotton-wool and oil, from the
Lachadive Islands. We had also on board coir, jaggeree,
ghee, cocoanuts, and a few cases of opium. The stowage
was clumsily done, and the vessel consequently crank.

We got under way with a mere breath of wind, and
for many days stood along the eastern coast of Java,
without any other incident to beguile the monotony of
our course than the occasional meeting with some of
the small grabs of the Archipelago to which we were
bound.

One evening, leaning over the taffrail, I observed a
very singular isolated cloud, to the N. W. It was re-
markable, as well from its color as from its being the
first we had seen since our departure from Batavia. I
watched it attentively until sunset, when it spread all at
once to the eastward and westward, girting in the hori-
zon with a narrow strip of vapor, and looking like a long
line of low beach. My notice was soon afterward at-
tracted by the dusky-red appearance of the moon, and
the peculiar character of the sea. The latter was under-
going a rapid change, and the water seemed more than
usually transparent. Although I could distinctly see the
bottom, yet, heaving the lead, I found the ship in fifteen
fathoms. The air now became intolerably hot, and was
loaded with spiral exhalations similar to those arising
from heated iron. As night came on, every breath of
wind died away, and a more entire calm it is impossible
to conceive. The flame of a candle burned upon the
poop without the least perceptible motion, and a long
hair, held between the finger and thumb, hung without
the possibility of detecting a vibration. However, as the
captain said he could perceive no indication of danger,
and as we were drifting in bodily to shore, he ordered
the sails to be furled, and the anchor let go. No watch
was set, and the crew, consisting principally of Malays,
stretched themselves deliberately upon deck. I went be-
low—not without a full presentiment of evil. Indeed, every
appearance warranted me in apprehending a simoon. I
told the captain of my fears; but he paid no attention to

what I said, and left me without deigning to give a reply. My uneasiness, however, prevented me from sleeping, and about midnight I went upon deck. As I placed my foot upon the upper step of the companion-ladder, I was startled by a loud, humming noise, like that occasioned by the rapid revolution of a mill-wheel, and before I could ascertain its meaning, I found the ship quivering to its centre. In the next instant a wilderness of foam hurled us upon our beam-ends, and, rushing over us fore and aft, swept the entire decks from stem to stern.

The extreme fury of the blast proved, in a great measure, the salvation of the ship. Although completely water-logged, yet, as her masts had gone by the board, she rose, after a minute, heavily from the sea, and, staggering awhile beneath the immense pressure of the tempest, finally righted.

By what miracle I escaped destruction, it is impossible to say. Stunned by the shock of the water, I found myself, upon recovery, jammed in between the stern-post and rudder. With great difficulty I regained my feet and looking dizzily around, was at first struck with the idea of our being among breakers; so terrific, beyond the wildest imagination, was the whirlpool of mountainous and foaming ocean within which we were engulfed. After a while I heard the voice of an old Swede, who had shipped with us at the moment of leaving port. I hallooed to him with all my strength, and presently he came reeling aft. We soon discovered that we were the sole survivors of the accident. All on deck, with the exception of ourselves, had been swept overboard; the captain and mates must have perished while they slept, for the cabins were deluged with water. Without assistance we could expect to do little for the security of the ship, and our exertions were at first paralyzed by the momentary expectation of going down. Our cable had, of course, parted like pack-thread, at the first breath of the hurricane, or we should have been instantaneously overwhelmed. We scudded with frightful velocity before the sea, and the water made clear breaches over us. The framework of our stern was shattered excessively, and, in almost every respect, we had received considerable injury; but to our extreme joy we found the pumps unchoked, and that we had made no great shifting of our

ballast. The main fury of the blast had already blown over, and we apprehended little danger from the violence of the wind; but we looked forward to its total cessation with dismay; well believing, that in our shattered condition, we should inevitably perish in the tremendous swell which would ensue. But this very just apprehension seemed by no means likely to be soon verified. For five entire days and nights—during which our only subsistence was a small quantity of jaggeree, procured with great difficulty from the forecastle—the hulk flew at a rate defying computation, before rapidly succeeding flaws of wind, which, without equalling the first violence of the simoon, were still more terrific than any tempest I had before encountered. Our course for the first four days was, with trifling variations, S. E. and by S.; and we must have run down the coast of New Holland. On the fifth day the cold became extreme, although the wind had hauled round a point more to the northward. The sun arose with a sickly yellow lustre, and clambered a very few degrees above the horizon—emitting no decisive light. There were no clouds apparent, yet the wind was upon the increase, and blew with a fitful and unsteady fury. About noon, as nearly as we could guess, our attention was again arrested by the appearance of the sun. It gave out no light, properly so called, but a dull and sullen glow without reflection, as if all its rays were polarized. Just before sinking within the turgid sea, its central fires suddenly went out, as if hurriedly extinguished by some unaccountable power. It was a dim, silver-like rim, alone, as it rushed down the unfathomable ocean.

We waited in vain for the arrival of the sixth day—that day to me has not yet arrived—to the Swede never did arrive. Thenceforward we were enshrouded in pitch darkness, so that we could not have seen an object at twenty paces from the ship. Eternal night continued to envelop us, all unrelieved by the phosphoric sea-brilliancy to which we had been accustomed in the tropics. We observed, too, that, although the tempest continued to rage with unabated violence, there was no longer to be discovered the usual appearance of surf, or foam, which had hitherto attended us. All around were horror, and thick gloom, and a black sweltering desert of ebony. Superstitious terror crept by degrees into the spirit of

the old Swede, and my own soul was wrapt in silent wonder. We neglected all care of the ship, as worse than useless, and securing ourselves as well as possible, to the stump of the mizen-mast, looked out bitterly into the world of ocean. We had no means of calculating time, nor could we form any guess of our situation. We were, however, well aware of having made farther to the southward than any previous navigators, and felt great amazement at not meeting with the usual impediments of ice. In the meantime every moment threatened to be our last—every mountainous billow hurried to overwhelm us. The swell surpassed anything I had imagined possible, and that we were not instantly buried is a miracle. My companion spoke of the lightness of our cargo, and reminded me of the excellent qualities of our ship; but I could not help feeling the utter hopelessness of hope itself, and prepared myself gloomily for that death which I thought nothing could defer beyond an hour, as, with every knot of way the ship made, the swelling of the black stupendous seas became more dismally appalling. At times we gasped for breath at an elevation beyond the albatross—at times became dizzy with the velocity of our descent into some watery hell, where the air grew stagnant, and no sound disturbed the slumbers of the kraken.

We were at the bottom of one of these abysses, when a quick scream from my companion broke fearfully upon the night. "See! see!" cried he, shrieking in my ears, "Almighty God! see! see!" As he spoke I became aware of a dull sullen glare of red light which streamed down the sides of the vast chasm where we lay, and threw a fitful brilliancy upon our deck. Casting my eyes upwards, I beheld a spectacle which froze the current of my blood. At a terrific height directly above us, and upon the very verge of the precipitous descent, hovered a gigantic ship of perhaps four thousand tons. Although upreared upon the summit of a wave more than a hundred times her own altitude, her apparent size still exceeded that of any ship of the line or East Indiaman in existence. Her huge hull was of a deep dingy black, unrelieved by any of the customary carvings of a ship. A single row of brass cannon protruded from her open ports, and dashed from the polished surfaces the fires of innumerable battle-lanterns which swung to and fro about her rig-

ging. But what mainly inspired us with horror and astonishment, was that she bore up under a press of sail in the very teeth of that supernatural sea, and of that ungovernable hurricane. When we first discovered her, her bows were alone to be seen, as she rose slowly from the dim and horrible gulf beyond her. For a moment of intense terror she paused upon the giddy pinnacle as if in contemplation of her own sublimity, then trembled, and tottered, and—came down.

At this instant, I know not what sudden self-possession came over my spirit. Staggering as far aft as I could, I awaited fearlessly the ruin that was to overwhelm. Our own vessel was at length ceasing from her struggles, and sinking with her head to the sea. The shock of the descending mass struck her, consequently in that portion of her frame which was nearly under water, and the inevitable result was to hurl me, with irresistible violence, upon the rigging of the stranger.

As I fell, the ship hove in stays, and went about; and to the confusion ensuing I attributed my escape from the notice of the crew. With little difficulty I made my way, unperceived, to the main hatchway, which was partially open, and soon found an opportunity of secreting myself in the hold. Why I did so I can hardly tell. An indefinite sense of awe, which at first sight of the navigators of the ship had taken hold of my mind, was perhaps the principle of my concealment. I was unwilling to trust myself with a race of people who had offered, to the cursory glance I had taken, so many points of vague novelty, doubt, and apprehension. I therefore thought proper to contrive a hiding-place in the hold. This I did by removing a small portion of the shifting-boards, in such a manner as to afford me a convenient retreat between the huge timbers of the ship.

I had scarcely completed my work, when a footstep in the hold forced me to make use of it. A man passed by my place of concealment with a feeble and unsteady gait. I could not see his face, but had an opportunity of observing his general appearance. There was about it an evidence of great age and infirmity. His knees tottered beneath a load of years, and his entire frame quivered under the burthen. He muttered to himself, in a low broken tone, some words of a language which I could not understand, and groped in a corner among a pile of

singular-looking instruments, and decayed charts of navigation. His manner was a wild mixture of the peevishness of second childhood, and the solemn dignity of a God. He at length went on deck, and I saw him no more.

* * * * *

A feeling, for which I have no name, has taken possession of my soul—a sensation which will admit of no analysis, to which the lessons of bygone time are inadequate, and for which I fear futurity itself will offer me no key. To a mind constituted like my own, the latter consideration is an evil. I shall never—I know that I shall never—be satisfied with regard to the nature of my conceptions. Yet it is not wonderful that these conceptions are indefinite, since they have their origin in sources so utterly novel. A new sense—a new entity is added to my soul.

* * * * *

It is long since I first trod the deck of this terrible ship, and the rays of my destiny are, I think, gathering to a focus. Incomprehensible men! Wrapped up in meditations of a kind which I cannot divine, they pass me by unnoticed. Concealment is utter folly on my part, for the people *will not* see. It is but just now that I passed directly before the eyes of the mate; it was no long while ago that I ventured into the captain's own private cabin, and took thence the materials with which I write, and have written. I shall from time to time continue this journal. It is true that I may not find an opportunity of transmitting it to the world, but I will not fail to make the endeavor. At the last moment I will enclose the MS. in a bottle, and cast it within the sea.

* * * / * *

An incident has occurred which has given me new room for meditation. Are such things the operation of ungoverned chance? I had ventured upon deck and thrown myself down, without attracting any notice, among a pile of ratlin-stuff and old sails, in the bottom of the yawl. While musing upon the singularity of my fate, I unwittingly daubed with a tar-brush the edges of a neatly-folded studding-sail which lay near me on a barrel. The studding-sail is now bent upon the ship, and the thought-

less touches of the brush are spread out into the word
DISCOVERY.

I have made my observations lately upon the structure
of the vessel. Although well armed, she is not, I think, a
ship of war. Her rigging, build, and general equipment, all
negative a supposition of this kind. What she *is not,* I
can easily perceive; what she *is,* I fear it is impossible to
say. I know not how it is, but in scrutinizing her strange
model and singular cast of spars, her huge size and over-
grown suits of canvas, her severely simple bow and
antiquated stern, there will occasionally flash across my
mind a sensation of familiar things, and there is always
mixed up with such indistinct shadows of recollection, an
unaccountable memory of old foreign chronicles and ages
long ago. * * *

I have been looking at the timbers of the ship. She is
built of a material to which I am a stranger. There is a
peculiar character about the wood which strikes me as
rendering it unfit for the purpose to which it has been
applied. I mean its extreme *porousness,* considered in-
dependently of the worm-eaten condition which is a con-
sequence of navigation in these seas, and apart from
the rottenness attendant upon age. It will appear perhaps
an observation somewhat over-curious, but this would
have every characteristic of Spanish oak, if Spanish oak
were distended by any unnatural means.

In reading the above sentence, a curious apothegm of an
old weatherbeaten Dutch navigator comes full upon my
recollection. "It is as sure," he was wont to say, when
any doubt was entertained of his veracity, "as sure as
there is a sea where the ship itself will grow in bulk like
the living body of the seaman." * * *

About an hour ago, I made bold to trust myself among
a group of the crew. They paid me no manner of atten-
tion, and, although I stood in the very midst of them all,
seemed utterly unconscious of my presence. Like the one
I had at first seen in the hold, they all bore about them
the marks of a hoary old age. Their knees trembled with
infirmity; their shoulders were bent double with decrepi-
tude; their shrivelled skins rattled in the wind; their
voices were low, tremulous, and broken; their eyes glis-
tened with the rheum of years; and their gray hairs
streamed terribly in the tempest. Around them, on every
part of the deck, lay scattered mathematical instru-

ments of the most quaint and obsolete construction. * * *

I mentioned, some time ago, the bending of a studding-sail. From that period, the ship, being thrown dead off the wind, has continued her terrific course due south, with every rag of canvas packed upon her, from her truck to her lower studding-sail booms, and rolling every moment her top-gallant yard-arms into the most appalling hell of water which it can enter into the mind of man to imagine. I have just left the deck, where I find it impossible to maintain a footing, although the crew seem to experience little inconvenience. It appears to me a miracle of miracles that our enormous bulk is not swallowed up at once and forever. We are surely doomed to hover continually upon the brink of eternity, without taking a final plunge into the abyss. From billows a thousand times more stupendous than any I have ever seen, we glide away with the facility of the arrowy sea-gull; and the colossal waters rear their heads above us like demons of the deep, but like demons confined to simple threats, and forbidden to destroy. I am led to attribute these frequent escapes to the only natural cause which can account for such effect. I must suppose the ship to be within the influence of some strong current, or impetuous undertow. * * *

I have seen the captain face to face, and in his own cabin—but, as I expected, he paid me no attention. Although in his appearance there is, to a casual observer, nothing which might bespeak him more or less than man, still, a feeling of irrepressible reverence and awe mingled with the sensation of wonder with which I regarded him. In stature, he is nearly my own height; that is, about five feet eight inches. He is of a well-knit and compact frame of body, neither robust nor remarkable otherwise. But it is the singularity of the expression which reigns upon the face—it is the intense, the wonderful, the thrilling evidence of old age so utter, so extreme, which excites within my spirit a sense—a sentiment ineffable. His forehead, although little wrinkled, seems to bear upon it the stamp of a myriad of years. His gray hairs are records of the past, and his grayer eyes are sybils of the future. The cabin floor was thickly strewn with strange, iron-clasped folios, and mouldering instruments of science, and obsolete long-forgotten

charts. His head was bowed down upon his hands, and
he pored, with a fiery, unquiet eye, over a paper which I
took to be a commission, and which, at all events, bore
the signature of a monarch. He murmured to himself
—as did the first seaman whom I saw in the hold—some
low peevish syllables of a foreign tongue; and although
the speaker was close at my elbow, his voice seemed to
reach my ears from the distance of a mile. * * *

The ship and all in it are imbued with the spirit of Eld.
The crew glide to and fro like the ghosts of buried cen-
turies; their eyes have an eager and uneasy meaning;
and when their fingers fall athwart my path in the wild
glare of the battle-lanterns, I feel as I have never felt
before, although I have been all my life a dealer in an-
tiquities, and have imbibed the shadows of fallen columns
at Balbec, and Tadmor, and Persepolis, until my very soul
has become a ruin. * * *

When I look around me, I feel ashamed of my former
apprehension. If I trembled at the blast which has hither-
to attended us, shall I not stand aghast at a warring of
wind and ocean, to convey any idea of which, the words
tornado and simoon are trivial and ineffective? All
in the immediate vicinity of the ship, is the blackness of
eternal night, and a chaos of foamless water; but, about a
league on either side of us, may be seen, indistinctly and
at intervals, stupendous ramparts of ice, towering away
into the desolate sky, and looking like the walls of the
universe. * * *

As I imagined, the ship proves to be in a current—if
that appellation can properly be given to a tide which,
howling and shrieking by the white ice, thunders on to
the southward with a velocity like the headlong dashing
of a cataract. * * *

To conceive the horror of my sensations is, I presume,
utterly impossible; yet a curiosity to penetrate the mys-
teries of these awful regions, predominates even over my
despair, and will reconcile me to the most hideous aspect
of death. It is evident that we are hurrying onward
to some exciting knowledge—some never-to-be-imparted
secret, whose attainment is destruction. Perhaps this
current leads us to the southern pole itself. It must be
confessed that a supposition apparently so wild has every
probability in its favor. * * *

The crew pace the deck with unquiet and tremulous

step; but there is upon their countenance an expression more of the eagerness of hope than of the apathy of despair.

In the meantime the wind is still in our poop, and, as we carry a crowd of canvas, the ship is at times lifted bodily from out the sea! Oh, horror upon horror!—the ice opens suddenly to the right, and to the left, and we are whirling dizzily, in immense concentric circles, round and round the borders of a gigantic amphitheatre, the summit of whose walls is lost in the darkness and the distance. But little time will be left me to ponder upon my destiny! The circles rapidly grow small—we are plunging madly within the grasp of the whirlpool—and amid a roaring, and bellowing, and thundering of ocean and tempest, the ship is quivering—oh God! and——going down!

Note.—The "MS. Found in a Bottle," was originally published in 1831, and it was not until many years afterward that I became acquainted with the maps of Mercator, in which the ocean is represented as rushing, by four mouths into the (northern) Polar Gulf, to be absorbed into the bowels of the earth; the Pole itself being represented by a black rock, towering to a prodigious height.

A Descent into the Maelström

> The ways of God in Nature, as in Provi-
> dence, are not as *our* ways; nor are the
> models that we frame in any way commen-
> surate to the vastness, profundity, and un-
> searchableness of His works, *which have*
> *a depth in them greater than the well of*
> *Democritus.*
>
> —*Joseph Glanville*

W<small>E</small> <small>HAD NOW</small> reached the summit of the loftiest crag.
For some minutes the old man seemed too much ex-
hausted to speak.

"Not long ago," said he at length, "and I could have
guided you on this route as well as the youngest of my
sons; but, about three years past, there happened to
me an event such as never happened before to mortal
man—or at least such as no man ever survived to tell
of—and the six hours of deadly terror which I then en-
dured have broken me up body and soul. You suppose me
a *very* old man—but I am not. It took less than a single
day to change these hairs from a jetty black to white,
to weaken my limbs, and to unstring my nerves, so that
I tremble at the least exertion, and am frightened at a
shadow. Do you know I can scarcely look over this little
cliff without getting giddy?"

The "little cliff," upon whose edge he had so carelessly
thrown himself down to rest that the weightier portion
of his body hung over it, while he was only kept from fall-
ing by the tenure of his elbow on its extreme and slip-
pery edge—this "little cliff" arose, a sheer unobstructed
precipice of black shining rock, some fifteen or sixteen
hundred feet from the world of crags beneath us.
Nothing would have tempted me to be within half a

dozen yards of its brink. In truth so deeply was I excited by the perilous position of my companion, that I fell at full length upon the ground, clung to the shrubs around me, and dared not even glance upward at the sky—while I struggled in vain to divest myself of the idea that the very foundations of the mountain were in danger from the fury of the winds. It was long before I could reason myself into sufficient courage to sit up and look out into the distance.

"You must get over these fancies," said the guide, "for I have brought you here that you might have the best possible view of the scene of that event I mentioned—and to tell you the whole story with the spot just under your eye.

"We are now," he continued, in that particularizing manner which distinguished him—"we are now close upon the Norwegian coast—in the sixty-eighth degree of latitude—in the great province of Nordland—and in the dreary district of Lofoden. The mountain upon whose top we sit is Helseggen, the Cloudy. Now raise yourself up a little higher—hold on to the grass if you feel giddy—so—and look out, beyond the belt of vapor beneath us, into the sea."

I looked dizzily, and beheld a wide expanse of ocean, whose waters were so inky a hue as to bring at once to my mind the Nubian geographer's account of the *Mare Tenebrarum*. A panorama more deplorably desolate no human imagination can conceive. To the right and left, as far as the eye could reach, there lay outstretched, like ramparts of the world, lines of horridly black and bee-tling cliff, whose character of gloom was but the more forcibly illustrated by the surf which reared high up against it its white and ghastly crest, howling and shrieking for ever. Just opposite the promontory upon whose apex we were placed, and at a distance of some five or six miles out at sea, there was visible a small, bleak-looking island; or, more properly, its position was discernible through the wilderness of surge in which it was enveloped. About two miles nearer the land, arose another of smaller size, hideously craggy and barren, and encompassed at various intervals by a cluster of dark rocks.

The appearance of the ocean, in the space between the more distant island and the shore, had something very

unusual about it. Although, at the time, so strong a gale was blowing landward that a brig in the remote offing lay to under a double-reefed trysail, and constantly plunged her whole hull out of sight, still there was here nothing like a regular swell, but only a short, quick, angry cross dashing of water in every direction—as well in the teeth of the wind as otherwise. Of foam there was little except in the immediate vicinity of the rocks.

"The island in the distance," resumed the old man, "is called by the Norwegians Vurrgh. The one midway is Moskoe. That a mile to the northward is Ambaaren. Yonder are Islesen, Hotholm, Keildhelm, Suarven, and Buckholm. Further off—between Moskoe and Vurrgh—are Otterholm, Flimen, Sandflesen, and Stockholm. These are the true names of the places—but why it has been thought necessary to name them at all, is more than either you or I can understand. Do you hear any thing? Do you see any change in the water?"

We had now been about ten minutes upon the top of Helseggen, to which we had ascended from the interior of Lofoden, so that we had caught no glimpse of the sea until it had burst upon us from the summit. As the old man spoke, I became aware of a loud and gradually increasing sound, like the moaning of a vast herd of buffaloes upon an American prairie; and at the same moment I perceived that what seamen term the *chopping* character of the ocean beneath us, was rapidly changing into a current which set to the eastward. Even while I gazed, this current acquired a monstrous velocity. Each moment added to its speed—to its headlong impetuosity. In five minutes the whole sea, as far as Vurrgh, was lashed into ungovernable fury; but it was between Moskoe and the coast that the main uproar held its sway. Here the vast bed of the waters, seamed and scarred into a thousand conflicting channels, burst suddenly into phrensied convulsion—heaving, boiling, hissing—gyrating in gigantic and innumerable vortices, and all whirling and plunging on to the eastward with a rapidity which water never elsewhere assumes, except in precipitous descents.

In a few minutes more, there came over the scene another radical alteration. The general surface grew somewhat more smooth, and the whirlpools, one by one, disappeared, while prodigious streaks of foam became ap-

parent where none had been seen before. These streaks,
at length, spreading out to a great distance, and entering
into combination, took unto themselves the gyratory mo-
tion of the subsided vortices, and seemed to form the
germ of another more vast. Suddenly—very suddenly—
this assumed a distinct and definite existence, in a circle
of more than a mile in diameter. The edge of the whirl
was represented by a broad belt of gleaming spray; but
no particle of this slipped into the mouth of the terrific
funnel, whose interior, as far as the eye could fathom it,
was a smooth, shining, and jet-black wall of water, in-
clined to the horizon at an angle of some forty-five de-
grees, speeding dizzily round and round with a swaying
and sweltering motion, and sending forth to the winds an
appalling voice, half shriek, half roar, such as not even
the mighty cataract of Niagara ever lifts up in its agony
to Heaven.

The mountain trembled to its very base, and the rock
rocked. I threw myself upon my face, and clung to the
scant herbage in an excess of nervous agitation.

"This," said I at length, to the old man—"this *can* be
nothing else than the great whirlpool of the Maelström."

"So it is sometimes termed," said he. "We Norwegians
call it the Moskoe-ström, from the island of Moskoe in
the midway."

The ordinary account of this vortex had by no means
prepared me for what I saw. That of Jonas Ramus, which
is perhaps the most circumstantial of any, cannot impart
the faintest conception either of the magnificence, or of
the horror of the scene—or of the wild bewildering
sense of *the novel* which confounds the beholder. I am
not sure from what point of view the writer in question
surveyed it, nor at what time; but it could neither have
been from the summit of Helseggen, nor during a storm.
There are some passages of his description, nevertheless,
which may be quoted for their details, although their ef-
fect is exceedingly feeble in conveying an impression of
the spectacle.

"Between Lofoden and Moskoe," he says, "the depth
of the water is between thirty-six and forty fathoms;
but on the other side, toward Ver (Vurrgh) this depth de-
creases so as not to afford a convenient passage for a
vessel, without the risk of splitting on the rocks, which
happens even in the calmest weather. When it is flood,

the stream runs up the country between Lofoden and
Moskoe with a boisterous rapidity; but the roar of its
impetuous ebb to the sea is scarce equalled by the loudest
and most dreadful cataracts; the noise being heard sev-
eral leagues off, and the vortices or pits are of such an
extent and depth, that if a ship comes within its attrac-
tion, it is inevitably absorbed and carried down to the
bottom, and there beat to pieces against the rocks; and
when the water relaxes, the fragments thereof are thrown
up again. But these intervals of tranquillity are only at
the turn of the ebb and flood, and in calm weather, and
last but a quarter of an hour, its violence gradually re-
turning. When the stream is most boisterous, and its fury
heightened by a storm, it is dangerous to come within a
Norway mile of it. Boats, yachts, and ships have been
carried away by not guarding against it before they were
carried within its reach. It likewise happens frequently,
that whales come too near the stream, and are overpow-
ered by its violence; and then it is impossible to describe
their howlings and bellowings in their fruitless struggles
to disengage themselves. A bear once, attempting to swim
from Lofoden to Moskoe, was caught by the stream
and borne down, while he roared terribly, so as to be
heard on shore. Large stocks of firs and pine trees, after
being absorbed by the current, rise again broken and
torn to such a degree as if bristles grew upon them. This
plainly shows the bottom to consist of craggy rocks,
among which they are whirled to and fro. This stream is
regulated by the flux and reflux of the sea—it being con-
stantly high and low water every six hours. In the year
1645, early in the morning of Sexagesima Sunday, it raged
with such noise and impetuosity that the very stones of
the houses on the coast fell to the ground."

In regard to the depth of the water, I could not see
how this could have been ascertained at all in the imme-
diate vicinity of the vortex. The "forty fathoms" must
have reference only to portions of the channel close
upon the shore either of Moskoe or Lofoden. The depth
in the centre of the Moskoe-ström must be unmeas-
urably greater; and no better proof of this fact is neces-
sary than can be obtained from even the sidelong glance
into the abyss of the whirl which may be had from
the highest crag of Helseggen. Looking down from this
pinnacle upon the howling Phlegethon below, I could not

help smiling, at the simplicity with which the honest Jonas Ramus records, as a matter difficult of belief, the anecdotes of the whales and the bears, for it appeared to me, in fact, a self-evident thing, that the largest ships of the line in existence, coming within the influence of that deadly attraction, could resist it as little as a feather the hurricane, and must disappear bodily and at once.

The attempts to account for the phenomenon—some of which, I remember, seemed to me sufficiently plausible in perusal—now wore a very different and unsatisfactory aspect. The idea generally received is that this, as well as three smaller vortices among the Ferroe Islands, "have no other cause than the collision of waves rising and falling, at flux and reflux, against a ridge of rocks and shelves, which confines the water so that it precipitates itself like a cataract; and thus the higher the flood rises, the deeper must the fall be, and the natural result of all is a whirlpool or vortex, the prodigious suction of which is sufficiently known by lesser experiments."—These are the words of the Encyclopædia Britannica. Kircher and others imagine that in the centre of the channel of the maelström is an abyss penetrating the globe, and issuing in some very remote part—the Gulf of Bothnia being somewhat decidedly named in one instance. This opinion, idle in itself, was the one to which, as I gazed, my imagination most readily assented; and, mentioning it to the guide, I was rather surprised to hear him say that, although it was the view almost universally entertained of the subject by the Norwegians, it nevertheless was not his own. As to the former notion he confessed his inability to comprehend it; and here I agreed with him—for, however conclusive on paper, it becomes altogether unintelligible, and even absurd, amid the thunder of the abyss.

"You have had a good look at the whirl now," said the old man, "and if you will creep round this crag, so as to get in its lee, and deaden the roar of the water, I will tell you a story that will convince you I ought to know something of the Moskoe-ström."

I placed myself as desired, and he proceeded.

"Myself and my two brothers once owned a schooner-rigged smack of about seventy tons burthen, with which we were in the habit of fishing among the islands beyond Moskoe, nearly to Vurrgh. In all violent eddies at sea there is good fishing, at proper opportunities, if

one has only the courage to attempt it; but among the whole of the Lofoden coastmen, we three were the only ones who made a regular business of going out to the islands, as I tell you. The usual grounds are a great way lower down to the southward. There fish can be got at all hours, without much risk, and therefore these places are preferred. The choice spots over here among the rocks, however, not only yield the finest variety, but in far greater abundance; so that we often got in a single day, what the more timid of the craft could not scrape together in a week. In fact, we made it a matter of desperate speculation—the risk of life standing instead of labor, and courage answering for capital.

"We kept the smack in a cove about five miles higher up the coast than this; and it was our practice, in fine weather, to take advantage of the fifteen minutes' slack to push across the main channel of the Moskoe-ström, far above the pool, and then drop down upon anchorage somewhere near Otterholm, or Sandflesen, where the eddies are not so violent as elsewhere. Here we used to remain until nearly time for slack-water again, when we weighed and made for home. We never set out upon this expedition without a steady side wind for going and coming—one that we felt sure would not fail us before our return—and we seldom made a miscalculation upon this point. Twice, during six years, we were forced to stay all night at anchor on account of a dead calm, which is a rare thing indeed just about here; and once we had to remain on the grounds nearly a week, starving to death, owing to a gale which blew up shortly after our arrival, and made the channel too boisterous to be thought of. Upon this occasion we should have been driven out to sea in spite of every thing (for the whirlpools threw us round and round so violently, that, at length, we fouled our anchor and dragged it), if it had not been that we drifted into one of the innumerable cross currents—here to-day and gone to-morrow—which drove us under the lee of Flimen, where, by good luck, we brought up.

"I could not tell you the twentieth part of the difficulties we encountered 'on the ground'—it is a bad spot to be in, even in good weather—but we make shift always to run the gauntlet of the Moskoe-ström itself without accident; although at times my heart has been

in my mouth when we happened to be a minute or so behind or before the slack. The wind sometimes was not as strong as we thought it at starting, and then we made rather less way than we could wish, while the current rendered the smack unmanageable. My eldest brother had a son eighteen years old, and I had two stout boys of my own. These would have been of great assistance at such times, in using the sweeps as well as afterward in fishing—but, somehow, although we ran the risk ourselves, we had not the heart to let the young ones get into the danger—for, after all said and done, it *was* a horrible danger, and that is the truth.

"It is now within a few days of three years since what I am going to tell you occurred. It was on the tenth of July, 18—, a day which the people of this part of the world will never forget—for it was one in which blew the most terrible hurricane that ever came out of the heavens. And yet all the morning, and indeed until late in the afternoon, there was a gentle and steady breeze from the southwest, while the sun shone brightly, so that the oldest seaman among us could not have foreseen what was to follow.

"The three of us—my two brothers and myself—had crossed over to the islands about two o'clock P.M., and soon nearly loaded the smack with fine fish, which, we all remarked, were more plenty that day than we had ever known them. It was just seven, *by my watch,* when we weighed and started for home, so as to make the worst of the Ström at slack water, which we knew would be at eight.

"We set out with a fresh wind on our starboard quarter, and for some time spanked along at a great rate, never dreaming of danger, for indeed we saw not the slightest reason to apprehend it. All at once we were taken aback by a breeze from over Helseggen. This was most unusual—something that had never happened to us before—and I began to feel a little uneasy, without exactly knowing why. We put the boat on the wind, but could make no headway at all for the eddies, and I was upon the point of proposing to return to the anchorage, when, looking astern, we saw the whole horizon covered with a singular copper-colored cloud that rose with the most amazing velocity.

"In the meantime the breeze that had headed us off

fell away and we were dead becalmed, drifting about in every direction. This state of things, however, did not last long enough to give us time to think about it. In less than a minute the storm was upon us—in less than two the sky was entirely overcast—and what with this and the driving spray, it became suddenly so dark that we could not see each other in the smack.

"Such a hurricane as then blew it is folly to attempt describing. The oldest seaman in Norway never experienced any thing like it. We had let our sails go by the run before it cleverly took us; but, at the first puff, both our masts went by the board as if they had been sawed off—the mainmast taking with it my youngest brother, who had lashed himself to it for safety.

"Our boat was the lightest feather of a thing that ever sat upon water. It had a complete flush deck, with only a small hatch near the bow, and this hatch it had always been our custom to batten down when about to cross the Ström, by way of precaution against the chopping seas. But for this circumstance we should have foundered at once—for we lay entirely buried for some moments. How my elder brother escaped destruction I cannot say, for I never had an opportunity of ascertaining. For my part as soon as I had let the foresail run, I threw myself flat on deck, with my feet against the narrow gunwale of the bow, and with my hands grasping a ring-bolt near the foot of the foremast. It was mere instinct that prompted me to do this—which was undoubtedly the very best thing I could have done—for I was too much flurried to think.

"For some moments we were completely deluged, as I say, and all this time I held my breath, and clung to the bolt. When I could stand it no longer I raised myself upon my knees, still keeping hold with my hands, and thus got my head clear. Presently our little boat gave herself a shake, just as a dog does in coming out of the water, and thus rid herself, in some measure, of the seas. I was now trying to get the better of the stupor that had come over me, and to collect my senses so as to see what was to be done, when I felt somebody grasp my arm. It was my elder brother, and my heart leaped for joy, for I had made sure that he was overboard—but the next moment all this joy was turned into horror—for

he put his mouth close to my ear, and screamed out the word '*Moskoe-ström!*'

"No one ever will know what my feelings were at that moment. I shook from head to foot as if I had had the most violent fit of the ague. I knew what he meant by that one word well enough—I knew what he wished to make me understand. With the wind that now drove us on, we were bound for the whirl of the Ström, and nothing could save us!

"You perceive that in crossing the Ström *channel*, we always went a long way up above the whirl, even in the calmest weather, and then had to wait and watch carefully for the slack—but now we were driving right upon the pool itself, and in such a hurricane as this! 'To be sure,' I thought, 'we shall get there just about the slack—there is some little hope in that'—but in the next moment I cursed myself for being so great a fool as to dream of hope at all. I knew very well that we were doomed, had we been ten times a ninety-gun ship.

"By this time the first fury of the tempest had spent itself, or perhaps we did not feel it so much, as we scudded before it, but at all events the seas, which at first had been kept down by the wind, and lay flat and frothing, now got up into absolute mountains. A singular change, too, had come over the heavens. Around in every direction it was still as black as pitch, but nearly overhead there burst out, all at once, a circular rift of clear sky—as clear as I ever saw—and of a deep bright blue—and through it there blazed forth the full moon with a lustre that I never before knew her to wear. She lit up every thing about us with the greatest distinctness—but, oh God, what a scene it was to light up!

"I now made one or two attempts to speak to my brother—but in some manner which I could not understand, the din had so increased that I could not make him hear a single word, although I screamed at the top of my voice in his ear. Presently he shook his head, looking as pale as death, and held up one of his fingers, as if to say '*listen!*'

"At first I could not make out what he meant—but soon a hideous thought flashed upon me. I dragged my watch from its fob. It was not going. I glanced at its face by the moonlight, and then burst into tears as I flung it far away into the ocean. *It had run down at seven*

o'clock! We were behind the time of the slack, and the whirl of the Ström was in full fury!

"When a boat is well built, properly trimmed, and not deep laden, the waves in a strong gale, when she is going large, seem always to slip from beneath her—which appears strange to a landsman—and this is what is called *riding,* in sea phrase.

"Well, so far we had ridden the swells very cleverly; but presently a gigantic sea happened to take us right under the counter, and bore us with it as it rose—up—up—as if into the sky. I would not have believed that any wave could rise so high. And then down we came with a sweep, a slide, and a plunge that made me feel sick and dizzy, as if I was falling from some lofty mountain-top in a dream. But while we were up I had thrown a quick glance around—and that one glance was all-sufficient. I saw our exact position in an instant. The Moskoe-ström whirlpool was about a quarter of a mile dead ahead—but no more like the every-day Moskoe-ström than the whirl, as you now see it, is like a mill-race. If I had not known where we were, and what we had to expect, I should not have recognized the place at all. As it was, I involuntarily closed my eyes in horror. The lids clenched themselves together as if in a spasm.

"It could not have been more than two minutes afterwards until we suddenly felt the waves subside, and were enveloped in foam. The boat made a sharp half turn to larboard, and then shot off in its new direction like a thunderbolt. At the same moment the roaring noise of the water was completely drowned in a kind of shrill shriek—such a sound as you might imagine given out by the water-pipes of many thousand steam-vessels letting off their steam all together. We were now in the belt of surf that always surrounds the whirl; and I thought, of course, that another moment would plunge us into the abyss, down which we could only see indistinctly on account of the amazing velocity with which we were borne along. The boat did not seem to sink into the water at all, but to skim like an air-bubble upon the surface of the surge. Her starboard side was next the whirl, and on the larboard arose the world of ocean we had left. It stood like a huge writhing wall between us and the horizon.

"It may appear strange, but now, when we were in the very jaws of the gulf, I felt more composed than when we were only approaching it. Having made up my mind to hope no more, I got rid of a great deal of that terror which unmanned me at first. I supposed it was despair that strung my nerves.

"It may look like boasting—but what I tell you is truth—I began to reflect how magnificent a thing it was to die in such a manner, and how foolish it was in me to think of so paltry a consideration as my own individual life, in view of so wonderful a manifestation of God's power. I do believe that I blushed with shame when this idea crossed my mind. After a little while I became possessed with the keenest curiosity about the whirl itself. I positively felt a *wish* to explore its depths, even at the sacrifice I was going to make; and my principal grief was that I should never be able to tell my old companions on shore about the mysteries I should see. These, no doubt, were singular fancies to occupy a man's mind in such extremity—and I have often thought since, that the revolutions of the boat around the pool might have rendered me a little light-headed.

"There was another circumstance which tended to restore my self-possession and this was the cessation of the wind, which could not reach us in our present situation—for, as you saw for yourself, the belt of the surf is considerably lower than the general bed of the ocean, and this latter now towered above us, a high, black, mountainous ridge. If you have never been at sea in a heavy gale, you can form no idea of the confusion of mind occasioned by the wind and spray together. They blind, deafen, and strangle you, and take away all power of action or reflection. But we were now, in a great measure, rid of these annoyances—just as death-condemned felons in prison are allowed petty indulgences, forbidden them while their doom is yet uncertain.

"How often we made the circuit of the belt it is impossible to say. We careered round and round for perhaps an hour, flying rather than floating, getting gradually more and more into the middle of the surge, and then nearer and nearer to its horrible inner edge. All this time I had never let go of the ring-bolt. My brother was at the stern, holding on to a small empty water-cask which had been securely lashed under the coop of

the counter, and was the only thing on deck that had not been swept overboard when the gale first took us. As we approached the brink of the pit he let go his hold upon this, and made for the ring, from which, in the agony of his terror, he endeavored to force my hands, as it was not large enough to afford us both a secure grasp. I never felt deeper grief than when I saw him attempt this act—although I knew he was a madman when he did it—a raving maniac through sheer fright. I did not care, however, to contest the point with him. I knew it could make no difference whether either of us held on at all; so I let him have the bolt, and went astern to the cask. This there was no great difficulty in doing; for the smack flew round steadily enough, and upon an even keel—only swaying to and fro with the immense sweeps and swelters of the whirl. Scarcely had I secured myself in my new position, when we gave a wild lurch to starboard, and rushed headlong into the abyss. I muttered a hurried prayer to God, and thought all was over.

"As I felt the sickening sweep of the descent, I had instinctively tightened my hold upon the barrel, and closed my eyes. For some seconds I dared not open them—while I expected instant destruction, and wondered that I was not already in my death-struggles with the water. But moment after moment elapsed. I still lived. The sense of falling had ceased; and the motion of the vessel seemed much as it had been before, while in the belt of foam, with the exception that she now lay more along. I took courage and looked once again upon the scene.

"Never shall I forget the sensation of awe, horror, and admiration with which I gazed about me. The boat appeared to be hanging, as if by magic, midway down, upon the interior surface of a funnel vast in circumference, prodigious in depth, and whose perfectly smooth sides might have been mistaken for ebony, but for the bewildering rapidity with which they spun around, and for the gleaming and ghastly radiance they shot forth, as the rays of the full moon, from that circular rift amid the clouds which I have already described, streamed in a flood of golden glory along the black walls, and far away down into the inmost recesses of the abyss.

"At first I was too much confused to observe any thing accurately. The general burst of terrific grandeur was all

that I beheld. When I recovered myself a little, however, my gaze fell instinctively downward. In this direction I was able to obtain an unobstructed view, from the manner in which the smack hung on the inclined surface of the pool. She was quite upon an even keel—that is to say, her deck lay in a plane parallel with that of the water—but this latter sloped at an angle of more than forty-five degrees, so that we seemed to be lying upon our beam-ends. I could not help observing, nevertheless, that I had scarcely more difficulty in maintaining my hold and footing in this situation, than if we had been upon a dead level; and this, I suppose, was owing to the speed at which we revolved.

"The rays of the moon seemed to search the very bottom of the profound gulf; but still I could make out nothing distinctly on account of a thick mist in which every thing there was enveloped, and over which there hung a magnificent rainbow, like that narrow and tottering bridge which Mussulmen say is the only pathway between Time and Eternity. This mist, or spray, was no doubt occasioned by the clashing of the great walls of the funnel, as they all met together at the bottom—but the yell that went up to the Heavens from out of that mist I dare not attempt to describe.

"Our first slide into the abyss itself, from the belt of foam above, had carried us to a great distance down the slope; but our farther descent was by no means proportionate. Round and round we swept—not with any uniform movement—but in dizzying swings and jerks, that sent us sometimes only a few hundred yards—sometimes nearly the complete circuit of the whirl. Our progress downward, at each revolution, was slow, but very perceptible.

"Looking about me upon the wide waste of liquid ebony on which we were thus borne, I perceived that our boat was not the only object in the embrace of the whirl. Both above and below us were visible fragments of vessels, large masses of building-timber and trunks of trees, with many smaller articles, such as pieces of house furniture, broken boxes, barrels and staves. I have already described the unnatural curiosity which had taken the place of my original terrors. It appeared to grow upon me as I drew nearer and nearer to my dreadful doom. I now began to watch, with a strange interest,

the numerous things that floated in our company. I *must* have been delirious, for I even sought *amusement* in speculating upon the relative velocities of their several descents toward the foam below. 'This fir-tree,' I found myself at one time saying, 'will certainly be the next thing that takes the awful plunge and disappears,'—and then I was disappointed to find that the wreck of a Dutch merchant ship overtook it and went down before. At length, after making several guesses of this nature, and being deceived in all—this fact—the fact of my invariable miscalculation, set me upon a train of reflection that made my limbs again tremble, and my heart beat heavily once more.

"It was not a new terror that thus affected me, but the dawn of a more exciting *hope*. This hope arose partly from memory, and partly from present observation. I called to mind the great variety of buoyant matter that strewed the coast of Lofoden, having been absorbed and then thrown forth by the Moskoe-ström. By far the greater number of the articles were shattered in the most extraordinary way—so chafed and roughened as to have the appearance of being stuck full of splinters—but then I distinctly recollected that there were *some* of them which were not disfigured at all. Now I could not account for this difference except by supposing that the roughened fragments were the only ones which had been *completely absorbed*—that the others had entered the whirl at so late a period of the tide, or, from some reason, had descended so slowly after entering, that they did not reach the bottom before the turn of the flood came, or of the ebb, as the case might be. I conceived it possible, in either instance, that they might thus be whirled up again to the level of the ocean, without undergoing the fate of those which had been drawn in more early or absorbed more rapidly. I made, also, three important observations. The first was, that as a general rule, the larger the bodies were, the more rapid their descent—the second, that, between two masses of equal extent, the one spherical, and the other *of any other shape,* the superiority in speed of descent was with the sphere—the third, that, between two masses of equal size, the one cylindrical, and the other of any other shape, the cylinder was absorbed the more slowly. Since my escape, I have had several conversations on

this subject with an old school-master of the district; and it was from him that I learned the use of the words 'cylinder' and 'sphere.' He explained to me—although I have forgotten the explanation—how what I observed was, in fact, the natural consequence of the forms of the floating fragments—and showed me how it happened that a cylinder, swimming in a vortex, offered more resistance to its suction, and was drawn in with greater difficulty than an equally bulky body, of any form whatever.[1]

"There was one startling circumstance which went a great way in enforcing these observations, and rendering me anxious to turn them to account, and this was that, at every revolution, we passed something like a barrel, or else the yard or the mast of a vessel, while many of these things, which had been on our level when I first opened my eyes upon the wonders of the whirlpool, were now high up above us, and seemed to have moved but little from their original station.

"I no longer hesitated what to do. I resolved to lash myself securely to the water-cask upon which I now held, to cut it loose from the counter, and to throw myself with it into the water. I attracted my brother's attention by signs, pointed to the floating barrels that came near us, and did every thing in my power to make him understand what I was about to do. I thought at length that he comprehended my design—but, whether this was the case or not, he shook his head despairingly, and refused to move from his station by the ring-bolt. It was impossible to reach him; the emergency admitted of no delay; and so, with a bitter struggle, I resigned him to his fate, fastened myself to the cask by means of the lashings which secured it to the counter, and precipitated myself with it into the sea, without another moment's hesitation.

"The result was precisely what I had hoped it might be. As it is myself who now tell you this tale—as you see that I *did* escape—and as you are already in possession of the mode in which this escape was effected, and must therefore anticipate all that I have farther to say—I will bring my story quickly to conclusion. It might have been an hour, or thereabouts, after my quit-

[1] See Archimedes, *"De Incidentibus in Fluido."*—lib. 2.

ting the smack, when, having descended to a vast distance beneath me, it made three or four wild gyrations in rapid succession, and, bearing my loved brother with it, plunged headlong, at once and forever, into the chaos of foam below. The barrel to which I was attached sunk very little farther than half the distance between the bottom of the gulf and the spot at which I leaped overboard, before a great change took place in the character of the whirlpool. The slope of the sides of the vast funnel became momently less and less steep. The gyrations of the whirl grew, gradually, less and less violent. By degrees, the froth and the rainbow disappeared, and the bottom of the gulf seemed slowly to uprise. The sky was clear, the winds had gone down, and the full moon was setting radiantly in the west, when I found myself on the surface of the ocean, in full view of the shores of Lofoden, and above the spot where the pool of the Moskoe-ström *had been*. It was the hour of the slack—but the sea still heaved in mountainous waves from the effects of the hurricane. I was borne violently into the channel of the Ström, and in a few minutes, was hurried down the coast into the 'grounds' of the fishermen. A boat picked me up—exhausted from fatigue—and (now that the danger was removed) speechless from the memory of its horror. Those who drew me on board were my old mates and daily companions—but they knew me no more than they would have known a traveller from the spirit-land. My hair, which had been raven black the day before, was as white as you see it now. They say too that the whole expression of my countenance had changed. I told them my story—they did not believe it. I now tell it to *you*—and I can scarcely expect you to put more faith in it than did the merry fishermen of Lofoden."

The Murders in the Rue Morgue

What song the Syrens sang, or what
name Achilles assumed when he hid him-
self among women, although puzzling ques-
tions, are not beyond *all* conjecture.
Sir Thomas Browne

THE MENTAL FEATURES discoursed of as the analyti-
cal, are, in themselves, but little susceptible of analysis.
We appreciate them only in their effects. We know of
them, among other things, that they are always to their
possessor, when inordinately possessed, a source of the
liveliest enjoyment. As the strong man exults in his
physical ability, delighting in such exercises as call his
muscles into action, so glories the analyst in that moral
activity which *disentangles*. He derives pleasure from
even the most trivial occupations bringing his talent into
play. He is fond of enigmas, of conundrums, hiero-
glyphics; exhibiting in his solutions of each a degree of
acumen which appears to the ordinary apprehension
præternatural. His results, brought about by the very soul
and essence of method, have, in truth, the whole air of
intuition.

The faculty of re-solution is possibly much invigorated
by mathematical study, and especially by that highest
branch of it which, unjustly, and merely on account of
its retrograde operations, has been called, as if *par
excellence*, analysis. Yet to calculate is not in itself to
analyze. A chess-player, for example, does the one, with-
out effort at the other. It follows that the game of chess,
in its effect upon mental character, is greatly misunder-
stood. I am not now writing a treatise, but simply pref-
acing a somewhat peculiar narrative by observations
very much at random; I will, therefore, take occasion to

assert that the higher powers of the reflective intellect are more decidedly and more usefully tasked by the un-ostentatious game of draughts than by all the elaborate frivolity of chess. In this latter, where the pieces have different and *bizarre* motions, with various and variable values, what is only complex, is mistaken (a not unusual error) for what is profound. The *attention* is here called powerfully into play. If it flag for an instant, an over-sight is committed, resulting in injury or defeat. The pos-sible moves being not only manifold, but involute, the chances of such oversights are multiplied; and in nine cases out of ten, it is the more concentrative rather than the more acute player who conquers. In draughts, on the contrary, where the moves are *unique* and have but lit-tle variation, the probabilities of inadvertence are di-minished, and the mere attention being left comparatively unemployed, what advantages are obtained by either party are obtained by superior *acumen*. To be less ab-stract, let us suppose a game of draughts where the pieces are reduced to four kings, and where, of course, no oversight is to be expected. It is obvious that here the victory can be decided (the players being at all equal) only by some *recherché* movement, the result of some strong exertion of the intellect. Deprived of ordinary resources, the analyst throws himself into the spirit of his opponent, identifies himself therewith, and not un-frequently sees thus, at a glance, the sole methods (sometimes indeed absurdly simple ones) by which he may seduce into error or hurry into miscalculation.

Whist has long been known for its influence upon what is termed the calculating power; and men of the highest order of intellect have been known to take an apparently unaccountable delight in it, while eschewing chess as frivolous. Beyond doubt there is nothing of a similar nature so greatly tasking the faculty of analysis. The best chess-player in Christendom *may* be little more than the best player of chess; but proficiency in whist implies capacity for success in all these more important undertakings where mind struggles with mind. When I say proficiency, I mean that perfection in the game which includes a comprehension of *all* the sources whence legitimate advantage may be derived. These are not only manifold, but multiform, and lie frequently among re-cesses of thought altogether inaccessible to the ordinary

understanding. To observe attentively is to remember distinctly; and, so far, the concentrative chess-player will do very well at whist; while the rules of Hoyle (themselves based upon the mere mechanism of the game) are sufficiently and generally comprehensible. Thus to have a retentive memory, and proceed by "the book" are points commonly regarded as the sum total of good playing. But it is in matters beyond the limits of mere rule that the skill of the analyst is evinced. He makes, in silence, a host of observations and inferences. So, perhaps, do his companions; and the difference in the extent of the information obtained, lies not so much in the validity of the inference as in the quality of the observation. The necessary knowledge is that of *what* to observe. Our player confines himself not at all; nor, because the game is the object, does he reject deductions from things external to the game. He examines the countenance of his partner, comparing it carefully with that of each of his opponents. He considers the mode of assorting the cards in each hand; often counting trump by trump, and honor by honor, through the glances bestowed by their holders upon each. He notes every variation of face as the play progresses, gathering a fund of thought from the differences in the expression of certainty, of surprise, of triumph, or chagrin. From the manner of gathering up a trick he judges whether the person taking it, can make another in the suit. He recognizes what is played through feint, by the manner with which it is thrown upon the table. A casual or inadvertent word; the accidental dropping or turning of a card, with the accompanying anxiety or carelessness in regard to its concealment; the counting of the tricks, with the order of their arrangement; embarrassment, hesitation, eagerness, or trepidation—all afford, to his apparently intuitive perception, indications of the true state of affairs. The first two or three rounds having been played, he is in full possession of the contents of each hand, and thenceforward puts down his cards with as absolute a precision of purpose as if the rest of the party had turned outward the faces of their own.

The analytical power should not be confounded with simple ingenuity; for while the analyst is necessarily ingenious, the ingenious man is often remarkably incapable of analysis. The constructive or combining power,

by which ingenuity is usually manifested, and to which the phrenologists (I believe erroneously) have assigned a separate organ, supposing it a primitive faculty, has been so frequently seen in those whose intellect bordered otherwise upon idiocy, as to have attracted general observation among writers on morals. Between ingenuity and the analytic ability there exists a difference far greater, indeed, than that between the fancy and the imagination, but of a character very strictly analogous. It will be found, in fact, that the ingenious are always fanciful, and the *truly* imaginative never otherwise than analytic.

The narrative which follows will appear to the reader somewhat in the light of a commentary upon the propositions just advanced.

Residing in Paris during the spring and part of the summer of 18—, I there became acquainted with a Monsieur C. Auguste Dupin. This young gentleman was of an excellent, indeed of an illustrious family, but, by a variety of untoward events, had been reduced to such poverty that the energy of his character succumbed beneath it, and he ceased to bestir himself in the world, or to care for the retrieval of his fortunes. By courtesy of his creditors, there still remained in his possession a small remnant of his patrimony; and, upon the income arising from this, he managed, by means of a rigorous economy, to procure the necessities of life, without troubling himself about its superfluities. Books, indeed, were his sole luxuries, and in Paris these are easily obtained.

Our first meeting was at an obscure library in the Rue Montmartre, where the accident of our both being in search of the same very rare and very remarkable volume, brought us into closer communion. We saw each other again and again. I was deeply interested in the little family history which he detailed to me with all that candor which a Frenchman indulges whenever mere self is the theme. I was astonished, too, at the vast extent of his reading; and, above all, I felt my soul enkindled within me by the wild fervor, and the vivid freshness of his imagination. Seeking in Paris the objects I then sought, I felt that the society of such a man would be to me a treasure beyond price; and this feeling I frankly confided to him. It was at length arranged that

we should live together during my stay in the city; and
as my worldly circumstances were somewhat less em-
barrassed than his own, I was permitted to be at the
expense of renting, and furnishing in a style which suited
the rather fantastic gloom of our common temper, a
time-eaten and grotesque mansion, long deserted through
superstitions into which we did not inquire, and totter-
ing to its fall in a retired and desolate portion of the
Faubourg St. Germain.

Had the routine of our life at this place been known
to the world, we should have been regarded as madmen
—although, perhaps, as madmen of a harmless nature.
Our seclusion was perfect. We admitted no visitors. In-
deed the locality of our retirement had been carefully
kept a secret from my own former associates; and it
had been many years since Dupin had ceased to know
or be known in Paris. We existed within ourselves alone.

It was a freak of fancy in my friend (for what else
shall I call it?) to be enamored of the night for her
own sake; and into this *bizarrerie,* as into all his others,
I quietly fell; giving myself up to his wild whims with a
perfect *abandon.* The sable divinity would not herself
dwell with us always; but we could counterfeit her pres-
ence. At the first dawn of the morning we closed all
the massy shutters of our old building; lighted a couple
of tapers which, strongly perfumed, threw out only the
ghastliest and feeblest of rays. By the aid of these we then
busied our souls in dreams—reading, writing, or con-
versing, until warned by the clock of the advent of the
true Darkness. Then we sallied forth into the streets,
arm in arm, continuing the topics of the day, or roam-
ing far and wide until a late hour, seeking, amid the wild
lights and shadows of the populous city, that infinity
of mental excitement which quiet observation can af-
ford.

At such times I could not help remarking and admir-
ing (although from his rich ideality I had been prepared
to expect it) a peculiar analytic ability in Dupin. He
seemed, too, to take an eager delight in its exercise—
if not exactly in its display—and did not hesitate to
confess the pleasure thus derived. He boasted to me,
with a low chuckling laugh, that most men, in respect to
himself, wore windows in their bosoms, and was wont
to follow up such assertions by direct and very startling

proofs of his intimate knowledge of my own. His manner at these moments was frigid and abstract; his eyes were vacant in expression; while his voice, usually a rich tenor, rose into a treble which would have sounded petulant but for the deliberateness and entire distinctness of the enunciation. Observing him in these moods, I often dwelt meditatively upon the old philosophy of the Bi-Part Soul, and amused myself with the fancy of a double Dupin—the creative and the resolvent.

Let it not be supposed, from what I have just said, that I am detailing any mystery, or penning any romance. What I have described in the Frenchman was merely the result of an excited, or perhaps of a diseased, intelligence. But of the character of his remarks at the periods in question an example will best convey the idea.

We were strolling one night down a long dirty street, in the vicinity of the Palais Royal. Being both, apparently, occupied with thought, neither of us had spoken a syllable for fifteen minutes at least. All at once Dupin broke forth with these words:

"He is a very little fellow, that's true, and would do better for the *Théâtre des Variétés*."

"There can be no doubt of that," I replied, unwittingly, and not at first observing (so much had I been absorbed in reflection) the extraordinary manner in which the speaker had chimed in with my meditations. In an instant afterward I recollected myself, and my astonishment was profound.

"Dupin," said I, gravely, "this is beyond my comprehension. I do not hesitate to say that I am amazed, and can scarcely credit my senses. How was it possible you should know I was thinking of ——?" Here I paused, to ascertain beyond a doubt whether he really knew of whom I thought.

"—— of Chantilly," said he, "why do you pause? You were remarking to yourself that his diminutive figure unfitted him for tragedy."

This was precisely what had formed the subject of my reflections. Chantilly was a *quondam* cobbler of the Rue St. Denis, who, becoming stage-mad, had attempted the *rôle* of Xerxes, in Crébillon's tragedy so called, and been notoriously Pasquinaded for his pains.

"Tell me, for Heaven's sake," I exclaimed, "the method—if method there is—by which you have been

enabled to fathom my soul in this matter." In fact, I was even more startled than I would have been willing to express.

"It was the fruiterer," replied my friend, "who brought you to the conclusion that the mender of soles was not of sufficient height for Xerxes *et id genus omne.*"

"The fruiterer!—you astonish me—I know no fruiterer whomsoever."

"The man who ran up against you as we entered the street—it may have been fifteen minutes ago."

I now remembered that, in fact, a fruiterer, carrying upon his head a large basket of apples, had nearly thrown me down, by accident, as we passed from the Rue C—— into the thoroughfare where we stood; but what this had to do with Chantilly I could not possibly understand.

There was not a particle of *charlatânerie* about Dupin. "I will explain," he said, "and that you may comprehend all clearly, we will first retrace the course of your meditations, from the moment in which I spoke to you until that of the *rencontre* with the fruiterer in question. The larger links of the chain run thus—Chantilly, Orion, Dr. Nichols, Epicurus, Stereotomy, the street stones, the fruiterer."

There are few persons who have not, at some period of their lives, amused themselves in retracing the steps by which particular conclusions of their own minds have been attained. The occupation is often full of interest; and he who attempts it for the first time is astonished by the apparently illimitable distance and incoherence between the starting-point and the goal. What, then, must have been my amazement, when I heard the Frenchman speak what he had just spoken, and when I could not help acknowledging that he had spoken the truth. He continued:

"We had been talking of horses, if I remember aright, just before leaving the Rue C——. This was the last subject we discussed. As we crossed into this street, a fruiterer, with a large basket upon his head, brushing quickly past us, thrust you upon a pile of paving-stones collected at a spot where the causeway is undergoing repair. You stepped upon one of the loose fragments, slipped, slightly strained your ankle, appeared vexed or sulky, muttered a few words, turned to look at the pile, and then proceeded in silence. I was not particularly at-

tentive to what you did; but observation has become
with me, of late, a species of necessity.

"You kept your eyes upon the ground—glancing, with
a petulant expression, at the holes and ruts in the pave-
ment (so that I saw you were still thinking of the stones),
until we reached the little alley called Lamartine, which
has been paved, by way of experiment, with the
overlapping and riveted blocks. Here your countenance
brightened up, and, perceiving your lips move, I could
not doubt that you murmured the word 'stereotomy,' a
term very affectedly applied to this species of pavement.
I knew that you could not say to yourself 'stereotomy'
without being brought to think of atomies, and thus
of the theories of Epicurus; and since, when we dis-
cussed this subject not very long ago, I mentioned to
you how singularly, yet with how little notice, the vague
guesses of that noble Greek had met with confirmation in
the late nebular cosmogony, I felt that you could not
avoid casting your eyes upward to the great *nebula* in
Orion, and I certainly expected that you would do so.
You did look up; and I was now assured that I had cor-
rectly followed your steps. But in that bitter *tirade* upon
Chantilly, which appeared in yesterday's *'Musée,'* the
satirist, making some disgraceful allusions to the cob-
bler's change of name upon assuming the buskin, quoted
a Latin line about which we have often conversed. I mean
the line

Perdidit antiquum litera prima sonum.

I had told you that this was in reference to Orion, form-
erly written Urion; and, from certain pungencies con-
nected with this explanation, I was aware that you could
not have forgotten it. It was clear, therefore, that you
would not fail to combine the two ideas of Orion and
Chantilly. That you did combine them I saw by the
character of the smile which passed over your lips. You
thought of the poor cobbler's immolation. So far, you
had been stooping in your gait; but now I saw you draw
yourself up to your full height. I was then sure that you
reflected upon the diminutive figure of Chantilly. At this
point I interrupted your meditations to remark that as,
in fact, he *was* a very little fellow—that Chantilly—he
would do better at the *Théâtre des Variétés.*"

Not long after this, we were looking over an evening edition of the *Gazette des Tribunaux,* when the following paragraphs arrested our attention.

"EXTRAORDINARY MURDERS.—This morning, about three o'clock, the inhabitants of the Quartier St. Roch were roused from sleep by a succession of terrific shrieks, issuing, apparently, from the fourth story of a house in the Rue Morgue, known to be in the sole occupancy of one Madame L'Espanaye, and her daughter, Mademoiselle Camille L'Espanaye. After some delay, occasioned by a fruitless attempt to procure admission in the usual manner, the gateway was broken in with a crowbar, and eight or ten of the neighbors entered, accompanied by two *gendarmes.* By this time the cries had ceased; but, as the party rushed up the first flight of stairs, two or more rough voices, in angry contention, were distinguished, and seemed to proceed from the upper part of the house. As the second landing was reached, these sounds, also, had ceased, and every thing remained perfectly quiet. The party spread themselves, and hurried from room to room. Upon arriving at a large back chamber in the fourth story (the door of which, being found locked, with the key inside, was forced open), a spectacle presented itself which struck every one present not less with horror than with astonishment.

"The apartment was in the wildest disorder—the furniture broken and thrown about in all directions. There was only one bedstead; and from this the bed had been removed, and thrown into the middle of the floor. On a chair lay a razor, besmeared with blood. On the hearth were two or three long and thick tresses of gray human hair, also dabbled with blood, and seeming to have been pulled out by the roots. Upon the floor were found four Napoleons, an ear-ring of topaz, three large silver spoons, three smaller of *métal d'Alger,* and two bags, containing nearly four thousand francs in gold. The drawers of a *bureau,* which stood in one corner, were open, and had been, apparently, rifled, although many articles still remained in them. A small iron safe was discovered under the *bed* (not under the bedstead). It was open, with the key still in the door. It had no contents beyond a few old letters, and other papers of little consequence.

"Of Madame L'Espanaye no traces were here seen;

but an unusual quantity of soot being observed in the
fire-place, a search was made in the chimney, and (hor-
rible to relate!) the corpse of the daughter, head down-
ward, was dragged therefrom; it having been thus forced
up the narrow aperture for a considerable distance. The
body was quite warm. Upon examining it, many excoria-
tions were perceived, no doubt occasioned by the vio-
lence with which it had been thrust up and disengaged.
Upon the face were many severe scratches, and, upon
the throat, dark bruises, and deep indentations of finger
nails, as if the deceased had been throttled to death.

"After a thorough investigation of every portion of
the house without farther discovery, the party made its
way into a small paved yard in the rear of the building,
where lay the corpse of the old lady, with her throat so
entirely cut that, upon an attempt to raise her, the
head fell off. The body, as well as the head, was fear-
fully mutilated—the former so much so as scarcely to
retain any semblance of humanity.

"To this horrible mystery there is not as yet, we be-
lieve, the slightest clew."

The next day's paper had these additional particulars:

"The Tragedy in the Rue Morgue.—Many individuals
have been examined in relation to this most extraordi-
nary and frightful affair," [the word *'affaire'* has not yet,
in France, that levity of import which it conveys with us]
"but nothing whatever has transpired to throw light upon
it. We give below all the material testimony elicited.

"Pauline Dubourg, laundress, deposes that she has
known both the deceased for three years, having washed
for them during that period. The old lady and her daugh-
ter seemed on good terms—very affectionate toward
each other. They were excellent pay. Could not speak in
regard to their mode or means of living. Believe that
Madame L. told fortunes for a living. Was reputed to
have money put by. Never met any person in the house
when she called for the clothes or took them home.
Was sure that they had no servant in employ. There
appeared to be no furniture in any part of the building
except in the fourth story.

"Pierre Moreau, tobacconist, deposes that he has been
in the habit of selling small quantities of tobacco and
snuff to Madame L'Espanaye for nearly four years. Was
born in the neighborhood, and has always resided there.

The deceased and her daughter had occupied the house in which the corpses were found, for more than six years. It was formerly occupied by a jeweller, who under-let the upper rooms to various persons. The house was the property of Madame L. She became dissatisfied with the abuse of the premises by her tenant, and moved into them herself, refusing to let any portion. The old lady was childish. Witness had seen the daughter some five or six times during the six years. The two lived an exceedingly retired life—were reputed to have money. Had heard it said among the neighbors that Madame L. told fortunes—did not believe it. Had never seen any person enter the door except the old lady and her daughter, a porter once or twice, and a physician some eight or ten times.

"Many other persons, neighbors, gave evidence to the same effect. No one was spoken of as frequenting the house. It was not known whether there were any living connections of Madame L. and her daughter. The shutters of the front windows were seldom opened. Those in the rear were always closed, with the exception of the large back room, fourth story. The house was a good house—not very old.

"*Isidore Musèt, gendarme,* deposes that he was called to the house about three o'clock in the morning, and found some twenty or thirty persons at the gateway, endeavoring to gain admittance. Forced it open, at length, with a bayonet—not with a crowbar. Had but little difficulty in getting it open, on account of its being a double or folding gate, and bolted neither at bottom nor top. The shrieks were continued until the gate was forced—and then suddenly ceased. They seemed to be screams of some person (or persons) in great agony—were loud and drawn out, not short and quick. Witness led the way up stairs. Upon reaching the first landing, heard two voices in loud and angry contention—the one a gruff voice, the other much shriller— a very strange voice. Could distinguish some words of the former, which was that of a Frenchman. Was positive that it was not a woman's voice. Could distinguish the words '*sacré*' and '*diable.*' The shrill voice was that of a foreigner. Could not be sure whether it was the voice of a man or of a woman. Could not make out what was said, but believed the language to be Spanish. The state of the room and of the

bodies was described by this witness as we described them yesterday.

"*Henri Duval,* a neighbor, and by trade a silver-smith, deposes that he was one of the party who first entered the house. Corroborates the testimony of Musèt in general. As soon as they forced an entrance, they reclosed the door, to keep out the crowd, which collected very fast, notwithstanding the lateness of the hour. The shrill voice, this witness thinks, was that of an Italian. Was certain it was not French. Could not be sure that it was a man's voice. It might have been a woman's. Was not acquainted with the Italian language. Could not distinguish the words, but was convinced by the intonations that the speaker was an Italian. Knew Madame L. and her daughter. Had conversed with both frequently. Was sure that the shrill voice was not that of either of the deceased.

"———*Odenheimer, restaurateur.*—This witness volunteered his testimony. Not speaking French, was examined through an interpreter. Is a native of Amsterdam. Was passing the house at the time of the shrieks. They lasted for several minutes—probably ten. They were long and loud—very awful and distressing. Was one of those who entered the building. Corroborated the previous evidence in every respect but one. Was sure that the shrill voice was that of a man—of a Frenchman. Could not distinguish the words uttered. They were loud and quick —unequal—spoken apparently in fear as well as in anger. The voice was harsh—not so much shrill as harsh. Could not call it a shrill voice. The gruff voice said repeatedly, '*sacré*,' '*diable*,' and once '*mon Dieu.*'

"*Jules Mignaud,* banker, of the firm of Mignaud et Fils, Rue Deloraine. Is the elder Mignaud. Madame L'Espanaye had some property. Had opened an account with his banking house in the spring of the year —— (eight years previously). Made frequent deposits in small sums. Had checked for nothing until the third day before her death, when she took out in person the sum of 4000 francs. This sum was paid in gold, and a clerk sent home with the money.

"*Adolphe Le Bon,* clerk to Mignaud et Fils, deposes that on the day in question, about noon, he accompanied Madame L'Espanaye to her residence with the 4000 francs, put up in two bags. Upon the door being opened,

Mademoiselle L. appeared and took from his hands one of the bags, while the old lady relieved him of the other. He then bowed and departed. Did not see any person in the street at the time. It is a bystreet—very lonely.

"*William Bird,* tailor, deposes that he was one of the party who entered the house. Is an Englishman. Has lived in Paris two years. Was one of the first to ascend the stairs. Heard the voices in contention. The gruff voice was that of a Frenchman. Could make out several words, but cannot now remember all. Heard distinctly '*sacré*' and '*mon Dieu.*' There was a sound at the moment as if of several persons struggling—a scraping and scuffling sound. The shrill voice was very loud—louder than the gruff one. Is sure that it was not the voice of an Englishman. Appeared to be that of a German. Might have been a woman's voice. Does not understand German.

"Four of the above-named witnesses, being recalled, deposed that the door of the chamber in which was found the body of Mademoiselle L. was locked on the inside when the party reached it. Every thing was perfectly silent—no groans or noises of any kind. Upon forcing the door no person was seen. The windows, both of the back and front room, were down and firmly fastened from within. A door between the two rooms was closed but not locked. The door leading from the front room into the passage was locked, with the key on the inside. A small room in the front of the house, on the fourth story, at the head of the passage, was open, the door being ajar. This room was crowded with old beds, boxes, and so forth. These were carefully removed and searched. There was not an inch of any portion of the house which was not carefully searched. Sweeps were sent up and down the chimneys. The house was a four-story one, with garrets (*mansardes*). A trap-door on the roof was nailed down very securely—did not appear to have been opened for years. The time elapsing between the hearing of the voices in contention and the breaking open of the room door was variously stated by the witnesses. Some made it as short as three minutes—some as long as five. The door was opened with difficulty.

"*Alfonzo Garcio,* undertaker, deposes that he resides in the Rue Morgue. Is a native of Spain. Was one of the party who entered the house. Did not proceed up stairs. Is nervous, and was apprehensive of the consequences of

agitation. Heard the voices in contention. The gruff voice
was that of a Frenchman. Could not distinguish what was
said. The shrill voice was that of an Englishman—is sure
of this. Does not understand the English language, but
judges by the intonation.

"*Alberto Montani,* confectioner, deposes that he was
among the first to ascend the stairs. Heard the voices in
question. The gruff voice was that of a Frenchman. Dis-
tinguished several words. The speaker appeared to be ex-
postulating. Could not make out the words of the shrill
voice. Spoke quick and unevenly. Thinks it the voice of a
Russian. Corroborates the general testimony. Is an
Italian. Never conversed with a native of Russia.

"Several witnesses, recalled, here testified that the
chimneys of all the rooms on the fourth story were too
narrow to admit the passage of a human being. By
'sweeps' were meant cylindrical sweeping-brushes, such as
are employed by those who clean chimneys. These brushes
were passed up and down every flue in the house. There
is no back passage by which any one could have de-
scended while the party proceeded up stairs. The body of
Mademoiselle L'Espanaye was so firmly wedged in the
chimney that it could not be got down until four or five of
the party united their strength.

"*Paul Dumas,* physician, deposes that he was called
to view the bodies about daybreak. They were both then
lying on the sacking of the bedstead in the chamber
where Mademoiselle L. was found. The corpse of the
young lady was much bruised and excoriated. The fact
that it had been thrust up the chimney would sufficiently
account for these appearances. The throat was greatly
chafed. There were several deep scratches just below the
chin, together with a series of livid spots which were evi-
dently the impression of fingers. The face was fearfully
discolored, and the eyeballs protruded. The tongue had
been partially bitten through. A large bruise was discov-
ered upon the pit of the stomach, produced, apparently,
by the pressure of a knee. In the opinion of M. Dumas,
Mademoiselle L'Espanaye had been throttled to death by
some person or persons unknown. The corpse of the
mother was horribly mutilated. All the bones of the right
leg and arm were more or less shattered. The left *tibia*
much splintered, as well as all the ribs of the left side.
Whole body dreadfully bruised and discolored. It was not

possible to say how the injuries had been inflicted. A heavy club of wood, or a broad bar of iron—a chair—any large, heavy, and obtuse weapon would have produced such results, if wielded by the hands of a very powerful man. No woman could have inflicted the blows with any weapon. The head of the deceased, when seen by witness, was entirely separated from the body, and was also greatly shattered. The throat had evidently been cut with some very sharp instrument—probably with a razor.

"*Alexandre Etienne,* surgeon, was called with M. Dumas to view the bodies. Corroborated the testimony, and the opinions of M. Dumas.

"Nothing further of importance was elicited, although several other persons were examined. A murder so mysterious, and so perplexing in all its particulars, was never before committed in Paris—if indeed a murder has been committed at all. The police are entirely at fault—an unusual occurrence in affairs of this nature. There is not, however, the shadow of a clew apparent."

The evening edition of the paper stated that the greatest excitement still continued in the Quartier St. Roch—that the premises in question had been carefully researched, and fresh examinations of witnesses instituted, but all to no purpose. A postscript, however, mentioned that Adolphe Le Bon had been arrested and imprisoned —although nothing appeared to criminate him beyond the facts already detailed.

Dupin seemed singularly interested in the progress of this affair—at least so I judged from his manner, for he made no comments. It was only after the announcement that Le Bon had been imprisoned, that he asked me my opinion respecting the murders.

I could merely agree with all Paris in considering them an insoluble mystery. I saw no means by which it would be possible to trace the murderer.

"We must not judge of the means," said Dupin, "by this shell of an examination. The Parisian police, so much extolled for *acumen,* are cunning, but no more. There is no method in their proceedings, beyond the method of the moment. They make a vast parade of measures; but, not unfrequently, these are so ill-adapted to the objects proposed, as to put us in mind of Monsieur Jourdain's calling for his *robe-de-chambre*—*pour mieux entendre la musique.* The results attained by them are not

unfrequently surprising, but, for the most part, are brought about by simple diligence and activity. When these qualities are unavailing, their schemes fail. Vidocq, for example, was a good guesser, and a persevering man. But, without educated thought, he erred continually by the very intensity of his investigations. He impaired his vision by holding the object too close. He might see, perhaps, one or two points with unusual clearness, but in so doing he, necessarily, lost sight of the matter as a whole. Thus there is such a thing as being too profound. Truth is not always in a well. In fact, as regards the more important knowledge, I do believe that she is invariably superficial. The depth lies in the valleys where we seek her, and not upon the mountain-tops where she is found. The modes and sources of this kind of error are well typified in the contemplation of the heavenly bodies. To look at a star by glances—to view it in a side-long way, by turning toward it the exterior portions of the *retina* (more susceptible of feeble impressions of light than the interior), is to behold the star distinctly— is to have the best appreciation of its lustre—a lustre which grows dim just in proportion as we turn our vision *fully* upon it. A greater number of rays actually fall upon the eye in the latter case, but in the former, there is the more refined capacity for comprehension. By undue profundity we perplex and enfeeble thought; and it is possible to make even Venus herself vanish from the firmament by a scrutiny too sustained, too concentrated, or too direct.

"As for these murders, let us enter into some examinations for ourselves, before we make up an opinion respecting them. An inquiry will afford us amusement," [I thought this an odd term, so applied, but said nothing] "and besides, Le Bon once rendered me a service for which I am not ungrateful. We will go and see the premises with our own eyes. I know G——, the Prefect of Police, and shall have no difficulty in obtaining the necessary permission."

The permission was obtained, and we proceeded at once to the Rue Morgue. This is one of those miserable thoroughfares which intervene between the Rue Richelieu and the Rue St. Roch. It was late in the afternoon when we reached it, as this quarter is at a great distance from that in which we resided. The house was readily

found; for there were still many persons gazing up at the closed shutters, with an objectless curiosity, from the opposite side of the way. It was an ordinary Parisian house, with a gateway, on one side of which was a glazed watch-box, with a sliding panel in the window, indicating a *loge de concierge*. Before going in we walked up the street, turned down an alley, and then, again turning, passed in the rear of the building—Dupin, meanwhile, examining the whole neighborhood, as well as the house, with a minuteness of attention for which I could see no possible object.

Retracing our steps we came again to the front of the dwelling, rang, and, having shown our credentials, were admitted by the agents in charge. We went up stairs —into the chamber where the body of Mademoiselle L'Espanaye had been found, and where both the deceased still lay. The disorders of the room had, as usual, been suffered to exist. I saw nothing beyond what had been stated in the *Gazette des Tribunaux*. Dupin scrutinized every thing—not excepting the bodies of the victims. We then went into the other rooms, and into the yard; a *gendarme* accompanying us throughout. The examination occupied us until dark, when we took our departure. On our way home my companion stepped in for a moment at the office of one of the daily papers.

I have said that the whims of my friend were manifold, and that *Je les ménagais:*—for this phrase there is no English equivalent. It was his humor, now, to decline all conversation on the subject of the murder, until about noon the next day. He then asked me, suddenly, if I had observed any thing *peculiar* at the scene of the atrocity.

There was something in his manner of emphasizing the word *"peculiar,"* which caused me to shudder, without knowing why.

"No, nothing *peculiar*," I said; "nothing more, at least, than we both saw stated in the paper."

"The *Gazette*," he replied, "has not entered, I fear, into the unusual horror of the thing. But dismiss the idle opinions of this print. It appears to me that this mystery is considered insoluble, for the very reason which should cause it to be regarded as easy of solution—I mean for the *outré* character of its features. The police are confounded by the seeming absence of motive—not for the

murder itself—but for the atrocity of the murder. They
are puzzled, too, by the seeming impossibility of recon-
ciling the voices heard in contention, with the facts
that no one was discovered upstairs but the assassinated
Mademoiselle L'Espanaye, and that there were no means
of egress without the notice of the party ascending. The
wild disorder of the room; the corpse thrust, with the head
downward, up the chimney; the frightful mutilation of the
body of the old lady; these considerations, with those
just mentioned, and others which I need not mention,
have sufficed to paralyze the powers, by putting com-
pletely at fault the boasted *acumen,* of the government
agents. They have fallen into the gross but common error
of confounding the unusual with the abstruse. But it is
by these deviations from the plane of the ordinary, that
reason feels its way, if at all, in its search for the true.
In investigations such as we are now pursuing, it should
not be so much asked 'what has occurred,' as 'what has
occurred that has never occurred before.' In fact, the
facility with which I shall arrive, or have arrived, at the
solution of this mystery, is in the direct ratio of its ap-
parent insolubility in the eyes of the police."

I stared at the speaker in mute astonishment.

"I am now awaiting," continued he, looking toward the
door of our apartment—"I am now awaiting a person
who, although perhaps not the perpetrator of these
butcheries, must have been in some measure implicated
in their perpetration. Of the worst portion of the crimes
committed, it is probable that he is innocent. I hope
that I am right in this supposition; for upon it I build my
expectation of reading the entire riddle. I look for the
man here—in this room—every moment. It is true that
he may not arrive; but the probability is that he will.
Should he come, it will be necessary to detain him. Here
are pistols; and we both know how to use them when oc-
casion demands their use."

I took the pistols, scarcely knowing what I did, or be-
lieving what I heard, while Dupin went on, very much as
if in a soliloquy. I have already spoken of his abstract
manner at such times. His discourse was addressed to
myself; but his voice, although by no means loud, had that
intonation which is commonly employed in speaking to
some one at a great distance. His eyes, vacant in expres-
sion, regarded only the wall.

"That the voices heard in contention," he said, "by the party upon the stairs, were not the voices of the women themselves, was fully proved by the evidence. This relieves us of all doubt upon the question whether the old lady could have first destroyed the daughter, and afterward have committed suicide. I speak of this point chiefly for the sake of method; for the strength of Madame L'Espanaye would have been utterly unequal to the task of thrusting her daughter's corpse up the chimney as it was found; and the nature of the wounds upon her own person entirely precludes the idea of self-destruction. Murder, then, has been committed by some third party; and the voices of this third party were those heard in contention. Let me now advert—not to the whole testimony respecting these voices—but to what was *peculiar* in that testimony. Did you observe any thing peculiar about it?"

I remarked that, while all the witnesses agreed in supposing the gruff voice to be that of a Frenchman, there was much disagreement in regard to the shrill, or, as one individual termed it, the harsh voice.

"That was the evidence itself," said Dupin, "but it was not the peculiarity of the evidence. You have observed nothing distinctive. Yet there *was* something to be observed. The witnesses, as you remark, agreed about the gruff voice; they were here unanimous. But in regard to the shrill voice, the peculiarity is—not that they disagreed—but that, while an Italian, an Englishman, a Spaniard, a Hollander, and a Frenchman attempted to describe it, each one spoke of it as that *of a foreigner*. Each is sure that it was not the voice of one of his own countrymen. Each likens it—not to the voice of an individual of any nation with whose language he is conversant —but the converse. The Frenchman supposes it the voice of a Spaniard, and 'might have distinguished some words *had he been acquainted with the Spanish.*' The Dutchman maintains it to have been that of a Frenchman; but we find it stated that '*not understanding French this witness was examined through an interpreter.*' The Englishman thinks it the voice of a German, and '*does not understand German.*' The Spaniard 'is sure' that it was that of an Englishman, but 'judges by the intonation' altogether, '*as he has no knowledge of the English.*' The Italian believes it the voice of a Russian, but '*has never

conversed with a native of Russia.' A second Frenchman
differs, moreover, with the first, and is positive that the
voice was that of an Italian; but, *not being cognizant of
that tongue,* is, like the Spaniard, 'convinced by the in-
tonation.' Now, how strangely unusual must that voice
have really been, about which such testimony as this
could have been elicited!—in whose *tones,* even, denizens
of the five great divisions of Europe could recognize noth-
ing familiar! You will say that it might have been the
voice of an Asiatic—of an African. Neither Asiatics nor
Africans abound in Paris; but, without denying the in-
ference, I will now merely call your attention to three
points. The voice is termed by one witness 'harsh rather
than shrill.' It is represented by two others to have been
'quick and *unequal.*' No words—no sounds resembling
words—were by any witness mentioned as distinguish-
able.

"I know not," continued Dupin, "what impression I
may have made, so far, upon your own understanding;
but I do not hesitate to say that legitimate deductions
even from this portion of the testimony—the portion re-
specting the gruff and shrill voices—are in themselves
sufficient to engender a suspicion which should give di-
rection to all farther progress in the investigation of the
mystery. I said 'legitimate deductions'; but my meaning
is not thus fully expressed. I designed to imply that the
deductions are the *sole* proper ones, and that the suspi-
cion arises *inevitably* from them as the single result. What
the suspicion is, however, I will not say just yet. I merely
wish you to bear in mind that, with myself, it was suffi-
ciently forcible to give a definite form—a certain ten-
dency—to my inquiries in the chamber.

"Let us now transport ourselves, in fancy, to this cham-
ber. What shall we first seek here? The means of egress
employed by the murderers. It is not too much to say
that neither of us believe in præternatural events. Mad-
ame and Mademoiselle L'Espanaye were not destroyed
by spirits. The doers of the deed were material and es-
caped materially. Then how? Fortunately there is but one
mode of reasoning upon the point, and that mode *must*
lead us to a definite decision. Let us examine, each by
each, the possible means of egress. It is clear that the
assassins were in the room where Mademoiselle L'Es-
panaye was found, or at least in the room adjoin-

ing, when the party ascended the stairs. It is, then, only from these two apartments that we have to seek issues. The police have laid bare the floors, the ceiling, and the masonry of the walls, in every direction. No *secret* issues could, have escaped their vigilance. But, not trusting to *their* eyes, I examined with my own. There were, then, *no* secret issues. Both doors leading from the rooms into the passage were securely locked, with the keys inside. Let us turn to the chimneys. These, although of ordinary width for some eight or ten feet above the hearths, will not admit, throughout their extent, the body of a large cat. The impossibility of egress, by means already stated, being thus absolute, we are reduced to the windows. Through those of the front room no one could have escaped without notice from the crowd in the street. The murderers *must* have passed, then, through those of the back room. Now, brought to this conclusion in so unequivocal a manner as we are, it is not our part, as reasoners, to reject it on account of apparent impossibilities. It is only left for us to prove that these apparent 'impossibilities' are, in reality, not such.

"There are two windows in the chamber. One of them is unobstructed by furniture, and is wholly visible. The lower portion of the other is hidden from view by the head of the unwieldy bedstead which is thrust close up against it. The former was found securely fastened from within. It resisted the utmost force of those who endeavored to raise it. A large gimlet-hole had been pierced in its frame to the left, and a very stout nail was found fitted therein, nearly to the head. Upon examining the other window, a similar nail was seen similarly fitted in it; and a vigorous attempt to raise this sash failed also. The police were now entirely satisfied that egress had not been in these directions. And, *therefore,* it was thought a matter of supererogation to withdraw the nails and open the windows.

"My own examination was somewhat more particular, and was so for the reason I have just given—because here it was, I knew, that all apparent impossibilities *must* be proved to be not such in reality.

"I proceeded to think thus—*a posteriori*. The murderers *did* escape from one of these windows. This being so, they could not have re-fastened the sashes from the inside, as they were found fastened;—the consideration

which put a stop, through its obviousness, to the scrutiny of the police in this quarter. Yet the sashes *were* fastened. They *must,* then, have the power of fastening themselves. There was no escape from this conclusion. I stepped to the unobstructed casement, withdrew the nail with some difficulty, and attempted to raise the sash. It resisted all my efforts, as I had anticipated. A concealed spring must, I now knew, exist; and this corroboration of my idea convinced me that my premises, at least, were correct, however mysterious still appeared the circumstances attending the nails. A careful search soon brought to light the hidden spring. I pressed it, and, satisfied with the discovery, forbore to upraise the sash.

"I now replaced the nail and regarded it attentively. A person passing out through this window might have reclosed it, and the spring would have caught—but the nail could not have been replaced. The conclusion was plain, and again narrowed in the field of my investigations. The assassins *must* have escaped through the other window. Supposing, then, the springs upon each sash to be the same, as was probable, there *must* be found a difference between the nails, or at least between the modes of their fixture. Getting upon the sacking of the bedstead, I looked over the head-board minutely at the second casement. Passing my hand down behind the board, I readily discovered and pressed the spring, which was, as I had supposed, identical in character with its neighbor. I now looked at the nail. It was as stout as the other, and apparently fitted in the same manner—driven in nearly up to the head.

"You will say that I was puzzled; but, if you think so, you must have misunderstood the nature of the inductions. To use a sporting phrase, I had not been once 'at fault.' The scent had never for an instant been lost. There was no flaw in any link of the chain. I had traced the secret to its ultimate result,—and that result was *the nail*. It had, I say, in every respect, the appearance of its fellow in the other window; but this fact was an absolute nullity (conclusive as it might seem to be) when compared with the consideration that here, at this point, terminated the clew. 'There *must* be something wrong,' I said, 'about the nail.' I touched it; and the head, with about a quarter of an inch of the shank, came off in my fingers. The rest of the shank was in the gimlet-

hole, where it had been broken off. The fracture was an old one (for its edges were incrusted with rust), and had apparently been accomplished by the blow of a hammer, which had partially imbedded, in the top of the bottom sash, the head portion of the nail. I now carefully replaced this head portion in the indentation whence I had taken it, and the resemblance to a perfect nail was complete—the fissure was invisible. Pressing the spring, I gently raised the sash for a few inches; the head went up with it, remaining firm in its bed. I closed the window, and the semblance of the whole nail was again perfect.

"This riddle, so far, was now unriddled. The assassin had escaped through the window which looked upon the bed. Dropping of its own accord upon his exit (or perhaps purposely closed), it had become fastened by the spring; and it was the retention of this spring which had been mistaken by the police for that of the nail,—farther inquiry being thus considered unnecessary.

"The next question is that of the mode of descent. Upon this point I had been satisfied in my walk with you around the building. About five feet and a half from the casement in question there runs a lightning-rod. From this rod it would have been impossible for any one to reach the window itself, to say nothing of entering it. I observed, however, that the shutters of the fourth story were of the peculiar kind called by ·Parisian carpenters *ferrades*—a kind rarely employed at the present day, but frequently seen upon very old mansions at Lyons and Bordeaux. They are in the form of an ordinary door (a single, not a folding door), except that the lower half is latticed or worked in open trellis—thus affording an excellent hold for the hands. In the present instance these shutters are fully three feet and a half broad. When we saw them from the rear of the house, they were both about half open—that is to say they stood off at right angles from the wall. It is probable that the police, as well as myself, examined the back of the tenement; but, if so, in looking at these *ferrades* in the line of their breadth (as they must have done), they did not perceive this great breadth itself, or, at all events, failed to take it into due consideration. In fact, having once satisfied themselves that no egress could have been made in this quarter, they would naturally bestow here a very

cursory examination. It was clear to me, however, that the shutter belonging to the window at the head of the bed, would, if swung fully back to the wall, reach to within two feet of the lightning-rod. It was also evident that, by exertion of a very unusual degree of activity and courage, an entrance into the window, from the rod, might have been thus effected. By reaching to the distance of two feet and a half (we now suppose the shutter open to its whole extent) a robber might have taken a firm grasp upon the trellis-work. Letting go, then, his hold upon the rod, placing his feet securely against the wall, and springing boldly from it, he might have swung the shutter so as to close it, and, if we imagine the window open at the time, might even have swung himself into the room.

"I wish you to bear especially in mind that I have spoken of a *very* unusual degree of activity as requisite to success in so hazardous and so difficult a feat. It is my design to show you first, that the thing might possibly have been accomplished:—but, secondly and *chiefly,* I wish to impress upon your understanding the *very extraordinary*—the almost præternatural character of that agility which could have accomplished it.

"You will say, no doubt, using the language of the law, that 'to make out my case,' I should rather undervalue than insist upon a full estimation of the activity required in this matter. This may be the practice in law, but it is not the usage of reason. My ultimate object is only the truth. My immediate purpose is to lead you to place in juxtaposition, that *very unusual* activity of which I have just spoken, with that *very peculiar* shrill (or harsh) and *unequal* voice, about whose nationality no two persons could be found to agree, and in whose utterance no syllabification could be detected."

At these words a vague and half-formed conception of the meaning of Dupin flitted over my mind. I seemed to be upon the verge of comprehension, without power to comprehend—as men, at times, find themselves upon the brink of remembrance, without being able, in the end, to remember. My friend went on with his discourse.

"You will see," he said, "that I have shifted the question from the mode of egress to that of ingress. It was my design to convey the idea that both were effected in the same manner, at the same point. Let us now revert

to the interior of the room. Let us survey the appearances
here. The drawers of the bureau, it is said, had been
rifled, although many articles of apparel still remained
within them. The conclusion here is absurd. It is a mere
guess—a very silly one—and no more. How are we to
know that the articles found in the drawers were not
all these drawers had originally contained? Madame
L'Espanaye and her daughter lived an exceedingly re-
tired life—saw no company—seldom went out—had lit-
tle use for numerous changes of habiliment. Those found
were at least of as good quality as any likely to be
possessed by these ladies. If a thief had taken any, why
did he not take the best—why did he not take all? In a
word, why did he abandon four thousand francs in gold
to encumber himself with a bundle of linen? The gold
was abandoned. Nearly the whole sum mentioned by
Monsieur Mignaud, the banker, was discovered, in bags,
upon the floor. I wish you, therefore, to discard from
your thoughts the blundering idea of *motive,* engendered
in the brains of the police by that portion of the evidence
which speaks of money delivered at the door of the
house. Coincidences ten times as remarkable as this (the
delivery of the money, and murder committed within
three days upon the party receiving it), happen to all of
us every hour of our lives, without attracting even mo-
mentary notice. Coincidences, in general, are great
stumbling-blocks in the way of that class of thinkers
who have been educated to know nothing of the theory
of probabilities—that theory to which the most glorious
objects of human research are indebted for the most
glorious of illustration. In the present instance, had the
gold been gone, the fact of its delivery three days be-
fore would have formed something more than a coinci-
dence. It would have been corroborative of this idea of
motive. But, under the real circumstances of the case, if
we are to suppose gold the motive of this outrage, we
must also imagine the perpetrator so vacillating an idiot
as to have abandoned his gold and his motive together.

"Keeping now steadily in mind the points to which I
have drawn your attention—that peculiar voice, that un-
usual agility, and that startling absence of motive in a
murder so singularly atrocious as this—let us glance at
the butchery itself. Here is a woman strangled to death
by manual strength, and thrust up a chimney·head

downward. Ordinary assassins employ no such mode of murder as this. Least of all, do they thus dispose of the murdered. In the manner of thrusting the corpse up the chimney, you will admit that there was something *excessively outré*—something altogether irreconcilable with our common notions of human action, even when we suppose the actors the most depraved of men. Think, too, how great must have been that strength which could have thrust the body *up* such an aperture so forcibly that the united vigor of several persons was found barely sufficient to drag it *down!*

"Turn, now, to other indications of the employment of a vigor most marvellous. On the hearth were thick tresses —very thick tresses—of gray human hair. These had been torn out by the roots. You are aware of the great force necessary in tearing thus from the head even twenty or thirty hairs together. You saw the locks in question as well as myself. Their roots (a hideous sight!) were clotted with fragments of the flesh of the scalp—sure token of the prodigious power which had been exerted in uprooting perhaps half a million hairs at a time. The throat of the old lady was not merely cut, but the head absolutely severed from the body: the instrument was a mere razor. I wish you also to look at the *brutal* ferocity of these deeds. Of the bruises upon the body of Madame L'Espanaye I do not speak. Monsieur Dumas, and his worthy coadjutor Monsieur Etienne, have pronounced that they were inflicted by some obtuse instrument; and so far these gentlemen are very correct. The obtuse instrument was clearly the stone pavement in the yard, upon which the victim had fallen from the window which looked in upon the bed. This idea, however simple it may now seem, escaped the police for the same reason that the breadth of the shutters escaped them—because, by the affair of the nails, their perceptions had been hermetically sealed against the possibility of the windows having ever been opened at all.

"If now, in addition to all these things, you have properly reflected upon the odd disorder of the chamber, we have gone so far as to combine the ideas of an agility astounding, a strength superhuman, a ferocity brutal, a butchery without motive, a *grotesquerie* in horror absolutely alien from humanity, and a voice foreign in tone to the ears of men of many nations, and devoid of all

distinct or intelligible syllabification. What result, then, has ensued? What impression have I made upon your fancy?"

I felt a creeping of the flesh as Dupin asked me the question. "A madman," I said, "has done this deed—some raving maniac, escaped from a neighboring *Maison de Santé.*"

"In some respects," he replied, "your idea is not ir-relevant. But the voices of madmen, even in their wildest paroxysms, are never found to tally with that peculiar voice heard upon the stairs. Madmen are of some nation, and their language, however incoherent in its words, has always the coherence of syllabification. Besides, the hair of a madman is not such as I now hold in my hand. I disentangled this little tuft from the rigidly clutched fingers of Madame L'Espanaye. Tell me what you can make of it."

"Dupin!" I said, completely unnerved; "this hair is most unusual—this is no *human* hair."

"I have not asserted that it is," said he; "but, before we decide this point, I wish you to glance at the little sketch I have here traced upon this paper. It is a *fac-simile* drawing of what has been described in one por-tion of the testimony as 'dark bruises and deep in-dentations of finger nails' upon the throat of Mademoi-selle L'Espanaye, and in another (by Messrs. Dumas and Etienne) as a 'series of livid spots, evidently the im-pression of fingers.'

"You will perceive," continued my friend, spreading out the paper upon the table before us, "that this draw-ing gives the idea of a firm and fixed hold. There is no *slipping* apparent. Each finger has retained—possibly until the death of the victim—the fearful grasp by which it originally imbedded itself. Attempt, now, to place all your fingers, at the same time, in the respective impres-sions as you see them."

I made the attempt in vain.

"We are possibly not giving this matter a fair trial," he said. "The paper is spread out upon a plane surface; but the human throat is cylindrical. Here is a billet of wood, the circumference of which is about that of the throat. Wrap the drawing around it, and try the experi-ment again."

I did so; but the difficulty was even more obvious

than before. "This," I said, "is the mark of no human hand."

"Read now," replied Dupin, "this passage from Cuvier."

It was a minute anatomical and generally descriptive account of the large fulvous Ourang-Outang of the East Indian Islands. The gigantic stature, the prodigious strength and activity, the wild ferocity, and the imitative propensities of these mammalia are sufficiently well known to all. I understood the full horrors of the murder at once.

"The description of the digits," said I, as I made an end of the reading, "is in exact accordance with this drawing. I see that no animal but an Ourang-Outang, of the species here mentioned, could have impressed the indentations as you have traced them. This tuft of tawny hair, too, is identical in character with that of the beast of Cuvier. But I cannot possibly comprehend the particulars of this frightful mystery. Besides, there were *two* voices heard in contention, and one of them was unquestionably the voice of a Frenchman."

"True; and you will remember an expression attributed almost unanimously, by the evidence, to this voice,—the expression, '*mon Dieu!*' This, under the circumstances, has been justly characterized by one of the witnesses (Montani, the confectioner) as an expression of remonstrance or expostulation. Upon these two words, therefore, I have mainly built my hopes of a full solution of the riddle. A Frenchman was cognizant of the murder. It is possible—indeed it is far more than probable —that he was innocent of all participation in the bloody transactions which took place. The Ourang-Outang may have escaped from him. He may have traced it to the chamber; but, under the agitating circumstances which ensued, he could never have recaptured it. It is still at large. I will not pursue these guesses—for I have no right to call them more—since the shades of reflection upon which they are based are scarcely of sufficient depth to be appreciable by my own intellect, and since I could not pretend to make them intelligible to the understanding of another. We will call them guesses, then, and speak of them as such. If the Frenchman in question is indeed, as I suppose, innocent of this atrocity, this advertisement, which I left last night, upon our return home, at the office of *Le Monde* (a paper devoted to

the shipping interest, and much sought by sailors), will bring him to our residence."

He handed me a paper, and I read thus:

"CAUGHT—*In the Bois de Boulogne, early in the morning of the —— inst.* (the morning of the murder), *a very large, tawny Ourang-Outang of the Bornese species. The owner (who is ascertained to be a sailor, belonging to a Maltese vessel) may have the animal again, upon identifying it satisfactorily, and paying a few charges arising from its capture and keeping. Call at No. —— Rue ——, Faubourg St. Germain—au troisième.*"

"How was it possible," I asked, "that you should know the man to be a sailor, and belonging to a Maltese vessel?"

"I do *not* know it," said Dupin. "I am not *sure* of it. Here, however, is a small piece of ribbon, which from its form, and from its greasy appearance, has evidently been used in tying the hair in one of those long *queues* of which sailors are so fond. Moreover, this knot is one which few besides sailors can tie, and is peculiar to the Maltese. I picked the ribbon up at the foot of the lightning-rod. It could not have belonged to either of the deceased. Now if, after all, I am wrong in my induction from this ribbon, that the Frenchman was a sailor belonging to a Maltese vessel, still I can have done no harm in saying what I did in the advertisement. If I am in error, he will merely suppose that I have been misled by some circumstance into which he will not take the trouble to inquire. But if I am right, a great point is gained. Cognizant although innocent of the murder, the Frenchman will naturally hesitate about replying to the advertisement—about demanding the Ourang-Outang. He will reason thus:—'I am innocent; I am poor; my Ourang-Outang is of great value—to one in my circumstances a fortune of itself—why should I lose it through idle apprehensions of danger? Here it is, within my grasp. It was found in the Bois de Boulogne—at a vast distance from the scene of that butchery. How can it ever be suspected that a brute beast should have done the deed? The police are at fault—they have failed to procure the slightest clew. Should they even trace the animal, it would

be impossible to prove me cognizant of the murder or to
implicate me in guilt on account of that cognizance.
Above all, *I am known*. The advertiser designates me as
the possessor of the beast. I am not sure to what limit
his knowledge may extend. Should I avoid claiming a
property of so great value, which it is known that I possess,
I will render the animal, at least, liable to suspicion.
It is not my policy to attract attention either to myself
or to the beast. I will answer the advertisement, get the
Ourang-Outang, and keep it close until this matter has
blown over.' "

At this moment we heard a step upon the stairs.

"Be ready," said Dupin, "with your pistols, but neither
use them nor show them until at a signal from myself."

The front door of the house had been left open, and
the visitor had entered, without ringing, and advanced
several steps upon the staircase. Now, however, he
seemed to hesitate. Presently we heard him descending.
Dupin was moving quickly to the door, when we again
heard him coming up. He did not turn back a second
time, but stepped up with decision, and rapped at the
door of our chamber.

"Come in," said Dupin, in a cheerful and hearty tone.

A man entered. He was a sailor, evidently,—a tall,
stout, and muscular-looking person, with a certain dare-
devil expression of countenance, not altogether unprepos-
sessing. His face, greatly sunburnt, was more than half
hidden by whisker and *mustachio*. He had with him a
huge oaken cudgel, but appeared to be otherwise un-
armed. He bowed awkwardly, and bade us "good eve-
ning," in French accents, which, although somewhat
Neufchatelish, were still sufficiently indicative of a Pari-
sian origin.

"Sit down, my friend," said Dupin. "I suppose you have
called about the Ourang-Outang. Upon my word, I al-
most envy you the possession of him; a remarkably fine,
and no doubt a very valuable animal. How old do you
suppose him to be?"

The sailor drew a long breath, with the air of a man
relieved of some intolerable burden, and then replied, in
an assured tone:

"I have no way of telling—but he can't be more than
four or five years old. Have you got him here?"

"Oh, no; we had no conveniences for keeping him

here. He is at a livery stable in the Rue Dubourg, just by. You can get him in the morning. Of course you are prepared to identify the property?"

"To be sure I am, sir."

"I shall be sorry to part with him," said Dupin.

"I don't mean that you should be at all this trouble for nothing, sir," said the man. "Couldn't expect it. Am very willing to pay a reward for the finding of the animal—that is to say, any thing in reason."

"Well," replied my friend, "that is all very fair, to be sure. Let me think!—what should I have? Oh! I will tell you. My reward shall be this. You shall give me all the information in your power about these murders in the Rue Morgue."

Dupin said the last words in a very low tone, and very quietly. Just as quietly, too, he walked toward the door, locked it, and put the key in his pocket. He then drew a pistol from his bosom and placed it, without the least flurry, upon the table.

The sailor's face flushed up as if he were struggling with suffocation. He started to his feet and grasped his cudgel; but the next moment he fell back into his seat, trembling violently, and with the countenance of death itself. He spoke not a word. I pitied him from the bottom of my heart.

"My friend," said Dupin, in a kind tone, "you are alarming yourself unnecessarily—you are indeed. We mean you no harm whatever. I pledge you the honor of a gentleman, and of a Frenchman, that we intend you no injury. I perfectly well know that you are innocent of the atrocities in the Rue Morgue. It will not do, however, to deny that you are in some measure implicated in them. From what I have already said, you must know that I have had means of information about this matter—means of which you could never have dreamed. Now the thing stands thus. You have done nothing which you could have avoided—nothing, certainly, which renders you culpable. You were not even guilty of robbery, when you might have robbed with impunity. You have nothing to conceal. You have no reason for concealment. On the other hand, you are bound by every principle of honor to confess all you know. An innocent man is now imprisoned, charged with that crime of which you can point out the perpetrator."

The sailor had recovered his presence of mind, in a great measure, while Dupin uttered these words; but his original boldness of bearing was all gone.

"So help me God!" said he, after a brief pause, "I *will* tell you all I know about this affair;—but I do not expect you to believe one half I say—I would be a fool indeed if I did. Still, I *am* innocent, and I will make a clean breast if I die for it."

What he stated was, in substance, this. He had lately made a voyage to the Indian Archipelago. A party, of which he formed one, landed at Borneo, and passed into the interior on an excursion of pleasure. Himself and a companion had captured the Ourang-Outang. This companion dying, the animal fell into his own exclusive possession. After great trouble, occasioned by the intractable ferocity of his captive during the home voyage, he at length succeeded in lodging it safely at his own residence in Paris, where, not to attract toward himself the unpleasant curiosity of his neighbors, he kept it carefully secluded, until such time as it should recover from a wound in the foot, received from a splinter on board ship. His ultimate design was to sell it.

Returning home from some sailors' frolic on the night, or rather in the morning, of the murder, he found the beast occupying his own bedroom, into which it had broken from a closet adjoining, where it had been, as was thought, securely confined. Razor in hand, and fully lathered, it was sitting before a looking-glass, attempting the operation of shaving, in which it had no doubt previously watched its master through the keyhole of the closet. Terrified at the sight of so dangerous a weapon in the possession of an animal so ferocious, and so well able to use it, the man, for some moments, was at a loss what to do. He had been accustomed, however, to quiet the creature, even in its fiercest moods, by the use of a whip, and to this he now resorted. Upon sight of it, the Ourang-Outang sprang at once through the door of the chamber, down the stairs, and thence, through a window, unfortunately open, into the street.

The Frenchman followed in despair; the ape, razor still in hand, occasionally stopping to look back and gesticulate at his pursuer, until the latter had nearly come up with it. It then again made off. In this manner the chase continued for a long time. The streets were pro-

foundly quiet, as it was nearly three o'clock in the morn-
ing. In passing down an alley in the rear of the Rue
Morgue, the fugitive's attention was arrested by a light
gleaming from the open window of Madame L'Espanaye's
chamber, in the fourth story of her house. Rushing to the
building, it perceived the lightning-rod, clambered up
with inconceivable agility, grasped the shutter, which
was thrown fully back against the wall, and, by its
means, swung itself directly upon the headboard of the
bed. The whole feat did not occupy a minute. The shutter
was kicked open again by the Ourang-Outang as it en-
tered the room.

The sailor, in the meantime, was both rejoiced and per-
plexed. He had strong hopes of now recapturing the brute,
as it could scarcely escape from the trap into which it had
ventured, except by the rod, where it might be inter-
cepted as it came down. On the other hand, there was
much cause for anxiety as to what it might do in the
house. This latter reflection urged the man still to follow
the fugitive. A lightning-rod is ascended without diffi-
culty, especially by a sailor; but, when he had arrived as
high as the window, which lay far to his left, his career
was stopped; the most that he could accomplish was to
reach over so as to obtain a glimpse of the interior of the
room. At this glimpse he nearly fell from his hold through
excess of horror. Now it was that those hideous shrieks
arose upon the night, which had startled from slumber
the inmates of the Rue Morgue. Madame L'Espanaye
and her daughter, habited in their night clothes, had ap-
parently been occupied in arranging some papers in the
iron chest already mentioned, which had been wheeled
into the middle of the room. It was open, and its con-
tents lay beside it on the floor. The victims must have
been sitting with their backs toward the window; and,
from the time elapsing between the ingress of the beast
and the screams, it seems probable that it was not im-
mediately perceived. The flapping-to of the shutter would
naturally have been attributed to the wind.

As the sailor looked in, the gigantic animal had seized
Madame L'Espanaye by the hair (which was loose, as
she had been combing it), and was flourishing the razor
about her face, in imitation of the motions of a barber.
The daughter lay prostrate and motionless; she had
swooned. The screams and struggles of the old lady (dur-

ing which the hair was torn from her head) had the effect
of changing the probably pacific purposes of the Ourang-
Outang into those of wrath. With one determined sweep
of its muscular arm it nearly severed her head from her
body. The sight of blood inflamed its anger into phrensy.
Gnashing its teeth, and flashing fire from its eyes, it flew
upon the body of the girl, and imbedded its fearful talons
in her throat, retaining its grasp until she expired. Its
wandering and wild glances fell at this moment upon the
head of the bed, over which the face of its master, rigid
with horror, was just discernible. The fury of the beast,
who no doubt bore still in mind the dreaded whip, was
instantly converted into fear. Conscious of having de-
served punishment, it seemed desirous of concealing its
bloody deeds, and skipped about the chamber in an
agony of nervous agitation; throwing down and breaking
the furniture as it moved, and dragging the bed from the
bedstead. In conclusion, it seized first the corpse of the
daughter, and thrust it up the chimney, as it was found;
then that of the old lady, which it immediately hurled
through the window headlong.

As the ape approached the casement with its mutilated
burden, the sailor shrank aghast to the rod, and, rather
gliding than clambering down it, hurried at once home—
dreading the consequences of the butchery, and gladly
abandoning, in his terror, all solicitude about the fate of
the Ourang-Outang. The words heard by the party upon
the staircase were the Frenchman's exclamations of hor-
ror and affright, commingled with the fiendish jabberings
of the brute.

I have scarcely any thing to add. The Ourang-Outang
must have escaped from the chamber, by the rod, just be-
fore the breaking of the door. It must have closed the
window as it passed through it. It was subsequently caught
by the owner himself, who obtained for it a very large
sum at the *Jardin des Plantes*. Le Bon was instantly re-
leased, upon our narration of the circumstances (with
some comments from Dupin) at the *bureau* of the Prefect
of Police. This functionary, however well disposed to my
friend, could not altogether conceal his chagrin at the
turn which affairs had taken, and was fain to indulge
in a sarcasm or two about the propriety of every person
minding his own business.

"Let him talk," said Dupin, who had not thought it

necessary to reply. "Let him discourse; it will ease his conscience. I am satisfied with having defeated him in his own castle. Nevertheless, that he failed in the solution of this mystery, is by no means that matter for wonder which he supposes it; for, in truth, our friend the Prefect is somewhat too cunning to be profound. In his wisdom is no *stamen*. It is all head and no body, like the pictures of the Goddess Laverna—or, at best, all head and shoulders, like a codfish. But he is a good creature after all. I like him especially for one master stroke of cant, by which he has attained his reputation for ingenuity. I mean the way he has *'de nier ce qui est, et d'expliquer ce qui n'est pas.'* " [1]

[1] Rousseau—Nouvelle Héloise.

The Purloined Letter

Nil sapientiæ odiosius acumine nimio.—*Seneca*

AT PARIS, just after dark one gusty evening in the autumn of 18—, I was enjoying the twofold luxury of meditation and a meerschaum, in company with my friend, C. Auguste Dupin, in his little back library, or book-closet, *au troisième,* No. 33 *Rue Dunôt, Faubourg St. Germain.* For one hour at least we had maintained a profound silence; while each, to any casual observer, might have seemed intently and exclusively occupied with the curling eddies of smoke that oppressed the atmosphere of the chamber. For myself, however, I was mentally discussing certain topics which had formed matter for conversation between us at an earlier period of the evening; I mean the affair of the Rue Morgue, and the mystery attending the murder of Marie Rogêt. I looked upon it, therefore, as something of a coincidence, when the door of our apartment was thrown open and admitted our old acquaintance, Monsieur G——, the Prefect of the Parisian police.

We gave him a hearty welcome; for there was nearly half as much of the entertaining as of the contemptible about the man, and we had not seen him for several years. We had been sitting in the dark, and Dupin now arose for the purpose of lighting a lamp, but sat down again, without doing so, upon G.'s saying that he had called to consult us, or rather to ask the opinion of my friend, about some official business which had occasioned a great deal of trouble.

"If it is any point requiring reflection," observed Dupin, as he forbore to enkindle the wick, "we shall examine it to better purpose in the dark."

"That is another of your odd notions," said the Prefect, who had the fashion of calling everything "odd" that was beyond his comprehension, and thus lived amid an absolute legion of "oddities."

"Very true," said Dupin, as he supplied his visitor with a pipe, and rolled toward him a comfortable chair.

"And what is the difficulty now?" I asked. "Nothing more in the assassination way I hope?"

"Oh, no; nothing of that nature. The fact is, the business is *very* simple indeed, and I make no doubt that we can manage it sufficiently well ourselves; but then I thought Dupin would like to hear the details of it because it is so excessively *odd*."

"Simple and odd," said Dupin.

"Why, yes; and not exactly that either. The fact is, we have all been a good deal puzzled because the affair *is* so simple, and yet baffles us altogether."

"Perhaps it is the very simplicity of the thing which puts you at fault," said my friend.

"What nonsense you *do* talk!" replied the Prefect, laughing heartily.

"Perhaps the mystery is a little *too* plain," said Dupin.

"Oh, good heavens! who ever heard of such an idea?"

"A little *too* self-evident."

"Ha! ha! ha!—ha! ha! ha!—ho! ho! ho!" roared our visitor, profoundly amused, "oh, Dupin, you will be the death of me yet!"

"And what, after all, *is* the matter on hand?" I asked.

"Why, I will tell you," replied the Prefect, as he gave a long, steady, and contemplative puff, and settled himself in his chair. "I will tell you in a few words; but, before I begin, let me caution you that this is an affair demanding the greatest secrecy, and that I should most probably lose the position I now hold, were it known that I confided it to any one."

"Proceed," said I.

"Or not," said Dupin.

"Well, then; I have received personal information, from a very high quarter, that a certain document of the last importance has been purloined from the royal apartments. The individual who purloined it is known; this beyond a doubt; he was seen to take it. It is known, also, that it still remains in his possession."

"How is this known?" asked Dupin.

"It is clearly inferred," replied the Prefect, "from the nature of the document, and from the non-appearance of certain results which would at once arise from its passing *out* of the robber's possession—that is to say, from his employing it as he must design in the end to employ it."

"Be a little more explicit," I said.

"Well, I may venture so far as to say that the paper gives its holder a certain power in a certain quarter where such power is immensely valuable." The Prefect was fond of the cant of diplomacy.

"Still I do not quite understand," said Dupin.

"No? Well; the disclosure of the document to a third person, who shall be nameless, would bring in question the honor of a personage of most exalted station; and this fact gives the holder of the document an ascendancy over the illustrious personage whose honor and peace are so jeopardized."

"But this ascendancy," I interposed, "would depend upon the robber's knowledge of the loser's knowledge of the robber. Who would dare—"

"The thief," said G., "is the Minister D——, who dares all things, those unbecoming as well as those becoming a man. The method of the theft was not less ingenious than bold. The document in question—a letter, to be frank—had been received by the personage robbed while alone in the royal *boudoir*. During its perusal she was suddenly interrupted by the entrance of the other exalted personage from whom especially it was her wish to conceal it. After a hurried and vain endeavor to thrust it in a drawer, she was forced to place it, open as it was, upon a table. The address, however, was uppermost, and, the contents thus unexposed, the letter escaped notice. At this juncture enters the Minister D——. His lynx eye immediately perceives the paper, recognizes the handwriting of the address, observes the confusion of the personage addressed, and fathoms her secret. After some business transactions, hurried through in his ordinary manner, he produces a letter somewhat similar to the one in question, opens it, pretends to read it, and then places it in close juxtaposition to the other. Again he converses, for some fifteen minutes, upon the public affairs. At length, in taking leave, he takes also from the table the letter to which he had no claim. Its rightful

owner saw, but, of course, dared not call attention to the act, in the presence of the third personage who stood at her elbow. The minister decamped; leaving his own letter—one of no importance—upon the table."

"Here, then," said Dupin to me, "you have precisely what you demand to make the ascendancy complete —the robber's knowledge of the loser's knowledge of the robber."

"Yes," replied the Prefect; "and the power thus attained has, for some months past, been wielded, for political purposes, to a very dangerous extent. The personage robbed is more thoroughly convinced, every day, of the necessity of reclaiming her letter. But this, of course, cannot be done openly. In fine, driven to despair, she has committed the matter to me."

"Than whom," said Dupin, amid a perfect whirlwind of smoke, "no more sagacious agent could, I suppose, be desired, or even imagined."

"You flatter me," replied the Prefect; "but it is possible that some such opinion may have been entertained."

"It is clear," said I, "as you observe, that the letter is still in the possession of the minister; since it is this possession, and not any employment of the letter, which bestows the power. With the employment the power departs."

"True," said G.; "and upon this conviction I proceeded. My first care was to make thorough search of the minister's hotel; and here my chief embarrassment lay in the necessity of searching without his knowledge. Beyond all things, I have been warned of the danger which would result from giving him reason to suspect our design."

"But," said I, "you are quite *au fait* in these investigations. The Parisian police have done this thing often before."

"Oh, yes; and for this reason I did not despair. The habits of the minister gave me, too, a great advantage. He is frequently absent from home all night. His servants are by no means numerous. They sleep at a distance from their master's apartment, and, being chiefly Neapolitans, are readily made drunk. I have keys, as you know, with which I can open any chamber or cabinet in Paris. For three months a night has not passed, during the greater part of which I have not been engaged, personally, in ransacking the D—— Hotel. My honor is in-

terested, and, to mention a great secret, the reward is enormous. So I did not abandon the search until I had become fully satisfied that the thief is a more astute man than myself. I fancy that I have investigated every nook and corner of the premises in which it is possible that the paper can be concealed."

"But is it not possible," I suggested, "that although the letter may be in possession of the minister, as it unquestionably is, he may have concealed it elsewhere than upon his own premises?"

"This is barely possible," said Dupin. "The present peculiar condition of affairs at court, and especially of those intrigues in which D—— is known to be involved, would render the instant availability of the document—its susceptibility of being produced at a moment's notice—a point of nearly equal importance with its possession."

"Its susceptibility of being produced?" said I.

"That is to say, of being *destroyed*," said Dupin.

"True," I observed; "the paper is clearly then upon the premises. As for its being upon the person of the minister, we may consider that as out of the question."

"Entirely," said the Prefect. "He has been twice waylaid, as if by footpads, and his person rigidly searched under my own inspection."

"You might have spared yourself this trouble," said Dupin. "D——, I presume, is not altogether a fool, and, if not, must have anticipated these waylayings, as a matter of course."

"Not *altogether* a fool," said G., "but then he is a poet, which I take to be only one remove from a fool."

"True," said Dupin, after a long and thoughtful whiff from his meerschaum, "although I have been guilty of certain doggerel myself."

"Suppose you detail," said I, "the particulars of your search."

"Why, the fact is, we took our time, and we searched *everywhere*. I have had long experience in these affairs. I took the entire building, room by room; devoting the nights of a whole week to each. We examined, first, the furniture of each apartment. We opened every possible drawer; and I presume you know that, to a properly trained police-agent, such a thing as a *'secret'* drawer is impossible. Any man is a dolt who permits a 'secret' drawer to escape him in a search of this kind.

The thing is *so* plain. There is a certain amount of bulk
—of space—to be accounted for in every cabinet. Then
we have accurate rules. The fiftieth part of a line
could not escape us. After the cabinets we took the
chairs. The cushions we probed with the fine long needles
you have seen me employ. From the tables we removed
the tops."

"Why so?"

"Sometimes the top of a table, or other similarly
arranged piece of furniture, is removed by the person
wishing to conceal an article; then the leg is excavated,
the article deposited within the cavity, and the top re-
placed. The bottoms and tops of bedposts are employed in
the same way."

"But could not the cavity be detected by sounding?" I
asked.

"By no means, if, when the article is deposited, a
sufficient wadding of cotton be placed around it. Be-
sides, in our case, we were obliged to proceed without
noise."

"But you could not have removed—you could not have
taken to pieces *all* articles of furniture in which it would
have been possible to make a deposit in the manner you
mention. A letter may be compressed into a thin spiral
roll, not differing much in shape or bulk from a large
knitting-needle, and in this form it might be inserted into
the rung of a chair, for example. You did not take to
pieces all the chairs?"

"Certainly not; but we did better—we examined the
rungs of every chair in the hotel, and, indeed, the joint-
ings of every description of furniture, by the aid of a most
powerful microscope. Had there been any traces of re-
cent disturbance we should not have failed to detect it in-
stantly. A single grain of gimlet-dust, for example,
would have been as obvious as an apple. Any disorder in
the gluing—any unusual gaping in the joints—would
have sufficed to insure detection."

"I presume you looked to the mirrors, between the
boards and the plates, and you probed the beds and the
bedclothes, as well as the curtains and carpets."

"That of course; and when we had absolutely com-
pleted every particle of the furniture in this way, then we
examined the house itself. We divided its entire surface
into compartments, which we numbered, so that none

might be missed; then we scrutinized each individual square inch throughout the premises, including the two houses immediately adjoining, with the microscope, as before."

"The two houses adjoining!" I exclaimed; "you must have had a great deal of trouble."

"We had; but the reward offered is prodigious."

"You included the *grounds* about the houses?"

"All the grounds are paved with brick. They gave us comparatively little trouble. We examined the moss between the bricks, and found it undisturbed."

"You looked among D——'s papers, of course, and into the books of the library?"

"Certainly; we opened every package and parcel; we not only opened every book, but we turned over every leaf in each volume, not contenting ourselves with a mere shake, according to the fashion of some of our police officers. We also measured the thickness of every book-*cover*, with the most accurate admeasurement, and applied to each the most jealous scrutiny of the microscope. Had any of the bindings been recently meddled with, it would have been utterly impossible that the fact should have escaped observation. Some five or six volumes, just from the hands of the binder, we carefully probed, longitudinally, with the needles."

"You explored the floors beneath the carpets?"

"Beyond doubt. We removed every carpet, and examined the boards with the microscope."

"And the paper on the walls?"

"Yes."

"You looked into the cellars?"

"We did."

"Then," I said, "you have been making a miscalculation, and the letter is *not* upon the premises, as you suppose."

"I fear you are right there," said the Prefect. "And now, Dupin, what would you advise me to do?"

"To make a thorough research of the premises."

"That is absolutely needless," replied G——. "I am not more sure that I breathe than I am that the letter is not at the hotel."

"I have no better advice to give you," said Dupin. "You have, of course, an accurate description of the letter?"

"Oh, yes!"—And here the Prefect, producing a memorandum-book, proceeded to read aloud a minute account of the internal, and especially of the external, appearance of the missing document. Soon after finishing the perusal of this description, he took his departure, more entirely depressed in spirits than I had ever known the good gentleman before.

In about a month afterward he paid us another visit, and found us occupied very nearly as before. He took a pipe and a chair and entered into some ordinary conversation. At length I said:

"Well, but G., what of the purloined letter? I presume you have at last made up your mind that there is no such thing as overreaching the Minister?"

"Confound him, say I—yes; I made the re-examination, however, as Dupin suggested—but it was all labor lost, as I knew it would be."

"How much was the reward offered, did you say?" asked Dupin.

"Why, a very great deal—a *very* liberal reward—I don't like to say how much, precisely; but one thing I *will* say, that I wouldn't mind giving my individual check for fifty thousand francs to any one who could obtain me that letter. The fact is, it is becoming of more and more importance every day; and the reward has been lately doubled. If it were trebled, however, I could do no more than I have done."

"Why, yes," said Dupin, drawlingly, between the whiffs of his meerschaum, "I really—think, G., you have not exerted yourself—to the utmost in this matter. You might —do a little more, I think, eh?"

"How?—in what way?"

"Why—puff, puff—you might—puff, puff—employ counsel in the matter, eh?—puff, puff, puff. Do you remember the story they tell of Abernethy?"

"No; hang Abernethy!"

"To be sure! hang him and welcome. But, once upon a time, a certain rich miser conceived the design of spunging upon this Abernethy for a medical opinion. Getting up, for this purpose, an ordinary conversation in a private company, he insinuated his case to the physician, as that of an imaginary individual.

" 'We will suppose,' said the miser, 'that his symptoms

are such and such; now, doctor, what would *you* have directed him to take?'

" 'Take!' said Abernethy, 'why, take *advice,* to be sure.' "

"But," said the Prefect, a little discomposed, "*I* am *perfectly* willing to take advice, and to pay for it. I would *really* give fifty thousand francs to any one who would aid me in the matter."

"In that case," replied Dupin, opening a drawer, and producing a check-book, "you may as well fill me up a check for the amount mentioned. When you have signed it, I will hand you the letter."

I was astounded. The Prefect appeared absolutely thunder-stricken. For some minutes he remained speechless and motionless, looking incredulously at my friend with open mouth, and eyes that seemed starting from their sockets; then apparently recovering himself in some measure, he seized a pen, and after several pauses and vacant stares, finally filled up and signed a check for fifty thousand francs, and handed it across the table to Dupin. The latter examined it carefully and deposited it in his pocket-book; then, unlocking an *escritoire,* took thence a letter and gave it to the prefect. This functionary grasped it in a perfect agony of joy, opened it with a trembling hand, cast a rapid glance at its contents, and then, scrambling and struggling to the door, rushed at length unceremoniously from the room and from the house, without having uttered a syllable since Dupin had requested him to fill up the check.

When he had gone, my friend entered into some explanations.

"The Parisian police," he said, "are exceedingly able in their way. They are persevering, ingenious, cunning, and thoroughly versed in the knowledge which their duties seem chiefly to demand. Thus, when G—— detailed to us his mode of searching the premises at the Hotel D——, I felt entire confidence in his having made a satisfactory investigation—so far as his labors extended."

"So far as his labors extended?" said I.

"Yes," said Dupin. "The measures adopted were not only the best of their kind, but carried out to absolute perfection. Had the letter been deposited within the range

of their search, these fellows would, beyond a question, have found it."

I merely laughed—but he seemed quite serious in all that he said.

"The measures, then," he continued, "were good in their kind, and well executed; their defect lay in their being inapplicable to the case and to the man. A certain set of highly ingenious resources are, with the Prefect, a sort of Procrustean bed, to which he forcibly adapts his designs. But he perpetually errs by being too deep or too shallow for the matter in hand; and many a school-boy is a better reasoner than he. I knew one about eight years of age, whose success at guessing in the game of 'even and odd' attracted universal admiration. This game is simple, and is played with marbles. One player holds in his hand a number of these toys, and demands of another whether that number is even or odd. If the guess is right, the guesser wins one; if wrong, he loses one. The boy to whom I allude won all the marbles of the school. Of course he had some principle of guessing; and this lay in mere observation and admeasurements of the astuteness of his opponents. For example, an arrant simpleton is his opponent, and, holding up his closed hand, asks, 'Are they even or odd?' Our school-boy replies, 'Odd,' and loses; but upon the second trial he wins, for he then says to himself: 'The simpleton had them even upon the first trial, and his amount of cunning is just sufficient to make him have them odd upon the second; I will therefore guess odd';—he guesses odd, and wins. Now, with a simpleton a degree above the first, he would have reasoned thus: 'This fellow finds that in the first instance I guessed odd, and, in the second, he will propose to himself, upon the first impulse, a simple variation from even to odd, as did the first simpleton; but then a second thought will suggest that this is too simple a variation, and finally he will decide upon putting it even as before. I will therefore guess even';—he guesses even, and wins. Now this mode of reasoning in the school-boy, whom his fellows termed 'lucky,'—what, in its last analysis, is it?"

"It is merely," I said, "an identification of the reasoner's intellect with that of his opponent."

"It is," said Dupin; "and, upon inquiring of the boy by what means he effected the *thorough* identification in which his success consisted, I received answer as follows:

'When I wish to find out how wise, or how stupid or how good, or how wicked is any one, or what are his thoughts at the moment, I fashion the expression of my face, as accurately as possible, in accordance with the expression of his, and then wait to see what thoughts or sentiments arise in my mind or heart, as if to match or correspond with the expression.' This response of the school-boy lies at the bottom of all the spurious profundity which has been attributed to Rochefoucault, to La Bougive, to Machiavelli, and to Campanella."

"And the identification," I said, "of the reasoner's intellect with that of his opponent, depends, if I understand you aright, upon the accuracy with which the opponent's intellect is admeasured."

"For its practical value it depends upon this," replied Dupin; "and the Prefect and his cohort fail so frequently, first, by default of this identification, and, secondly, by ill-admeasurement, or rather through non-admeasurement, of the intellect with which they are engaged. They consider only their *own* ideas of ingenuity; and, in searching for any thing hidden, advert only to the modes in which *they* would have hidden it. They are right in this much —that their own ingenuity is a faithful representative of that of the *mass;* but when the cunning of the individual felon is diverse in character from their own, the felon foils them, of course. This always happens when it is above their own, and very usually when it is below. They have no variation of principle in their investigations; at best, when urged by some unusual emergency—by some extraordinary reward—they extend or exaggerate their old modes of *practice,* without touching their principles. What, for example, in this case of D——, has been done to vary the principle of action? What is all this boring, and probing, and sounding, and scrutinizing with the microscope, and dividing the surface of the building into registered square inches—what is it all but an exaggeration *of the application* of the one principle or set of principles of search, which are based upon the one set of notions regarding human ingenuity, to which the Prefect, in the long routine of his duty, has been accustomed? Do you not see he has taken it for granted that *all* men proceed to conceal a letter, not exactly in a gimlet-hole bored in a chair-leg, but, at least, in *some* out-of-the-way hole or corner suggested by the

same tenor of thought which would urge a man to secrete
a letter in a gimlet-hole bored in a chair-leg? And do
you not see also, that such *recherchés* nooks for con-
cealment are adapted only for ordinary occasions, and
would be adopted only by ordinary intellects; for, in all
cases of concealment, a disposal of the article concealed
—a disposal of it in this *recherché* manner,—is, in the
very first instance, presumable and presumed; and thus
its discovery depends, not at all upon the acumen, but al-
together upon the mere care, patience, and determina-
tion of the seekers; and where the case is of importance
—or, what amounts to the same thing in the political
eyes, when the reward is of magnitude,—the qualities in
question have *never* been known to fail. You will now
understand what I meant in suggesting that, had the
purloined letter been hidden anywhere within the limits
of the Prefect's examination—in other words, had the
principle of its concealment been comprehended within
the principles of the Prefect—its discovery would have
been a matter altogether beyond question. This function-
ary, however, has been thoroughly mystified; and the
remote source of his defeat lies in the supposition that
the Minister is a fool, because he has acquired renown as
a poet. All fools are poets; this the Prefect *feels;* and he
is merely guilty of a *non distributio medii* in thence in-
ferring that all poets are fools."

"But is this really the poet?" I asked. "There are
two brothers, I know; and both have attained reputation
in letters. The Minister I believe has written learnedly on
the Differential Calculus. He is a mathematician, and no
poet."

"You are mistaken; I know him well; he is both. As
poet *and* mathematician, he would reason well; as mere
mathematician, he could not have reasoned at all, and
thus would have been at the mercy of the Prefect."

"You surprise me," I said, "by these opinions, which
have been contradicted by the voice of the world. You
do not mean to set at naught the well-digested idea of cen-
turies. The mathematical reason has long been regarded
as *the* reason *par excellence.*"

" '*Il y a à parier,*' " replied Dupin, quoting from Cham-
fort, " '*que toute idée publique, toute convention reçue,
est une sottise, car elle a convenu au plus grand nom-
bre.*' The mathematicians, I grant you, have done their

best to promulgate the popular error to which you allude, and which is none the less an error for its promulgation as truth. With an art worthy a better cause, for example, they have insinuated the term 'analysis' into application to algebra. The French are the originators of this particular deception; but if a term is of any importance—if words derive any value from applicability—then 'analysis' conveys 'algebra' about as much as, in Latin, *'ambitus'* implies 'ambition,' *'religio'* 'religion,' or *'homines honesti'* a set of *honorable* men."

"You have a quarrel on hand, I see," said I, "with some of the algebraists of Paris; but proceed."

"I dispute the availability, and thus the value, of that reason which is cultivated in any especial form other than the abstractly logical. I dispute, in particular, the reason educed by mathematical study. The mathematics are the science of form and quantity; mathematical reasoning is merely logic applied to observation upon form and quantity. The great error lies in supposing that even the truths of what is called *pure* algebra are abstract or general truths. And this error is so egregious that I am confounded at the universality with which it has been received. Mathematical axioms are *not* axioms of general truth. What is true of *relation*—of form and quantity—is often grossly false in regard to morals, for example. In this latter science it is very usually *un*true that the aggregated parts are equal to the whole. In chemistry also the axiom fails. In the consideration of motive it fails; for two motives, each of a given value, have not, necessarily, a value when united, equal to the sum of their values apart. There are numerous other mathematical truths which are only truths within the limits of *relation*. But the mathematician argues from his *finite truths*, through habit, as if they were of an absolutely general applicability—as the world indeed imagines them to be. Bryant, in his very learned 'Mythology,' mentions an analogous source of error, when he says that 'although the pagan fables are not believed, yet we forget ourselves continually, and make inferences from them as existing realities.' With the algebraists, however, who are pagans themselves, the 'pagan fables' *are* believed, and the inferences are made, not so much through lapse of memory as through an unaccountable addling of the brains. In short, I never yet encountered the mere mathemati-

cian who would be trusted out of equal roots, or one who did not clandestinely hold it as a point of his faith that $x^2 + px$ was absolutely and unconditionally equal to q. Say to one of these gentlemen, by way of experiment, if you please, that you believe occasions may occur where $x^2 + px$ is *not* altogether equal to q, and, having made him understand what you mean, get out of his reach as speedily as convenient, for, beyond doubt, he will endeavor to knock you down.

"I mean to say," continued Dupin, while I merely laughed at his last observations, "that if the Minister had been no more than a mathematician, the Prefect would have been under no necessity of giving me this check. I knew him, however, as both mathematician and poet, and my measures were adapted to his capacity, with reference to the circumstances by which he was surrounded. I knew him as a courtier, too, and as a bold *intriguant*. Such a man, I considered, could not fail to be aware of the ordinary policial modes of action. He could not have failed to anticipate—and events have proved that he did not fail to anticipate—the waylayings to which he was subjected. He must have foreseen, I reflected, the secret investigations of his premises. His frequent absences from home at night, which were hailed by the Prefect as certain aids to his success, I regarded only as *ruses*, to afford opportunity for thorough search to the police, and thus the sooner to impress them with the conviction to which G——, in fact, did finally arrive —the conviction that the letter was not upon the premises. I felt, also, that the whole train of thought, which I was at some pains in detailing to you just now, concerning the invariable principle of policial action in searches for articles concealed—I felt that this whole train of thought would necessarily pass through the mind of the minister. It would imperatively lead him to despise all the ordinary *nooks* of concealment. *He* could not, I reflected, be so weak as not to see that the most intricate and remote recess of his hotel would be as open as his commonest closets to the eyes, to the probes, to the gimlets, and to the microscopes of the Prefect. I saw, in fine, that he would be driven, as a matter of course, to *simplicity*, if not deliberately induced to it as a matter of choice. You will remember, perhaps, how desperately the Prefect laughed when I suggested, upon our first inter-

view, that it was just possible this mystery troubled him
so much on account of its being so *very* self-evident."

"Yes," said I, "I remember his merriment well. I really
thought he would have fallen into convulsions."

"The material world," continued Dupin, "abounds with
very strict analogies to the immaterial; and thus some
color of truth has been given to the rhetorical dogma,
that metaphor, or simile, may be made to strengthen an
argument as well as to embellish a description. The prin-
ciple of the *vis inertiæ*, for example, seems to be identi-
cal in physics and metaphysics. It is not more true in the
former, that a large body is with more difficulty set in
motion than a smaller one, and that its subsequent
momentum is commensurate with this difficulty, than it is,
in the latter, that intellects of the vaster capacity, while
more forcible, more constant, and more eventful in their
movements than those of inferior grade, are yet the less
readily moved, and more embarrassed, and full of hesi-
tation in the first few steps of their progress. Again:
have you ever noticed which of the street signs, over the
shop doors, are the most attractive of attention?"

"I have never given the matter a thought," I said.

"There is a game of puzzles," he resumed, "which is
played upon a map. One party playing requires another
to find a given word—the name of town, river, state, or
empire—any word, in short, upon the motley and per-
plexed surface of the chart. A novice in the game gen-
erally seeks to embarrass his opponents by giving them
the most minutely lettered names; but the adept selects
such words as stretch, in large characters, from one end
of the chart to the other. These, like the over-largely
lettered signs and placards of the street, escape observa-
tion by dint of being excessively obvious; and here the
physical oversight is precisely analogous with the moral
inapprehension by which the intellect suffers to pass un-
noticed those considerations which are too obtrusively
and too palpably self-evident. But this is a point, it ap-
pears, somewhat above or beneath the understanding of
the Prefect. He never once thought it probable, or pos-
sible, that the minister had deposited the letter immedi-
ately beneath the nose of the whole world, by way of
best preventing any portion of that world from perceiv-
ing it.

"But the more I reflected upon the daring, dashing, and

discriminating ingenuity of D——; upon the fact that the document must always have been *at hand,* if he intended to use it to good purpose; and upon the decisive evidence, obtained by the Prefect, that it was not hidden within the limits of that dignitary's ordinary search—the more satisfied I became that, to conceal this letter, the minister had resorted to the comprehensive and sagacious expedient of not attempting to conceal it at all.

"Full of these ideas, I prepared myself with a pair of green spectacles, and called one fine morning, quite by accident, at the Ministerial hotel. I found D—— at home, yawning, lounging, and dawdling, as usual, and pretending to be in the last extremity of *ennui.* He is, perhaps, the most really energetic human being now alive—but that is only when nobody sees him.

"To be even with him, I complained of my weak eyes, and lamented the necessity of the spectacles, under cover of which I cautiously and thoroughly surveyed the whole apartment, while seemingly intent only upon the conversation of my host.

"I paid especial attention to a large writing-table near which he sat, and upon which lay confusedly, some miscellaneous letters and other papers, with one or two musical instruments and a few books. Here, however, after a long and very deliberate scrutiny, I saw nothing to excite particular suspicion.

"At length my eyes, in going the circuit of the room, fell upon a trumpery filigree card-rack of pasteboard, that hung dangling by a dirty blue ribbon, from a little brass knob just beneath the middle of the mantelpiece. In this rack, which had three or four compartments, were five or six visiting cards and a solitary letter. This last was much soiled and crumpled. It was torn nearly in two, across the middle—as if a design, in the first instance, to tear it entirely up as worthless, had been altered, or stayed, in the second. It had a large black seal, bearing the D—— cipher *very* conspicuously, and was addressed, in a diminutive female hand, to D——, the minister, himself. It was thrust carelessly, and even, as it seemed, contemptuously, into one of the uppermost divisions of the rack.

"No sooner had I glanced at this letter than I concluded it to be that of which I was in search. To be sure, it was, to all appearance, radically different from the one

of which the Prefect had read us so minute a description.
Here the seal was large and black, with the D—— cipher;
there it was small and red, with the ducal arms of the
S—— family. Here, the address, to the minister, was
diminutive and feminine; there the superscription, to
a certain royal personage, was markedly bold and de-
cided; the size alone formed a point of correspondence.
But, then, the *radicalness* of these differences, which was
excessive; the dirt; the soiled and torn condition of the
paper, so inconsistent with the *true* methodical habits
of D——, and so suggestive of a design to delude the
beholder into an idea of the worthlessness of the docu-
ment;—these things, together with the hyperobtrusive
situation of this document, full in the view of every visi-
tor, and thus exactly in accordance with the conclusions
to which I had previously arrived; these things, I say,
were strongly corroborative of suspicion, in one who
came with the intention to suspect.

"I protracted my visit as long as possible, and, while
I maintained a most animated discussion with the min-
ister, upon a topic which I knew well had never failed to
interest and excite him, I kept my attention really riveted
upon the letter. In this examination, I committed to mem-
ory its external appearance and arrangement in the rack;
and also fell, at length, upon a discovery which set at
rest whatever trivial doubt I might have entertained. In
scrutinizing the edges of the paper, I observed them to be
more *chafed* than seemed necessary. They presented the
broken appearance which is manifested when a stiff pa-
per, having been once folded and pressed with a folder,
is refolded in a reversed direction, in the same creases
or edges which had formed the original fold. This dis-
covery was sufficient. It was clear to me that the letter
had been turned, as a glove, inside out, re-directed and
re-sealed. I bade the minister good-morning, and took
my departure at once, leaving a gold snuff-box upon the
table.

"The next morning I called for the snuff-box, when we
resumed, quite eagerly, the conversation of the preceding
day. While thus engaged, however, a loud report, as if
of a pistol, was heard immediately beneath the windows
of the hotel, and was succeeded by a series of fearful
screams, and the shoutings of a terrified mob. D——
rushed to a casement, threw it open, and looked out. In

the meantime I stepped to the card-rack, took the letter, put it in my pocket, and replaced it by a *fac-simile,* (so far as regards externals) which I had carefully prepared at my lodgings—imitating the D—— cipher, very readily, by means of a seal formed of bread.

"The disturbance in the street had been occasioned by the frantic behavior of a man with a musket. He had fired it among a crowd of women and children. It proved, however, to have been without ball, and the fellow was suffered to go his way as a lunatic or a drunkard. When he had gone, D—— came from the window, whither I had followed him immediately upon securing the object in view. Soon afterward I bade him farewell. The pretended lunatic was a man in my own pay."

"But what purpose had you," I asked, "in replacing the letter by a *fac-simile?* Would it not have been better, at the first visit, to have seized it openly, and departed?"

"D——," replied Dupin, "is a desperate man, and a man of nerve. His hotel, too, is not without attendants devoted to his interests. Had I made the wild attempt you suggest, I might never have left the Ministerial presence alive. The good people of Paris might have heard of me no more. But I had an object apart from these considerations. You know my political prepossessions. In this matter, I act as a partisan of the lady concerned. For eighteen months the Minister has had her in his power. She has now him in hers—since, being unaware that the letter is not in his possession, he will proceed with his exactions as if it was. Thus will he inevitably commit himself, at once, to his political destruction. His downfall, too, will not be more precipitate than awkward. It is all very well to talk about the *facilis descensus Averni*; but in all kinds of climbing, as Catalani said of singing, it is far more easy to get up than to come down. In the present instance I have no sympathy—at least no pity—for him who descends. He is that *monstrum horrendum,* an unprincipled man of genius. I confess, however, that I should like very well to know the precise character of his thoughts, when, being defied by her whom the Prefect terms 'a certain personage,' he is reduced to opening the letter which I left for him in the card-rack."

"How? did you put any thing particular in it?"

"Why—it did not seem altogether right to leave the

interior blank—that would have been insulting. D——, at
Vienna once, did me an evil turn, which I told him,
quite good-humoredly, that I should remember. So, as I
knew he would feel some curiosity in regard to the
identity of the person who had outwitted him, I thought
it a pity not to give him a clew. He is well acquainted
with my MS., and I just copied into the middle of the
blank sheet the words—

 " '—— ——Un dessein si funeste,
 S'il n'est digne d'Atrée, est digne de Thyeste.'

They are to be found in Crébillon's 'Atrée.' "

The Black Cat

FOR THE MOST wild yet most homely narrative which I am about to pen, I neither expect nor solicit belief. Mad indeed would I be to expect it, in a case where my very senses reject their own evidence. Yet, mad am I not —and very surely do I not dream. But to-morrow I die, and to-day I would unburden my soul. My immediate purpose is to place before the world, plainly, succinctly, and without comment, a series of mere household events. In their consequences, these events have terrified—have tortured—have destroyed me. Yet I will not attempt to expound them. To me, they have presented little but horror—to many they will seem less terrible than *baroques*. Hereafter, perhaps, some intellect may be found which will reduce my phantasm to the commonplace—some intellect more calm, more logical, and far less excitable than my own, which will perceive, in the circumstances I detail with awe, nothing more than an ordinary succession of very natural causes and effects.

From my infancy I was noted for the docility and humanity of my disposition. My tenderness of heart was even so conspicuous as to make me the jest of my companions. I was especially fond of animals, and was indulged by my parents with a great variety of pets. With these I spent most of my time, and never was so happy as when feeding and caressing them. This peculiarity of character grew with my growth, and, in my manhood, I derived from it one of my principal sources of pleasure. To those who have cherished an affection for a faithful and sagacious dog, I need hardly be at the trouble of explaining the nature or the intensity of the gratification thus derivable. There is something in the unselfish and self-sacrificing love of a brute, which goes directly to the heart of him who has had frequent occasion to

test the paltry friendship and gossamer fidelity of mere *Man*.

I married early, and was happy to find in my wife a disposition not uncongenial with my own. Observing my partiality for domestic pets, she lost no opportunity of procuring those of the most agreeable kind. We had birds, gold-fish, a fine dog, rabbits, a small monkey, and a *cat*.

This latter was a remarkably large and beautiful animal, entirely black, and sagacious to an astonishing degree. In speaking of his intelligence, my wife, who at heart was not a little tinctured with superstition, made frequent allusion to the ancient popular notion, which regarded all black cats as witches in disguise. Not that she was ever *serious* upon this point—and I mention the matter at all for no better reason than that it happens, just now, to be remembered.

Pluto—this was the cat's name—was my favorite pet and playmate. I alone fed him, and he attended me wherever I went about the house. It was even with difficulty that I could prevent him from following me through the streets.

Our friendship lasted, in this manner, for several years, during which my general temperament and character—through the instrumentality of the Fiend Intemperance—had (I blush to confess it) experienced a radical alteration for the worse. I grew, day by day, more moody, more irritable, more regardless of the feelings of others. I suffered myself to use intemperate language to my wife. At length, I even offered her personal violence. My pets, of course, were made to feel the change in my disposition. I not only neglected, but ill-used them. For Pluto, however, I still retained sufficient regard to restrain me from maltreating him, as I made no scruple of maltreating the rabbits, the monkey, or even the dog, when, by accident, or through affection, they came in my way. But my disease grew upon me—for what disease is like Alcohol!—and at length even Pluto, who was now becoming old, and consequently somewhat peevish—even Pluto began to experience the effects of my ill temper.

One night, returning home, much intoxicated, from one of my haunts about town, I fancied that the cat avoided my presence. I seized him; when, in his fright

at my violence, he inflicted a slight wound upon my hand with his teeth. The fury of a demon instantly possessed me. I knew myself no longer. My original soul seemed, at once, to take its flight from my body; and a more than fiendish malevolence, gin-nurtured, thrilled every fibre of my frame. I took from my waistcoat-pocket a penknife, opened it, grasped the poor beast by the throat, and deliberately cut one of its eyes from the socket! I blush, I burn, I shudder, while I pen the damnable atrocity.

When reason returned with the morning—when I had slept off the fumes of the night's debauch—I experienced a sentiment half of horror, half of remorse, for the crime of which I had been guilty; but it was, at best, a feeble and equivocal feeling, and the soul remained untouched. I again plunged into excess, and soon drowned in wine all memory of the deed.

In the meantime the cat slowly recovered. The socket of the lost eye presented, it is true, a frightful appearance, but he no longer appeared to suffer any pain. He went about the house as usual, but, as might be expected, fled in extreme terror at my approach. I had so much of my old heart left, as to be at first grieved by this evident dislike on the part of a creature which had once so loved me. But this feeling soon gave place to irritation. And then came, as if to my final and irrevocable overthrow, the spirit of PERVERSENESS. Of this spirit philosophy takes no account. Yet I am not more sure that my soul lives, than I am that perverseness is one of the primitive impulses of the human heart—one of the indivisible primary faculties, or sentiments, which give direction to the character of Man. Who has not, a hundred times, found himself committing a vile or a stupid action, for no other reason than because he knows he should *not?* Have we not a perpetual inclination, in the teeth of our best judgment, to violate that which is *Law,* merely because we understand it to be such? This spirit of perverseness, I say, came to my final overthrow. It was this unfathomable longing of the soul *to vex itself*—to offer violence to its own nature—to do wrong for the wrong's sake only—that urged me to continue and finally to consummate the injury I had inflicted upon the unoffending brute. One morning, in cold blood, I slipped a noose about its neck and hung it to the limb of a tree;—

hung it with the tears streaming from my eyes, and with the bitterest remorse at my heart;—hung it *because* I knew that it had loved me, and *because* I felt it had given me no reason of offence;—hung it *because* I knew that in so doing I was committing a sin—a deadly sin that would so jeopardize my immortal soul as to place it —if such a thing were possible—even beyond the reach of the infinite mercy of the Most Merciful and Most Terrible God.

On the night of the day on which this most cruel deed was done, I was aroused from sleep by the cry of fire. The curtains of my bed were in flames. The whole house was blazing. It was with great difficulty that my wife, a servant, and myself, made our escape from the conflagration. The destruction was complete. My entire worldly wealth was swallowed up, and I resigned myself thenceforward to despair.

I am above the weakness of seeking to establish a sequence of cause and effect, between the disaster and the atrocity. But I am detailing a chain of facts—and wish not to leave even a possible link imperfect. On the day succeeding the fire, I visited the ruins. The walls, with one exception, had fallen in. This exception was found in a compartment wall, not very thick, which stood about the middle of the house, and against which had rested the head of my bed. The plastering had here, in great measure, resisted the action of the fire—a fact which I attributed to its having been recently spread. About this wall a dense crowd were collected, and many persons seemed to be examining a particular portion of it with very minute and eager attention. The words "strange!" "singular!" and other similar expressions, excited my curiosity. I approached and saw, as if graven in *bas-relief* upon the white surface, the figure of a gigantic *cat*. The impression was given with an accuracy truly marvelous. There was a rope about the animal's neck.

When I first beheld this apparition—for I could scarcely regard it as less—my wonder and my terror were extreme. But at length reflection came to my aid. The cat, I remembered, had been hung in a garden adjacent to the house. Upon the alarm of fire, this garden had been immediately filled by the crowd—by some one of whom the animal must have been cut from the tree and thrown, through an open window, into my chamber. This had prob-

ably been done with the view of arousing me from sleep. The falling of other walls had compressed the victim of my cruelty into the substance of the freshly-spread plaster; the lime of which, with the flames, and the *ammonia* from the carcass, had then accomplished the portraiture as I saw it.

Although I thus readily accounted to my reason, if not altogether to my conscience, for the startling fact just detailed, it did not the less fail to make a deep impression upon my fancy. For months I could not rid myself of the phantasm of the cat; and, during this period, there came back into my spirit a half-sentiment that seemed, but was not, remorse. I went so far as to regret the loss of the animal, and to look about me, among the vile haunts which I now habitually frequented, for another pet of the same species, and of somewhat similar appearance, with which to supply its place.

One night as I sat, half stupefied, in a den of more than infamy, my attention was suddenly drawn to some black object, reposing upon the head of one of the immense hogsheads of gin, or of rum, which constituted the chief furniture of the apartment. I had been looking steadily at the top of this hogshead for some minutes, and what now caused me surprise was the fact that I had not sooner perceived the object thereupon. I approached it, and touched it with my hand. It was a black cat—a very large one—fully as large as Pluto, and closely resembling him in every respect but one. Pluto had not a white hair upon any portion of his body; but this cat had a large, although indefinite splotch of white, covering nearly the whole region of the breast.

Upon my touching him, he immediately arose, purred loudly, rubbed against my hand, and appeared delighted with my notice. This, then, was the very creature of which I was in search. I at once offered to purchase it of the landlord; but this person made no claim to it—knew nothing of it—had never seen it before.

I continued my caresses, and when I prepared to go home, the animal evinced a disposition to accompany me. I permitted it to do so; occasionally stooping and patting it as I proceeded. When it reached the house it domesticated itself at once, and became immediately a great favorite with my wife.

For my own part, I soon found a dislike to it arising

within me. This was just the reverse of what I had anticipated; but—I knew not how or why it was—its evident fondness for myself rather disgusted and annoyed me. By slow degrees these feelings of disgust and annoyance rose into the bitterness of hatred. I avoided the creature; a certain sense of shame, and the remembrance of my former deed of cruelty, preventing me from physically abusing it. I did not, for some weeks, strike, or otherwise violently ill use it; but gradually—very gradually—I came to look upon it with unutterable loathing, and to flee silently from its odious presence, as from the breath of a pestilence.

What added, no doubt, to my hatred of the beast, was the discovery, on the morning after I brought it home, that, like Pluto, it also had been deprived of one of its eyes. This circumstance, however, only endeared it to my wife, who, as I have already said, possessed, in a high degree, that humanity of feeling which had once been my distinguishing trait, and the source of many of my simplest and purest pleasures.

With my aversion to this cat, however, its partiality for myself seemed to increase. It followed my footsteps with a pertinacity which it would be difficult to make the reader comprehend. Whenever I sat, it would crouch beneath my chair, or spring upon my knees, covering me with its loathsome caresses. If I arose to walk it would get between my feet and thus nearly throw me down, or, fastening its long and sharp claws in my dress, clamber, in this manner, to my breast. At such times, although I longed to destroy it with a blow, I was yet withheld from so doing, partly by a memory of my former crime, but chiefly—let me confess it at once—by absolute *dread* of the beast.

This dread was not exactly a dread of physical evil— and yet I should be at a loss how otherwise to define it. I am almost ashamed to own—yes, even in this felon's cell, I am almost ashamed to own—that the terror and horror with which the animal inspired me, had been heightened by one of the merest chimeras it would be possible to conceive. My wife had called my attention, more than once, to the character of the mark of white hair, of which I have spoken, and which constituted the sole visible difference between the strange beast and the one I had destroyed. The reader will remember that

this mark, although large, had been originally very indefinite; but, by slow degrees—degrees nearly imperceptible, and which for a long time my reason struggled to reject as fanciful—it had, at length, assumed a rigorous distinctness of outline. It was now the representation of an object that I shudder to name—and for this, above all, I loathed, and dreaded, and would have rid myself of the monster *had I dared*—it was now, I say, the image of a hideous—of a ghastly thing—of the GALLOWS!—oh, mournful and terrible engine of Horror and of Crime— of Agony and of Death!

And now was I indeed wretched beyond the wretchedness of mere Humanity. And *a brute beast*—whose fellow I had contemptuously destroyed—*a brute beast* to work out for *me*—for me, a man fashioned in the image of the High God—so much of insufferable woe! Alas! neither by day nor by night knew I the blessing of rest any more! During the former the creature left me no moment alone, and in the latter I started hourly from dreams of unutterable fear to find the hot breath of *the thing* upon my face, and its vast weight—an incarnate nightmare that I had no power to shake off— incumbent eternally upon my *heart!*

Beneath the pressure of torments such as these the feeble remnant of the good within me succumbed. Evil thoughts became my sole intimates—the darkest and most evil of thoughts. The moodiness of my usual temper increased to hatred of all things and of all mankind; while from the sudden, frequent, and ungovernable outbursts of a fury to which I now blindly abandoned myself, my uncomplaining wife, alas, was the most usual and the most patient of sufferers.

One day she accompanied me, upon some household errand, into the cellar of the old building which our poverty compelled us to inhabit. The cat followed me down the steep stairs, and, nearly throwing me headlong, exasperated me to madness. Uplifting an axe, and forgetting in my wrath the childish dread which had hitherto stayed my hand, I aimed a blow at the animal, which, of course, would have proved instantly fatal had it descended as I wished. But this blow was arrested by the hand of my wife. Goaded by the interference into a rage more than demoniacal, I withdrew my arm from her

grasp and buried the axe in her brain. She fell dead upon the spot without a groan.

This hideous murder accomplished, I set myself forthwith, and with entire deliberation, to the task of concealing the body. I knew that I could not remove it from the house, either by day or by night, without the risk of being observed by the neighbors. Many projects entered my mind. At one period I thought of cutting the corpse into minute fragments, and destroying them by fire. At another, I resolved to dig a grave for it in the floor of the cellar. Again, I deliberated about casting it in the well in the yard—about packing it in a box, as if merchandise, with the usual arrangements, and so getting a porter to take it from the house. Finally I hit upon what I considered a far better expedient than either of these. I determined to wall it up in the cellar, as the monks of the Middle Ages are recorded to have walled up their victims.

For a purpose such as this the cellar was well adapted. Its walls were loosely constructed, and had lately been plastered throughout with a rough plaster, which the dampness of the atmosphere had prevented from hardening. Moreover, in one of the walls was a projection, caused by a false chimney, or fireplace, that had been filled up and made to resemble the rest of the cellar. I made no doubt that I could readily displace the bricks at this point, insert the corpse, and wall the whole up as before, so that no eye could detect any thing suspicious.

And in this calculation I was not deceived. By means of a crowbar I easily dislodged the bricks, and, having carefully deposited the body against the inner wall, I propped it in that position, while with little trouble I relaid the whole structure as it originally stood. Having procured mortar, sand, and hair, with every possible precaution, I prepared a plaster which could not be distinguished from the old, and with this I very carefully went over the new brick-work. When I had finished, I felt satisfied that all was right. The wall did not present the slightest appearance of having been disturbed. The rubbish on the floor was picked up with the minutest care. I looked around triumphantly, and said to myself: "Here at least, then, my labor has not been in vain."

My next step was to look for the beast which had been the cause of so much wretchedness; for I had, at length,

firmly resolved to put it to death. Had I been able to meet with it at the moment, there could have been no doubt of its fate; but it appeared that the crafty animal had been alarmed at the violence of my previous anger, and forbore to present itself in my present mood. It is impossible to describe or to imagine the deep, the blissful sense of relief which the absence of the detested creature occasioned in my bosom. It did not make its appearance during the night; and thus for one night, at least, since its introduction into the house, I soundly and tranquilly slept; aye, *slept* even with the burden of murder upon my soul.

The second and the third day passed, and still my tormentor came not. Once again I breathed as a freeman. The monster, in terror, had fled the premises for ever! I should behold it no more! My happiness was supreme! The guilt of my dark deed disturbed me but little. Some few inquiries had been made, but these had been readily answered. Even a search had been instituted—but of course nothing was to be discovered. I looked upon my future felicity as secured.

Upon the fourth day of the assassination, a party of the police came, very unexpectedly, into the house, and proceeded again to make rigorous investigation of the premises. Secure, however, in the inscrutability of my place of concealment, I felt no embarrassment whatever. The officers bade me accompany them in their search. They left no nook or corner unexplored. At length, for the third or fourth time, they descended into the cellar. I quivered not in a muscle. My heart beat calmly as that of one who slumbers in innocence. I walked the cellar from end to end. I folded my arms upon my bosom, and roamed easily to and fro. The police were thoroughly satisfied and prepared to depart. The glee at my heart was too strong to be restrained. I burned to say if but one word, by way of triumph, and to render doubly sure their assurance of my guiltlessness.

"Gentlemen," I said at last, as the party ascended the steps, "I delight to have allayed your suspicions. I wish you all health and a little more courtesy. By the bye, gentlemen, this—this is a very well-constructed house," (in the rabid desire to say something easily, I scarcely knew what I uttered at all),—"I may say an *excellently* well-constructed house. These walls—are you going, gen-

tlemen?—these walls are solidly put together"; and here, through the mere frenzy of bravado, I rapped heavily with a cane which I held in my hand, upon that very portion of the brickwork behind which stood the corpse of the wife of my bosom.

But may God shield and deliver me from the fangs of the Arch-Fiend! No sooner had the reverberation of my blows sunk into silence, than I was answered by a voice from within the tomb!—by a cry, at first muffled and broken, like the sobbing of a child, and then quickly swelling into one long, loud, and continuous scream, utterly anomalous and inhuman—a howl—a wailing shriek, half of horror and half of triumph, such as might have arisen only out of hell, conjointly from the throats of the damned in their agony and of the demons that exult in the damnation.

Of my own thoughts it is folly to speak. Swooning, I staggered to the opposite wall. For one instant the party on the stairs remained motionless, through extremity of terror and awe. In the next a dozen stout arms were toiling at the wall. It fell bodily. The corpse, already greatly decayed and clotted with gore, stood erect before the eyes of the spectators. Upon its head, with red extended mouth and solitary eye of fire, sat the hideous beast whose craft had seduced me into murder, and whose informing voice had consigned me to the hangman. I had walled the monster up within the tomb.

The Fall of the House of Usher

Son cœur est un luth suspendu;
Sitôt qu'on le touche il résonne.

—*De Béranger*

DURING THE WHOLE of a dull, dark, and soundless day
in the autumn of the year, when the clouds hung
oppressively low in the heavens, I had been passing
alone, on horseback, through a singularly dreary tract
of country, and at length found myself, as the shades of
the evening drew on, within view of the melancholy
House of Usher. I know not how it was—but, with the
first glimpse of the building, a sense of insufferable gloom
pervaded my spirit. I say insufferable; for the feeling was
unrelieved by any of that half-pleasurable, because po-
etic, sentiment with which the mind usually receives even
the sternest natural images of the desolate or terrible. I
looked upon the scene before me—upon the mere house,
and the simple landscape features of the domain—upon
the bleak walls—upon the vacant eye-like windows—
upon a few rank sedges—and upon a few white trunks
of decayed trees—with an utter depression of soul which
I can compare to no earthly sensation more properly than
to the after-dream of the reveller upon opium—the bitter
lapse into every-day life—the hideous dropping off of the
veil. There was an iciness, a sinking, a sickening of the
heart—an unredeemed dreariness of thought which no
goading of the imagination could torture into aught of the
sublime. What was it—I paused to think—what was it
that so unnerved me in the contemplation of the House
of Usher? It was a mystery all insoluble; nor could I
grapple with the shadowy fancies that crowded upon
me as I pondered. I was forced to fall back upon the

unsatisfactory conclusion, that while, beyond doubt, there
are combinations of very simple natural objects which
have the power of thus affecting us, still the analysis of
this power lies among considerations beyond our depth.
It was possible, I reflected, that a mere different arrange-
ment of the particulars of the scene, of the details of the
picture, would be sufficient to modify, or perhaps to an-
nihilate its capacity for sorrowful impression; and, acting
upon this idea, I reined my horse to the precipitous brink
of a black and lurid tarn that lay in unruffled lustre
by the dwelling, and gazed down—but with a shud-
der even more thrilling than before—upon the remodelled
and inverted images of the gray sedge, and the ghastly
tree-stems, and the vacant and eye-like windows.

Nevertheless, in this mansion of gloom I now proposed
to myself a sojourn of some weeks. Its proprietor, Rod-
erick Usher, had been one of my boon companions in
boyhood; but many years had elapsed since our last meet-
ing. A letter, however, had lately reached me in a distant
part of the country—a letter from him—which, in its
wildly importunate nature, had admitted of no other than
a personal reply. The MS. gave evidence of nervous
agitation. The writer spoke of acute bodily illness—of a
mental disorder which oppressed him—and of an earnest
desire to see me, as his best and indeed his only personal
friend, with a view of attempting, by the cheerfulness of
my society, some alleviation of his malady. It was the
manner in which all this, and much more, was said—
it was the apparent *heart* that went with his request—
which allowed me no room for hesitation; and I accord-
ingly obeyed forthwith what I still considered a very
singular summons.

Although, as boys, we had been even intimate associ-
ates, yet I really knew little of my friend. His reserve had
been always excessive and habitual. I was aware, how-
ever, that his very ancient family had been noted, time
out of mind, for a peculiar sensibility of temperament,
displaying itself, through long ages, in many works of
exalted art, and manifested, of late, in repeated deeds of
munificent yet unobtrusive charity, as well as in a pas-
sionate devotion to the intricacies, perhaps even more
than to the orthodox and easily recognizable beauties, of
musical science. I had learned, too, the very remarkable
fact, that the stem of the Usher race, all time-honored

as it was, had put forth, at no period, any enduring branch; in other words, that the entire family lay in the direct line of descent, and had always, with very trifling and very temporary variation, so lain. It was this deficiency, I considered, while running over in thought the perfect keeping of the character of the premises with the accredited character of the people, and while speculating upon the possible influence which the one, in the long lapse of centuries, might have exercised upon the other —it was this deficiency, perhaps, of collateral issue, and the consequent undeviating transmission, from sire to son, of the patrimony with the name, which had, at length, so identified the two as to merge the original title of the estate in the quaint and equivocal appellation of the "House of Usher"—an appellation which seemed to include, in the minds of the peasantry who used it, both the family and the family mansion.

I have said that the sole effect of my somewhat childish experiment—that of looking down within the tarn— had been to deepen the first singular impression. There can be no doubt that the consciousness of the rapid increase of my superstition—for why should I not so term it?—served mainly to accelerate the increase itself. Such, I have long known, is the paradoxical law of all sentiments having terror as a basis. And it might have been for this reason only, that, when I again uplifted my eyes to the house itself, from its image in the pool, there grew in my mind a strange fancy—a fancy so ridiculous, indeed, that I but mention it to show the vivid force of the sensations which oppressed me. I had so worked upon my imagination as really to believe that about the whole mansion and domain there hung an atmosphere peculiar to themselves and their immediate vicinity—an atmosphere which had no affinity with the air of heaven, but which had reeked up from the decayed trees, and the gray wall, and the silent tarn—a pestilent and mystic vapor, dull, sluggish, faintly discernible, and leaden-hued.

Shaking off from my spirit what *must* have been a dream, I scanned more narrowly the real aspect of the building. Its principal feature seemed to be that of an excessive antiquity. The discoloration of ages had been great. Minute fungi overspread the whole exterior, hanging in a fine tangled web-work from the eaves. Yet all this was apart from any extraordinary dilapidation. No

portion of the masonry had fallen; and there appeared to
be a wild inconsistency between its still perfect adap-
tation of parts, and the crumbling condition of the in-
dividual stones. In this there was much that reminded me
of the specious totality of old wood-work which has
rotted for long years in some neglected vault, with
no disturbance from the breath of the external air. Be-
yond this indication of extensive decay, however, the
fabric gave little token of instability. Perhaps the eye of
a scrutinizing observer might have discovered a barely
perceptible fissure, which, extending from the roof of the
building in front, made its way down the wall in a zigzag
direction, until it became lost in the sullen waters of the
tarn.

Noticing these things, I rode over a short causeway
to the house. A servant in waiting took my horse, and I
entered the Gothic archway of the hall. A valet, of
stealthy step, thence conducted me, in silence, through
many dark and intricate passages in my progress to the
studio of his master. Much that I encountered on the way
contributed, I know not how, to heighten the vague senti-
ments of which I have already spoken. While the objects
around me—while the carvings of the ceilings, the sombre
tapestries of the walls, the ebon blackness of the floors,
and the phantasmagoric armorial trophies which rattled
as I strode, were but matters to which, or to such
as which, I had been accustomed from my infancy—
while I hesitated not to acknowledge how familiar was
all this—I still wondered to find how unfamiliar were the
fancies which ordinary images were stirring up. On one
of the staircases, I met the physician of the family. His
countenance, I thought, wore a mingled expression of
low cunning and perplexity. He accosted me with trepi-
dation and passed on. The valet now threw open a door
and ushered me into the presence of his master.

The room in which I found myself was very large and
lofty. The windows were long, narrow, and pointed, and
at so vast a distance from the black oaken floor as to
be altogether inaccessible from within. Feeble gleams of
encrimsoned light made their way through the trellissed
panes, and served to render sufficiently distinct the more
prominent objects around; the eye, however, struggled
in vain to reach the remoter angles of the chamber, or the
recesses of the vaulted and fretted ceiling. Dark draperies

hung upon the walls. The general furniture was profuse, comfortless, antique, and tattered. Many books and musical instruments lay scattered about, but failed to give any vitality to the scene. I felt that I breathed an atmosphere of sorrow. An air of stern, deep, and irredeemable gloom hung over and pervaded all.

Upon my entrance, Usher arose from a sofa on which he had been lying at full length, and greeted me with a vivacious warmth which had much in it, I at first thought, of an overdone cordiality—of the constrained effort of the *ennuyé* man of the world. A glance, however, at his countenance convinced me of his perfect sincerity. We sat down; and for some moments, while he spoke not, I gazed upon him with a feeling half of pity, half of awe. Surely, man had never before so terribly altered, in so brief a period, as had Roderick Usher! It was with difficulty that I could bring myself to admit the identity of the wan being before me with the companion of my early boyhood. Yet the character of his face had been at all times remarkable. A cadaverousness of complexion; an eye large, liquid, and luminous beyond comparison; lips somewhat thin and very pallid, but of a surpassingly beautiful curve; a nose of a delicate Hebrew model, but with a breadth of nostril unusual in similar formations; a finely moulded chin, speaking, in its want of prominence, of a want of moral energy; hair of a more than web-like softness and tenuity;—these features, with an inordinate expansion above the regions of the temple, made up altogether a countenance not easily to be forgotten. And now in the mere exaggeration of the prevailing character of these features, and of the expression they were wont to convey, lay so much of change that I doubted to whom I spoke. The now ghastly pallor of the skin, and the now miraculous lustre of the eye, above all things startled and even awed me. The silken hair, too, had been suffered to grow all unheeded, and as, in its wild gossamer texture, it floated rather than fell about the face, I could not, even with effort, connect its Arabesque expression with any idea of simple humanity.

In the manner of my friend I was at once struck with an incoherence—an inconsistency; and I soon found this to arise from a series of feeble and futile struggles to overcome an habitual trepidancy—an excessive nervous agitation. For something of this nature I had indeed been

prepared, no less by his letter, than by reminiscences
of certain boyish traits, and by conclusions deduced from
his peculiar physical conformation and temperament. His
action was alternately vivacious and sullen. His voice
varied rapidly from a tremulous indecision (when the ani-
mal spirits seemed utterly in abeyance) to that species
of energetic concision—that abrupt, weighty, unhurried,
and hollow-sounding enunciation—that leaden, self-bal-
anced, and perfectly modulated guttural utterance, which
may be observed in the lost drunkard, or the irreclaim-
able ·eater of opium, during the periods of his most in-
tense excitement.

It was thus that he spoke of the object of my visit, of
his earnest desire to see me, and of the solace he ex-
pected me to afford him. He entered, at some length, into
what he conceived to be the nature of his malady. It
was, he said, a constitutional and a family evil, and
one for which he despaired to find a remedy—a mere
nervous affection, he immediately added, which would
undoubtedly soon pass off. It displayed itself in a host of
unnatural sensations. Some of these, as he detailed them,
interested and bewildered me; although, perhaps, the
terms and the general manner of their narration had
their weight. He suffered much from a morbid acute-
ness of the senses; the most insipid food was alone en-
durable; he could wear only garments of certain texture;
the odors of all flowers were oppressive; his eyes were
tortured by even a faint light; and there were but peculiar
sounds, and these from stringed instruments, which did
not inspire him with horror.

To an anomalous species of terror I found him a
bounden slave. "I shall perish," said he, "I *must* perish
in this deplorable folly. Thus, thus, and not otherwise,
shall I be lost. I dread the events of the future, not in
themselves, but in their results. I shudder at the thought
of any, even the most trivial, incident, which may oper-
ate upon this intolerable agitation of soul. I have, indeed,
no abhorrence of danger, except in its absolute effect
—in terror. In this unnerved, in this pitiable, condition
I feel that the period will sooner or later arrive when
I must abandon life. and reason together, in some struggle
with the grim phantasm, FEAR."

I learned, moreover, at intervals, and through broken
and equivocal hints, another singular feature of his men-

tal condition. He was enchained by certain superstitious impressions in regard to the dwelling which he tenanted, and whence, for many years, he had never ventured forth —in regard to an influence whose supposititious force was conveyed in terms too shadowy here to be re-stated —an influence which some peculiarities in the mere form and substance of his family mansion had, by dint of long sufferance, he said, obtained over his spirit—an effect which the *physique* of the gray walls and turrets, and of the dim tarn into which they all looked down, had, at length, brought about upon the *morale* of his existence.

He admitted, however, although with hesitation, that much of the peculiar gloom which thus afflicted him could be traced to a more natural and far more palpable origin—to the severe and long-continued illness—indeed to the evidently approaching dissolution—of a tenderly beloved sister, his sole companion for long years, his last and only relative on earth. "Her decease," he said, with a bitterness which I can never forget, "would leave him (him, the hopeless and the frail) the last of the ancient race of the Ushers." While he spoke, the lady Madeline (for so was she called) passed through a remote portion of the apartment, and, without having noticed my presence, disappeared. I regarded her with an utter astonishment not unmingled with dread; and yet I found it impossible to account for such feelings. A sensation of stupor oppressed me as my eyes followed her retreating steps. When a door, at length, closed upon her, my glance sought instinctively and eagerly the countenance of the brother; but he had buried his face in his hands, and I could only perceive that a far more than ordinary wanness had overspread the emaciated fingers through which trickled many passionate tears.

The disease of the lady Madeline had long baffled the skill of her physicians. A settled apathy, a gradual wasting away of the person, and frequent although transient affections of a partially cataleptical character were the unusual diagnosis. Hitherto she had steadily borne up against the pressure of her malady, and had not betaken herself finally to bed; but on the closing in of the evening of my arrival at the house, she succumbed (as her brother told me at night with inexpressible agitation) to the prostrating power of the destroyer; and I learned

that the glimpse I had obtained of her person would thus
probably be the last I should obtain—that the lady, at
least while living, would be seen by me no more.

For several days ensuing, her name was unmentioned
by either Usher or myself; and during this period I was
busied in earnest endeavors to alleviate the melancholy
of my friend. We painted and read together, or I lis-
tened, as if in a dream, to the wild improvisations of his
speaking guitar. And thus, as a closer and still closer
intimacy admitted me more unreservedly into the re-
cesses of his spirit, the more bitterly did I perceive the
futility of all attempt at cheering a mind from which
darkness, as if an inherent positive quality, poured forth
upon all objects of the moral and physical universe in
one unceasing radiation of gloom.

I shall ever bear about me a memory of the many
solemn hours I thus spent alone with the master of the
House of Usher. Yet I should fail in any attempt to con-
vey an idea of the exact character of the studies, or
of the occupations, in which he involved me, or led me
the way. An excited and highly distempered ideality
threw a sulphureous lustre over all. His long improvised
dirges will ring forever in my ears. Among other things,
I hold painfully in mind a certain singular perversion
and amplification of the wild air of the last waltz of Von
Weber. From the paintings over which his elaborate fancy
brooded, and which grew, touch by touch, into
vagueness at which I shuddered the more thrillingly, be-
cause I shuddered knowing not why—from these paint-
ings (vivid as their images now are before me) I would
in vain endeavor to educe more than a small portion
which should lie within the compass of merely written
words. By the utter simplicity, by the nakedness of his
designs, he arrested and overawed attention. If ever
mortal painted an ideal, that mortal was Roderick
Usher. For me at least, in the circumstances then sur-
rounding me, there arose out of the pure abstractions
which the hypochondriac contrived to throw upon his
canvas, an intensity of intolerable awe, no shadow of
which felt I ever yet in the contemplation of the cer-
tainly glowing yet too concrete reveries of Fuseli.

One of the phantasmagoric conceptions of my friend,
partaking not so rigidly of the spirit of abstraction, may

be shadowed forth, although feebly, in words. A small picture presented the interior of an immensely long and rectangular vault or tunnel, with low walls, smooth, white, and without interruption or device. Certain accessory points of the design served well to convey the idea that this excavation lay at an exceeding depth below the surface of the earth. No outlet was observed in any portion of its vast extent, and no torch or other artificial source of light was discernible; yet a flood of intense rays rolled throughout, and bathed the whole in a ghastly and inappropriate splendor.

I have just spoken of that morbid condition of the auditory nerve which rendered all music intolerable to the sufferer, with the exception of certain effects of stringed instruments. It was, perhaps, the narrow limits to which he thus confined himself upon the guitar which gave birth, in great measure, to the fantastic character of his performances. But the fervid *facility* of his *impromptus* could not be so accounted for. They must have been, and were, in the notes, as well as in the words of his wild fantasias (for he not unfrequently accompanied himself with rhymed verbal improvisations), the result of that intense mental collectedness and concentration to which I have previously alluded as observable only in particular moments of the highest artificial excitement. The words of one of these rhapsodies I have easily remembered. I was, perhaps, the more forcibly impressed with it as he gave it, because, in the under or mystic current of its meaning, I fancied that I perceived, and for the first time, a full consciousness on the part of Usher of the tottering of his lofty reason upon her throne. The verses, which were entitled "The Haunted Palace," ran very nearly, if not accurately, thus:—

I.

In the greenest of our valleys,
 By good angels tenanted,
Once a fair and stately palace—
 Radiant palace—reared its head.
In the monarch Thought's dominion—
 It stood there!
Never seraph spread a pinion
 Over fabric half so fair.

II.

Banners yellow, glorious, golden,
 On its roof did float and flow
(This—all this—was in the olden
 Time long ago);
And every gentle air that dallied,
 In that sweet day,
Along the ramparts plumed and pallid,
 A winged odor went away.

III.

Wanderers in that happy valley
 Through two luminous windows saw
Spirits moving musically
 To a lute's well-tunèd law;
Round about a throne, where sitting
 (Porphyrogene!)
In state his glory well befitting,
 The ruler of the realm was seen.

IV.

And all with pearl and ruby glowing
 Was the fair palace door,
Through which came flowing, flowing, flowing
 And sparkling evermore,
A troop of Echoes whose sweet duty
 Was but to sing,
In voices of surpassing beauty,
 The wit and wisdom of their king.

V.

But evil things, in robes of sorrow,
 Assailed the monarch's high estate;
(Ah, let us mourn, for never morrow
 Shall dawn upon him, desolate!)
And, round about his home, the glory
 That blushed and bloomed
Is but a dim-remembered story
 Of the old time entombed.

VI.

And travellers now within that valley,
 Through the red-litten windows see
Vast forms that move fantastically
 To a discordant melody;
While, like a rapid ghastly river,
 Through the pale door;
A hideous throng rush out forever,
 And laugh—but smile no more.

I well remember that suggestions arising from this ballad led us into a train of thought wherein there became manifest an opinion of Usher's which I mention not so much on account of its novelty (for other men [1] have thought thus), as on account of the pertinacity with which he maintained it. This opinion, in its general form, was that of the sentience of all vegetable things. But, in his disordered fancy, the idea had assumed a more daring character, and trespassed, under certain conditions, upon the kingdom of inorganization. I lack words to express the full extent, or the earnest *abandon* of his persuasion. The belief, however, was connected (as I have previously hinted) with the gray stones of the home of his forefathers. The conditions of the sentience had been here, he imagined, fulfilled in the method of collocation of these stones—in the order of their arrangement, as well as in that of the many *fungi* which overspread them, and of the decayed trees which stood around—above all, in the long undisturbed endurance of this arrangement, and in its reduplication in the still waters of the tarn. Its evidence—the evidence of the sentience—was to be seen, he said (and I here started as he spoke), in the gradual yet certain condensation of an atmosphere of their own about the waters and the walls. The result was discoverable, he added, in that silent yet importunate and terrible influence which for centuries had moulded the destinies of his family, and which made *him* what I now saw him—what he was. Such opinions need no comment, and I will make none.

Our books—the books which, for years, had formed no small portion of the mental existence of the invalid —were, as might be supposed, in strict keeping with this character of phantasm. We pored together over such works as the "Ververt et Chartreuse" of Gresset; the "Belphegor" of Machiavelli; the "Heaven and Hell" of Swedenborg; the "Subterranean Voyage of Nicholas Klimm" of Holberg; the "Chiromancy" of Robert Flud, of Jean D'Indaginé, and of Dela Chambre; the "Journey into the Blue Distance" of Tieck; and the "City of the Sun" of Campanella. One favorite volume was a small octavo edition of the "Directorium Inquisitorium," by

[1] Watson, Dr. Percival, Spallanzani, and especially the Bishop of Landaff.—See "Chemical Essays," vol. v.

the Dominican Eymeric de Gironne; and there were passages in Pomponius Mela, about the old African Satyrs and Ægipans, over which Usher would sit dreaming for hours. His chief delight, however, was found in the perusal of an exceedingly rare and curious book in quarto Gothic—the manual of a forgotten church—the *Vigiliæ Mortuorum secundum Chorum Ecclesiæ Maguntinæ.*

I could not help thinking of the wild ritual of this work, and of its probable influence upon the hypochondriac, when, one evening, having informed me abruptly that the lady Madeline was no more, he stated his intention of preserving her corpse for a fortnight (previously to its final interment), in one of the numerous vaults within the main walls of the building. The worldly reason, however, assigned for this singular proceeding, was one which I did not feel at liberty to dispute. The brother had been led to his resolution (so he told me) by consideration of the unusual character of the malady of the deceased, of certain obtrusive and eager inquiries on the part of her medical men, and of the remote and exposed situation of the burial-ground of the family. I will not deny that when I called to mind the sinister countenance of the person whom I met upon the staircase, on the day of my arrival at the house, I had no desire to oppose what I regarded as at best but a harmless, and by no means an unnatural, precaution.

At the request of Usher, I personally aided him in the arrangements for the temporary entombment. The body having been encoffined, we two alone bore it to its rest. The vault in which we placed it (and which had been so long unopened that our torches, half smothered in its oppressive atmosphere, gave us little opportunity for investigation) was small, damp, and entirely without means of admission for light; lying, at great depth, immediately beneath that portion of the building in which was my own sleeping apartment. It had been used, apparently, in remote feudal times, for the worst purpose of a donjon-keep, and, in later days, as a place of deposit for powder, or some other highly combustible substance, as a portion of its floor, and the whole interior of a long archway through which we reached it, were carefully sheathed with copper. The door, of massive iron, had been, also, similarly protected. Its immense weight caused

an unusually sharp, grating sound, as it moved upon its hinges.

Having deposited our mournful burden upon tressels within this region of horror, we partially turned aside the yet unscrewed lid of the coffin, and looked upon the face of the tenant. A striking similitude between the brother and sister now first arrested my attention; and Usher, divining, perhaps, my thoughts, murmured out some few words from which I learned that the deceased and himself had been twins, and that sympathies of a scarcely intelligible nature had always existed between them. Our glances, however, rested not long upon the dead— for we could not regard her unawed. The disease which had thus entombed the lady in the maturity of youth, had left, as usual in all maladies of a strictly cataleptical character, the mockery of a faint blush upon the bosom and the face, and that suspiciously lingering smile upon the lip which is so terrible in death. We replaced and screwed down the lid, and, having secured the door of iron, made our way, with toil, into the scarcely less gloomy apartments of the upper portion of the house.

And now, some days of bitter grief having elapsed, an observable change came over the features of the mental disorder of my friend. His ordinary manner had vanished. His ordinary occupations were neglected or forgotten. He roamed from chamber to chamber with hurried, unequal, and objectless step. The pallor of his countenance had assumed, if possible, a more ghastly hue— but the luminousness of his eye had utterly gone out. The once occasional huskiness of his tone was heard no more; and a tremulous quaver, as if of extreme terror, habitually characterized his utterance. There were times, indeed, when I thought his unceasingly agitated mind was laboring with some oppressive secret, to divulge which he struggled for the necessary courage. At times, again, I was obliged to resolve all into the mere inexplicable vagaries of madness, for I beheld him gazing upon vacancy for long hours, in an attitude of the profoundest attention, as if listening to some imaginary sound. It was no wonder that his condition terrified— that it infected me. I felt creeping upon me, by slow yet certain degrees, the wild influences of his own fantastic yet impressive superstitions.

It was, especially, upon retiring to bed late in the night

of the seventh or eighth day after the placing of the lady
Madeline within the donjon, that I experienced the full
power of such feelings. Sleep came not near my couch
—while the hours waned and waned away. I struggled to
reason off the nervousness which had dominion over me.
I endeavored to believe that much, if not all of what I
felt, was due to the bewildering influence of the gloomy
furniture of the room—of the dark and tattered dra-
peries, which, tortured into motion by the breath of a
rising tempest, swayed fitfully to and fro upon the walls,
and rustled uneasily about the decorations of the bed.
But my efforts were fruitless. An irrepressible tremor
gradually pervaded my frame; and, at length, there sat
upon my very heart an incubus of utterly causeless
alarm. Shaking this off with a gasp and a struggle, I
uplifted myself upon the pillows, and, peering earnestly
within the intense darkness of the chamber, hearkened
—I know not why, except that an instinctive spirit
prompted me—to certain low and indefinite sounds
which came, through the pauses of the storm, at long in-
tervals, I knew not whence. Overpowered by an intense
sentiment of horror, unaccountable yet unendurable, I
threw on my clothes with haste (for I felt that I should
sleep no more during the night), and endeavored to
arouse myself from the pitiable condition into which I
had fallen, by pacing rapidly to and fro through the
apartment.

I had taken but few turns in this manner, when a light
step on an adjoining staircase arrested my attention. I
presently recognized it as that of Usher. In an instant
afterward he rapped, with a gentle touch, at my door,
and entered, bearing a lamp. His countenance was, as
usual, cadaverously wan—but, moreover, there was a
species of mad hilarity in his eyes—an evidently re-
strained *hysteria* in his whole demeanor. His air ap-
palled me—but any thing was preferable to the solitude
which I had so long endured, and I even welcomed his
presence as a relief.

"And you have not seen it?" he said abruptly, after
having stared about him for some moments in silence—
"you have not then seen it?—but, stay! you shall." Thus
speaking, and having carefully shaded his lamp, he hur-
ried to one of the casements, and threw it freely open to
the storm.

The impetuous fury of the entering gust nearly lifted us from our feet. It was, indeed, a tempestuous yet sternly beautiful night, and one wildly singular in its terror and its beauty. A whirlwind had apparently collected its force in our vicinity; for there were frequent and violent alterations in the direction of the wind; and the exceeding density of the clouds (which hung so low as to press upon the turrets of the house) did not prevent our perceiving the life-like velocity with which they flew careering from all points against each other, without passing away into the distance. I say that even their exceeding density did not prevent our perceiving this— yet we had no glimpse of the moon or stars, nor was there any flashing forth of the lightning. But the under surfaces of the huge masses of agitated vapor, as well as all terrestrial objects immediately around us, were glowing in the unnatural light of a faintly luminous and distinctly visible gaseous exhalation which hung about and enshrouded the mansion.

"You must not—you shall not behold this!" said I, shuddering, to Usher, as I led him, with a gentle violence, from the window to a seat. "These appearances, which bewilder you, are merely electrical phenomena not uncommon—or it may be that they have their ghastly origin in the rank miasma of the tarn. Let us close this casement; —the air is chilling and dangerous to your frame. Here is one of your favorite romances. I will read, and you shall listen:—and so we will pass away this terrible night together."

The antique volume which I had taken up was the "Mad Trist" of Sir Launcelot Canning; but I had called it a favorite of Usher's more in sad jest than in earnest; for, in truth, there is little in its uncouth and unimaginative prolixity which could have had interest for the lofty and spiritual ideality of my friend. It was, however, the only book immediately at hand; and I indulged a vague hope that the excitement which now agitated the hypochondriac, might find relief (for the history of mental disorder is full of similar anomalies) even in the extremeness of the folly which I should read. Could I have judged, indeed, by the wild overstrained air of vivacity with which he hearkened, or apparently hearkened, to the words of the tale, I might well have congratulated myself upon the success of my design.

I had arrived at that well-known portion of the story where Ethelred, the hero of the Trist, having sought in vain for peaceable admission into the dwelling of the hermit, proceeds to make good an entrance by force. Here, it will be remembered, the words of the narrative run thus:

"And Ethelred, who was by nature of a doughty heart, and who was now mighty withal, on account of the powerfulness of the wine which he had drunken, waited no longer to hold parley with the hermit, who, in sooth, was of an obstinate and maliceful turn, but, feeling the rain upon his shoulders, and fearing the rising of the tempest, uplifted his mace outright, and, with blows, made quickly room in the plankings of the door for his gauntleted hand; and now pulling therewith sturdily, he so cracked, and ripped, and tore all asunder, that the noise of the dry and hollow-sounding wood alarumed and reverberated throughout the forest."

At the termination of this sentence I started and, for a moment, paused; for it appeared to me (although I at once concluded that my excited fancy had deceived me) —it appeared to me that, from some very remote portion of the mansion, there came, indistinctly, to my ears, what might have been, in its exact similarity of character, the echo (but a stifled and dull one certainly) of the very cracking and ripping sound which Sir Launcelot had so particularly described. It was, beyond doubt, the coincidence alone which had arrested my attention; for, amid the rattling of the sashes of the casements, and the ordinary commingled noises of the still increasing storm, the sound, in itself, had nothing, surely, which should have interested or disturbed me. I continued the story:

"But the good champion Ethelred, now entering within the door, was sore enraged and amazed to perceive no signal of the maliceful hermit; but, in the stead thereof, a dragon of a scaly and prodigious demeanor, and of a fiery tongue, which sate in guard before a palace of gold, with a floor of silver; and upon the wall there hung a shield of shining brass with this legend enwritten—

Who entereth herein, a conqueror hath bin;
Who slayeth the dragon, the shield he shall win.

And Ethelred uplifted his mace, and struck upon the

head of the dragon, which fell before him, and gave up his pesty breath, with a shriek so horrid and harsh, and withal so piercing, that Ethelred had fain to close his ears with his hands against the dreadful noise of it, the like whereof was never before heard."

Here again I paused abruptly, and now with a feeling of wild amazement—for there could be no doubt whatever that, in this instance, I did actually hear (although from what direction it proceeded I found it impossible to say) a low and apparently distant, but harsh, protracted, and most unusual screaming or grating sound —the exact counterpart of what my fancy had already conjured up for the dragon's unnatural shriek as described by the romancer.

Oppressed, as I certainly was, upon the occurrence of this second and most extraordinary coincidence, by a thousand conflicting sensations, in which wonder and extreme terror were predominant, I still retained sufficient presence of mind to avoid exciting, by any observation, the sensitive nervousness of my companion. I was by no means certain that he had noticed the sounds in question; although, assuredly, a strange alteration had, during the last few minutes, taken place in his demeanor. From a position fronting my own, he had gradually brought round his chair, so as to sit with his face to the door of the chamber; and thus I could but partially perceive his features, although I saw that his lips trembled as if he were murmuring inaudibly. His head had dropped upon his breast—yet I knew that he was not asleep, from the wide and rigid opening of the eye as I caught a glance of it in profile. The motion of his body, too, was at variance with this idea—for he rocked from side to side with a gentle yet constant and uniform sway. Having rapidly taken notice of all this, I resumed the narrative of Sir Launcelot, which thus proceeded:

"And now, the champion, having escaped from the terrible fury of the dragon, bethinking himself of the brazen shield, and of the breaking up of the enchantment which was upon it, removed the carcass from out of the way before him, and approached valorously over the silver pavement of the castle to where the shield was upon the wall; which in sooth tarried not for his full coming, but fell down at his feet upon the silver floor, with a mighty great and terrible ringing sound."

No sooner had these syllables passed my lips, than—as if a shield of brass had indeed, at the moment, fallen heavily upon a floor of silver—I became aware of a distinct, hollow, metallic, and clangorous, yet apparently muffled, reverberation. Completely unnerved, I leaped to my feet; but the measured rocking movement of Usher was undisturbed. I rushed to the chair in which he sat. His eyes were bent fixedly before him, and throughout his whole countenance there reigned a stony rigidity. But, as I placed my hand upon his shoulder, there came a strong shudder over his whole person; a sickly smile quivered about his lips; and I saw that he spoke in a low, hurried, and gibbering murmur, as if unconscious of my presence. Bending closely over him, I at length drank in the hideous import of his words.

"Not hear it?—yes, I hear it, and *have* heard it. Long—long—long—many minutes, many hours, many days, have I heard it—yet I dared not—oh, pity me, miserable wretch that I am!—I dared not—I *dared* not speak! *We have put her living in the tomb!* Said I not that my senses were acute? I *now* tell you that I heard her first feeble movements in the hollow coffin. I heard them—many, many days ago—yet I dared not—*I dared not speak!* And now—to-night—Ethelred—ha ha!—the breaking of the hermit's door, and the death-cry of the dragon, and the clangor of the shield—say, rather, the rending of her coffin, and the grating of the iron hinges of her prison, and her struggles within the coppered archway of the vault! Oh! whither shall I fly? Will she not be here anon? Is she not hurrying to upbraid me for my haste? Have I not heard her footstep on the stair? Do I not distinguish that heavy and horrible beating of her heart? Madman!"—here he sprang furiously to his feet, and shrieked out his syllables, as if in the effort he were giving up his soul—"*Madman! I tell you that she now stands without the door!*"

As if in the superhuman energy of his utterance there had been found the potency of a spell, the huge antique panels to which the speaker pointed threw slowly back, upon the instant, their ponderous and ebony jaws. It was the work of the rushing gust—but then without those doors there *did* stand the lofty and enshrouded figure of the lady Madeline of Usher. There was blood upon her white robes, and the evidence of some bitter struggle

upon every portion of her emaciated frame. For a moment she remained trembling and reeling to and fro upon the threshold—then, with a low moaning cry, fell heavily inward upon the person of her brother, and in her violent and now final death-agonies, bore him to the floor a corpse, and a victim to the terrors he had anticipated.

From that chamber, and from that mansion, I fled aghast. The storm was still abroad in all its wrath as I found myself crossing the old causeway. Suddenly there shot along the path a wild light, and I turned to see whence a gleam so unusual could have issued; for the vast house and its shadows were alone behind me. The radiance was that of the full, setting, and blood-red moon, which now shone vividly through that once barely discernible fissure, of which I have spoken as extending from the roof of the building, in a zigzag direction, to the base. While I gazed, this fissure rapidly widened—there came a fierce breath of the whirlwind—the entire orb of the satellite burst at once upon my sight—my brain reeled as I saw the mighty walls rushing asunder—there was a long tumultuous shouting sound like the voice of a thousand waters—and the deep and dank tarn at my feet closed sullenly and silently over the fragments of the *"House of Usher."*

The Pit and the Pendulum

Impia tortorum longas hic turba furores
Sanguinis innocui, non satiata, aluit.
Sospite nunc patria, fracto nunc funeris antro,
Mors ubi dira fuit vita salusque patent.

[*Quatrain composed for the gates of a market to be
erected upon the site of the Jacobin Club House at Paris.*]

I WAS SICK—SICK unto death with that long agony;
and when they at length unbound me, and I was permitted to sit, I felt that my senses were leaving me.
The sentence—the dread sentence of death—was the
last of distinct accentuation which reached my ears. After
that, the sound of the inquisitorial voices seemed
merged in one dreamy indeterminate hum. It conveyed
to my soul the idea of *revolution*—perhaps from its association in fancy with the burr of a mill-wheel. This only
for a brief period, for presently I heard no more. Yet,
for a while, I saw—but with how terrible an exaggeration! I saw the lips of the black-robed judges. They appeared to me white—whiter than the sheet upon which
I trace these words—and thin even to grotesqueness;
thin with the intensity of their expression of firmness—
of immovable resolution—of stern contempt of human
torture. I saw that the decrees of what to me was Fate
were still issuing from those lips. I saw them writhe with
a deadly locution. I saw them fashion the syllables of my
name; and I shuddered because no sound succeeded. I
saw, too, for a few moments of delirious horror, the
soft and nearly imperceptible waving of the sable draperies which enwrapped the walls of the apartment. And
then my vision fell upon the seven tall candles upon the
table. At first they wore the aspect of charity, and

seemed white slender angels who would save me; but then, all at once, there came a most deadly nausea over my spirit, and I felt every fibre in my frame thrill as if I had touched the wire of a galvanic battery, while the angel forms became meaningless spectres, with heads of flame, and I saw that from them there would be no help. And then there stole into my fancy, like a rich musical note, the thought of what sweet rest there must be in the grave. The thought came gently and stealthily, and it seemed long before it attained full appreciation; but just as my spirit came at length properly to feel and entertain it, the figures of the judges vanished, as if magically, from before me; the tall candles sank into nothingness; their flames went out utterly; the blackness of darkness supervened; all sensations appeared swallowed up in a mad rushing descent as of the soul into Hades. Then silence, and stillness, and night were the universe.

I had swooned; but still will not say that all of consciousness was lost. What of it there remained I will not attempt to define, or even to describe; yet all was not lost. In the deepest slumber—no! In delirium—no! In a swoon—no! In death—no! even in the grave all *is not* lost. Else there is no immortality for man. Arousing from the most profound of slumbers, we break the gossamer web of *some* dream. Yet in a second afterward (so frail may that web have been) we remember not that we have dreamed. In the return to life from the swoon there are two stages: first, that of the sense of mental or spiritual; secondly, that of the sense of physical, existence. It seems probable that if, upon reaching the second stage, we could recall the impressions of the first, we should find these impressions eloquent in memories of the gulf beyond. And that gulf is—what? How at least shall we distinguish its shadows from those of the tomb? But if the impressions of what I have termed the first stage are not, at will, recalled, yet, after long interval, do they not come unbidden, while we marvel whence they come? He who has never swooned, is not he who finds strange palaces and wildly familiar faces in coals that glow; is not he who beholds floating in mid-air the sad visions that the many may not view; is not he who ponders over the perfume of some novel flower; is not he whose brain grows bewildered with the

meaning of some musical cadence which has never before arrested his attention.

Amid frequent and thoughtful endeavors to remember, amid earnest struggles to regather some token of the state of seeming nothingness into which my soul had lapsed, there have been moments when I have dreamed of success; there have been brief, very brief periods when I have conjured up remembrances which the lucid reason of a later epoch assures me could have had reference only to that condition of seeming unconsciousness. These shadows of memory tell, indistinctly, of tall figures that lifted and bore me in silence down—down—still down—till a hideous dizziness oppressed me at the mere idea of the interminableness of the descent. They tell also of a vague horror at my heart, on account of that heart's unnatural stillness. Then comes a sense of sudden motionlessness throughout all things; as if those who bore me (a ghastly train!) had outrun, in their descent, the limits of the limitless, and paused from the wearisomeness of their toil. After this I call to mind flatness and dampness; and then all is *madness*—the madness of a memory which busies itself among forbidden things.

Very suddenly there came back to my soul motion and sound—the tumultuous motion of the heart, and, in my ears, the sound of its beating. Then a pause in which all is blank. Then again sound, and motion, and touch—a tingling sensation pervading my frame. Then the mere consciousness of existence, without thought—a condition which lasted long. Then, very suddenly, *thought,* and shuddering terror, and earnest endeavor to comprehend my true state. Then a strong desire to lapse into insensibility. Then a rushing revival of soul and a successful effort to move. And now a full memory of the trial, of the judges, of the sable draperies, of the sentence, of the sickness, of the swoon. Then entire forgetfulness of all that followed; of all that a later day and much earnestness of endeavor have enabled me vaguely to recall.

So far, I had not opened my eyes. I felt that I lay upon my back, unbound. I reached out my hand, and it fell heavily upon something damp and hard. There I suffered it to remain for many minutes, while I strove to imagine where and *what* I could be. I longed, yet dared not, to employ my vision. I dreaded the first glance at

objects around me. It was not that I feared to look upon things horrible, but that I grew aghast lest there should be *nothing* to see. At length, with a wild desperation at heart, I quickly unclosed my eyes. My worst thoughts, then, were confirmed. The blackness of eternal night encompassed me. I struggled for breath. The intensity of the darkness seemed to oppress and stifle me. The atmosphere was intolerably close. I lay still quietly, and made effort to exercise my reason. I brought to mind the inquisitorial proceedings, and attempted from that point to deduce my real condition. The sentence had passed; and it appeared to me that a very long interval of time had since elapsed. Yet not for a moment did I suppose myself actually dead. Such a supposition, notwithstanding what we read in fiction, is altogether inconsistent with real existence;—but where and in what state was I? The condemned to death, I knew, perished usually at the *auts-da-fé*, and one of these had been held on the very night of the day of my trial. Had I been remanded to my dungeon, to await the next sacrifice, which would not take place for many months? This I at once saw could not be. Victims had been in immediate demand. Moreover, my dungeon, as well as all the condemned cells at Toledo, had stone floors, and light was not altogether excluded.

A fearful idea now suddenly drove the blood in torrents upon my heart, and for a brief period I once more relapsed into insensibility. Upon recovering, I at once started to my feet, trembling convulsively in every fibre. I thrust my arms wildly above and around me in all directions. I felt nothing; yet dreaded to move a step, lest I should be impeded by the walls of a *tomb*. Perspiration burst from every pore, and stood in cold big beads upon my forehead. The agony of suspense grew at length intolerable, and I cautiously moved forward, with my arms extended, and my eyes straining from their sockets in the hope of catching some faint ray of light. I proceeded for many paces; but still all was blackness and vacancy. I breathed more freely. It seemed evident that mine was not, at least, the most hideous of fates.

And now, as I still continued to step cautiously onward, there came thronging upon my recollection a thousand vague rumors of the horrors of Toledo. Of the dungeons there had been strange things narrated—fables

I had always deemed them,—but yet strange, and too ghastly to repeat, save in a whisper. Was I left to perish of starvation in this subterranean world of darkness; or what fate, perhaps even more fearful, awaited me? That the result would be death, and a death of more than customary bitterness, I knew too well the character of my judges to doubt. The mode and the hour were all that occupied or distracted me.

My outstretched hands at length encountered some solid obstruction. It was a wall, seemingly of stone masonry—very smooth, slimy, and cold. I followed it up; stepping with all the careful distrust with which certain antique narratives had inspired me. This process, however, afforded me no means of ascertaining the dimensions of my dungeon, as I might make its circuit and return to the point whence I set out without being aware of the fact, so perfectly uniform seemed the wall. I therefore sought the knife which had been in my pocket when led into the inquisitorial chamber; but it was gone; my clothes had been exchanged for a wrapper of coarse serge. I had thought of forcing the blade in some minute crevice of the masonry, so as to identify my point of departure. The difficulty, nevertheless, was but trivial; although, in the disorder of my fancy, it seemed at first insuperable. I tore a part of the hem from the robe and placed the fragment at full length, and at right angles to the wall. In groping my way around the prison, I could not fail to encounter this rag upon completing the circuit. So, at least, I thought; but I had not counted upon the extent of the dungeon, or upon my own weakness. The ground was moist and slippery. I staggered onward for some time, when I stumbled and fell. My excessive fatigue induced me to remain prostrate; and sleep soon overtook me as I lay.

Upon awaking, and stretching forth an arm, I found beside me a loaf and a pitcher with water. I was too much exhausted to reflect upon this circumstance, but ate and drank with avidity. Shortly afterward, I resumed my tour around the prison, and with much toil, came at last upon the fragment of the serge. Up to the period when I fell, I had counted fifty-two paces, and upon resuming my walk, I had counted forty-eight more—when I arrived at the rag. There were in all, then, a hundred paces; and, admitting two paces to the yard, I presumed

the dungeon to be fifty yards in circuit. I had met, how-
ever, with many angles in the wall, and thus I could
form no guess at the shape of the vault, for vault I
could not help supposing it to be.

I had little object—certainly no hope—in these re-
searches; but a vague curiosity prompted me to continue
them. Quitting the wall, I resolved to cross the area of
the enclosure. At first, I proceeded with extreme cau-
tion, for the floor, although seemingly of solid material,
was treacherous with slime. At length, however, I took
courage, and did not hesitate to step firmly—endeavor-
ing to cross in as direct a line as possible. I had ad-
vanced some ten or twelve paces in this manner, when
the remnant of the torn hem of my robe became en-
tangled between my legs. I stepped on it, and fell vio-
lently on my face.

In the confusion attending my fall, I did not immedi-
ately apprehend a somewhat startling circumstance,
which yet, in a few seconds afterward, and while I still
lay prostrate, arrested my attention. It was this: my
chin rested upon the floor of the prison, but my lips,
and the upper portion of my head, although seem-
ingly at a less elevation than the chin, touched nothing.
At the same time, my forehead seemed bathed in a
clammy vapor, and the peculiar smell of decayed fungus
arose to my nostrils. I put forward my arm, and shud-
dered to find that I had fallen at the very brink of a
circular pit, whose extent, of course, I had no means of
ascertaining at the moment. Groping about the masonry
just below the margin, I succeeded in dislodging a small
fragment, and let it fall into the abyss. For many sec-
onds I hearkened to its reverberations as it dashed
against the sides of the chasm in its descent; at length,
there was a sullen plunge into water, succeeded by loud
echoes. At the same moment, there came a sound re-
sembling the quick opening and as rapid closing of a
door overhead, while a faint gleam of light flashed sud-
denly through the gloom, and as suddenly faded away.

I saw clearly the doom which had been prepared for
me, and congratulated myself upon the timely accident
by which I had escaped. Another step before my fall,
and the world had seen me no more. And the death just
avoided was of that very character which I had regarded
as fabulous and frivolous in the tales respecting the

Inquisition. To the victims of its tyranny, there was the choice of death with its direst physical agonies, or death with its most hideous moral horrors. I had been reserved for the latter. By long suffering my nerves had been unstrung, until I trembled at the sound of my own voice, and had become in every respect a fitting subject for the species of torture which awaited me.

Shaking in every limb, I groped my way back to the wall—resolving there to perish rather than risk the terrors of the wells, of which my imagination now pictured many in various positions about the dungeon. In other conditions of mind, I might have had courage to end my misery at once, by a plunge into one of these abysses; but now I was the veriest of cowards. Neither could I forget what I had read of these pits—that the *sudden* extinction of life formed no part of their most horrible plan.

Agitation of spirit kept me awake for many long hours, but at length I again slumbered. Upon arousing, I found by my side, as before, a loaf and a pitcher of water. A burning thirst consumed me, and I emptied the vessel at a draught. It must have been drugged—for scarcely had I drunk, before I became irresistibly drowsy. A deep sleep fell upon me—a sleep like that of death. How long it lasted, of course I know not; but when, once again, I unclosed my eyes, the objects around me were visible. By a wild, sulphurous lustre, the origin of which I could not at first determine, I was enabled to see the extent and aspect of the prison.

In its size I had been greatly mistaken. The whole circuit of its walls did not exceed twenty-five yards. For some minutes this fact occasioned me a world of vain trouble; vain indeed—for what could be of less importance, under the terrible circumstances which environed me, than the mere dimensions of my dungeon? But my soul took a wild interest in trifles, and I busied myself in endeavors to account for the error I had committed in my measurement. The truth at length flashed upon me. In my first attempt at exploration I had counted fifty-two paces, up to the period when I fell: I must then have been within a pace or two of the fragment of serge; in fact, I had nearly performed the circuit of the vault. I then slept—and, upon awaking, I must have returned upon my steps—thus supposing the circuit nearly

double what it actually was. My confusion of mind prevented me from observing that I began my tour with the wall to the left, and ended it with the wall to the right.

I had been deceived, too, in respect to the shape of the enclosure. In feeling my way I had found many angles, and thus deduced an idea of great irregularity; so potent is the effect of total darkness upon one arousing from lethargy or sleep! The angles were simply those of a few slight depressions, or niches, at odd intervals. The general shape of the prison was square. What I had taken for masonry seemed now to be iron, or some other metal, in huge plates, whose sutures or joints occasioned the depression. The entire surface of this metallic enclosure was rudely daubed in all the hideous and repulsive devices to which the charnel superstition of the monks has given rise. The figures of fiends in aspects of menace, with skeleton forms, and other more really fearful images, overspread and disfigured the walls. I observed that the outlines of these monstrosities were sufficiently distinct, but that the colors seemed faded and blurred, as if from the effects of a damp atmosphere. I now noticed the floor, too, which was of stone. In the centre yawned the circular pit from whose jaws I had escaped; but it was the only one in the dungeon.

All this I saw indistinctly and by much effort—for my personal condition had been greatly changed during slumber. I now lay upon my back, and at full length, on a species of low framework of wood. To this I was securely bound by a long strap resembling a surcingle. It passed in many convolutions about my limbs and body, leaving at liberty only my head, and my left arm to such extent, that I could, by dint of much exertion, supply myself with food from an earthen dish which lay by my side on the floor. I saw, to my horror, that the pitcher had been removed. I say to my horror—for I was consumed with intolerable thirst. This thirst it appeared to be the design of my persecutors to stimulate —for the food in the dish was meat pungently seasoned.

Looking upward, I surveyed the ceiling of my prison. It was some thirty or forty feet overhead, and constructed much as the side walls. In one of its panels a very singular figure riveted my whole attention. It was the painted figure of Time as he is commonly represented,

save that, in lieu of a scythe, he held what, at a casual glance, I supposed to be the pictured image of a huge pendulum, such as we see on antique clocks. There was something, however, in the appearance of this machine which caused me to regard it more attentively. While I gazed directly upward at it (for its position was immediately over my own) I fancied that I saw it in motion. In an instant afterward the fancy was confirmed. Its sweep was brief, and of course slow. I watched it for some minutes somewhat in fear, but more in wonder. Wearied at length with observing its dull movement, I turned my eyes upon the other objects in the cell.

A slight noise attracted my notice, and, looking to the floor, I saw several enormous rats traversing it. They had issued from the well which lay just within view to my right. Even then, while I gazed, they came up in troops, hurriedly, with ravenous eyes, allured by the scent of the meat. From this it required much effort and attention to scare them away.

It might have been half an hour, perhaps, even an hour (for I could take but imperfect note of time), before I again cast my eyes upward. What I then saw confounded and amazed me. The sweep of the pendulum had increased in extent by nearly a yard. As a natural consequence its velocity was also much greater. But what mainly disturbed me was the idea that it had perceptibly *descended*. I now observed—with what horror it is needless to say—that its nether extremity was formed of a crescent of glittering steel, about a foot in length from horn to horn; the horns upward, and the under edge evidently as keen as that of a razor. Like a razor also, it seemed massy and heavy, tapering from the edge into a solid and broad structure above. It was appended to a weighty rod of brass, and the whole *hissed* as it swung through the air.

I could no longer doubt the doom prepared for me by monkish ingenuity in torture. My cognizance of the pit had become known to the inquisitorial agents—*the pit,* whose horrors had been destined for so bold a recusant as myself—the pit, typical of hell and regarded by rumor as the Ultima Thule of all their punishments. The plunge into this pit I had avoided by the merest of accidents, and I knew that surprise, or entrapment into torment, formed an important portion of all

the grotesquerie of these dungeon deaths. Having failed
to fall, it was no part of the demon plan to hurl me
into the abyss, and thus (there being no alternative) a
different and milder destruction awaited me. Milder! I
half smiled in my agony as I thought of such application
of such a term.

What boots it to tell of the long, long hours of horror
more than mortal, during which I counted the rushing
oscillations of the steel! Inch by inch, line by line—
with a descent only appreciable at intervals that seemed
ages—down and still down it came! Days passed—it
might have been that many days passed—ere it swept so
closely over me as to fan me with its acrid breath. The
odor of the sharp steel forced itself into my nostrils. I
prayed—I wearied heaven with my prayer for its more
speedy descent. I grew frantically mad, and struggled to
force myself upward against the sweep of the fearful
scimitar. And then I fell suddenly calm, and lay smiling
at the glittering death, as a child at some rare bauble.

There was another interval of utter insensibility; it was
brief; for, upon again lapsing into life, there had been
no perceptible descent in the pendulum. But it might
have been long—for I knew there were demons who took
note of my swoon, and who could have arrested the
vibration at pleasure. Upon my recovery, too, I felt very
—oh! inexpressibly—sick and weak, as if through long
inanition. Even amid the agonies of that period, the human
nature craved food. With painful effort I outstretched my
arm as far as my bonds permitted, and took possession of
the small remnant which had been spared me by the
rats. As I put a portion of it within my lips, there rushed
to my mind a half-formed thought of joy—of hope. Yet
what business had *I* with hope? It was, as I say, a half-
formed thought—man has many such, which are never
completed. I felt that it was of joy—of hope; but I felt
also that it had perished in its formation. In vain I strug-
gled to perfect—to regain it. Long suffering had nearly
annihilated all my ordinary powers of mind. I was an
imbecile—an idiot.

The vibration of the pendulum was at right angles to
my length. I saw that the crescent was designed to cross
the region of the heart. It would fray the serge of my
robe—it would return and repeat its operations—again
—and again. Notwithstanding its terrifically wide sweep

(some thirty feet or more), and the hissing vigor of its descent, sufficient to sunder these very walls of iron, still the fraying of my robe would be all that, for several minutes, it would accomplish. And at this thought I paused. I dared not go further than this reflection. I dwelt upon it with a pertinacity of attention—as if, in so dwelling, I could arrest *here* the descent of the steel. I forced myself to ponder upon the sound of the crescent as it should pass across the garment—upon the peculiar thrilling sensation which the friction of cloth produces on the nerves. I pondered upon all this frivolity until my teeth were on edge.

Down—steadily down it crept. I took a frenzied pleasure in contrasting its downward with its lateral velocity. To the right—to the left—far and wide—with the shriek of a damned spirit! to my heart, with the stealthy pace of the tiger! I alternately laughed and howled, as the one or the other idea grew predominant.

Down—certainly, relentlessly down! It vibrated within three inches of my bosom! I struggled violently—furiously—to free my left arm. This was free only from the elbow to the hand. I could reach the latter, from the platter beside me, to my mouth, with great effort, but no farther. Could I have broken the fastenings above the elbow, I would have seized and attempted to arrest the pendulum. I might as well have attempted to arrest an avalanche!

Down—still unceasingly—still inevitably down! I gasped and struggled at each vibration. I shrunk convulsively at its every sweep. My eyes followed its outward or upward whirls with the eagerness of the most unmeaning despair; they closed themselves spasmodically at the descent, although death would have been a relief, oh, how unspeakable! Still I quivered in every nerve to think how slight a sinking of the machinery would precipitate that keen, glistening axe upon my bosom. It was *hope* that prompted the nerve to quiver—the frame to shrink. It was *hope*—the hope that triumphs on the rack—that whispers to the death-condemned even in the dungeons of the Inquisition.

I saw that some ten or twelve vibrations would bring the steel in actual contact with my robe—and with this observation there suddenly came over my spirit all the keen, collected calmness of despair. For the first time

during many hours—or perhaps days—I *thought*. It now
occurred to me, that the bandage, or surcingle, which en-
veloped me, was *unique*. I was tied by no separate cord.
The first stroke of the razor-like crescent athwart any
portion of the band would so detach it that it might be
unwound from my person by means of my left hand.
But how fearful, in that case, the proximity of the steel!
The result of the slightest struggle, how deadly! Was it
likely, moreover, that the minions of the torturer had
not foreseen and provided for this possibility? Was it
probable that the bandage crossed my bosom in the
track of the pendulum? Dreading to find my faint and,
as it seemed, my last hope frustrated, I so far elevated
my head as to obtain a distinct view of my breast. The
surcingle enveloped my limbs and body close in all di-
rections—*save in the path of the destroying crescent*.

Scarcely had I dropped my head back into its original
position, when there flashed upon my mind what I can-
not better describe than as the unformed half of that
idea of deliverance to which I have previously alluded,
and of which a moiety only floated indeterminately
through my brain when I raised food to my burning lips.
The whole thought was now present—feeble, scarcely
sane, scarcely definite—but still entire. I proceeded at
once, with the nervous energy of despair, to attempt its
execution.

For many hours the immediate vicinity of the low
framework upon which I lay had been literally swarming
with rats. They were wild, bold, ravenous—their red eyes
glaring upon me as if they waited but for motionlessness
on my part to make me their prey. "To what food," I
thought, "have they been accustomed in the well?"

They had devoured, in spite of all my efforts to prevent
them, all but a small remnant of the contents of the
dish. I had fallen into an habitual see-saw or wave of the
hand about the platter; and, at length, the unconscious
uniformity of the movement deprived it of effect. In
their voracity, the vermin frequently fastened their sharp
fangs in my fingers. With the particles of the oily and
spicy viand which now remained, I thoroughly rubbed
the bandage wherever I could reach it; then, raising my
hand from the floor, I lay breathlessly still.

At first, the ravenous animals were startled and terri-
fied at the change—at the cessation of movement.

They shrank alarmedly back; many sought the well. But this was only for a moment. I had not counted in vain upon their voracity. Observing that I remained without motion, one or two of the boldest leaped upon the framework, and smelt at the surcingle. This seemed the signal for a general rush. Forth from the well they hurried in fresh troops. They clung to the wood—they overran it, and leaped in hundreds upon my person. The measured movement of the pendulum disturbed them not at all. Avoiding its strokes, they busied themselves with the anointed bandage. They pressed—they swarmed upon me in ever accumulating heaps. They writhed upon my throat; their cold lips sought my own; I was half stifled by their thronging pressure; disgust, for which the world has no name, swelled my bosom, and chilled, with a heavy clamminess, my heart. Yet one minute, and I felt that the struggle would be over. Plainly I perceived the loosening of the bandage. I knew that in more than one place it must be already severed. With a more than human resolution I lay *still*.

Nor had I erred in my calculations—nor had I endured in vain. I at length felt that I was *free*. The surcingle hung in ribands from my body. But the stroke of the pendulum already pressed upon my bosom. It had divided the serge of the robe. It had cut through the linen beneath. Twice again it swung, and a sharp sense of pain shot through every nerve. But the moment of escape had arrived. At a wave of my hand my deliverers hurried tumultuously away. With a steady movement—cautious, sidelong, shrinking, and slow—I slid from the embrace of the bandage and beyond the reach of the scimitar. For the moment, at least, *I was free*.

Free!—and in the grasp of the Inquisition! I had scarcely stepped from my wooden bed of horror upon the stone floor of the prison, when the motion of the hellish machine ceased, and I beheld it drawn up, by some invisible force, through the ceiling. This was a lesson which I took desperately to heart. My every motion was undoubtedly watched. Free!—I had but escaped death in one form of agony, to be delivered unto worse than death in some other. With that thought I rolled my eyes nervously around on the barriers of iron that hemmed me in. Something unusual—some change which, at first, I could not appreciate distinctly—it was obvious,

had taken place in the apartment. For many minutes of a dreamy and trembling abstraction, I busied myself in vain, unconnected conjecture. During this period, I became aware, for the first time, of the origin of the sulphurous light which illumined the cell. It proceeded from a fissure, about half an inch in width, extending entirely around the prison at the base of the walls, which thus appeared, and were, completely separated from the floor. I endeavored, but of course in vain, to look through the aperture.

As I arose from the attempt, the mystery of the alteration in the chamber broke at once upon my understanding. I have observed that, although the outlines of the figures upon the walls were sufficiently distinct, yet the colors seemed blurred and indefinite. These colors had now assumed, and were momentarily assuming, a startling and most intense brilliancy, that gave to the spectral and fiendish portraitures an aspect that might have thrilled even firmer nerves than my own. Demon eyes, of a wild and ghastly vivacity, glared upon me in a thousand directions, where none had been visible before, and gleamed with the lurid lustre of a fire that I could not force my imagination to regard as unreal.

Unreal!—Even while I breathed there came to my nostrils the breath of the vapor of heated iron! A suffocating odor pervaded the prison! A deeper glow settled each moment in the eyes that glared at my agonies! A richer tint of crimson diffused itself over the pictured horrors of blood. I panted! I gasped for breath! There could be no doubt of the design of my tormentors—oh! most unrelenting! oh! most demoniac of men! I shrank from the glowing metal to the centre of the cell. Amid the thought of the fiery destruction that impended, the idea of the coolness of the well came over my soul like balm. I rushed to its deadly brink. I threw my straining vision below. The glare from the enkindled roof illumined its inmost recesses. Yet, for a wild moment, did my spirit refuse to comprehend the meaning of what I saw. At length it forced—it wrestled its way into my soul—it burned itself in upon my shuddering reason. Oh! for a voice to speak!—oh! horror!—oh! any horror but this! With a shriek, I rushed from the margin, and buried my face in my hands—weeping bitterly.

The heat rapidly increased, and once again I looked

up, shuddering as with a fit of the ague. There had been a second change in the cell—and now the change was obviously in the *form*. As before, it was in vain that I at first endeavored to appreciate or understand what was taking place. But not long was I left in doubt. The Inquisitorial vengeance had been hurried by my two-fold escape, and there was to be no more dallying with the King of Terrors. The room had been square. I saw that two of its iron angles were now acute—two, consequently, obtuse. The fearful difference quickly increased with a low rumbling or moaning sound. In an instant the apartment had shifted its form into that of a lozenge. But the alteration stopped not here—I neither hoped nor desired it to stop. I could have clasped the red walls to my bosom as a garment of eternal peace. "Death," I said, "any death but that of the pit!" Fool! might I not have known that *into the pit* it was the object of the burning iron to urge me? Could I resist its glow? or if even that, could I withstand its pressure? And now, flatter and flatter grew the lozenge, with a rapidity that left me no time for contemplation. Its centre, and of course its greatest width, came just over the yawning gulf. I shrank back—but the closing walls pressed me resistlessly onward. At length for my seared and writhing body there was no longer an inch of foothold on the firm floor of the prison. I struggled no more, but the agony of my soul found vent in one loud, long, and final scream of despair. I felt that I tottered upon the brink—I averted my eyes—

There was a discordant hum of human voices! There was a loud blast as of many trumpets! There was a harsh grating as of a thousand thunders! The fiery walls rushed back! An outstretched arm caught my own as I fell, fainting, into the abyss. It was that of General Lasalle. The French army had entered Toledo. The Inquisition was in the hands of its enemies.

The Masque of the Red Death

THE "RED DEATH" had long devastated the country. No pestilence had ever been so fatal, or so hideous. Blood was its Avatar and its seal—the redness and the horror of blood. There were sharp pains, and sudden dizziness, and then profuse bleeding at the pores, with dissolution. The scarlet stains upon the body and especially upon the face of the victim, were the pest ban which shut him out from the aid and from the sympathy of his fellow-men. And the whole seizure, progress, and termination of the disease, were the incidents of half an hour.

But the Prince Prospero was happy and dauntless and sagacious. When his dominions were half depopulated, he summoned to his presence a thousand hale and light-hearted friends from among the knights and dames of his court, and with these retired to the deep seclusion of one of his castellated abbeys. This was an extensive and magnificent structure, the creation of the prince's own eccentric yet august taste. A strong and lofty wall girdled it in. This wall had gates of iron. The courtiers, having entered, brought furnaces and massy hammers and welded the bolts. They resolved to leave means neither of ingress nor egress to the sudden impulses of despair or of frenzy from within. The abbey was amply provisioned. With such precautions the courtiers might bid defiance to contagion. The external world could take care of itself. In the meantime it was folly to grieve, or to think. The prince had provided all the appliances of pleasure. There were buffoons, there were improvisatori, there were ballet-dancers, there were musicians, there was Beauty, there was wine. All these and security were within. Without was the "Red Death."

It was toward the close of the fifth or sixth month of his seclusion, and while the pestilence raged most

furiously abroad, that the Prince Prospero entertained
his thousand friends at a masked ball of the most un-
usual magnificence.

It was a voluptuous scene, that masquerade. But
first let me tell of the rooms in which it was held. There
were seven—an imperial suite. In many palaces, how-
ever, such suites form a long and straight vista, while the
folding doors slide back nearly to the walls on either
hand, so that the view of the whole extent is scarcely
impeded. Here the case was very different; as might have
been expected from the duke's love of the *bizarre*. The
apartments were so irregularly disposed that the vision
embraced but little more than one at a time. There was a
sharp turn at every twenty or thirty yards, and at each
turn a novel effect. To the right and left, in the middle of
each wall, a tall and narrow Gothic window looked out
upon a closed corridor which pursued the windings of
the suite. These windows were of stained glass whose
color varied in accordance with the prevailing hue of
the decorations of the chamber into which it opened.
That at the eastern extremity was hung, for example,
in blue—and vividly blue were its windows. The second
chamber was purple in its ornaments and tapestries,
and here the panes were purple. The third was green
throughout, and so were the casements. The fourth was
furnished and lighted with orange—the fifth with white—
the sixth with violet. The seventh apartment was closely
shrouded in black velvet tapestries that hung all over
the ceiling and down the walls, falling in heavy folds upon
a carpet of the same material and hue. But in this cham-
ber only, the color of the windows failed to correspond
with the decorations. The panes here were scarlet—a
deep blood color. Now in no one of the seven apartments
was there any lamp or candelabrum, amid the profusion
of golden ornaments that lay scattered to and fro or de-
pended from the roof. There was no light of any kind
emanating from lamp or candle within the suite of
chambers. But in the corridors that followed the suite,
there stood, opposite to each window, a heavy tripod,
bearing a brazier of fire, that projected its rays through
the tinted glass and so glaringly illumined the room. And
thus were produced a multitude of gaudy and fantastic
appearances. But in the western or black chamber the
effect of the fire-light that streamed upon the dark hang-

ings through the blood-tinted panes was ghastly in the
extreme, and produced so wild a look upon the counte-
nances of those who entered, that there were few of the
company bold enough to set foot within its precincts at
all.

It was in this apartment, also, that there stood against
the western wall, a gigantic clock of ebony. Its pendulum
swung to and fro with a dull, heavy, monotonous clang;
and when the minute-hand made the circuit of the face,
and the hour was to be stricken, there came from the
brazen lungs of the clock a sound which was clear and
loud and deep and exceedingly musical, but of so peculiar
a note and emphasis that, at each lapse of an hour, the
musicians of the orchestra were constrained to pause,
momentarily, in their performance, to hearken to the
sound; and thus the waltzers perforce ceased their evolu-
tions; and there was a brief disconcert of the whole gay
company; and, while the chimes of the clock yet rang,
it was observed that the giddiest grew pale, and the
more aged and sedate passed their hands over their
brows as if in confused reverie or meditation. But when
the echoes had fully ceased, a light laughter at once
pervaded the assembly; the musicians looked at each
other and smiled as if at their own nervousness and
folly, and made whispering vows, each to the other, that
the next chiming of the clock should produce in them no
similar emotion; and then, after the lapse of sixty
minutes (which embrace three thousand and six hun-
dred seconds of the Time that flies), there came yet an-
other chiming of the clock, and then were the same dis-
concert and tremulousness and meditation as before.

But, in spite of these things, it was a gay and magnif-
icent revel. The tastes of the duke were peculiar. He had
a fine eye for colors and effects. He disregarded the
decora of mere fashion. His plans were bold and fiery,
and his conceptions glowed with barbaric lustre. There
are some who would have thought him mad. His fol-
lowers felt that he was not. It was necessary to hear
and see and touch him to be *sure* that he was not.

He had directed, in great part, the movable embellish-
ments of the seven chambers, upon occasion of this great
fête; and it was his own guiding taste which had given
character to the masqueraders. Be sure they were gro-
tesque. There were much glare and glitter and piquancy

and phantasm—much of what has·been since seen in
"Hernani." There were arabesque figures with unsuited
limbs and appointments. There were delirious fancies
such as the madman fashions. There was much of the
beautiful, much of the wanton, much of the *bizarre,*
something of the terrible, and not a little of that which
might have excited disgust. To and fro in the seven cham-
bers there stalked, in fact, a multitude of dreams. And
these—the dreams—writhed in and about, taking hue
from the rooms, and causing the wild music of the or-
chestra to seem as the echo of their steps. And, anon,
there strikes the ebony clock which stands in the hall of
the velvet. And then, for a moment, all is still, and all is
silent save the voice of the clock. The dreams are stiff-
frozen as they stand. But the echoes of the chime die
away—they have endured but an instant—and a light,
half-subdued laughter floats after them as they depart.
And now again the music swells, and the dreams live,
and writhe to and fro more merrily than ever, taking hue
from the many-tinted windows through which stream the
rays from the tripods. But to the chamber which lies most
westwardly of the seven there are now none of the mask-
ers who venture; for the night is waning away; and there
flows a ruddier light through the blood-colored panes;
and the blackness of the sable drapery appals; and to
him whose foot falls upon the sable carpet, there comes
from the near clock of ebony a muffled peal more sol-
emnly emphatic than any which reaches *their* ears who
indulge in the more remote gaieties of the other apart-
ments.

But these other apartments were densely crowded, and
in them beat feverishly the heart of life. And the revel
went whirlingly on, until at length there commenced the
sounding of midnight upon the clock. And then the music
ceased, as I have told; and the evolutions of the waltzers
were quieted; and there was an uneasy cessation of all
things as before. But now there were twelve strokes to
be sounded by the bell of the clock; and thus it hap-
pened, perhaps, that more of thought crept, with more
of time, into the meditations of the thoughtful among
those who revelled. And thus too, it happened, perhaps,
that before the last echoes of the last chime had utterly
sunk into silence, there were many individuals in the
crowd who had found leisure to become aware of the

presence of a masked figure which had arrested the
attention of no single individual before. And the rumor of
this new presence having spread itself whisperingly
around, there arose at length from the whole company
a buzz, or murmur, expressive of disapprobation and sur-
prise—then, finally, of terror, of horror, and of disgust.

In an assembly of phantasms such as I have painted,
it may well be supposed that no ordinary appearance
could have excited such sensation. In truth the mas-
querade license of the night was nearly unlimited; but
the figure in question had out-Heroded Herod, and gone
beyond the bounds of even the prince's indefinite de-
corum. There are chords in the hearts of the most reck-
less which cannot be touched without emotion. Even with
the utterly lost, to whom life and death are equally jests,
there are matters of which no jest can be made. The
whole company, indeed, seemed now deeply to feel
that in the costume and bearing of the stranger neither
wit nor propriety existed. The figure was tall and gaunt,
and shrouded from head to foot in the habiliments of the
grave. The mask which concealed the visage was made
so nearly to resemble the countenance of a stiffened
corpse that the closest scrutiny must have had difficulty
in detecting the cheat. And yet all this might have been
endured, if not approved, by the mad revellers around.
But the mummer had gone so far as to assume the type
of the Red Death. His vesture was dabbled in *blood*—and
his broad brow, with all the features of the face, was be-
sprinkled with the scarlet horror.

When the eyes of Prince Prospero fell upon this spec-
tral image (which, with a slow and solemn movement,
as if more fully to sustain its *rôle,* stalked to and fro
among the waltzers) he was seen to be convulsed, in the
first moment with a strong shudder either of terror or dis-
taste; but, in the next, his brow reddened with rage.

"Who dares"—he demanded hoarsely of the courtiers
who stood near him—"who dares insult us with this
blasphemous mockery? Seize him and unmask him—that
we may know whom we have to hang, at sunrise, from
the battlements!"

It was in the eastern or blue chamber in which stood
the Prince Prospero as he uttered these words. They rang
throughout the seven rooms loudly and clearly, for the

prince was a bold and robust man, and the music had become hushed at the waving of his hand.

It was in the blue room where stood the prince, with a group of pale courtiers by his side. At first, as he spoke, there was a slight rushing movement of this group in the direction of the intruder, who, at the moment was also near at hand, and now, with deliberate and stately step, made closer approach to the speaker. But from a certain nameless awe with which the mad assumptions of the mummer had inspired the whole party, there were found none who put forth hand to seize him; so that, unimpeded, he passed within a yard of the prince's person; and, while the vast assembly, as if with one impulse, shrank from the centres of the rooms to the walls, he made his way uninterruptedly, but with the same solemn and measured step which had distinguished him from the first, through the blue chamber to the purple—through the purple to the green—through the green to the orange —through this again to the white—and even thence to the violet, ere a decided movement had been made to arrest him. It was then, however, that the Prince Prospero, maddening with rage and the shame of his own momentary cowardice, rushed hurriedly through the six chambers, while none followed him on account of a deadly terror that had seized upon all. He bore aloft a drawn dagger, and had approached, in rapid impetuosity, to within three or four feet of the retreating figure, when the latter, having attained the extremity of the velvet apartment turned suddenly and confronted his pursuer. There was a sharp cry—and the dagger dropped gleaming upon the sable carpet, upon which, instantly afterward, fell prostrate in death the Prince Prospero. Then, summoning the wild courage of despair, a throng of the revellers at once threw themselves into the black apartment, and, seizing the mummer whose tall figure stood erect and motionless within the shadow of the ebony clock, gasped in unutterable horror at finding the grave cerements and corpse-like mask, which they handled with so violent a rudeness, untenanted by any tangible form.

And now was acknowledged the presence of the Red Death. He had come like a thief in the night. And one by one dropped the revellers in the blood-bedewed halls of their revel, and died each in the despairing posture of

his fall. And the life of the ebony clock went out with that of the last of the gay. And the flames of the tripods expired. And Darkness and Decay and the Red Death held illimitable dominion over all.

blessed myself him, that I thought I should never have done wringing his hand.

"I said to him, 'My dear Fortunato, you are luckily

The Cask of Amontillado

THE THOUSAND injuries of Fortunato I had borne as I best could; but when he ventured upon insult, I vowed revenge. You, who so well know the nature of my soul, will not suppose, however, that I gave utterance to a threat. *At length* I would be avenged; this was a point definitively settled—but the very definitiveness with which it was resolved, precluded the idea of risk. I must not only punish, but punish with impunity. A wrong is unredressed when retribution overtakes its redresser. It is equally unredressed when the avenger fails to make himself felt as such to him who has done the wrong.

It must be understood, that neither by word nor deed had I given Fortunato cause to doubt my good-will. I continued, as was my wont, to smile in his face, and he did not perceive that my smile *now* was at the thought of his immolation.

He had a weak point—this Fortunato—although in other regards he was a man to be respected and even feared. He prided himself on his connoisseurship in wine. Few Italians have the true virtuoso spirit. For the most part their enthusiasm is adopted to suit the time and opportunity—to practise imposture upon the British and Austrian *millionaires*. In painting and gemmary Fortunato, like his countrymen, was a quack—but in the matter of old wines he was sincere. In this respect I did not differ from him materially: I was skilful in the Italian vintages myself, and bought largely whenever I could.

It was about dusk, one evening during the supreme madness of the carnival season, that I encountered my friend. He accosted me with excessive warmth, for he had been drinking much. The man wore motley. He had on a tight-fitting parti-striped dress, and his head was surmounted by the conical cap and bells. I was so

pleased to see him, that I thought I should never have done wringing his hand.

I said to him: "My dear Fortunato, you are luckily met. How remarkably well you are looking to-day! But I have received a pipe of what passes for Amontillado, and I have my doubts."

"How?" said he. "Amontillado? A pipe? Impossible! And in the middle of the carnival!"

"I have my doubts," I replied; "and I was silly enough to pay the full Amontillado price without consulting you in the matter. You were not to be found, and I was fearful of losing a bargain."

"Amontillado!"

"I have my doubts."

"Amontillado!"

"And I must satisfy them."

"Amontillado!"

"As you are engaged, I am on my way to Luchesi. If any one has a critical turn, it is he. He will tell me——"

"Luchesi cannot tell Amontillado from Sherry."

"And yet some fools will have it that his taste is a match for your own."

"Come, let us go."

"Whither?"

"To your vaults."

"My friend, no; I will not impose upon your good nature. I perceive you have an engagement. Luchesi——"

"I have no engagement;—come."

"My friend, no. It is not the engagement, but the severe cold with which I perceive you are afflicted. The vaults are insufferably damp. They are encrusted with nitre."

"Let us go, nevertheless. The cold is merely nothing. Amontillado! You have been imposed upon. And as for Luchesi, he cannot distinguish Sherry from Amontillado."

Thus speaking, Fortunato possessed himself of my arm. Putting on a mask of black silk, and drawing a *roquelaire* closely about my person, I suffered him to hurry me to my palazzo.

There were no attendants at home; they had absconded to make merry in honor of the time. I had told them that I should not return until the morning, and had given them explicit orders not to stir from the house. These orders were sufficient, I well knew, to insure their

immediate disappearance, one and all, as soon as my back was turned.

I took from their sconces two flambeaux, and giving one to Fortunato, bowed him through several suites of rooms to the archway that led into the vaults. I passed down a long and winding staircase, requesting him to be cautious as he followed. We came at length to the foot of the descent, and stood together on the damp ground of the catacombs of the Montresors.

The gait of my friend was unsteady, and the bells upon his cap jingled as he strode.

"The pipe?" said he.

"It is farther on," said I; "but observe the white web-work which gleams from these cavern walls."

He turned toward me, and looked into my eyes with two filmy orbs that distilled the rheum of intoxication.

"Nitre?" he asked, at length.

"Nitre," I replied. "How long have you had that cough?"

"Ugh! ugh! ugh!—ugh! ugh! ugh!—ugh! ugh! ugh!—ugh! ugh! ugh!—ugh! ugh! ugh!"

My poor friend found it impossible to reply for many minutes.

"It is nothing," he said at last.

"Come," I said, with decision, "we will go back; your health is precious. You are rich, respected, admired, beloved; you are happy, as once I was. You are a man to be missed. For me it is no matter. We will go back; you will be ill, and I cannot be responsible. Besides, there is Luchesi——"

"Enough," he said; "the cough is a mere nothing; it will not kill me. I shall not die of a cough."

"True—true," I replied; "and, indeed, I had no intention of alarming you unnecessarily; but you should use all proper caution. A draught of this Medoc will defend us from the damps."

Here I knocked off the neck of a bottle which I drew from a long row of its fellows that lay upon the mould.

"Drink," I said, presenting him the wine.

He raised it to his lips with a leer. He paused and nodded to me familiarly, while his bells jingled.

"I drink," he said, "to the buried that repose around us."

"And I to your long life."

He again took my arm, and we proceeded.

"These vaults," he said, "are extensive."

"The Montresors," I replied, "were a great and numerous family."

"I forget your arms."

"A huge human foot d'or, in a field azure; the foot crushes a serpent rampant whose fangs are imbedded in the heel."

"And the motto?"

"Nemo me impune lacessit."

"Good!" he said.

The wine sparkled in his eyes and the bells jingled. My own fancy grew warm with the Medoc. We had passed through walls of piled bones, with casks and puncheons intermingling, into the inmost recesses of the catacombs. I paused again, and this time I made bold to seize Fortunato by an arm above the elbow.

"The nitre!" I said; "see, it increases. It hangs like moss upon the vaults. We are below the river's bed. The drops of moisture trickle among the bones. Come, we will go back ere it is too late. Your cough——"

"It is nothing," he said; "let us go on. But first, another draught of the Medoc."

I broke and reached him a flagon of De Grâve. He emptied it at a breath. His eyes flashed with a fierce light. He laughed and threw the bottle upward with a gesticulation I did not understand.

I looked at him in surprise. He repeated the movement —a grotesque one.

"You do not comprehend?" he said.

"Not I," I replied.

"Then you are not of the brotherhood."

"How?"

"You are not of the masons."

"Yes, yes," I said; "yes, yes."

"You? Impossible! A mason?"

"A mason," I replied.

"A sign," he said.

"It is this," I answered, producing a trowel from beneath the folds of my *roquelaire*.

"You jest," he exclaimed, recoiling a few paces. "But let us proceed to the Amontillado."

"Be it so," I said, replacing the tool beneath the cloak, and again offering him my arm. He leaned upon it

heavily. We continued our route in search of the Amontillado. We passed through a range of low arches, descended, passed on, and descending again, arrived at a deep crypt, in which the foulness of the air caused our flambeaux rather to glow than flame.

At the most remote end of the crypt there appeared another less spacious. Its walls had been lined with human remains, piled to the vault overhead, in the fashion of the great catacombs of Paris. Three sides of this interior crypt were still ornamented in this manner. From the fourth the bones had been thrown down, and lay promiscuously upon the earth, forming at one point a mound of some size. Within the wall thus exposed by the displacing of the bones, we perceived a still interior recess, in depth about four feet, in width three, in height six or seven. It seemed to have been constructed for no especial use within itself, but formed merely the interval between two of the colossal supports of the roof of the catacombs, and was backed by one of their circumscribing walls of solid granite.

It was in vain that Fortunato, uplifting his dull torch, endeavored to pry into the depth of the recess. Its termination the feeble light did not enable us to see.

"Proceed," I said; "herein is the Amontillado. As for Luchesi——"

"He is an ignoramus," interrupted my friend, as he stepped unsteadily forward, while I followed immediately at his heels. In an instant he had reached the extremity of the niche, and finding his progress arrested by the rock, stood stupidly bewildered. A moment more and I had fettered him to the granite. In its surface were two iron staples, distant from each other about two feet, horizontally. From one of these depended a short chain, from the other a padlock. Throwing the links about his waist, it was but the work of a few seconds to secure it. He was too much astounded to resist. Withdrawing the key I stepped back from the recess.

"Pass your hand," I said, "over the wall; you cannot help feeling the nitre. Indeed it is *very* damp. Once more let me *implore* you to return. No? Then I must positively leave you. But I must first render you all the little attentions in my power."

"The Amontillado!" ejaculated my friend, not yet recovered from his astonishment.

"True," I replied; "the Amontillado."

As I said these words I busied myself among the pile of bones of which I have before spoken. Throwing them aside, I soon uncovered a quantity of building stone and mortar. With these materials and with the aid of my trowel, I began vigorously to wall up the entrance of the niche.

I had scarcely laid the first tier of the masonry when I discovered that the intoxication of Fortunato had in a great measure worn off. The earliest indication I had of this was a low moaning cry from the depth of the recess. It was *not* the cry of a drunken man. There was then a long and obstinate silence. I laid the second tier, and the third, and the fourth; and then I heard the furious vibrations of the chain. The noise lasted for several minutes, during which, that I might hearken to it with the more satisfaction, I ceased my labors and sat down upon the bones. When at last the clanking subsided, I resumed the trowel, and finished without interruption the fifth, the sixth, and the seventh tier. The wall was now nearly upon a level with my breast. I again paused, and holding the flambeaux over the mason-work, threw a few feeble rays upon the figure within.

A succession of loud and shrill screams, bursting suddenly from the throat of the chained form, seemed to thrust me violently back. For a brief moment I hesitated —I trembled. Unsheathing my rapier, I began to grope with it about the recess; but the thought of an instant reassured me. I placed my hand upon the solid fabric of the catacombs, and felt satisfied. I reapproached the wall. I replied to the yells of him who clamored. I re-echoed —I aided—I surpassed them in volume and in strength. I did this, and the clamorer grew still.

It was now midnight, and my task was drawing to a close. I had completed the eighth, the ninth, and the tenth tier. I had finished a portion of the last and the eleventh; there remained but a single stone to be fitted and plastered in. I struggled with its weight; I placed it partially in its destined position. But now there came from out the niche a low laugh that erected the hairs upon my head. It was succeeded by a sad voice, which I had difficulty in recognizing as that of the noble Fortunato. The voice said—

"Ha! ha! ha!—he! he!—a very good joke indeed—an

excellent jest. We will have many a rich laugh about it at
the palazzo—he! he! he!—over our wine—he! he! he!"

"The Amontillado!" I said.

"He! he! he!—he! he! he!—yes, the Amontillado. But
is it not getting late? Will not they be awaiting us at the
palazzo, the Lady Fortunato and the rest? Let us be
gone."

"Yes," I said, "let us be gone."

"For the love of God, Montresor!"

"Yes," I said, "for the love of God!"

But to these words I hearkened in vain for a reply. I
grew impatient. I called aloud:

"Fortunato!"

No answer. I called again:

"Fortunato!"

No answer still. I thrust a torch through the remain-
ing aperture and let it fall within. There came forth in
return only a jingling of the bells. My heart grew sick—
on account of the dampness of the catacombs. I hastened
to make an end of my labor. I forced the last stone into
its position; I plastered it up. Against the new masonry
I re-erected the old rampart of bones. For the half of a
century no mortal has disturbed them. *In pace requiescat!*

The Assignation

Stay for me there! I will not fail
To meet thee in that hollow vale.

[*Exequy on the death of his wife, by Henry King, Bishop
of Chichester*]

ILL-FATED and mysterious man!—bewildered in the
brilliancy of thine own imagination, and fallen in the
flames of thine own youth! Again in fancy I behold
thee! Once more thy form hath risen before me!—not—
oh! not as thou art—in the cold valley and shadow—but
as thou *shouldst be*—squandering away a life of magnif-
icent meditation in that city of dim visions, thine own
Venice—which is a star-beloved Elysium of the sea, and
the wide windows of whose Palladian palaces look down
with a deep and bitter meaning upon the secrets of her
silent waters. Yes! I repeat it—as thou *shouldst be*.
There are surely other worlds than this—other thoughts
than the thoughts of the multitude—other speculations
than the speculations of the sophist. Who then shall call
thy conduct into question? who blame thee for thy vision-
ary hours, or denounce those occupations as a wasting
away of life, which were but the overflowings of thine
everlasting energies?

It was at Venice, beneath the covered archway there
called the *Ponte di Sospiri*, that I met, for the third or
fourth time the person of whom I speak. It is with a
confused recollection that I bring to mind the circum-
stances of that meeting. Yet I remember—ah! how
should I forget?—the deep midnight, the Bridge of Sighs,

the beauty of woman, and the Genius of Romance that stalked up and down the narrow canal.

It was a night of unusual gloom. The great clock of the Piazza had sounded the fifth hour of the Italian evening. The square of the Campanile lay silent and deserted, and the lights in the old Ducal Palace were dying fast away. I was returning home from the Piazetta, by way of the Grand Canal. But as my gondola arrived opposite the mouth of the canal San Marco, a female voice from its recesses broke suddenly upon the night, in one wild, hysterical, and long-continued shriek. Startled at the sound, I sprang upon my feet; while the gondolier, letting slip his single oar, lost it in the pitchy darkness beyond a chance of recovery, and we were consequently left to the guidance of the current which here sets from the greater into the smaller channel. Like some huge and sable-feathered condor, we were slowly drifting down toward the Bridge of Sighs, when a thousand flambeaux flashing from the windows, and down the staircases of the Ducal Palace, turned all at once that deep gloom into a livid and preternatural day.

A child, slipping from the arms of its own mother, had fallen from an upper window of the lofty structure into the deep and dim canal. The quiet waters had closed placidly over their victim; and, although my own gondola was the only one in sight, many a stout swimmer, already in the stream, was seeking in vain upon the surface, the treasure which was to be found, alas! only within the abyss. Upon the broad black marble flagstones at the entrance of the palace, and a few steps above the water, stood a figure which none who then saw can have ever since forgotten. It was the Marchesa Aphrodite—the adoration of all Venice—the gayest of the gay—the most lovely where all were beautiful—but still the young wife of the old and intriguing Mentoni, and the mother of that fair child, her first and only one, who now, deep beneath the murky water, was thinking in bitterness of heart upon her sweet caresses, and exhausting its little life in struggles to call upon her name.

She stood alone. Her small, bare and silvery feet gleamed in the black mirror of marble beneath her. Her hair, not as yet more than half loosened for the night from its ball-room array, clustered, amid a shower of diamonds, round and round her classical head, in

curls like those of the young hyacinth. A snowy-white and gauze-like drapery seemed to be nearly the sole covering to her delicate form; but the mid-summer and midnight air was hot, sullen, and still, and no motion in the statue-like form itself, stirred even the folds of that raiment of very vapor which hung around it as the heavy marble hangs around the Niobe. Yet—strange to say!—her large lustrous eyes were not turned downward upon that grave wherein her brightest hope lay buried—but riveted in a widely different direction! The prison of the Old Republic is, I think, the stateliest building in all Venice—but how could that lady gaze so fixedly upon it, when beneath her lay stifling her own child? Yon dark, gloomy niche, too, yawns right opposite her chamber window—what, then, *could* there be in its shadows—in its architecture—in its ivy-wreathed and solemn cornices —that the Marchesa di Mentoni had not wondered at a thousand times before? Nonsense!—Who does not remember that, at such a time as this, the eye, like a shattered mirror, multiplies the images of its sorrow, and sees in innumerable far-off places, the woe which is close at hand?

Many steps above the Marchesa, and within the arch of the water-gate, stood, in full dress, the Satyr-like figure of Mentoni himself. He was occasionally occupied in thrumming a guitar, and seemed *ennuyé* to the very death, as at intervals he gave directions for the recovery of his child. Stupefied and aghast, I had myself no power to move from the upright position I had assumed upon first hearing the shriek, and must have presented to the eyes of the agitated group a spectral and ominous appearance, as with pale countenance and rigid limbs, I floated down among them in that funereal gondola.

All efforts proved in vain. Many of the most energetic in the search were relaxing their exertions, and yielding to a gloomy sorrow. There seemed but little hope for the child; (how much less than for the mother!) but now, from the interior of that dark niche which has been already mentioned as forming a part of the Old Republican prison, and as fronting the lattice of the Marchesa, a figure muffled in a cloak, stepped out within reach of the light, and, pausing a moment upon the verge of the giddy descent, plunged headlong into the canal. As, in an instant afterward, he stood with the still living and

breathing child within his grasp, upon the marble flag-stones by the side of the Marchesa, his cloak, heavy with the drenching water, became unfastened, and, falling in folds about his feet, discovered to the wonder-stricken spectators the graceful person of a very young man, with the sound of whose name the greater part of Europe was then ringing.

No word spoke the deliverer. But the Marchesa! She will now receive her child—she will press it to her heart —she will cling to its little form, and smother it with her caresses. Alas! *another's* arms have taken it from the stranger—*another's* arms have taken it away, and borne it afar off, unnoticed, into the palace! And the Marchesa! Her lip—her beautiful lip trembles; tears are gathering in her eyes—those eyes which, like Pliny's acanthus, are "soft and almost liquid." Yes! tears are gathering in those eyes—and see! the entire woman thrills throughout the soul, and the statue has started into life! The pallor of the marble countenance, the swelling of the marble bosom, the very purity of the marble feet, we behold suddenly flushed over with a tide of ungovernable crimson; and a slight shudder quivers about her delicate frame, as a gentle air at Napoli about the rich silver lilies in the grass.

Why *should* that lady blush! To this demand there is no answer—except that, having left, in the eager haste and terror of a mother's heart, the privacy of her own *boudoir*, she has neglected to enthral her tiny feet in their slippers, and utterly forgotten to throw over her Venetian shoulders that drapery which is their due. What other possible reason could there have been for her so blushing?—for the glance of those wild appealing eyes? —for the unusual tumult of that throbbing bosom?— for the convulsive pressure of that trembling hand?— that hand which fell, as Mentoni turned into the palace, accidentally, upon the hand of the stranger. What reason could there have been for the low—the singularly low tone of those unmeaning words which the lady uttered hurriedly in bidding him adieu? "Thou hast conquered," she said, or the murmurs of the water deceived me; "thou hast conquered—one hour after sunrise—we shall meet—so let it be!"

* * * * * *

The tumult had subsided, the lights had died away within the palace, and the stranger, whom I now recognized, stood alone upon the flags. He shook with inconceivable agitation, and his eye glanced around in search of a gondola. I could not do less than offer him the service of my own; and he accepted the civility. Having obtained an oar at the water-gate, we proceeded together to his residence, while he rapidly recovered his self-possession, and spoke of our former slight acquaintance in terms of great apparent cordiality.

There are some subjects upon which I take pleasure in being minute. The person of the stranger—let me call him by this title, who to all the world was still a stranger —the person of the stranger is one of these subjects. In height he might have been below rather than above the medium size: although there were moments of intense passion when his frame actually *expanded* and belied the assertion. The light, almost slender symmetry of his figure promised more of that ready activity which he evinced at the Bridge of Sighs, than of that Herculean strength which he has been known to wield without an effort, upon occasions of more dangerous emergency. With the mouth and chin of a deity—singular, wild, full, liquid eyes, whose shadows varied from pure hazel to intense and brilliant jet—and a profusion of curling, black hair, from which a forehead of unusual breadth gleamed forth at intervals all light and ivory—his were features than which I have seen none more classically regular, except, perhaps, the marble ones of the Emperor Commodus. Yet his countenance was, nevertheless, one of those which all men have seen at some period of their lives, and have never afterward seen again. It had no peculiar, it had no settled predominant expression to be fastened upon the memory; a countenance seen and instantly forgotten, but forgotten with a vague and never-ceasing desire of recalling it to mind. Not that the spirit of each rapid passion failed, at any time, to throw its own distinct image upon the mirror of that face—but that the mirror, mirror-like, retained no vestige of the passion, when the passion had departed.

Upon leaving him on the night of our adventure, he solicited me, in what I thought an urgent manner, to call upon him *very* early the next morning. Shortly after sunrise, I found myself accordingly at his Palazzo, one

of those huge structures of gloomy yet fantastic pomp,
which tower above the waters of the Grand Canal in the
vicinity of the Rialto. I was shown up a broad winding
staircase of mosaics, into an apartment whose unparal-
leled splendor burst through the opening door with an
actual glare, making me blind and dizzy with luxurious-
ness.

I knew my acquaintance to be wealthy. Report had
spoken of his possessions in terms which I had even
ventured to call terms of ridiculous exaggeration. But as
I gazed about me, I could not bring myself to believe
that the wealth of any subject in Europe could have
supplied the princely magnificence which burned and
blazed around.

Although, as I say, the sun had arisen, yet the room
was still brilliantly lighted up. I judge from this circum-
stance, as well as from an air of exhaustion in the coun-
tenance of my friend, that he had not retired to bed
during the whole of the preceding night. In the architec-
ture and embellishments of the chamber, the evident
design had been to dazzle and astound. Little attention
had been paid to the *decora* of what is technically called
keeping, or to the proprieties of nationality. The eye wan-
dered from object to object, and rested upon none—
neither the *grotesques* of the Greek painters, nor the
sculptures of the best Italian days, nor the huge carvings
of untutored Egypt. Rich draperies in every part of the
room trembled to the vibration of low, melancholy mu-
sic, whose origin was not to be discovered. The senses
were oppressed by mingled and conflicting perfumes,
reeking up from strange convolute censers, together
with multitudinous flaring and flickering tongues of
emerald and violet fire. The rays of the newly risen sun
poured in upon the whole, through windows, formed each
of a single pane of crimson-tinted glass. Glancing to and
fro, in a thousand reflections, from curtains which rolled
from their cornices like cataracts of molten silver, the
beams of natural glory mingled at length fitfully with the
artificial light, and lay weltering in subdued masses upon
a carpet of rich, liquid-looking cloth of Chili gold.

"Ha! ha! ha!—ha! ha! ha!"—laughed the proprietor,
motioning me to a seat as I entered the room, and throw-
ing himself back at full-length upon an ottoman. "I see,"
said he, perceiving that I could not immediately recon-

cile myself to the *bienséance* of so singular a welcome,
—"I see you are astonished at my apartment—at my
statues—my pictures—my originality of conception in
architecture and upholstery! absolutely drunk, eh, with
my magnificence? But pardon me, my dear sir (here his
tone of voice dropped to the very spirit of cordiality);
pardon me for my uncharitable laughter. You appeared
so *utterly* astonished. Besides, some things are so com-
pletely ludicrous, that a man *must* laugh, or die. To die
laughing must be the most glorious of all glorious deaths!
Sir Thomas More—a very fine man was Sir Thomas
More—Sir Thomas More died laughing, you remember.
Also in the 'Absurdities' of Ravisius Textor, there is a
long list of characters who came to the same magnificent
end. Do you know, however," continued he, musingly,
"that at Sparta (which is now Palæochori), at Sparta,
I say, to the west of the citadel, among a chaos of
scarcely visible ruins, is a kind of *socle,* upon which are
still legible the letters ΛΑΣΜ. They are undoubtedly
part of ΓΕΛΑΣΜΑ. Now, at Sparta were a thousand
temples and shrines to a thousand different divinities.
How exceedingly strange that the altar of Laughter
should have survived all the others! But in the present
instance," he resumed, with a singular alteration of
voice and manner, "I have no right to be merry at your
expense. You might well have been amazed. Europe cannot
produce any thing so fine as this, my little regal cabinet.
My other apartments are by no means of the same order
—mere *ultras* of fashionable insipidity. This is better than
fashion—is it not? Yet this has but to be seen to be-
come the rage—that is, with those who could afford it at
the cost of their entire patrimony. I have guarded,
however, against any such profanation. With one excep-
tion, you are the only human being, besides myself and
my *valet,* who has been admitted within the mysteries
of these imperial precincts, since they have been be-
dizened as you see!"

I bowed in acknowledgment—for the overpowering
sense of splendor and perfume and music, together with
the unexpected eccentricity of his address and manner,
prevented me from expressing, in words, my apprecia-
tion of what I might have construed into a compliment.

"Here," he resumed, arising and leaning on my arm
as he sauntered around the apartment, "here are paint-

ings from the Greeks to Cimabue, and from Cimabue
to the present hour. Many are chosen, as you see, with
little deference to the opinions of Virtu. They are all, how-
ever, fitting tapestry for a chamber such as this. Here,
too, are some *chef-d'œuvres* of the unknown great; and
here, unfinished designs by men, celebrated in their day,
whose very names the perspicacity of the academies has
left to silence and to me. What think you," said he,
turning abruptly as he spoke,—"what think you of this
Madonna della Pietà?"

"It is Guido's own!" I said, with all the enthusiasm of
my nature, for I had been poring intently over its sur-
passing loveliness. "It is Guido's own!—how *could* you
have obtained it? she is undoubtedly in painting what
the Venus is in sculpture."

"Ha!" said he, thoughtfully, "the Venus?—the beau-
tiful Venus?—the Venus of the Medici?—she of the
diminutive head and the gilded hair? Part of the left arm
[here his voice dropped so as to be heard with difficul-
ty], and all the right, are restorations, and in the
coquetry of that right arm lies, I think, the quintessence
of all affectation. Give *me* the Canova! The Apollo, too,
is a copy—there can be no doubt of it—blind fool that
I am, who cannot behold the boasted inspiration of the
Apollo! I cannot help—pity me!—I cannot help prefer-
ring the Antinous. Was it not Socrates who said that the
statuary found his statue in the block of marble? Then
Michael Angelo was by no means original in his couplet—

'Non ha l'ottimo artista alcun concetto
 Che un marmo solo in se non circunscriva.' "

It has been, or should be remarked, that, in the man-
ner of the true gentleman, we are always aware of a dif-
ference from the bearing of the vulgar, without being at
once precisely able to determine in what such difference
consists. Allowing the remark to have applied in its
full force to the outward demeanor of my acquaintance,
I felt it, on that eventful morning, still more fully ap-
plicable to his moral temperament and character. Nor
can I better define that peculiarity of spirit which
seemed to place him so essentially apart from all other
human beings, than by calling it a *habit* of intense and
continual thought, pervading even his most trivial ac-

tions—intruding upon his moments of dalliance—and interweaving itself with his very flashes of merriment—like adders which writhe from out the eyes of the grinning masks in the cornices around the temples of Persepolis.

I could not help, however, repeatedly observing, through the mingled tone of levity and solemnity with which he rapidly descanted upon matters of little importance, a certain air of trepidation—a degree of nervous *unction* in action and in speech—an unquiet excitability of manner which appeared to me at all times unaccountable, and upon some occasions even filled me with alarm. Frequently, too, pausing in the middle of a sentence whose commencement he had apparently forgotten, he seemed to be listening in the deepest attention, as if either in momentary expectation of a visitor, or to sounds which must have had existence in his imagination alone.

It was during one of these reveries or pauses of apparent abstraction, that, in turning over a page of the poet and scholar Politian's beautiful tragedy, "The Orfeo" (the first native Italian tragedy), which lay near me upon an ottoman, I discovered a passage underlined in pencil. It was a passage toward the end of the third act—a passage of the most heart-stirring excitement—a passage which, although tainted with impurity, no man shall read without a thrill of novel emotion—no woman without a sigh. The whole page was blotted with fresh tears; and, upon the opposite interleaf, were the following English lines, written in a hand so very different from the peculiar characters of my acquaintance, that I had some difficulty in recognizing it as his own:

> Thou wast that all to me, love,
> For which my soul did pine—
> A green isle in the sea, love,
> A fountain and a shrine,
> All wreathed with fairy fruits and flowers;
> And all the flowers were mine.
>
> Ah, dream too bright to last!
> Ah, starry Hope, that didst arise
> But to be overcast!
> A voice from out the Future cries,
> "Onward!"—but o'er the Past
> (Dim gulf!) my spirit hovering lies,
> Mute—motionless—aghast!

For alas! alas! with me
 The light of life is o'er.
No more—no more—no more,
 (Such language holds the solemn sea
To the sands upon the shore),
 Shall bloom the thunder-blasted tree,
Or the stricken eagle soar!

Now all my hours are trances;
 And all my nightly dreams
Are where thy dark eye glances,
 And where thy footstep gleams
In what ethereal dances,
 By what Italian streams.

Alas! for that accursed time
 They bore thee o'er the billow,
From Love to titled age and crime,
 And an unholy pillow!—
From me, and from our misty clime,
 Where weeps the silver willow!

That these lines were written in English—a language
with which I had not believed their author acquainted—
afforded me little matter for surprise. I was too well aware
of the extent of his acquirements, and of the singular
pleasure he took in concealing them from observation,
to be astonished at any similar discovery; but the place
of date, I must confess, occasioned me no little amaze-
ment. It had been originally *London,* and afterward
carefully overscored—not, however, so effectually as to
conceal the word from a scrutinizing eye. I say, this oc-
casioned me no little amazement; for I well remember
that, in a former conversation with my friend, I particu-
larly inquired if he had at any time met in London the
Marchesa di Mentoni (who for some years previous to
her marriage had resided in that city), when his answer,
if I mistake not, gave me to understand that he had
never visited the metropolis of Great Britain. I might as
well here mention, that I have more than once heard
(without, of course, giving credit to a report involving
so many improbabilities), that the person of whom I
speak, was not only by birth, but in education, an *Eng-
lishman.*

* * * * * *

"There is one painting," said he, without being aware
of my notice of the tragedy,—"there is still one painting

which you have not seen." And throwing aside a drapery, he discovered a full-length portrait of the Marchesa Aphrodite.

Human art could have done no more in the delineation of her superhuman beauty. The same ethereal figure which stood before me the preceding night upon the steps of the Ducal Palace, stood before me once again. But in the expression of the countenance, which was beaming all over with smiles, there still lurked (incomprehensible anomaly!) that fitful stain of melancholy which will ever be found inseparable from the perfection of the beautiful. Her right arm lay folded over her bosom. With her left she pointed downward to a curiously fashioned vase. One small, fairy foot, alone visible, barely touched the earth; and, scarcely discernible in the brilliant atmosphere which seemed to encircle and enshrine her loveliness, floated a pair of the most delicately imagined wings. My glance fell from the painting to the figure of my friend, and the vigorous words of Chapman's *Bussy D'Ambois* quivered instinctively upon my lips:

> "He is up
> There like a Roman statue! He will stand
> Till Death hath made him marble!"

"Come," he said at length, turning toward a table of richly enamelled and massive silver, upon which were a few goblets fantastically stained, together with two large Etruscan vases, fashioned in the same extraordinary model as that in the foreground of the portrait, and filled with what I supposed to be Johannisberger. "Come," he said, abruptly, "let us drink! It is early—but let us drink. It is *indeed* early," he continued, musingly, as a cherub with a heavy golden hammer made the apartment ring with the first hour after sunrise: "It is *indeed* early—but what matters it? let us drink! Let us pour out an offering to yon solemn sun which these gaudy lamps and censers are so eager to subdue!" And having made me pledge him in a bumper, he swallowed in rapid succession several goblets of the wine.

"To dream," he continued, resuming the tone of his desultory conversation, as he held up to the rich light of a censer one of the magnificent vases—"to dream

has been the business of my life, I have therefore framed
for myself, as you see, a bower of dreams. In the heart
of Venice could I have erected a better? You behold
around you, it is true, a medley of architectural embel-
lishments. The chastity of Ionia is offended by antedilu-
vian devices, and the sphynxes of Egypt are outstretched
upon carpets of gold. Yet the effect is incongruous to the
timid alone. Proprieties of place, and especially of time,
are the bugbears which terrify mankind from the con-
templation of the magnificent. Once I was myself a
decorist; but that sublimation of folly has palled upon my
soul. All this is now the fitter for my purpose. Like these
arabesque censers, my spirit is writhing in fire, and the
delirium of this scene is fashioning me for the wilder
visions of that land of real dreams whither I am now
rapidly departing." He here paused abruptly, bent his
head to his bosom, and seemed to listen to a sound
which I could not hear. At length, erecting his frame,
he looked upwards, and ejaculated the lines of the
Bishop of Chichester:

> "Stay for me there! I will not fail
> To meet thee in that hollow vale."

In the next instant, confessing the power of the wine, he
threw himself at full length upon an ottoman.

A quick step was now heard upon the staircase, and a
loud knock at the door rapidly succeeded. I was hastening
to anticipate a second disturbance, when a page of
Mentoni's household burst into the room, and faltered
out, in a voice choking with emotion, the incoherent
words, "My mistress!—my mistress!—Poisoned!—poi-
soned! Oh, beautiful—oh, beautiful Aphrodite!"

Bewildered, I flew to the ottoman, and endeavored to
arouse the sleeper to a sense of the startling intelligence.
But his limbs were rigid—his lips were livid—his lately
beaming eyes were riveted in *death*. I staggered back
toward the table—my hand fell upon a cracked and
blackened goblet—and a consciousness of the entire and
terrible truth flashed suddenly over my soul.

The Tell-Tale Heart

TRUE!—nervous—very, very dreadfully nervous I had been and am; but why *will* you say that I am mad? The disease had sharpened my senses—not destroyed—not dulled them. Above all was the sense of hearing acute. I heard all things in the heaven and in the earth. I heard many things in hell. How, then, am I mad? Hearken! and observe how healthily—how calmly I can tell you the whole story.

It is impossible to say how first the idea entered my brain; but once conceived, it haunted me day and night. Object there was none. Passion there was none. I loved the old man. He had never wronged me. He had never given me insult. For his gold I had no desire. I think it was his eye! yes, it was this! One of his eyes resembled that of a vulture—a pale blue eye, with a film over it. Whenever it fell upon me, my blood ran cold; and so by degrees—very gradually—I made up my mind to take the life of the old man, and thus rid myself of the eye for ever.

Now this is the point. You fancy me mad. Madmen know nothing. But you should have seen *me*. You should have seen how wisely I proceeded—with what caution—with what foresight—with what dissimulation I went to work! I was never kinder to the old man than during the whole week before I killed him. And every night, about midnight, I turned the latch of his door and opened it—oh, so gently! And then, when I had made an opening sufficient for my head, I put in a dark lantern, all closed, closed, so that no light shone out, and then I thrust in my head. Oh, you would have laughed to see how cunningly I thrust it in! I moved it slowly—very, very slowly, so that I might not disturb the old man's sleep. It took me an hour to place my whole head within the opening so far that I could see him as he lay upon

his bed. Ha!—would a madman have been so wise as this? And then, when my head was well in the room, I undid the lantern cautiously—oh, so cautiously—cautiously (for the hinges creaked)—I undid it just so much that a single thin ray fell upon the vulture eye. And this I did for seven long nights—every night just at midnight —but I found the eye always closed; and so it was impossible to do the work; for it was not the old man who vexed me, but his Evil Eye. And every morning, when the day broke, I went boldly into the chamber, and spoke courageously to him, calling him by name in a hearty tone, and inquiring how he had passed the night. So you see he would have been a very profound old man, indeed, to suspect that every night, just at twelve, I looked in upon him while he slept.

Upon the eighth night I was more than usually cautious in opening the door. A watch's minute hand moves more slowly than did mine. Never before that night had I *felt* the extent of my own powers—of my sagacity. I could scarcely contain my feelings of triumph. To think that there I was, opening the door, little by little, and he not even to dream of my secret deeds or thoughts. I fairly chuckled at the idea; and perhaps he heard me; for he moved on the bed suddenly, as if startled. Now you may think that I drew back—but no. His room was as black as pitch with the thick darkness (for the shutters were close fastened, through fear of robbers), and so I knew that he could not see the opening of the door, and I kept pushing it on steadily, steadily.

I had my head in, and was about to open the lantern, when my thumb slipped upon the tin fastening, and the old man sprang up in the bed, crying out—"Who's there?"

I kept quite still and said nothing. For a whole hour I did not move a muscle, and in the meantime I did not hear him lie down. He was still sitting up in the bed listening;—just as I have done, night after night, hearkening to the death watches in the wall.

Presently I heard a slight groan, and I knew it was the groan of mortal terror. It was not a groan of pain or of grief—oh, no!—it was the low stifled sound that arises from the bottom of the soul when overcharged with awe. I knew the sound well. Many a night, just at midnight, when all the world slept, it has welled up from my own

bosom, deepening, with its dreadful echo, the terrors that distracted me. I say I knew it well. I knew what the old man felt, and pitied him, although I chuckled at heart. I knew that he had been lying awake ever since the first slight noise, when he had turned in the bed. His fears had been ever since growing upon him. He had been trying to fancy them causeless, but could not. He had been saying to himself—"It is nothing but the wind in the chimney—it is only a mouse crossing the floor," or "it is merely a cricket which has made a single chirp." Yes, he had been trying to comfort himself with these suppositions; but he had found all in vain. *All in vain*; because Death, in approaching him, had stalked with his black shadow before him, and enveloped the victim. And it was the mournful influence of the unperceived shadow that caused him to feel—although he neither saw nor heard—to *feel* the presence of my head within the room.

When I had waited a long time, very patiently, without hearing him lie down, I resolved to open a little—a very, very little crevice in the lantern. So I opened it—you cannot imagine how stealthily, stealthily—until, at length, a single dim ray, like the thread of the spider, shot from out the crevice and full upon the vulture eye.

It was open—wide, wide open—and I grew furious as I gazed upon it. I saw it with perfect distinctness—all a dull blue, with a hideous veil over it that chilled the very marrow in my bones; but I could see nothing else of the old man's face or person: for I had directed the ray as if by instinct, precisely upon the damned spot.

And now have I not told you that what you mistake for madness is but over-acuteness of the senses?—now, I say, there came to my ears a low, dull, quick sound, such as a watch makes when enveloped in cotton. I knew *that* sound well too. It was the beating of the old man's heart. It increased my fury, as the beating of a drum stimulates the soldier into courage.

But even yet I refrained and kept still. I scarcely breathed. I held the lantern motionless. I tried how steadily I could maintain the ray upon the eye. Meantime the hellish tattoo of the heart increased. It grew quicker and quicker, and louder and louder every instant. The old man's terror *must* have been extreme! It grew louder, I say, louder every moment!—do you mark

me well? I have told you that I am nervous: so I am. And now at the dead hour of the night, amid the dreadful silence of that old house, so strange a noise as this excited me to uncontrollable terror. Yet, for some minutes longer I refrained and stood still. But the beating grew louder, louder! I thought the heart must burst. And now a new anxiety seized me—the sound would be heard by a neighbor! The old man's hour had come! With a loud yell, I threw open the lantern and leaped into the room. He shrieked once—once only. In an instant I dragged him to the floor, and pulled the heavy bed over him. I then smiled gaily, to find the deed so far done. But, for many minutes, the heart beat on with a muffled sound. This, however, did not vex me; it would not be heard through the wall. At length it ceased. The old man was dead. I removed the bed and examined the corpse. Yes, he was stone, stone dead. I placed my hand upon the heart and held it there many minutes. There was no pulsation. He was stone dead. His eye would trouble me no more.

If still you think me mad, you will think so no longer when I describe the wise precautions I took for the concealment of the body. The night waned, and I worked hastily, but in silence. First of all I dismembered the corpse. I cut off the head and the arms and the legs.

I then took up three planks from the flooring of the chamber, and deposited all between the scantlings. I then replaced the boards so cleverly, so cunningly, that no human eye—not even *his*—could have detected any thing wrong. There was nothing to wash out—no stain of any kind—no blood-spot whatever. I had been too wary for that. A tub had caught all—ha! ha!

When I had made an end to these labors, it was four o'clock—still dark as midnight. As the bell sounded the hour, there came a knocking at the street door. I went down to open it with a light heart,—for what had I *now* to fear? There entered three men, who introduced themselves, with perfect suavity, as officers of the police. A shriek had been heard by a neighbor during the night; suspicion of foul play had been aroused; information had been lodged at the police office, and they (the officers) had been deputed to search the premises.

I smiled,—for *what* had I to fear? I bade the gentlemen

welcome. The shriek, I said, was my own in a dream. The old man, I mentioned, was absent in the country. I took my visitors all over the house. I bade them search— search *well*. I led them, at length, to *his* chamber. I showed them his treasures, secure, undisturbed. In the enthusiasm of my confidence, I brought chairs into the room, and desired them *here* to rest from their fatigues, while I myself, in the wild audacity of my perfect triumph, placed my own seat upon the very spot beneath which reposed the corpse of the victim.

The officers were satisfied. My *manner* had convinced them. I was singularly at ease. They sat, and while I answered cheerily, they chatted familiar things. But, ere long, I felt myself getting pale and wished them gone. My head ached, and I fancied a ringing in my ears: but still they sat and still chatted. The ringing became more distinct:—it continued and became more distinct: I talked more freely to get rid of the feeling: but it continued and gained definitiveness—until, at length, I found that the noise was *not* within my ears.

No doubt I now grew *very* pale;—but I talked more fluently, and with a heightened voice. Yet the sound increased—and what could I do? It was *a low, dull, quick sound—much such a sound as a watch makes when enveloped in cotton.* I gasped for breath—and yet the officers heard it not. I talked more quickly—more vehemently; but the noise steadily increased. I arose and argued about trifles, in a high key and with violent gesticulations, but the noise steadily increased. Why *would* they not be gone? I paced the floor to and fro with heavy strides, as if excited to fury by the observation of the men—but the noise steadily increased. Oh God! what *could* I do? I foamed—I raved—I swore! I swung the chair upon which I had been sitting, and grated it upon the boards, but the noise arose over all and continually increased. It grew louder—louder—*louder!* And still the men chatted pleasantly, and smiled. Was it possible they heard not? Almighty God!—no, no! They heard!— they suspected!—they *knew!*—they were making a mockery of my horror!—this I thought, and this I think. But any thing was better than this agony! Any thing was more tolerable than this derision! I could bear those hypocritical smiles no longer! I felt that I must scream or die!—

and now—again!—hark! louder! louder! louder! *louder!*—
 "Villains!" I shrieked, "dissemble no more! I admit the
deed!—tear up the planks!—here, here!—it is the beating
of his hideous heart!"

Diddling

CONSIDERED AS ONE OF THE EXACT SCIENCES

> Hey, diddle diddle,
> The cat and the fiddle.

SINCE THE WORLD began there have been two Jeremys. The one wrote a Jeremiad about usury, and was called Jeremy Bentham. He has been much admired by Mr. John Neal, and was a great man in a small way. The other gave name to the most important of the Exact Sciences, and was a great man in a *great* way—I may say, indeed, in the very greatest of ways.

Diddling—or the abstract idea conveyed by the verb to diddle—is sufficiently well understood. Yet the fact, the deed, the thing, *diddling,* is somewhat difficult to define. We may get, however, at a tolerably distinct conception of the matter in hand, by defining—not the thing, diddling, in itself—but man, as an animal that diddles. Had Plato but hit upon this, he would have been spared the affront of the picked chicken.

Very pertinently it was demanded of Plato, why a picked chicken, which was clearly a "biped without feathers," was not, according to his own definition, a man? But I am not to be bothered by any similar query. Man is an animal that diddles, and there is *no* animal that diddles *but* man. It will take an entire hen-coop of picked chickens to get over that.

What constitutes the essence, the nare, the principle of diddling is, in fact, peculiar to the class of creatures that wear coats and pantaloons. A crow thieves; a fox cheats; a weasel outwits; a man diddles. To diddle is his

destiny. "Man was made to mourn," says the poet. But
not so:—he was made to diddle. This is his aim—his
object—his *end*. And for this reason when a man's
diddled we say he's *"done."*

Diddling, rightly considered, is a compound, of which
the ingredients are minuteness, interest, perseverance,
ingenuity, audacity, *nonchalance,* originality, imperti-
nence, and *grin*.

Minuteness:—Your diddler is minute. His operations
are upon a small scale. His business is retail, for cash,
or approved paper at sight. Should he ever be tempted
into magnificent speculation, he then, at once, loses his
distinctive features, and becomes what we term "fi-
nancier." This latter word conveys the diddling idea in
every respect except that of magnitude. A diddler may
thus be regarded as a banker *in petto*—a "financial
operation," as a diddle at Brobdignag. The one is to the
other, as Homer to "Flaccus"—as a mastodon to a mouse
—as the tail of a comet to that of a pig.

Interest:—Your diddler is guided by self-interest. He
scorns to diddle for the mere *sake* of the diddle. He has
an object in view—his pocket—and yours. He regards
always the main chance. He looks to Number One. You
are Number Two, and must look to yourself.

Perseverance:—Your diddler perseveres. He is not
readily discouraged. Should even the banks break, he
cares nothing about it. He steadily pursues his end, and

Ut canis a corio nunquam absterrebitur uncto,

so he lets go of his game.

Ingenuity:—Your diddler is ingenious. He has con-
structiveness large. He understands plot. He invents and
circumvents. Were he not Alexander he would be Diog-
enes. Were he not a diddler, he would be a maker of
patent rat-traps or an angler for trout.

Audacity:—Your diddler is audacious.—He is a bold
man. He carries the war into Africa. He conquers all
by assault. He would not fear the daggers of Frey Herren.
With a little more prudence Dick Turpin would have
made a good diddler; with a trifle less blarney, Daniel
O'Connell; with a pound or two more brains, Charles
the Twelfth.

Nonchalance:—Your diddler is *nonchalant*. He is not

at all nervous. He never *had* any nerves. He is never seduced into a flurry. He is never put out—unless put out of doors. He is cool—cool as a cucumber. He is calm—"calm as a smile from Lady Bury." He is easy—easy as an old glove, or the damsels of ancient Baiæ.

Originality:—Your diddler is original—conscientiously so. His thoughts are his own. He would scorn to employ those of another. A stale trick is his aversion. He would return a purse, I am sure, upon discovering that he had obtained it by an unoriginal diddle.

Impertinence:—Your diddler is impertinent. He swaggers. He sets his arms a-kimbo. He thrusts his hands in his trowsers' pocket. He sneers in your face. He treads on your corns. He eats your dinner, he drinks your wine, he borrows your money, he pulls your nose, he kicks your poodle, and he kisses your wife.

Grin:—Your *true* diddler winds up all with a grin. But this nobody sees but himself. He grins when his daily work is done—when his allotted labors are accomplished —at night in his own closet, and altogether for his own private entertainment. He goes home. He locks his door. He divests himself of his clothes. He puts out his candle. He gets into bed. He places his head upon the pillow. All this done, and your diddler *grins*. This is no hypothesis. It is a matter of course. I reason *a priori,* and a diddle would be *no* diddle without a grin.

The origin of the diddle is referable to the infancy of the Human Race. Perhaps the first diddler was Adam. At all events, we can trace the science back to a very remote period of antiquity. The moderns, however, have brought it to a perfection never dreamed of by our thick-headed progenitors. Without pausing to speak of the "old saws," therefore, I shall content myself with a compendious account of some of the more "modern instances."

A very good diddle is this. A housekeeper in want of a sofa, for instance, is seen to go in and out of several cabinet warehouses. At length she arrives at one offering an excellent variety. She is accosted, and invited to enter, by a polite and voluble individual at the door. She finds a sofa well adapted to her views, and upon inquiring the price, is surprised and delighted to hear a sum named at least twenty per cent. lower than her expectations. She hastens to make the purchase, gets a bill and receipt,

leaves her address, with a request that the article be sent home as speedily as possible, and retires amid a profusion of bows from the shop-keeper. The night arrives and no sofa. The next day passes, and still none. A servant is sent to make inquiry about the delay. The whole transaction is denied. No sofa has been sold—no money received—except by the diddler, who played shop-keeper for the nonce.

Our cabinet warehouses are left entirely unattended, and thus afford every facility for a trick of this kind. Visitors enter, look at furniture, and depart unheeded and unseen. Should any one wish to purchase, or to inquire the price of an article, a bell is at hand, and this is considered amply sufficient.

Again, quite a respectable diddle is this. A well-dressed individual enters a shop; makes a purchase to the value of a dollar; finds, much to his vexation, that he has left his pocket-book in another coat pocket; and so says to the shop-keeper—

"My dear sir, never mind!—just oblige me, will you, by sending the bundle home? But stay! I really believe that I have nothing less than a five dollar bill, even *there*. However, you can send four dollars in change *with* the bundle, you know."

"Very good, sir," replies the shop-keeper, who entertains, at once, a lofty opinion of the high-mindedness of his customer. "I know fellows," he says to himself, "who would just have put the goods under their arm, and walked off with a promise to call and pay the dollar as they came by in the afternoon."

A boy is sent with the parcel and change. On the route, quite accidentally, he is met by the purchaser, who exclaims:

"Ah! this is my bundle, I see—I thought you had been home with it, long ago. Well, go on! My wife, Mrs. Trotter, will give you the five dollars—I left instructions with her to that effect. The change you might as well give to *me*—I shall want some silver for the Post Office. Very good! One, two, is this a good quarter?—three, four—quite right! Say to Mrs. Trotter that you met me, and be sure now and *do* not loiter on the way."

The boy doesn't loiter at all—but he is a very long time in getting back from his errand—for no lady of the precise name of Mrs. Trotter is to be discovered. He con-

soles himself, however, that he has not been such a fool as to leave the goods without the money, and re-entering his shop with a self-satisfied air, feels sensibly hurt and indignant when his master asks him what has become of the change.

A very simple diddle, indeed, is this. The captain of a ship which is about to sail, is presented by an official looking person with an unusually moderate bill of city charges. Glad to get off so easily, and confused by a hundred duties pressing upon him all at once, he discharges the claim forthwith. In about fifteen minutes, another and less reasonable bill is handed him by one who soon makes it evident that the first collector was a diddler, and the original collection a diddle.

And here, too, is a somewhat similar thing. A steamboat is casting loose from the wharf. A traveller, portmanteau in hand, is discovered running toward the wharf, at full speed. Suddenly, he makes a dead halt, stoops, and picks up something from the ground in a very agitated manner. It is a pocket-book, and—"Has any gentleman lost a pocket-book?" he cries. No one can say that he has exactly lost a pocket-book; but a great excitement ensues, when the treasure trove is found to be of value. The boat however, must not be detained.

"Time and tide wait for no man," says the captain.

"For God's sake, stay only a few minutes," says the finder of the book—"the true claimant will presently appear."

"Can't wait!" replies the man in authority; "cast off there, d'ye hear?"

"What *am* I to do?" asks the finder, in great tribulation. "I am about to leave the country for some years, and I cannot conscientiously retain this large amount in my possession. I beg your pardon, sir," [here he addresses a gentleman on shore,] "but you have the air of an honest man. *Will* you confer upon me the favor of taking charge of this pocket-book—I *know* I can trust you—and of advertising it? The notes, you see, amount to a very considerable sum. The owner will, no doubt, insist upon rewarding you for your trouble—"

"*Me!*—no, *you!*—it was *you* who found the book."

"Well, if you *must* have it so—I will take a small reward—just to satisfy your scruples. Let me see—why these notes are all hundreds—bless my soul! a hundred

is too much to take—fifty would be quite enough, I am sure—"

"Cast off there!" says the captain.

"But then I have no change for a hundred, and upon the whole, *you* had better—"

"Cast off there!" says the captain.

"Never mind!" cries the gentleman on shore, who has been examining his own pocket-book for the last minute or so—"never mind! *I* can fix it—here is a fifty on the Bank of North America—throw me the book."

And the over-conscientious finder takes the fifty with marked reluctance, and throws the gentleman the book, as desired, while the steamboat fumes and fizzes on her way. In about half an hour after her departure, the "large amount" is seen to be a "counterfeit presentment," and the whole thing a capital diddle.

A bold diddle is this. A camp-meeting, or something similar, is to be held at a certain spot which is accessible only by means of a free bridge. A diddler stations himself upon this bridge, respectfully informs all passers by of the new county law, which establishes a toll of one cent for foot passengers, two for horses and donkeys, and so forth, and so forth. Some grumble but all submit, and the diddler goes home a wealthier man by some fifty or sixty dollars well earned. This taking a toll from a great crowd of people is an excessively troublesome thing.

A neat diddle is this. A friend holds one of the diddler's promises to pay, filled up and signed in due form, upon the ordinary blanks printed in red ink. The diddler purchases one or two dozen of these blanks, and every day dips one of them in his soup, makes his dog jump for it, and finally gives it to him as a *bonne bouche*. The note arriving at maturity, the diddler, with the diddler's dog, calls upon the friend, and the promise to pay is made the topic of discussion. The friend produces it from his *escritoire,* and is in the act of reaching it to the diddler, when up jumps the diddler's dog and devours it forthwith. The diddler is not only surprised but vexed and incensed at the absurd behavior of his dog, and expresses his entire readiness to cancel the obligation at any moment when the evidence of the obligation shall be forthcoming.

A very minute diddle is this. A lady is insulted in the

street by a diddler's accomplice. The diddler himself flies to her assistance, and, giving his friend a comfortable thrashing, insists upon attending the lady to her own door. He bows, with his hand upon his heart, and most respectfully bids her adieu. She intreats him, as her deliverer, to walk in and be introduced to her big brother and her papa. With a sigh, he declines to do so. "Is there no way, then, sir," she murmurs, "in which I may be permitted to testify my gratitude?"

"Why, yes, madam, there is. Will you be kind enough to lend me a couple of shillings?"

In the first excitement of the moment the lady decides upon fainting outright. Upon second thought, however, she opens her purse-strings and delivers the specie. Now this, I say, is a diddle minute—for one entire moiety of the sum borrowed has to be paid to the gentleman who had the trouble of performing the insult, and who had then to stand still and be thrashed for performing it.

Rather a small, but still a scientific diddle is this. The diddler approaches the bar of a tavern, and demands a couple of twists of tobacco. These are handed to him, when, having slightly examined them, he says:

"I don't much like this tobacco. Here, take it back, and give me a glass of brandy and water in its place."

The brandy and water is furnished and imbibed, and the diddler makes his way to the door. But the voice of the tavern-keeper arrests him.

"I believe, sir, you have forgotten to pay for your brandy and water."

"Pay for my brandy and water!—didn't I give you the tobacco for the brandy and water? What more would you have?"

"But, sir, if you please, I don't remember that you paid me for the tobacco."

"What do you mean by that, you scoundrel?—Didn't I give you back your tobacco? Isn't *that* your tobacco lying *there?* Do you expect me to pay for what I did not take?"

"But, sir," says the publican, now rather at a loss what to say, "but sir—"

"But me no buts, sir," interrupts the diddler, apparently in very high dudgeon, and slamming the door after

him, as he makes his escape.— "But me no buts, sir, and none of your tricks upon travellers."

Here again is a very clever diddle, of which the simplicity is not its least recommendation. A purse, or pocket-book, being really lost, the loser inserts in *one* of the daily papers of a large city a fully descriptive advertisement.

Whereupon our diddler copies the *facts* of this advertisement, with a change of heading, of general phraseology, and *address*. The original, for instance, is long, and verbose, is headed "A Pocket-Book Lost!" and requires the treasure, when found, to be left at No. 1 Tom Street. The copy is brief, and being headed with "Lost" only, indicates No. 2 Dick, or No. 3 Harry Street, as the locality in which the owner may be seen. Moreover, it is inserted in at least five or six of the daily papers of the day, while in point of time, it makes its appearance only a few hours after the original. Should it be read by the loser of the purse, he would hardly suspect it to have any reference to his own misfortune. But, of course, the chances are five or six to one, that the finder will repair to the address given by the diddler, rather than to that pointed out by the rightful proprietor. The former pays the reward, pockets the treasure and decamps.

Quite an analogous diddle is this. A lady of *ton* has dropped, somewhere in the street, a diamond ring of very unusual value. For its recovery, she offers some forty or fifty dollars reward—giving, in her advertisement, a very minute description of the gem, and of its settings, and declaring that, on its restoration at No. so and so, in such and such Avenue, the reward will be paid *instanter,* without a single question being asked. During the lady's absence from home, a day or two afterwards, a ring is heard at the door of No. so and so, in such and such Avenue; a servant appears; the lady of the house is asked for and is declared to be out, at which astounding information, the visitor expresses the most poignant regret. His business is of importance and concerns the lady herself. In fact, he had the good fortune to find her diamond ring. But perhaps it would be as well that he should call again. "By no means!" says the servant; and "By no means!" say the lady's sister and the lady's sister-in-law, who are summoned

forthwith. The ring is clamorously identified, the reward is paid, and the finder nearly thrust out of doors. The lady returns and expresses some little dissatisfaction with her sister and sister-in-law, because they happen to have paid forty or fifty dollars for a *fac-simile* of her diamond ring—a *fac-simile* made out of real pinchbeck and unquestionable paste.

But as there is really no end to diddling, so there would be none to this essay, were I even to hint at half the variations, or inflections, of which this science is susceptible. I must bring this paper, perforce, to a conclusion, and this I cannot do better than by a summary notice of a very decent, but rather elaborate diddle, of which our own city was made the theatre, not very long ago, and which was subsequently repeated with success, in other still more verdant localities of the Union. A middle-aged gentleman arrives in town from parts unknown. He is remarkably precise, cautious, staid, and deliberate in his demeanor. His dress is scrupulously neat, but plain, unostentatious. He wears a white cravat, an ample waistcoat, made with an eye to comfort alone; thick-soled cosy-looking shoes, and pantaloons without straps. He has the whole air, in fact, of your well-to-do, sober-sided, exact, and respectable "man of business," *par excellence*—one of the stern and outwardly hard, internally soft, sort of people that we see in the crack high comedies—fellows whose words are so many bonds, and who are noted for giving away guineas, in charity, with the one hand, while, in the way of mere bargain, they exact the uttermost fraction of a farthing with the other.

He makes much ado before he can get suited with a boarding-house. He dislikes children. He has been accustomed to quiet. His habits are methodical—and then he would prefer getting into a private and respectable small family, piously inclined. Terms, however, are no object —only he must insist upon settling his bill on the first of every month (it is now the second) and begs his landlady, when he finally obtains one to his mind, *not* on any account to forget his instructions upon this point —but to send in a bill, *and* receipt, precisely at ten o'clock, on the *first* day of every month, and under no circumstances to put it off to the second.

These arrangements made, our man of business rents an office in a reputable rather than a fashionable quarter

of the town. There is nothing he more despises than pretense. "Where there is much show," he says, "there is seldom any thing very solid behind"—an observation which so profoundly impresses his landlady's fancy, that she makes a pencil memorandum of it forthwith, in her great family Bible, on the broad margin of the Proverbs of Solomon.

The next step is to advertise, after some such fashion as this, in the principal business sixpennies of the city —the pennies are eschewed as not "respectable"—and as demanding payment for all advertisements in advance. Our man of business holds it as a point of his faith that work should never be paid for until done.

"WANTED.—The advertisers, being about to commence extensive business operations in this city, will require the services of three or four intelligent and competent clerks, to whom a liberal salary will be paid. The very best recommendations, not so much for capacity, as for integrity, will be expected. Indeed, as the duties to be performed, involve high responsibilities, and large amounts of money must necessarily pass through the hands of those engaged, it is deemed advisable to demand a deposit of fifty dollars from each clerk employed. No person need apply, therefore, who is not prepared to leave this sum in the possession of the advertisers, and who cannot furnish the most satisfactory testimonials of morality. Young gentlemen piously inclined will be preferred. Application should be made between the hours of ten and eleven A.M., and four and five P.M., of Messrs.

"BOGS, HOGS, LOGS, FROGS, & CO.,

"No. 110 Dog Street."

By the thirty-first day of the month, this advertisement has brought to the office of Messrs. Bogs, Hogs, Logs, Frogs, and Company, some fifteen or twenty young gentlemen piously inclined. But our man of business is in no hurry to conclude a contract with any—no man of business is *ever* precipitate—and it is not until the most rigid catechism in respect to the piety of each young gentleman's inclination, that his services are engaged and his fifty dollars receipted for, *just* by way of

proper precaution, on the part of the respectable firm of Bogs, Hogs, Logs, Frogs, and Company. On the morning of the first day of the next month, the landlady does *not* present her bill, according to promise—a piece of neglect for which the comfortable head of the house ending in *ogs* would no doubt have chided her severely, could he have been prevailed upon to remain in town a day or two for that purpose.

As it is, the constables have had a sad time of it, running hither and thither, and all they can do is to declare the man of business most emphatically, a "hen knee high"—by which some persons imagine them to imply that, in fast, he is n.e.i.—by which again the very classical phrase *non est inventus,* is supposed to be understood. In the meantime the young gentlemen, one and all, are somewhat less piously inclined than before, while the landlady purchases a shilling's worth of the best India rubber, and very carefully obliterates the pencil memorandum that some fool has made in her great family Bible, on the broad margin of the Proverbs of Solomon.

The Man That Was Used Up

A TALE OF THE LATE BUGABOO AND KICKAPOO CAMPAIGN

Pleurez, pleurez, mes yeux, et fondez vous en eau!
La moitié de ma vie a mis l'autre au tombeau.

—*Corneille*

I CANNOT just now remember when or where I first made the acquaintance of that truly fine-looking fellow, Brevet Brigadier-General John A. B. C. Smith. Some one *did* introduce me to the gentleman, I am sure—at some public meeting, I know very well—held about something of great importance, no doubt—at some place or other, I feel convinced,—whose name I have unaccountably forgotten. The truth is—that the introduction was attended, upon my part, with a degree of anxious embarrassment which operated to prevent any definite impressions of either time or place. I am constitutionally nervous—this, with me, is a family failing, and I can't help it. In especial, the slightest appearance of mystery —of any point I cannot exactly comprehend—puts me at once into a pitiable state of agitation.

There was something, as it were, remarkable—yes, *remarkable,* although this is but a feeble term to express my full meaning—about the entire individuality of the personage in question. He was, perhaps, six feet in height, and of a presence singularly commanding. There was an *air distingué* pervading the whole man, which spoke of high breeding, and hinted at high birth. Upon this topic—the topic of Smith's personal appearance—I have a kind of melancholy satisfaction in being minute. His head of hair would have done honor to a Brutus;

nothing could be more richly flowing, or possess a brighter gloss. It was of a jetty black; which was also the color, or more properly the no color, of his unimaginable whiskers. You perceive I cannot speak of these latter without enthusiasm; it is not too much to say that they were the handsomest pair of whiskers under the sun. At all events, they encircled, and at times partially over-shadowed, a mouth utterly unequalled. Here were the most entirely even, and the most brilliantly white of all conceivable teeth. From between them, upon every prop-er occasion, issued a voice of surpassing clearness, mel-ody, and strength. In the matter of eyes, also, my ac-quaintance was pre-eminently endowed. Either one of such a pair was worth a couple of the ordinary ocular organs. They were of a deep hazel exceedingly large and lustrous; and there was perceptible about them, ever and anon, just that amount of interesting obliquity which gives pregnancy to expression.

The bust of the General was unquestionably the finest bust I ever saw. For your life you could not have found a fault with its wonderful proportion. This rare peculiarity set off to great advantage a pair of shoulders which would have called up a blush of conscious inferiority into the countenance of the marble Apollo. I have a passion for fine shoulders, and may say that I never beheld them in perfection before. The arms altogether were admirably modelled. Nor were the lower limbs less superb. These were, indeed, the *ne plus ultra* of good legs. Every con-noisseur in such matters admitted the legs to be good. There was neither too much flesh nor too little,—neither rudeness nor fragility. I could not imagine a more graceful curve than that of the *os femoris,* and there was just that due gentle prominence in the rear of the *fibula* which goes to the conformation of a properly propor-tioned calf. I wish to God my young and talented friend Chiponchipino, the sculptor, had but seen the legs of Brevet Brigadier-General John A. B. C. Smith.

But although men so absolutely fine-looking are neither as plenty as reasons or blackberries, still I could not bring myself to believe that *the remarkable* something to which I alluded just now,—that the odd air of *je ne sais quoi* which hung about my new acquaintance,—lay alto-gether, or indeed at all, in the supreme excellence of his bodily endowments. Perhaps it might be traced to the

manner;—yet here again I could not pretend to be posi-
tive. There *was* a primness, not to say stiffness, in his
carriage—a degree of measured and, if I may so express
it, of rectangular precision attending his every move-
ment, which, observed in a more diminutive figure, would
have had the least little savor in the world of affectation,
pomposity, or constraint, but which, noticed in a gentle-
man of his undoubted dimensions, was readily placed to
the account of reserve, *hauteur*—of a commendable
sense, in short, of what is due to the dignity of colossal
proportion.

The kind friend who presented me to General Smith
whispered in my ear some few words of comment upon
the man. He was a *remarkable* man—a *very* remark-
able man—indeed one of the *most* remarkable men of the
age. He was an especial favorite, too, with the ladies—
chiefly on account of his high reputation for courage.

"In *that* point he is unrivalled—indeed he is a perfect
desperado—a downright fire-eater, and no mistake," said
my friend, here dropping his voice excessively low, and
thrilling me with the mystery of his tone.

"A downright fire-eater, and *no* mistake. Showed *that,*
I should say, to some purpose, in the late tremendous
swamp-fight, away down South, with the Bugaboo and
Kickapoo Indians." [Here my friend opened his eyes to
some extent.] "Bless my soul!—blood and thunder,
and all that!—*prodigies* of valor!—heard of him of
course?—you know he's the man——"

"Man alive, how *do* you do? why, how *are* ye? *very*
glad to see ye, indeed!" here interrupted the General
himself, seizing my companion by the hand as he drew
near, and bowing stiffly but profoundly, as I was pre-
sented. I then thought (and I think so still) that I never
heard a clearer nor a stronger voice, nor beheld a finer
set of teeth: but I *must* say that I was sorry for the in-
terruption just at that moment, as, owing to the whis-
pers and insinuations aforesaid, my interest had been
greatly excited in the hero of the Bugaboo and Kickapoo
campaign.

However, the delightfully luminous conversation of
Brevet Brigadier-General John A. B. C. Smith soon
completely dissipated this chagrin. My friend leaving us
immediately, we had quite a long *tête-à-tête,* and I was
not only pleased but *really*—instructed. I never heard a

more fluent talker, or a man of greater general informa-
tion. With becoming modesty, he forbore, nevertheless,
to touch upon the theme I had just then most at heart—I
mean the mysterious circumstances attending the Buga-
boo war—and, on my own part, what I conceive to be a
proper sense of delicacy forbade me to broach the sub-
ject; although, in truth, I was exceedingly tempted to do
so. I perceived, too, that the gallant soldier preferred
topics of philosophical interest, and that he delighted,
especially, in commenting upon the rapid march of me-
chanical invention. Indeed, lead him where I would, this
was a point to which he invariably came back.

"There is nothing at all like it," he would say; "we
are a wonderful people, and live in a wonderful age.
Parachutes and railroads—man-traps and spring-guns!
Our steam-boats are upon every sea, and the Nassau
balloon packet is about to run regular trips (fare either
way only twenty pounds sterling) between London and
Timbuctoo. And who shall calculate the immense in-
fluence upon social life—upon arts—upon commerce—
upon literature—which will be the immediate result of
the great principles of electro-magnetics! Nor, is this all,
let me assure you! There is really no end to the march of
invention. The most wonderful—the most ingenious—and
let me add, Mr.—Mr.—Thompson, I believe, is your
name—let me add, I say the most *useful*—the most truly
useful—mechanical contrivances are daily springing up
like mushrooms, if I may so express myself, or, more
figuratively, like—ah—grasshoppers—like grasshoppers,
Mr. Thompson—about us and ah—ah—ah—around us!"

Thompson, to be sure, is not my name; but it is need-
less to say that I left General Smith with a heightened
interest in the man, with an exalted opinion of his con-
versational powers, and a deep sense of the valuable
privileges we enjoy in living in this age of mechanical
invention. My curiosity, however, had not been alto-
gether satisfied, and I resolved to prosecute immediate
inquiry among my acquaintances touching the Brevet
Brigadier-General himself, and particularly respecting the
tremendous events *quorum pars magna fuit,* during the
Bugaboo and Kickapoo campaign.

The first opportunity which presented itself, and which
(*horresco referens*) I did not in the least scruple to
seize, occurred at the Church of the Reverend Doctor

Drummummupp, where I found myself established, one
Sunday, just at sermon time, not only in the pew, but by
the side of that worthy and communicative little friend
of mine, Miss Tabitha T. Thus seated, I congratulated
myself, and with much reason, upon the very flattering
state of affairs. If any person knew any thing about
Brevet Brigadier-General John A. B. C. Smith, that per-
son, it was clear to me, was Miss Tabitha T. We tele-
graphed a few signals and then commenced, *sotto voce*,
a brisk *tête-à-tête*.

"Smith!" said she, in reply to my very earnest inquiry;
"Smith!—why, not General A. B. C.? Bless me, I thought
you *knew* all about *him!* This is a wonderfully inventive
age! Horrid affair that!—a bloody set of wretches, those
Kickapoos!—fought like a hero—prodigies of valor—im-
mortal renown. Smith!—Brevet Brigadier-General John
A. B. C.!—why, you know he's the man——"

"Man," here broke in Doctor Dummummupp, at the
top of his voice, and with a thump that came near knock-
ing the pulpit about our ears—"man that is born of a
woman hath but a short time to live; he cometh up and
is cut down like a flower!" I started to the extremity of
the pew, and perceived by the animated looks of the di-
vine, that the wrath which had nearly proved fatal to the
pulpit had been excited by the whispers of the lady and
myself. There was no help for it; so I submitted with a
good grace, and listened, in all the martyrdom of dig-
nified silence, to the balance of that very capital dis-
course.

Next evening found me a somewhat late visitor at the
Rantipole Theatre, where I felt sure of satisfying my
curiosity at once, by merely stepping into the box of those
exquisite specimens of affability and omniscience, the
Misses Arabella and Miranda Cognoscenti. That fine
tragedian, Climax, was doing Iago to a very crowded
house, and I experienced some little difficulty in making
my wishes understood; especially as our box was next the
slips, and completely overlooked the stage.

"Smith!" said Miss Arabella, as she at length compre-
hended the purport of my query; "Smith!—why, not
General John A. B. C.?"

"Smith!" inquired Miranda, musingly. "God bless me,
did you ever behold a finer figure?"

"Never, madam, but *do* tell me——"

"Or so inimitable grace?"

"Never, upon my word! But pray, inform me——"

"Or so just an appreciation of stage effect?"

"Madam!"

"Or a more delicate sense of the true beauties of Shakespeare? Be so good as to look at that leg!"

"The devil!" and I turned again to her sister.

"Smith!" said she, "why, not General John A. B. C.? Horrid affair that, wasn't it?—great wretches, those Bugaboos—savage and so on—but we live in a wonderfully inventive age!—Smith!—O yes! great man!—perfect desperado!—immortal renown!—prodigies of valor! *Never heard!*" [This was given in a scream.] "Bless my soul!—why, he's the man——"

> "——mandragora
> Nor all the drowsy syrups of the world
> Shall ever medicine thee to that sweet sleep
> Which thou ow'dst yesterday!"

here roared out Climax just in my ear, and shaking his fist in my face all the time, in a way that I *couldn't* stand, and I *wouldn't.* I left the Misses Cognoscenti immediately, went behind the scenes forthwith, and gave the beggarly scoundrel such a thrashing as I trust he will remember till the day of his death.

At the *soirée* of the lovely widow, Mrs. Kathleen O'Trump, I was confident that I should meet with no similar disappointment. Accordingly, I was no sooner seated at the card-table, with my pretty hostess for a *vis-à-vis,* then I propounded those questions the solution of which had become a matter so essential to my peace.

"Smith!" said my partner, "why, not General John A. B. C.? Horrid affair that, wasn't it?—diamonds did you say?—terrible wretches those Kickapoos!—we are playing *whist,* if you please, Mr. Tattle—however, this is the age of invention, most certainly *the* age, one may say—*the* age *par excellence*—speak French?—oh, quite a hero—perfect desperado!—*no hearts,* Mr. Tattle? I don't believe it.—immortal renown and all that!—prodigies of valor! *Never heard!!*—why, bless me, he's the man——"

"Mann!—*Captain* Mann!" here screamed some little feminine interloper from the farthest corner of the room.

"Are you talking about Captain Mann and the duel?—oh, I *must* hear—do tell—go on, Mrs. O'Trump!—do now go on!" And go on Mrs. O'Trump did—all about a certain Captain Mann, who was either shot or hung, or should have been both shot and hung. Yes! Mrs. O'Trump, she went on, and I—I went off. There was no chance of hearing any thing further that evening in regard to Brevet Brigadier-General John A. B. C. Smith.

Still I consoled myself with the reflection that the tide of ill-luck would not run against me forever, and so determined to make a bold push for information at the rout of that bewitching little angel, the graceful Mrs. Pirouette.

"Smith!" said Mrs. P., as we twirled about together in a *pas de zephyr,* "Smith!—why, not General John A. B. C.? Dreadful business that of the Bugaboos, wasn't it?—dreadful creatures, those Indians!—*do* turn out your toes! I really am ashamed of you—man of great courage, poor fellow!—but this is a wonderful age for invention— O dear me, I'm out of breath—quite a desperado— prodigies of valor—*never heard!*—can't believe it—I shall have to sit down and enlighten you—Smith! why, he's the man——"

"Man-*Fred,* I tell you!" here bawled out Miss Bas-Bleu, as I led Mrs. Pirouette to a seat. "Did ever anybody hear the like? It's Man-*Fred,* I say,.and not at all by any means Man-*Friday.*" Here Miss Bas-Bleu beckoned to me in a very peremptory manner; and I was obliged, will I nill I, to leave Mrs. P. for the purpose of deciding a dispute touching the title of a certain poetical drama of Lord Byron's. Although I pronounced, with great promptness, that the true title was Man-*Frida*y, and not by any means Man-*Fred,* yet when I returned to seek Mrs. Pirouette she was not to be discovered, and I made my retreat from the house in a very bitter spirit of animosity against the whole race of the Bas-Bleus.

Matters had now assumed a really serious aspect, and I resolved to call at once upon my particular friend, Mr. Theodore Sinivate; for I knew that here at least I should get something like definite information.

"Smith!" said he, in his well-known peculiar way of drawling out his syllables; "Smith!—why, not General John A. B. C.? Savage affair that with the Kickapo-o-o-os, wasn't it? Say, don't you think so?—perfect despera-a-ado

—great pity, 'pon my honor!—wonderfully inventive age!
—pro-o-odigies of valor! By the by, did you ever hear
about Captain Ma-a-a-a-n?"

"Captain Mann be d——d!" said I; "please to go on
with your story."

"Hem!—oh well!—quite *la même cho-o-ose*, as we
say in France. Smith, eh? Brigadier-General John A——B
——C.? I say"—[here Mr. S. thought proper to put his
finger to the side of his nose]—"I say, you don't mean
to insinuate now, really and truly, and conscientiously,
that you don't know all about that affair of Smith's, as
well as I do, eh? Smith? John A——B——C.? Why, bless me,
he's the ma-a-an——"

"*Mr.* Sinivate," said I, imploringly, "*is* he the man in
the mask?"

"No-o-o!" said he, looking wise, "nor the man in the
mo-o-on."

This reply I considered a pointed and positive insult,
and so left the house at once in high dudgeon, with a
firm resolve to call my friend, Mr. Sinivate, to a speedy
account for his ungentlemanly conduct and ill-breeding.

In the meantime, however, I had no notion of being
thwarted touching the information I desired. There was
one resource left me yet. I would go to the fountain-head.
I would call forthwith upon the General himself, and
demand, in explicit terms, a solution of this abominable
piece of mystery. Here, at least, there should be no
chance for equivocation. I would be plain, positive,
peremptory—as short as pie-crust—as concise as Taci-
tus or Montesquieu.

It was early when I called, and the General was
dressing, but I pleaded urgent business, and was shown
at once into his bedroom by an old negro valet, who re-
mained in attendance during my visit. As I entered the
chamber, I looked about, of course, for the occupant,
but did not immediately perceive him. There was a large
and exceedingly odd-looking bundle of something which
lay close by my feet on the floor, and, as I was not in
the best humor in the world, I gave it a kick out of the
way.

"Hem! ahem! rather civil that, I should say!" said
the bundle, in one of the smallest, and altogether the
funniest little voices, between a squeak and a whistle,
that I ever heard in all the days of my existence.

"Ahem! rather civil that, I should observe."

I fairly shouted with terror, and made off, at a tangent, into the farthest extremity of the room.

"God bless me, my dear fellow!" here again whistled the bundle, "what—what—what—why, what *is* the matter? I really believe you don't know me at all."

What *could* I say to all this—what *could* I? I staggered into an armchair, and, with staring eyes and open mouth, awaited the solution of the wonder.

"Strange you shouldn't know me though, isn't it?" presently resqueaked the nondescript, which I now perceived was performing upon the floor some inexplicable evolution, very analogous to the drawing on of a stocking. There was only a single leg, however, apparent.

"Strange you shouldn't know me though, isn't it? Pompey, bring me that leg!" Here Pompey handed the bundle a very capital cork leg, already dressed, which it screwed on in a trice; and then it stood up before my eyes.

"And a bloody action it *was*," continued the thing, as if in a soliloquy; "but then one mustn't fight with the Bugaboos and Kickapoos, and think of coming off with a mere scratch. Pompey, I'll thank you now for that arm. Thomas" [turning to me] "is decidedly the best hand at a cork leg; but if you should ever want an arm, my dear fellow, you must really let me recommend you to Bishop." Here Pompey screwed on an arm.

"We had rather hot work of it, that you may say. Now, you dog, slip on my shoulders and bosom. Pettit makes the best shoulders, but for a bosom you will have to go to Ducrow."

"Bosom!" said I.

"Pompey, will you *never* be ready with that wig? Scalping is a rough process, after all; but then you can procure such a capital scratch at De L'Orme's."

"Scratch!"

"Now, you nigger, my teeth! For a *good* set of these you had better go to Parmly's at once; high prices, but excellent work. I swallowed some very capital articles, though, when the big Bugaboo rammed me down with the butt end of his rifle."

"Butt end! ram down!! my eye!!"

"O yes, by the by, my eye—here, Pompey, you scamp, screw it in! Those Kickapoos are not so very slow at a

gouge; but he's a belied man, that Dr. Williams, after all; you can't imagine how well I see with the eyes of his make."

I now began very clearly to perceive that the object before me was nothing more nor less than my new acquaintance, Brevet Brigadier-General John A. B. C. Smith. The manipulations of Pompey had made, I must confess, a very striking difference in the personal appearance of the man. The voice, however, still puzzled me no little; but even this apparent mystery was speedily cleared up.

"Pompey, you black rascal," squeaked the General, "I really do believe you would let me go out without my palate."

Hereupon, the negro, grumbling out an apology, went up to his master, opened his mouth with the knowing air of a horse-jockey, and adjusted therein a somewhat singular-looking machine, in a very dexterous manner, that I could not altogether comprehend. The alteration, however, in the entire expression of the General's countenance was instantaneous and surprising. When he again spoke, his voice had resumed all that rich melody and strength which I had noticed upon our original introduction.

"D——n the vagabonds!" said he, in so clear a tone that I positively started at the change, "D——n the vagabonds! they not only knocked in the roof of my mouth, but took the trouble to cut off at least seven eighths of my tongue. There isn't Bonfanti's equal, however, in America, for really good articles of this description. I can recommend you to him with confidence," [here the General bowed,] "and assure you that I have the greatest pleasure in so doing."

I acknowledged his kindness in my best manner, and took leave of him at once, with a perfect understanding of the true state of affairs—with a full comprehension of the mystery which had troubled me so long. It was evident. It was a clear case. Brevet Brigadier-General John A. B. C. Smith was the man—was *the man that was used up.*

Narrative of A. Gordon Pym

INTRODUCTORY NOTE

UPON MY RETURN to the United States a few months ago, after the extraordinary series of adventures in the South Seas and elsewhere, of which an account is given in the following pages, accident threw me into the society of several gentlemen in Richmond, Va., who felt deep interest in all matters relating to the regions I had visited, and who were constantly urging it upon me, as a duty, to give my narrative to the public. I had several reasons, however, for declining to do so, some of which were of a nature altogether private, and concern no person but myself; others not so much so. One consideration which deterred me was, that having kept no journal during a greater portion of the time in which I was absent, I feared I should not be able to write, from mere memory, a statement so minute and connected as to have the *appearance* of that truth it would really possess, barring only the natural and unavoidable exaggeration to which all of us are prone when detailing events which have had powerful influence in exciting the imaginative faculties. Another reason was, that the incidents to be narrated were of a nature so positively marvellous that, unsupported as my assertions must necessarily be (except by the evidence of a single individual, and he a half-breed Indian), I could only hope for belief among my family, and those of my friends who have had reason, through life, to put faith in my veracity—the probability being that the public at large would regard what I should put forth as merely an impudent and ingenious fiction. A distrust in my own abilities as a writer was, nevertheless, one of the principal causes which prevented me from complying with the suggestions of my advisers.

Among those gentlemen in Virginia who expressed the greatest interest in my statement, more particularly in regard to that portion of it which related to the Antarctic Ocean, was Mr. Poe, lately editor of the *Southern Literary Messenger*, a monthly magazine, published by Mr. Thomas W. White, in the city of Richmond. He strongly advised me, among others, to prepare at once a full account of what I had seen and undergone, and trust to the shrewdness and common-sense of the public—in-

sisting, with great plausibility, that however roughly, as regards mere authorship, my book should be got up, its very uncouthness, if there were any, would give it all the better chance of being received as truth.

Notwithstanding this representation, I did not make up my mind to do as he suggested. He afterward proposed (finding that I would not stir in the matter) that I should allow him to draw up, in his own words, a narrative of the earlier portion of my adventures, from facts afforded by myself, publishing it in the *Southern Messenger under the garb of fiction.* To this, perceiving no objection, I consented, stipulating only that my real name should be retained. Two numbers of the pretended fiction appeared, consequently, in the *Messenger* for January and February (1837), and, in order that it might certainly be regarded as fiction, the name of Mr. Poe was affixed to the articles in the table of contents of the magazine.

The manner in which this *ruse* was received has induced me at length to undertake a regular compilation and publication of the adventures in question; for I found that, in spite of the air of fable which had been so ingeniously thrown around that portion of my statement which appeared in the *Messenger* (without altering or distorting a single fact), the public were still not at all disposed to receive it as fable, and several letters were sent to Mr. P.'s address, distinctly expressing a conviction to the contrary. I thence concluded that the facts of my narrative would prove of such a nature as to carry with them sufficient evidence of their own authenticity, and that I had consequently little to fear on the score of popular incredulity.

This *exposé* being made, it will be seen at once how much of what follows I claim to be my own writing; and it will also be understood that no fact is misrepresented in the first few pages which were written by Mr. Poe. Even to those readers who have not seen the *Messenger,* it will be unnecessary to point out where his portion ends and my own commences; the difference in point of style will be readily perceived.

A. G. PYM

Narrative of A. Gordon Pym

CHAPTER I

My NAME is Arthur Gordon Pym. My father was a respectable trader in sea-stores at Nantucket, where I was born. My maternal grandfather was an attorney in good practice. He was fortunate in every thing, and had speculated very successfully in stocks of the Edgarton New Bank, as it was formerly called. By these and other means he had managed to lay by a tolerable sum of money. He was more attached to myself, I believe, than to any person in the world, and I expected to inherit the most of his property at his death. He sent me, at six years of age, to the school of old Mr. Ricketts, a gentleman with only one arm, and of eccentric manners—he is well known to almost every person who has visited New Bedford. I stayed at his school until I was sixteen, when I left him for Mr. E. Ronald's academy on the hill. Here I became intimate with the son of Mr. Barnard, a sea-captain, who generally sailed in the employ of Lloyd and Vredenburgh—Mr. Barnard is also very well known in New Bedford, and has many relations, I am certain, in Edgarton. His son was named Augustus, and he was nearly two years older than myself. He had been on a whaling voyage with his father in the John Donaldson, and was always talking to me of his adventures in the South Pacific Ocean. I used frequently to go home with him, and remain all day, and sometimes all night. We occupied the same bed, and he would be sure to keep me awake until almost light, telling me stories of the natives of the Island of Tinian, and other places he had visited in his travels. At last I could not help being interested in what he said, and by degrees I felt the greatest desire to go to sea. I owned a sail-boat called the Ariel, and worth

about seventy-five dollars. She had a half deck or cuddy, and was rigged sloop-fashion—I forget her tonnage, but she would hold ten persons without much crowding. In this boat we were in the habit of going on some of the maddest freaks in the world; and, when I now think of them, it appears to me a thousand wonders that I am alive to-day.

I will relate one of these adventures by way of introduction to a longer and more momentous narrative. One night there was a party at Mr. Barnard's, and both Augustus and myself were not a little intoxicated toward the close of it. As usual, in such cases, I took part of his bed in preference to going home. He went to sleep, as I thought, very quietly (it being near one when the party broke up), and without saying a word on his favorite topic. It might have been half an hour from the time of our getting in bed, and I was just about falling into a doze, when he suddenly started up, and swore with a terrible oath that he would not go to sleep for any Arthur Pym in Christendom, when there was so glorious a breeze from the southwest. I never was so astonished in my life, not knowing what he intended, and thinking that the wines and liquors he had drunk had set him entirely beside himself. He proceeded to talk very coolly, however, saying he knew that I supposed him intoxicated, but that he was never more sober in his life. He was only tired, he added of lying in bed on such a fine night like a dog, and was determined to get up and dress, and go out on a frolic with the boat. I can hardly tell what possessed me, but the words were no sooner out of his mouth than I felt a thrill of the greatest excitement and pleasure, and thought his mad idea one of the most delightful and most reasonable things in the world. It was blowing almost a gale, and the weather was very cold— it being late in October. I sprang out of bed, nevertheless, in a kind of ecstasy, and told him I was quite as brave as himself, and quite as tired as he was of lying in bed like a dog, and quite as ready for any fun or frolic as any Augustus Barnard in Nantucket.

We lost no time in getting on our clothes and hurrying down to the boat. She was lying at the old decayed wharf by the lumber-yard of Pankey & Co., and almost thumping her side out against the rough logs. Augustus got into her and bailed her, for she was nearly half full of

water. This being done, we hoisted jib and mainsail, kept full, and started boldly out to sea.

The wind, as I before said, blew freshly from the southwest. The night was very clear and cold. Augustus had taken the helm, and I stationed myself by the mast, on the deck of the cuddy. We flew along at a great rate —neither of us having said a word since casting loose from the wharf. I now asked my companion what course he intended to steer, and what time he thought it probable we should get back. He whistled for a few minutes, and then said crustily: "*I* am going to sea—*you* may go home if you think proper." Turning my eyes upon him, I perceived at once that in spite of his assumed *nonchalance,* he was greatly agitated. I could see him distinctly by the light of the moon—his face was paler than any marble, and his hand shook so excessively that he could scarcely retain hold of the tiller. I felt that something had gone wrong, and became seriously alarmed. At this period I knew little about the management of a boat, and was now depending entirely upon the nautical skill of my friend. The wind, too, had suddenly increased, and we were fast getting out of the lee of the land—still I was ashamed to betray any trepidation, and for almost half an hour maintained a resolute silence. I could stand it no longer, however, and spoke to Augustus about the propriety of turning back. As before, it was nearly a minute before he made answer, or took any notice of my suggestion. "By and by," said he at length—"time enough —home by and by." I had expected such a reply, but there was something in the tone of these words which filled me with an indescribable feeling of dread. I again looked at the speaker attentively. His lips were perfectly livid, and his knees shook so violently together that he seemed scarcely able to stand. "For God's sake, Augustus," I screamed, now heartily frightened, "what ails you?—what is the matter?—what *are* you going to do?" "Matter!" he stammered, in the greatest apparent surprise, letting go the tiller at the same moment, and falling forward into the bottom of the boat—"matter—why, nothing is the—matter—going home—d—d—don't you see?" The whole truth now flashed upon me. I flew to him and raised him up. He was drunk—beastly drunk—he could no longer either stand, speak, or see. His eyes were perfectly glazed; and as I let him go in the extremity

of my despair, he rolled like a mere log into the bilge-water, from which I had lifted him. It was evident that, during the evening, he had drunk far more than I suspected, and that his conduct in bed had been the result of a highly-concentrated state of intoxication—a state which, like madness, frequently enables the victim to imitate the outward demeanor of one in perfect possession of his senses. The coolness of the night air, however, had had its usual effect—the mental energy began to yield before its influence—and the confused perception which he no doubt then had of his perilous situation had assisted in hastening the catastrophe. He was now thoroughly insensible, and there was no probability that he would be otherwise for many hours.

It is hardly possible to conceive the extremity of my terror. The fumes of the wine lately taken had evaporated, leaving me doubly timid and irresolute. I knew that I was altogether incapable of managing the boat, and that a fierce wind and strong ebb-tide were hurrying us to destruction. A storm was evidently gathering behind us; we had neither compass nor provisions; and it was clear that, if we held our present course, we should be out of sight of land before daybreak. These thoughts, with a crowd of others, equally fearful, flashed through my mind with a bewildering rapidity, and for some moments paralyzed me beyond the possiblity of making any exertion. The boat was going through the water at a terrific rate —full before the wind—no reef in either jib or mainsail— running her bows completely under the foam. It was a thousand wonders she did not broach to—Augustus having let go the tiller, as I said before, and I being too much agitated to think of taking it myself. By good luck, however, she kept steady, and gradually I recovered some degree of presence of mind. Still the wind was increasing fearfully; and whenever we rose from a plunge forward, the sea behind fell combing over our counter, and deluged us with water. I was so utterly benumbed, too, in every limb, as to be nearly unconscious of sensation. At length I summoned up the resolution of despair, and rushing to the mainsail, let it go by the run. As might have been expected, it flew over the bows, and, getting drenched with water, carried away the mast short off by the board. This latter accident alone saved me from instant destruction. Under the jib only, I now boomed

along before the wind, shipping heavy seas occasionally, but relieved from the terror of immediate death. I took the helm, and breathed with greater freedom, as I found that there yet remained to us a chance of ultimate escape. Augustus still lay senseless in the bottom of the boat; and as there was imminent danger of his drowning (the water being nearly a foot deep just where he fell), I contrived to raise him partially up, and keep him in a sitting position, by passing a rope round his waist, and lashing it to a ring-bolt in the deck of the cuddy. Having thus arranged every thing as well as I could in my chilled and agitated condition, I recommended myself to God, and made up my mind to bear whatever might happen with all the fortitude in my power.

Hardly had I come to this resolution, when, suddenly, a loud and long scream or yell, as if from the throats of a thousand demons, seemed to pervade the whole atmosphere around and above the boat. Never while I live shall I forget the intense agony of terror I experienced at that moment. My hair stood erect on my head—I felt the blood congealing in my veins—my heart ceased utterly to beat, and without having once raised my eyes to learn the source of my alarm, I tumbled headlong and insensible upon the body of my fallen companion.

I found myself, upon reviving, in the cabin of a large whaling-ship (the Penguin) bound to Nantucket. Several persons were standing over me, and Augustus, paler than death, was busily occupied in chafing my hands. Upon seeing me open my eyes, his exclamations of gratitude and joy excited alternate laughter and tears from the rough-looking personages who were present. The mystery of our being in existence was now soon explained. We had been run down by the whaling-ship, which was close-hauled, beating up to Nantucket with every sail she could venture to set, and consequently running almost at right angles to our own course. Several men were on the look-out forward, but did not perceive our boat until it was an impossibility to avoid coming in contact—their shouts of warning upon seeing us were what so terribly alarmed me. The huge ship, I was told, rode immediately over us with as much ease as our own little vessel would have passed over a feather, and without the least perceptible impediment to her progress. Not a scream arose from the deck of the victim—there was a slight grating sound to be

heard mingling with the roar of wind and water, as the
frail bark which was swallowed up rubbed for a moment
along the keel of her destroyer—but this was all. Think-
ing our boat (which it will be remembered was dis-
masted) some mere shell cut adrift as useless, the captain
(Captain E. T. V. Block of New London) was for pro-
ceeding on his course without troubling himself further
about the matter. Luckily, there were two of the look-
out who swore positively to having seen some person at
our helm, and represented the possibility of yet saving
him. A discussion ensued, when Block grew angry, and,
after a while, said that "it was no business of his to be
eternally watching for eggshells; that the ship should *not*
put about for any such nonsense; and if there was a man
run down, it was nobody's fault but his own—he might
drown and be d—d," or some language to that effect.
Henderson, the first mate, now took the matter up, being
justly indignant, as well as the whole ship's crew, at a
speech evincing such a degree of heartless atrocity. He
spoke plainly, seeing himself upheld by the men, told the
captain he considered him a fit subject for the gallows,
and that he would disobey his orders if he were hanged
for it the moment he set his foot on shore. He strode aft,
jostling Block (who turned very pale and made no an-
swer) on one side, and seizing the helm, gave the word,
in a firm voice, *Hard-a-lee!* The men flew to their posts,
and the ship went cleverly about. All this had occupied
nearly five minutes, and it was supposed to be hardly
within the bounds of possibility that any individual could
be saved—allowing any to have been on board the boat.
Yet, as the reader has seen, both Augustus and myself
were rescued; and our deliverance seemed to have been
brought about by two of those almost inconceivable
pieces of good fortune which are attributed by the wise
and pious to the special interference of Providence.

While the ship was yet in stays, the mate lowered the
jolly-boat and jumped into her with the very two men, I
believe, who spoke up as having seen me at the helm.
They had just left the lee of the vessel (the moon still
shining brightly) when she made a long and heavy roll to
windward, and Henderson, at the same moment, starting
up in his seat, bawled out to his crew to *back water*. He
would say nothing else—repeating his cry impatiently,
back water! back water! The men put back as speedily as

possible; but by this time the ship had gone round, and gotten fully under headway, although all hands on board were making great exertions to take in sail. In despite of the danger of the attempt, the mate clung to the main-chains as soon as they came within his reach. Another huge lurch now brought the starboard side of the vessel out of the water neatly as far as her keel, when the cause of his anxiety was rendered obvious enough. The body of a man was seen to be affixed in the most singular manner to the smooth and shining bottom (the Penguin was coppered and copper-fastened), and beating violent-ly against it with every movement of the hull. After sev-eral ineffectual efforts, made during the lurches of the ship, and at the imminent risk of swamping the boat, I was finally disengaged from my perilous situation and taken on board—for the body proved to be my own. It ap-peared that one of the timber-bolts having started and broken a passage through the copper, it had arrested my progress as I passed under the ship, and fastened me in so extraordinary a manner to her bottom. The head of the bolt had made its way through the collar of the green baize jacket I had on, and through the back part of my neck, forcing itself out between two sinews and just below the right ear. I was immediately put to bed—although life seemed to be totally extinct. There was no surgeon on board. The captain, however, treated me with every attention—to make amends, I presume, in the eyes of his crew, for his atrocious behavior in the pre-vious portion of the adventure.

In the meantime, Henderson had again put off from the ship, although the wind was now blowing almost a hurri-cane. He had not been gone many minutes when he fell in with some fragments of our boat, and shortly after-ward one of the men with him asserted that he could distinguish a cry for help at intervals amid the roaring of the tempest. This induced the hardy seamen to persevere in their search for more than half an hour, although re-peated signals to return were made them by Captain Block, and although every moment on the water in so frail a boat was fraught to them with the most imminent and deadly peril. Indeed, it is nearly impossible to con-ceive how the small jolly they were in could have escaped destruction for a single instant. She was built, however,

for the whaling service, and was fitted, as I have since had reason to believe, with air-boxes, in the manner of some life-boats used on the coast of Wales.

After searching in vain for about the period of time just mentioned, it was determined to get back to the ship. They had scarcely made this resolve when a feeble cry arose from a dark object that floated rapidly by. They pursued and soon overtook it. It proved to be the entire deck of the Ariel's cuddy. Augustus was struggling near it, apparently in the last agonies. Upon getting hold of him it was found that he was attached by a rope to the floating timber. This rope, it will be remembered, I had myself tied round his waist, and made fast to a ring-bolt, for the purpose of keeping him in an upright position, and my so doing, it appeared, had been ultimately the means of preserving his life. The Ariel was slightly put together, and in going down her frame naturally went to pieces; the deck of the cuddy, as might have been expected, was lifted, by the force of the water rushing in, entirely from the main timbers, and floated (with other fragments, no doubt) to the surface —Augustus was buoyed up with it, and thus escaped a terrible death.

It was more than an hour after being taken on board the Penguin before he could give any account of himself, or be made to comprehend the nature of the accident which had befallen our boat. At length he became thoroughly aroused, and spoke much of his sensations while in the water. Upon his first attaining any degree of consciousness, he found himself beneath the surface, whirling round and round with inconceivable rapidity, and with a rope wound in three or four folds tightly about his neck. In an instant afterward he felt himself going rapidly upward, when, his head striking violently against a hard substance, he again relapsed into insensibility. Upon once more reviving he was in fuller possession of his reason—this was still, however, in the greatest degree clouded and confused. He now knew that some accident had occurred, and that he was in the water, although his mouth was above the surface, and he could breathe with some freedom. Possibly, at this period the deck was drifting rapidly before the wind, and drawing him after it as he floated upon his back. Of course, as long as he

could have retained this position, it would have been
nearly impossible that he should be drowned. Presently
a surge threw him directly athwart the deck; and this
post he endeavored to maintain, screaming at intervals
for help. Just before he was discovered by Mr. Hender-
son, he had been obliged to relax his hold through ex-
haustion, and, falling into the sea, had given himself up
for lost. During the whole period of his struggles he
had not the faintest recollection of the Ariel, nor of any
matters in connection with the source of his disaster. A
vague feeling of terror and despair had taken entire
possession of his faculties. When he was finally picked
up, every power of his mind had failed him; and, as be-
fore said, it was nearly an hour after getting on board
the Penguin before he became fully aware of his con-
dition. In regard to myself—I was resuscitated from a
state bordering very nearly upon death (and after every
other means had been tried in vain for three hours and a
half) by vigorous friction with flannels bathed in hot oil
—a proceeding suggested by Augustus. The wound in
my neck, although of an ugly appearance, proved of little
real consequence, and I soon recovered from its effects.

The Penguin got into port about nine o'clock in the
morning, after encountering one of the severest gales
ever experienced off Nantucket. Both Augustus and my-
self managed to appear at Mr. Barnard's in time for
breakfast—which, luckily, was somewhat late, owing to
the party overnight. I suppose, all at the table were too
much fatigued themselves to notice our jaded appearance
—of course, it would not have borne a very rigid scrutiny.
School-boys, however, can accomplish wonders in the
way of deception, and I verily believe not one of our
friends in Nantucket had the slightest suspicion that the
terrible story told by some sailors in town of their having
run down a vessel at sea and drowned some thirty or
forty poor devils, had reference either to the Ariel, my
companion, or myself. We two have since very frequently
talked the matter over—but never without a shudder. In
one of our conversations Augustus frankly confessed to
me, that in his whole life he had at no time experienced
so excruciating a sense of dismay, as when on board our
little boat he first discovered the extent of his intoxica-
tion, and felt himself sinking beneath its influence.

CHAPTER II

In no affairs of mere prejudice, *pro* or *con,* do we deduce inferences with entire certainty, even from the most simple data. It might be supposed that a catastrophe such as I have just related would have effectually cooled my incipient passion for the sea. On the contrary, I never experienced a more ardent longing for the wild adventures incident to the life of a navigator than within a week after our miraculous deliverance. This short period proved amply long enough to erase from my memory the shadows, and bring out in vivid light all the pleasurably exciting points of color, all the picturesqueness, of the late perilous accident. My conversations with Augustus grew daily more frequent and more intensely full of interest. He had a manner of relating his stories of the ocean (more than one half of which I now suspect to have been sheer fabrications) well adapted to have weight with one of my enthusiastic temperament and somewhat gloomy although glowing imagination. It is strange, too, that he most strongly enlisted my feelings in behalf of the life of a seaman, when he depicted his more terrible moments of suffering and despair. For the bright side of the painting I had a limited sympathy. My visions were of shipwreck and famine; of death or captivity among barbarian hordes; of a lifetime dragged out in sorrow and tears, upon some gray and desolate rock, in an ocean unapproachable and unknown. Such visions or desires—for they amounted to desires—are common, I have since been assured, to the whole numerous race of the melancholy among men—at the time of which I speak I regarded them only as prophetic glimpses of a destiny which I felt myself in a measure bound to fulfil. Augustus thoroughly entered into my state of mind. It is probable, indeed, that our intimate communion had resulted in a partial interchange of character.

About eighteen months after the period of the Ariel's disaster, the firm of Lloyd and Vredenburgh (a house connected in some manner with the Messieurs Enderby, I believe, of Liverpool) were engaged in repairing and fitting out the brig Grampus for a whaling voyage. She was an old hulk, and scarcely sea-worthy when all was

done to her that could be done. I hardly know why she
was chosen in preference to other and good vessels be-
longing to the same owners—but so it was. Mr. Barnard
was appointed to command her, and Augustus was going
with him. While the brig was getting ready, he frequently
urged upon me the excellency of the opportunity now
offered for indulging my desire of travel. He found me
by no means an unwilling listener—yet the matter could
not be so easily arranged. My father made no direct op-
position; but my mother went into hysterics at the bare
mention of the design; and, more than all, my grand-
father, from whom I expected much, vowed to cut me off
with a shilling if I should ever broach the subject to
him again. These difficulties, however, so far from abat-
ing my desire, only added fuel to the flame. I deter-
mined to go at all hazards; and, having made known my
intention to Augustus, we set about arranging a plan by
which it might be accomplished. In the meantime I for-
bore speaking to any of my relations in regard to the
voyage, and, as I busied myself ostensibly with my usual
studies, it was supposed that I had abandoned the design.
I have since frequently examined my conduct on this oc-
casion with sentiments of displeasure as well as of sur-
prise. The intense hypocrisy I made use of for the fur-
therance of my project—an hypocrisy pervading every
word and action of my life for so long a period of time
—could only have been rendered tolerable to myself by
the wild and burning expectation with which I looked
forward to the fulfilment of my long-cherished visions of
travel.

In pursuance of my scheme of deception, I was neces-
sarily obliged to leave much to the management of Au-
gustus, who was employed for the greater part of every
day on board the Grampus, attending to some arrange-
ments for his father in the cabin and cabin-hold. At
night, however, we were sure to have a conference, and
talk over our hopes. After nearly a month passed in this
manner, without our hitting upon any plan we thought
likely to succeed, he told me at last that he had deter-
mined upon every thing necessary. I had a relation living
in New Bedford, a Mr. Ross, at whose house I was in the
habit of spending occasionally two or three weeks at a
time. The brig was to sail about the middle of June
(June, 1827), and it was agreed that, a day or two before

her putting to sea, my father was to receive a note, as usual, from Mr. Ross, asking me to come over and spend a fortnight with Robert and Emmet (his sons). Augustus charged himself with the inditing of this note and getting it delivered. Having set out, as supposed, for New Bedford, I was then to report myself to my companion, who would contrive a hiding-place for me in the Grampus. This hiding-place, he assured me, would be rendered sufficiently comfortable for a residence of many days, during which I was not to make my appearance. When the brig had proceeded so far on her course as to make any turning back a matter out of question, I should then, he said, be formally installed in all the comforts of the cabin; and as to his father, he would only laugh heartily at the joke. Vessels enough would be met with by which a letter might be sent home explaining the adventure to my parents.

The middle of June at length arrived, and every thing had been matured. The note was written and delivered, and on a Monday morning I left the house for the New Bedford packet, as supposed. I went, however, straight to Augustus, who was waiting for me at the corner of a street. It had been our original plan that I should keep out of the way until dark, and then slip on board the brig; but, as there was now a thick fog in our favor, it was agreed to lose no time in secreting me. Augustus led the way to the wharf, and I followed at a little distance, enveloped in a thick seaman's-cloak, which he had brought with him, so that my person might not be easily recognized. Just as we turned the second corner, after passing Mr. Edmund's well, who should appear, standing right in front of me, and looking me full in the face, but old Mr. Peterson, my grandfather. "Why, bless my soul, Gordon," said he, after a long pause, "why, why,— *whose* dirty cloak is that you have on?" "Sir!" I replied, assuming, as well as I could, in the exigency of the moment, an air of offended surprise, and talking in the gruffest of all imaginable tones—"sir! you are a sum'mat mistaken—my name, in the first place, bee'nt nothing at all like Goddin, and I'd want you for to know better, you blackguard, than to call my new obercoat a darty one." For my life I could hardly refrain from screaming with laughter at the odd manner in which the old gentleman received this handsome rebuke. He started back two

or three steps, turned first pale and then excessively red, threw up his spectacles, then, putting them down, ran full tilt at me, with his umbrella uplifted. He stopped short, however, in his career, as if struck with a sudden recollection; and presently, turning round, hobbled off down the street, shaking all the while with rage, and muttering between his teeth: "Won't do—new glasses—thought it was Gordon—d——d good-for-nothing salt water Long Tom."

After this narrow escape we proceeded with greater caution, and arrived at our point of destination in safety. There were only one or two of the hands on board, and these were busy forward, doing something to the forecastle combings. Captain Barnard, we knew very well, was engaged at Lloyd and Vredenburgh's, and would remain there until late in the evening, so we had little to apprehend on his account. Augustus went first up the vessel's side, and in a short while I followed him, without being noticed by the men at work. We proceeded at once into the cabin, and found no person there. It was fitted up in the most comfortable style—a thing somewhat unusual in a whaling-vessel. There were four very excellent state-rooms, with wide and convenient berths. There was also a large stove, I took notice, and a remarkably thick and valuable carpet covering the floor of both the cabin and state-rooms. The ceiling was full seven feet high, and, in short, every thing appeared of a more roomy and agreeable nature than I had anticipated. Augustus, however, would allow me but little time for observation, insisting upon the necessity of my concealing myself as soon as possible. He led the way into his own state-room, which was on the starboard side of the brig, and next to the bulkheads. Upon entering, he closed the door and bolted it. I thought I had never seen a nicer little room than the one in which I now found myself. It was about ten feet long, and had only one berth, which, as I said before, was wide and convenient. In that portion of the closet nearest the bulkheads there was a space of four feet square, containing a table, a chair, and a set of hanging shelves full of books, chiefly books of voyages and travels. There were many other little comforts in the room, among which I ought not to forget a kind of safe or refrigerator, in which

Augustus pointed out to me a host of delicacies, both in the eating and drinking department.

He now pressed with his knuckles upon a certain spot of the carpet in one corner of the space just mentioned, letting me know that a portion of the flooring, about sixteen inches square, had been neatly cut out and again adjusted. As he pressed, this portion rose up at one end sufficiently to allow the passage of his finger beneath. In this manner he raised the mouth of the trap (to which the carpet was still fastened by tacks), and I found that it led into the after-hold. He next lit a small taper by means of a phosphorus match, and, placing the light in a dark lantern, descended with it through the opening, bidding me follow. I did so, and he then pulled the cover upon the hole, by means of a nail driven into the under side—the carpet, of course, resuming its original position on the floor of the state-room, and all traces of the aperture being concealed.

The taper gave out so feeble a ray that it was with the greatest difficulty I could grope my way through the confused mass of lumber among which I now found myself. By degrees, however, my eyes became accustomed to the gloom, and I proceeded with less trouble, holding on to the skirts of my friend's coat. He brought me, at length, after creeping and winding through innumerable narrow passages, to an iron-bound box, such as is used sometimes for packing fine earthenware. It was nearly four feet high, and full six long, but very narrow. Two large empty oil-casks lay on the top of it, and above these, again, a vast quantity of straw matting, piled up as high as the floor of the cabin. In every other direction around was wedged as closely as possible, even up to the ceiling, a complete chaos of almost every species of ship-furniture, together with a heterogeneous medley of crates, hampers, barrels, and bales, so that it seemed a matter no less than miraculous that we had discovered any passage at all to the box. I afterward found that Augustus had purposely arranged the stowage in his hold with a view to affording me a thorough concealment, having had only one assistant in the labor, a man not going out in the brig.

My companion now showed me that one of the ends of the box could be removed at pleasure. He slipped it aside and displayed the interior, at which I was excessive-

ly amused. A mattress from one of the cabin berths cov-
ered the whole of its bottom, and it contained almost
every article of mere comfort which could be crowded
into so small a space, allowing me, at the same time,
sufficient room for my accommodation, either in a sit-
ting position or lying at full length. Among other things,
there were some books, pen, ink, and paper, three blan-
kets, a large jug full of water, a keg of sea-biscuit, three
or four immense Bologna sausages, an enormous ham,
a cold leg of roast mutton, and half a dozen bottles of
cordials and liqueurs. I proceeded immediately to take
possession of my little apartment, and this with feelings of
higher satisfaction, I am sure, than any monarch ever
experienced upon entering a new palace. Augustus now
pointed out to me the method of fastening the open end
of the box, and then, holding the taper close to the deck,
showed me a piece of dark whipcord lying along it. This,
he said, extended from my hiding-place throughout all
the necessary windings among the lumber, to a nail
which was driven into the deck of the hold, immediately
beneath the trap-door leading into his state-room. By
means of this cord I should be enabled readily to trace
my way out without his guidance, provided any unlooked-
for accident should render such a step necessary. He now
took his departure, leaving with me the lantern, to-
gether with a copious supply of tapers and phosphorus,
and promising to pay me a visit as often as he could
contrive to do so without observation. This was on the
seventeenth of June.

I remained three days and nights (as nearly as I
could guess) in my hiding-place without getting out of it
at all, except twice for the purpose of stretching my limbs
by standing erect between two crates just opposite the
opening. During the whole period I saw nothing of Au-
gustus; but this occasioned me little uneasiness, as I
knew the brig was expected to put to sea every hour, and
in the bustle he would not easily find opportunities of
coming down to me. At length I heard the trap open and
shut, and presently he called in a low voice, asking if all
was well, and if there was anything I wanted. "Nothing,"
I replied: "I am as comfortable as can be; when will the
brig sail?" "She will be under weigh in less than half an
hour," he answered. "I came to let you know, and for
fear you should be uneasy at my absence. I shall not have

a chance of coming down again for some time—perhaps for three or four days more. All is going on right above-board. After I go up and close the trap, do you creep along by the whipcord to where the nail is driven in. You will find my watch there—it may be useful to you, as you have no daylight to keep time by. I suppose you can't tell how long you have been buried—only three days—this is the twentieth. I would bring the watch to your box, but am afraid of being missed." With this he went up.

In about an hour after he had gone I distinctly felt the brig in motion, and congratulated myself upon having at length fairly commenced a voyage. Satisfied with this idea, I determined to make my mind as easy as possible, and await the course of events until I should be permitted to exchange the box for the more roomy, although hardly more comfortable, accommodations of the cabin. My first care was to get the watch. Leaving the taper burning, I groped along in the dark, following the cord through windings innumerable, in some of which I discovered that, after toiling a long distance, I was brought back within a foot or two of a former position. At length I reached the nail, and securing the object of my journey, returned with it in safety. I now looked over the books which had been so thoughtfully provided, and selected the expedition of Lewis and Clark to the mouth of the Columbia. With this I amused myself for some time, when, growing sleepy, I extinguished the light with great care, and soon fell into a sound slumber.

Upon awaking I felt strangely confused in mind, and some time elapsed before I could bring to recollection all the various circumstances of my situation. By degrees, however, I remembered all. Striking a light, I looked at the watch; but it was run down, and there were, consequently, no means of determining how long I slept. My limbs were greatly cramped, and I was forced to relieve them by standing between the crates. Presently feeling an almost ravenous appetite, I bethought myself of the cold mutton, some of which I had eaten just before going to sleep, and found excellent. What was my astonishment in discovering it to be in a state of absolute putrefaction! This circumstance occasioned me great disquietude; for, connecting it with the disorder of mind I experienced upon awaking, I began to suppose that I must have slept

for an inordinately long period of time. The close atmosphere of the hold might have something to do with this, and might, in the end, be productive of the most serious results. My head ached excessively; I fancied that I drew every breath with difficulty; and, in short, I was oppressed with a multitude of gloomy feelings. Still I could not venture to make any disturbance by opening the trap or otherwise, and, having wound up the watch, contented myself as well as possible.

Throughout the whole of the next tedious twenty-four hours no person came to my relief, and I could not help accusing Augustus of the grossest inattention. What alarmed me chiefly was, that the water in my jug was reduced to about half a pint, and I was suffering much from thirst, having eaten freely of the Bologna sausages after the loss of my mutton. I became very uneasy, and could no longer take any interest in my books. I was overpowered, too, with a desire to sleep, yet trembled at the thought of indulging it, lest there might exist some pernicious influence, like that of burning charcoal, in the confined air of the hold. In the meantime the roll of the brig told me that we were far in the main ocean, and a dull humming sound, which reached my ears as if from an immense distance, convinced me no ordinary gale was blowing. I could not imagine a reason for the absence of Augustus. We were surely far enough advanced on our voyage to allow of my going up. Some accident might have happened to him—but I could think of none which would account for his suffering me to remain so long a prisoner, except, indeed, his having suddenly died or fallen overboard, and upon this idea I could not dwell with any degree of patience. It was possible that we had been baffled by head-winds, and were still in the near vicinity of Nantucket. This notion, however, I was forced to abandon; for such being the case, the brig must have frequently gone about; and I was entirely satisfied, from her continual inclination to the larboard, that she had been sailing all along with a steady breeze on her starboard quarter. Besides, granting that we were still in the neighborhood of the island, why should not Augustus have visited me and informed me of the circumstance? Pondering in this manner upon the difficulties of my solitary and cheerless condition, I resolved to wait yet another twenty-four hours, when, if no relief

were obtained, I would make my way to the trap, and endeavor either to hold a parley with my friend, or get at least a little fresh air through the opening, and a further supply of water from the state-room. While occupied with this thought, however, I fell, in spite of every exertion to the contrary, into a state of profound sleep, or rather stupor. My dreams were of the most terrific description. Every species of calamity and horror befell me. Among other miseries I was smothered to death between huge pillows, by demons of the most ghastly and ferocious aspect. Immense serpents held me in their embrace, and looked earnestly in my face with their fearfully shining eyes. Then deserts, limitless, and of the most forlorn and awe-inspiring character, spread themselves out before me. Immensely tall trunks of trees, gray and leafless, rose up in endless succession as far as the eye could reach. Their roots were concealed in widespreading morasses, whose dreary water lay intensely black, still, and altogether terrible, beneath. And the strange trees seemed endowed with a human vitality, and waving to and fro their skeleton arms, were crying to the silent waters for mercy, in the shrill and piercing accents of the most acute agony and despair. The scene changed; and I stood, naked and alone, amid the burning sand-plains of Zahara. At my feet lay crouched a fierce lion of the tropics. Suddenly his wild eyes opened and fell upon me. With a convulsive bound he sprang to his feet, and laid bare his horrible teeth. In another instant there burst from his red throat a roar like the thunder of the firmament, and I fell impetuously to the earth. Stifling in a paroxysm of terror, I at last found myself partially awake. My dream, then, was not all a dream. Now, at least, I was in possession of my senses. The paws of some huge and real monster were pressing heavily upon my bosom—his hot breath was in my ear —and his white and ghastly fangs were gleaming upon me through the gloom.

Had a thousand lives hung upon the movement of a limb or the utterance of a syllable, I could have neither stirred nor spoken. The beast, whatever it was, retained his position without attempting any immediate violence, while I lay in an utterly helpless, and, I fancied, a dying condition beneath him. I felt that my powers of body and mind were fast leaving me—in a word, that I was

perishing, and perishing of sheer fright. My brain swam —I grew deadly sick—my vision failed—even the glaring eyeballs above me grew dim. Making a last strong effort, I at length breathed a faint ejaculation to God, and resigned myself to die. The sound of my voice seemed to arouse all the latent fury of the animal. He precipitated himself at full length upon my body; but what was my astonishment, when, with a long and low whine, he commenced licking my face and hands with the greatest eagerness, and with the most extravagant demonstration of affection and joy! I was bewildered, utterly lost in amazement—but I could not forget the peculiar whine of my Newfoundland dog Tiger, and the odd manner of his caresses I well knew. It was he. I experienced a sudden rush of blood to my temples—a giddy and overpowering sense of deliverance and reanimation. I rose hurriedly from the mattress upon which I had been lying, and, throwing myself upon the neck of my faithful follower and friend, relieved the long oppression of my bosom in a flood of the most passionate tears.

As upon a former occasion my conceptions were in a state of the greatest indistinctness and confusion after leaving the mattress. For a long time I found it nearly impossible to connect any ideas; but, by very slow degrees, my thinking faculties returned, and I again called to memory the several incidents of my condition. For the presence of Tiger I tried in vain to account; and after busying myself with a thousand different conjectures respecting him, was forced to content myself with rejoicing that he was with me to share my dreary solitude, and render me comfort by his caresses. Most people love their dogs, but for Tiger I had an affection far more ardent than common; and never, certainly, did any creature more truly deserve it. For seven years he had been my inseparable companion, and in a multitude of instances had given evidence of all the noble qualities for which we value the animal. I had rescued him, when a puppy, from the clutches of a malignant little villain in Nantucket, who was leading him, with a rope around his neck, to the water; and the grown dog repaid the obligation, about three years afterward, by saving me from the bludgeon of a street robber.

Getting now hold of the watch, I found, upon applying it to my ear, that it had again run down; but at this I

was not at all surprised, being convinced, from the
peculiar state of my feelings, that I had slept, as before,
for a very long period of time; how long, it was of course
impossible to say. I was burning up with fever, and my
thirst was almost intolerable. I felt about the box for my
little remaining supply of water, for I had no light, the
taper having burnt to the socket of the lantern, and the
phosphorus-box not coming readily to hand. Upon finding
the jug, however, I discovered it to be empty—Tiger, no
doubt, having been tempted to drink it, as well as to
devour the remnant of mutton, the bone of which lay,
well picked, by the opening of the box. The spoiled meat
I could well spare but my heart sank as I thought of
the water. I was feeble in the extreme, so much so that I
shook all over, as with an ague, at the slightest move-
ment or exertion. To add to my troubles, the brig was
pitching and rolling with great violence, and the oil-
casks which lay upon my box were in momentary danger
of falling down, so as to block up the only way of ingress
or egress. I felt, also, terrible sufferings from sea-sickness.
These considerations determined me to make my way, at
all hazards, to the trap, and obtain immediate relief,
before I should be incapacitated from doing so alto-
gether. Having come to this resolve, I again felt about for
the phosphorus-box and tapers. The former I found after
some little trouble; but, not discovering the tapers as
soon as I had expected (for I remembered very nearly
the spot in which I had placed them), I gave up the
search for the present, and bidding Tiger lie quiet, began
at once my journey toward the trap.

In this attempt my great feebleness became more than
ever apparent. It was with the utmost difficulty I could
crawl along at all, and very frequently my limbs sank
suddenly from beneath me; when, falling prostrate on
my face, I would remain for some minutes in a state
bordering on insensibility. Still I struggled forward by
slow degrees, dreading every moment that I should swoon
amid the narrow and intricate windings of the lumber, in
which event I had nothing but death to expect as the
result. At length, upon making a push forward with all
the energy I could command, I struck my forehead
violently against the sharp corner of an iron-bound
crate. The accident only stunned me for a few moments;
but I found, to my inexpressible grief, that the quick

and violent roll of the vessel had thrown the crate entirely across my path, so as effectually to block up the passage. With my utmost exertions I could not move it a single inch from its position, it being closely wedged in among the surrounding boxes and ship-furniture. It became necessary, therefore, enfeebled as I was, either to leave the guidance of the whipcord and seek out a new passage, or to climb over the obstacle, and resume the path on the other side. The former alternative presented too many difficulties and dangers to be thought of without a shudder. In my present weak state of both mind and body, I should infallibly lose my way if I attempted it, and perish miserably amid the dismal and disgusting labyrinths of the hold. I proceeded, therefore, without hesitation, to summon up all my remaining strength and fortitude, and endeavor, as I best might, to clamber over the crate.

Upon standing erect, with this end in view, I found the undertaking even a more serious task than my fears had led me to imagine. On each side of the narrow passage arose a complete wall of various heavy lumber, which the least blunder on my part might be the means of bringing down upon my head; or, if this accident did not occur, the path might be effectually blocked up against my return by the descending mass, as it was in front by the obstacle there. The crate itself was a long and unwieldy box, upon which no foothold could be obtained. In vain I attempted, by every means in my power, to reach the top, with the hope of being thus enabled to draw myself up. Had I succeeded in reaching it, it is certain that my strength would have proved utterly inadequate to the task of getting over, and it was better in every respect that I failed. At length, in a desperate effort to force the crate from its ground, I felt a strong vibration in the side next me. I thrust my hand eagerly to the edge of the planks, and found that a very large one was loose. With my pocket-knife, which, luckily, I had with me, I succeeded, after great labor, in prying it entirely off; and getting through the aperture, discovered, to my exceeding joy, that there were no boards on the opposite side—in other words, that the top was wanting, it being the bottom through which I had forced my way. I now met with no important difficulty in proceeding along the line until I finally reached the nail. With a beating heart I

stood erect, and with a gentle touch pressed against the cover of the trap. It did not rise as soon as I had expected, and I pressed it with somewhat more determination, still dreading lest some other person than Augustus might be in his state-room. The door, however, to my astonishment, remained steady, and I became somewhat uneasy, for I knew that it had formerly required but little or no effort to remove it. I pushed it strongly—it was nevertheless firm; with all my strength—it still did not give way: with rage, with fury, with despair—it set at defiance my utmost efforts; and it was evident, from the unyielding nature of the resistance, that the hole had either been discovered and effectually nailed up, or that some immense weight had been placed upon it, which it was useless to think of removing.

My sensations were those of extreme horror and dismay. In vain I attempted to reason on the probable cause of my being thus entombed. I could summon up no connected chain of reflection, and, sinking on the floor, gave way, unresistingly, to the most gloomy imaginings, in which the dreadful deaths of thirst, famine, suffocation and premature interment crowded upon me as the prominent disasters to be encountered. At length there returned to me some portion of presence of mind. I arose, and felt with my fingers for the seams or cracks of the aperture. Having found them, I examined them closely to ascertain if they emitted any light from the state-room; but none was visible. I then forced the blade of my pen-knife through them, until I met with some hard obstacle. Scraping against it, I discovered it to be a solid mass of iron, which, from its peculiar wavy feel as I passed the blade along it, I concluded to be a chain-cable. The only course now left me was to retrace my way to the box, and there either yield to my sad fate, or try so to tranquilize my mind as to admit of my arranging some plan of escape. I immediately set about the attempt, and succeeded, after innumerable difficulties, in getting back. As I sank, utterly exhausted, upon the mattress, Tiger threw himself at full length by my side, and seemed as if desirous, by his caresses, of consoling me in my troubles, and urging me to bear them with fortitude.

The singularity of his behavior at length forcibly arrested my attention. After licking my face and hands for

some minutes, he would suddenly cease doing so, and utter a low whine. Upon reaching out my hand toward him, I then invariably found him lying on his back, with his paws uplifted. This conduct, so frequently repeated, appeared strange, and I could in no manner account for it. As the dog seemed distressed, I concluded that he had received some injury; and, taking his paws in my hands, I examined them one by one, but found no signs of any hurt. I then supposed him hungry, and gave him a large piece of ham, which he devoured with avidity—afterward, however, resuming his extraordinary manœuvres. I now imagined that he was suffering, like myself, the torments of thirst, and was about adopting this conclusion as the true one, when the idea occurred to me that I had as yet only examined his paws, and that there might possibly be a wound upon some portion of his body or head. The latter I felt carefully over, but found nothing. On passing my hand, however, along his back, I perceived a slight erection of the hair extending completely across it. Probing this with my finger, I discovered a string and tracing it up, found that it encircled the whole body. Upon a close scrutiny, I came across a small slip of what had the feeling of letter paper, through which the string had been fastened in such a manner as to bring it immediately beneath the left shoulder of the animal.

CHAPTER III

THE thought instantly occurred to me that the paper was a note from Augustus, and that some unaccountable accident having happened to prevent his relieving me from my dungeon, he had devised this method of acquainting me with the true state of affairs. Trembling with eagerness, I now commenced another search for my phosphorus matches and tapers. I had a confused recollection of having put them carefully away just before falling asleep; and, indeed, previously to my last journey to the trap, I had been able to remember the exact spot where I had deposited them. But now I endeavored in vain to call it to mind, and busied myself for a full hour in a fruitless and vexatious search for the missing articles; never, surely, was there a more tantalizing state of anxiety and suspense. At length, while groping about,

with my head close to the ballast, near the opening of the box, and outside of it, I perceived a faint glimmering of light in the direction of the steerage. Greatly surprised, I endeavored to make my way toward it, as it appeared to be but a few feet from my position. Scarcely had I moved with this intention, when I lost sight of the glimmer entirely, and, before I could bring it into view again, was obliged to feel along by the box until I had exactly resumed my original situation. Now, moving my head with caution to and fro, I found that, by proceeding slowly, with great care, in an opposite direction to that in which I had at first started, I was enabled to draw near the light, still keeping it in view. Presently I came directly upon it (having squeezed my way through innumerable narrow windings), and found that it proceeded from some fragments of my matches lying in an empty barrel turned upon its side. I was wondering how they came in such a place, when my hand fell upon two or three pieces of taper-wax, which had been evidently mumbled by the dog. I concluded at once that he had devoured the whole of my supply of candles, and I felt hopeless of being ever able to read the note of Augustus. The small remnants of the wax were so smashed up among other rubbish in the barrel, that I despaired of deriving any service from them, and left them as they were. The phosphorus, of which there was only a speck or two, I gathered up as well as I could, and returned with it, after much difficulty, to my box, where Tiger had all the while remained.

What to do next I could not tell. The hold was so intensely dark that I could not see my hand, however close I would hold it to my face. The white slip of paper could barely be discerned, and not even that when I looked at it directly; by turning the exterior portions of the retina toward it—that is to say, by surveying it slightly askance, I found that it became in some measure perceptible. Thus the gloom of my prison may be imagined, and the note of my friend, if indeed it were a note from him, seemed only likely to throw me into further trouble, by disquieting to no purpose my already enfeebled and agitated mind. In vain I revolved in my brain a multitude of absurd expedients for procuring light—such expedients precisely as a man in the perturbed sleep occasioned by opium would be apt to fall

upon for a similar purpose—each and all of which appear by turns to the dreamer the most reasonable and the most preposterous of conceptions, just as the reasoning or imaginative faculties flicker, alternately, one above the other. At last an idea occurred to me which seemed rational, and which gave me cause to wonder, very justly, that I had not entertained it before. I placed the slip of paper on the back of a book, and, collecting the fragments of the phosphorus matches which I had brought from the barrel, laid them together upon the paper. I then, with the palm of my hand, rubbed the whole over quickly, yet steadily. A clear light diffused itself immediately throughout the whole surface; and had there been any writing upon it, I should not have experienced the least difficulty, I am sure, in reading it. Not a syllable was there, however—nothing but a dreary and unsatisfactory blank; the illumination died away in a few seconds, and my heart died away within me as it went.

I have before stated more than once that my intellect, for some period prior to this, had been in a condition nearly bordering on idiocy. There were, to be sure, momentary intervals of perfect sanity, and, now and then, even of energy; but these were few. It must be remembered that I had been, for many days certainly, inhaling the almost pestilential atmosphere of a close hole in a whaling vessel, and for a long portion of that time but scantily supplied with water. For the last fourteen or fifteen hours I had none—nor had I slept during that time. Salt provisions of the most exciting kind had been my chief, and, indeed, since the loss of the mutton, my only supply of food, with the exception of the sea-biscuit; and these latter were utterly useless to me, as they were too dry and hard to be swallowed in the swollen and parched condition of my throat. I was now in a high state of fever, and in every respect exceedingly ill. This will account for the fact that many miserable hours of despondency elapsed after my last adventure with the phosphorus, before the thought suggested itself that I had examined only one side of the paper. I shall not attempt to describe my feelings of rage (for I believe I was more angry than any thing else) when the egregious oversight I had committed flashed suddenly upon my perception. The blunder itself would have been unimportant,

had not my own folly and impetuosity rendered it otherwise—in my disappointment at not finding some words upon the slip, I had childishly torn it in pieces and thrown it away, it was impossible to say where.

From the worst part of this dilemma I was relieved by the sagacity of Tiger. Having got, after a long search, a small piece of the note, I put it to the dog's nose, and endeavored to make him understand that he must bring me the rest of it. To my astonishment (for I had taught him none of the usual tricks for which his breed are famous), he seemed to enter at once into my meaning, and, rummaging about for a few moments, soon found another considerable portion. Bringing me this, he paused awhile, and, rubbing his nose against my hand, appeared to be waiting for my approval of what he had done. I patted him on the head, when he immediately made off again. It was now some minutes before he came back—but when he did come, he brought with him a large slip, which proved to be all the paper missing—it having been torn, it seems, only into three pieces. Luckily, I had no trouble in finding what few fragments of the phosphorus were left—being guided by the indistinct glow one or two of the particles still emitted. My difficulties had taught me the necessity of caution, and I now took time to reflect upon what I was about to do. It was very probable, I considered, that some words were written upon that side of the paper which had not been examined— but which side was that? Fitting the pieces together gave me no clue in this respect, although it assured me that the words (if there were any) would be found all on one side, and connected in a proper manner, as written. There was the greater necessity of ascertaining the point in question beyond a doubt, as the phosphorus remaining would be altogether insufficient for a third attempt, should I fail in the one I was now about to make. I placed the paper on a book as before, and sat for some minutes thoughtfully revolving the matter over in my mind. At last I thought it barely possible that the written side might have some unevenness on its surface, which a delicate sense of feeling might enable me to detect. I determined to make the experiment, and passed my finger very carefully over the side which first presented itself. Nothing, however, was perceptible, and I turned the paper, adjusting it on the book. I now again car-

ried my forefinger cautiously along, when I was aware of
an exceedingly slight, but still discernible glow, which
followed as it proceeded. This, I knew, must arise from
some very minute remaining particles of the phosphorus
with which I had covered the paper in my previous at-
tempt. The other, or under side, then, was that on which
lay the writing, if writing there should finally prove to be.
Again I turned the note, and went to work as I had
previously done. Having rubbed in the phosphorus, a
brilliancy ensued as before—but this time several lines
of MS. in a large hand, and apparently in red ink, be-
came distinctly visible. The glimmer, although sufficiently
bright, was but momentary. Still, had I not been too
greatly excited, there would have been ample time enough
for me to peruse the whole three sentences before me—
for I saw there were three. In my anxiety, however, to
read all at once, I succeeded only in reading the seven
concluding words, which thus appeared—*"blood—your
life depends upon lying close."*

Had I been able to ascertain the entire contents of the
note—the full meaning of the admonition which my
friend had thus attempted to convey, that admonition,
even although it should have revealed a story of dis-
aster the most unspeakable, could not, I am firmly con-
vinced, have imbued my mind with one tithe of the
harrowing and yet indefinable horror with which I was
inspired by the fragmentary warning thus received. And
"blood," too, that word of all words—so rife at all times
with mystery, and suffering, and terror—how trebly full
of import did it now appear—how chilly and heavily
(disjointed, as it thus was, from any foregoing words
to qualify or render it distinct) did its vague syllables fall
amid the deep gloom of my prison, into the innermost
recesses of my soul!

Augustus had, undoubtedly, good reasons for wishing
me to remain concealed, and I formed a thousand sur-
mises as to what they could be—but I could think of
nothing affording a satisfactory solution of the mystery.
Just after returning from my last journey to the trap,
and before my attention had been otherwise directed by
the singular conduct of Tiger, I had come to the resolu-
tion of making myself heard at all events by those on
board, or, if I could not succeed in this directly, of trying
to cut my way through the orlop deck. The half certainty

which I felt of being able to accomplish one of these two purposes in the last emergency, had given me courage (which I should not otherwise have had) to endure the evils of my situation. The few words I had been able to read, however, had cut me off from these final resources, and I now, for the first time, felt all the misery of my fate. In a paroxysm of despair I threw myself again upon the mattress, where, for about the period of a day and night, I lay in a kind of stupor, relieved only by momentary intervals of reason and recollection.

At length I once more arose, and busied myself in reflection upon the horrors which encompassed me. For another twenty-four hours it was barely possible that I might exist without water—for a longer time I could not do so. During the first portion of my imprisonment I had made free use of the cordials with which Augustus had supplied me, but they only served to excite fever, without in the least degree assuaging my thirst. I had now only about a gill left, and this was of a species of strong peach liqueur at which my stomach revolted. The sausages were entirely consumed; of the ham nothing remained but a small piece of the skin; and all the biscuit, except a few fragments of one, had been eaten by Tiger. To add to my troubles, I found that my headache was increasing momentarily, and with it the species of delirium which had distressed me more or less since my first falling asleep. For some hours past it had been with the greatest difficulty I could breathe at all, and now each attempt at so doing was attended with the most depressing spasmodic action of the chest. But there was still another and very different source of disquietude, and one, indeed, whose harassing terrors had been the chief means of arousing me to exertion from my stupor on the mattress. It arose from the demeanor of the dog.

I first observed an alteration in his conduct while rubbing in the phosphorus on the paper in my last attempt. As I rubbed, he ran his nose against my hand with a slight snarl; but I was too greatly excited at the time to pay much attention to the circumstance. Soon afterward, it will be remembered, I threw myself on the mattress, and fell into a species of lethargy. Presently I became aware of a singular hissing sound close at my ears, and discovered it to proceed from Tiger, who was panting

and wheezing in a state of the greatest apparent excite-
ment, his eyeballs flashing fiercely through the gloom. I
spoke to him, when he replied with a low growl, and
then remained quiet. Presently I relapsed into my stupor,
from which I was again awakened in a similar manner.
This was repeated three or four times, until finally his be-
havior inspired me with so great a degree of fear, that
I became fully aroused. He was now lying close by the
door of the box, snarling fearfully, although in a kind of
undertone, and grinding his teeth as if strongly convulsed.
I had no doubt whatever that the want of water or the
confined atmosphere of the hold had driven him mad,
and I was at a loss what course to pursue. I could not
endure the thought of killing him, yet it seemed absolute-
ly necessary for my own safety. I could distinctly per-
ceive his eyes fastened upon me with an expression of
the most deadly animosity, and I expected every instant
that he would attack me. At last I could endure my
terrible situation no longer, and determined to make my
way from the box at all hazards, and dispatch him, if
his opposition should render it necessary for me to do
so. To get out, I had to pass directly over his body, and
he already seemed to anticipate my design—raising him-
self upon his forelegs (as I perceived by the altered posi-
tion of his eyes), and displayed the whole of his white
fangs, which were easily discernible. I took the remains
of the ham-skin, and the bottle containing the liqueur,
and secured them about my person, together with a large
carving-knife which Augustus had left me—then, folding
my cloak around me as closely as possible, I made a
movement toward the mouth of the box. No sooner did
I do this, than the dog sprang with a loud growl toward
my throat. The whole weight of his body struck me on
the right shoulder, and I fell violently to the left, while
the enraged animal passed entirely over me. I had fallen
upon my knees, with my head buried among the blankets,
and these protected me from a second furious assault,
during which I felt the sharp teeth pressing vigorously
upon the woollen which enveloped my neck—yet, luckily,
without being able to penetrate all the folds. I was now
beneath the dog, and a few moments would place me
completely in his power. Despair gave me strength, and
I rose boldly up, shaking him from me by main force,
and dragging with me the blankets from the mattress.

These I now threw over him, and before he could extricate himself, I had got through the door and closed it effectually against his pursuit. In this struggle, however, I had been forced to drop the morsel of ham-skin, and I now found my whole stock of provisions reduced to a single gill of liqueur. As this reflection crossed my mind, I felt myself actuated by one of those fits of perverseness which might be supposed to influence a spoiled child in similar circumstances, and, raising the bottle to my lips, I drained it to the last drop, and dashed it furiously upon the floor.

Scarcely had the echo of the crash died away, when I heard my name pronounced in an eager but subdued voice, issuing from the direction of the steerage. So unexpected was any thing of the kind, and so intense was the emotion excited within me by the sound, that I endeavored in vain to reply. My powers of speech totally failed, and in an agony of terror lest my friend should conclude me dead, and return without attempting to reach me, I stood up between the crates near the door of the box, trembling convulsively, and gasping and struggling for utterance. Had a thousand words depended upon a syllable, I could not have spoken it. There was a slight movement now audible among the lumber somewhere forward of my station. The sound presently grew less distinct, then again less so, and still less. Shall I ever forget my feelings at this moment? He was going—my friend, my companion, from whom I had a right to expect so much—he was going—he would abandon me—he was gone! He would leave me to perish miserably, to expire in the most horrible and loathsome of dungeons—and one word, one little syllable, would save me—yet that single syllable I could not utter! I felt, I am sure, more than ten thousand times the agonies of death itself. My brain reeled, and I fell, deadly sick, against the end of the box.

As I fell, the carving-knife was shaken out from the waist-band of my pantaloons, and dropped with a rattling sound to the floor. Never did any strain of the richest melody come so sweetly to my ears! With the intensest anxiety I listened to ascertain the effect of the noise upon Augustus—for I knew that the person who called my name could be no one but himself. All was silent for some moments. At length I again heard the

word *"Arthur!"* repeated in a low tone, and one full of
hesitation. Reviving hope loosened at once my powers of
speech, and I now screamed at the top of my voice,
"Augustus! oh, Augustus!" "Hush, for God's sake be
silent!" he replied, in a voice trembling with agitation; "I
will be with you immediately—as soon as I can make
my way through the hold." For a long time I heard him
moving among the lumber, and every moment seemed
to me an age. At length I felt his hand upon my shoul-
der, and he placed, at the same moment, a bottle of
water to my lips. Those only who have been suddenly
redeemed from the jaws of the tomb, or who have
known the insufferable torments of thirst under circum-
stances as aggravated as those which encompassed me in
my dreary prison, can form any idea of the unutterable
transports which that one long draught of the richest of
all physical luxuries afforded.

When I had in some degree satisfied my thirst, Augus-
tus produced from his pocket three or four boiled po-
tatoes, which I devoured with the greatest avidity. He
had brought with him a light in a dark lantern, and the
grateful rays afforded me scarcely less comfort than
the food and drink. But I was impatient to learn the
cause of his protracted absence, and he proceeded to
recount what had happened on board during my incar-
ceration.

CHAPTER IV

THE brig put to sea, as I had supposed, in about an hour
after he had left the watch. This was on the twentieth of
June. It will be remembered that I had been in the hold
for three days; and, during this period, there was so con-
stant a bustle on board, and so much running to and
fro, especially in the cabin and state-rooms, that he
had had no chance of visiting me without the risk of
having the secret of the trap discovered. When at
length he did come, I had assured him that I was doing
as well as possible; and, therefore, for the two next
days he felt but little uneasiness on my account—still,
however, watching an opportunity of going down. It
was not *until the fourth day* that he found one. Several
times during this interval he had made up his mind to let

his father know of the adventure, and have me come up at once; but we were still within reaching distance of Nantucket, and it was doubtful, from some expressions which had escaped Captain Barnard, whether he would not immediately put back if he discovered me to be on board. Besides, upon thinking the matter over, Augustus, so he told me, could not imagine that I was in immediate want, or that I would hesitate, in such case, to make myself heard at the trap. When, therefore he considered every thing, he concluded to let me stay until he could meet with an opportunity of visiting me unobserved. This, as I said before, did not occur until the fourth day after his bringing me the watch, and the seventh since I had first entered the hold. He then went down without taking with him any water or provisions, intending in the first place merely to call my attention, and get me to come from the box to the trap—when he would go up to the state-room and thence hand me down a supply. When he descended for this purpose he found that I was asleep, for it seems that I was snoring very loudly. From all the calculations I can make on the subject, this must have been the slumber into which I fell just after my return from the trap with the watch, and which, consequently, must have lasted *for more than three entire days and nights* at the very least. Latterly, I have had reason both from my own experience and the assurance of others, to be acquainted with the strong soporific effects of the stench arising from old fish-oil when closely confined; and when I think of the condition of the hold in which I was imprisoned, and the long period during which the brig had been used as a whaling vessel, I am more inclined to wonder that I awoke at all, after once falling asleep, than that I should have slept uninterruptedly for the period specified above.

Augustus called to me at first in a low voice and without closing the trap—but I made him no reply. He then shut the trap, and spoke to me in a louder, and finally in a very loud tone—still I continued to snore. He was now at a loss what to do. It would take him some time to make his way through the lumber to my box, and in the meanwhile his absence would be noticed by Captain Barnard, who had occasion for his services every minute, in arranging and copying papers connected with the business of the voyage. He determined, therefore,

upon reflection, to ascend, and await another opportunity
of visiting me. He was the more easily induced to this
resolve, as my slumber appeared to be of the most tran-
quil nature, and he could not suppose that I had under-
gone any inconvenience from my incarceration. He had
just made up his mind on these points when his atten-
tion was arrested by an unusual bustle, the sound of
which proceeded apparently from the cabin. He sprang
through the trap as quickly as possible, closed it, and
threw open the door of his state-room. No sooner had
he put his foot over the threshold than a pistol flashed
in his face, and he was knocked down, at the same mo-
ment, by a blow from a handspike.

A strong hand held him on the cabin floor, with a
tight grasp upon his throat; still he was able to see what
was going on around him. His father was tied hand and
foot, and lying along the steps of the companion-way,
with his head down, and a deep wound in the forehead,
from which the blood was flowing in a continued stream.
He spoke not a word, and was apparently dying. Over
him stood the first mate, eyeing him with an expression
of fiendish derision, and deliberately searching his pock-
ets, from which he presently drew forth a large wallet
and a chronometer. Seven of the crew (among whom
was the cook, a negro) were rummaging the state-rooms
on the larboard for arms, where they soon equipped
themselves with muskets and ammunition. Besides Au-
gustus and Captain Barnard, there were nine men alto-
gether in the cabin, and these among the most ruffianly
of the brig's company. The villains now went upon deck,
taking my friend with them, after having secured his
arms behind his back. They proceeded straight to the
forecastle, which was fastened down—two of the muti-
neers standing by it with axes—two also at the main
hatch. The mate called out in a loud voice: "Do you hear
there below? tumble up with you, one by one—now,
mark that—and no grumbling!" It was some minutes be-
fore any one appeared;—at last an Englishman, who had
shipped as a raw hand, came up, weeping piteously, and
entreating the mate, in the most humble manner, to
spare his life. The only reply was a blow on the forehead
from an axe. The poor fellow fell to the deck without a
groan, and the black cook lifted him up in his arms as he
would a child, and tossed him deliberately into the sea.

Hearing the blow and the plunge of the body, the men below could now be induced to venture on deck neither by threats nor promises, until a proposition was made to smoke them out. A general rush then ensued, and for a moment it seemed possible that the brig might be re-taken. The mutineers, however, succeeded at last in clos-ing the forecastle effectually before more than six of their opponents could get up. These six, finding them-selves so greatly outnumbered and without arms, sub-mitted after a brief struggle. The mate gave them fair words—no doubt with a view of inducing those below to yield, for they had no difficulty in hearing all that was said on deck. The result proved his sagacity, no less than his diabolical villainy. All in the forecastle presently signified their intention of submitting, and, ascending one by one, were pinioned and then thrown on their backs, together with the first six—there being, in all of the crew who were not concerned in the mutiny, twenty-seven.

A scene of the most horrible butchery ensued. The bound seamen were dragged to the gangway. Here the cook stood with an axe, striking each victim on the head as he was forced over the side of the vessel by the other mutineers. In this manner twenty-two perished, and Au-gustus had given himself up for lost, expecting every moment his own turn to come next. But it seemed that the villains were now either weary, or in some measure disgusted with their bloody labor; for the four remaining prisoners, together with my friend, who had been thrown on the deck with the rest, were respited while the mate sent below for rum, and the whole murderous party held a drunken carouse, which lasted until sunset. They now fell to disputing in regard to the fate of the survivors, who lay not more than four paces off, and could dis-tinguish every word said. Upon some of the mutineers the liquor appeared to have a softening effect, for sev-eral voices were heard in favor of releasing the captives altogether, on condition of joining the mutiny and shar-ing the profits. The black cook, however (who in all re-spects was a perfect demon, and who seemed to exert as much influence, if not more, than the mate himself), would listen to no proposition of the kind, and rose re-peatedly for the purpose of resuming his work at the gangway. Fortunately he was so far overcome by in-

toxication as to be easily restrained by the less blood-thirsty of the party, among whom was a line-manager, who went by the name of Dirk Peters. This man was the son of an Indian woman of the tribe of Upsarokas, who live among the fastnesses of the Black Hills, near the source of the Missouri. His father was a fur-trader, I believe, or at least connected in some manner with the Indian trading-posts on Lewis river. Peters himself was one of the most ferocious-looking men I ever beheld. He was short in stature, not more than four feet eight inches high, but his limbs were of Herculean mould. His hands, especially, were so enormously thick and broad as hardly to retain a human shape. His arms, as well as legs, were *bowed* in the most singular manner, and appeared to possess no flexibility whatever. His head was equally deformed, being of immense size, with an indentation on the crown (like that on the head of most negroes), and entirely bald. To conceal this latter deficiency, which did not proceed from old age, he usually wore a wig formed of any hair-like material which presented itself —occasionally the skin of a Spanish dog or American grizzly bear. At the time spoken of, he had on a por-tion of one of these bear-skins; and it added no little to the natural ferocity of his countenance, which betook of the Upsaroka character. The mouth extended nearly from ear to ear; his lips were thin, and seemed, like some other portions of his frame, to be devoid of natural pliancy, so that the ruling expression never varied under the influence of any emotion whatever. This ruling ex-pression may be conceived when it is considered that the teeth were exceedingly long and protruding, and never even partially covered, in any instance, by the lips. To pass this man with a casual glance, one might imagine him to be convulsed with laughter; but a second look would induce a shuddering acknowledgment, that if such an expression were indicative of merriment, the merri-ment must be that of a demon. Of this singular being many anecdotes were prevalent among the seafaring men of Nantucket. These anecdotes went to prove his prodigious strength when under excitement, and some of them had given rise to a doubt of his sanity. But on board the Grampus, it seems, he was regarded, at the time of the mutiny, with feelings more of derision than of any thing else. I have been thus particular in speaking

of Dirk Peters, because, ferocious as he appeared, he proved the main instrument in preserving the life of Augustus, and because I shall have frequent occasion to mention him hereafter in the course of my narrative—a narrative, let me here say, which, in its later portions, will be found to include incidents of a nature so entirely out of the range of human experience, and for this reason so far beyond the limits of human credulity, that I proceed in utter hopelessness of obtaining credence for all that I shall tell, yet confidently trusting in time and progressing science to verify some of the most important and most improbable of my statements.

After much indecision and two or three violent quarrels, it was determined at last that all the prisoners (with the exception of Augustus, whom Peters insisted in a jocular manner upon keeping as his clerk) should be set adrift in one of the smallest whale-boats. The mate went down into the cabin to see if Captain Barnard was still living—for, it will be remembered, he was left below when the mutineers came up. Presently the two made their appearance, the captain pale as death, but somewhat recovered from the effects of his wound. He spoke to the men in a voice hardly articulate, entreated them not to set him adrift, but to return to their duty, and promising to land them wherever they chose, and to take no steps for bringing them to justice. He might as well have spoken to the winds. Two of the ruffians seized him by the arms and hurled him over the brig's side into the boat, which had been lowered while the mate went below. The four men who were lying on the deck were then untied and ordered to follow, which they did without attempting any resistance—Augustus being still left in his painful position, although he struggled and prayed only for the poor satisfaction of being permitted to bid his father farewell. A handful of sea-biscuits and a jug of water were now handed down; but neither mast, sail, oar, nor compass. The boat was towed astern for a few minutes, during which the mutineers held another consultation—it was then finally cast adrift. By this time night had come on—there was neither moon nor stars visible—and a short and ugly sea was running, although there was no great deal of wind. The boat was instantly out of sight, and little hope could be entertained for the unfortunate sufferers who were in it. This

event happened, however, in latitude 35° 30′ north, longitude 61° 20′ west, and consequently at no very great distance from the Bermuda Islands. Augustus therefore endeavored to console himself with the idea that the boat might either succeed in reaching the land, or come sufficiently near to be fallen in with by vessels off the coast.

All sail was now put upon the brig, and she continued her original course to the southwest—the mutineers being bent upon some piratical expedition, in which, from all that could be understood, a ship was to be intercepted on her way from the Cape Verd Islands to Porto Rico. No attention was paid to Augustus, who was untied and suffered to go about anywhere forward of the cabin companion-way. Dirk Peters treated him with some degree of kindness, and on one occasion saved him from the brutality of the cook. His situation was still one of the most precarious, as the men were continually intoxicated, and there was no relying upon their continued good-humor or carelessness in regard to himself. His anxiety on my account he represented, however, as the most distressing result of his condition; and, indeed, I had never reason to doubt the sincerity of his friendship. More than once he had resolved to acquaint the mutineers with the secret of my being on board, but was restrained from so doing, partly through recollection of the atrocities he had already beheld, and partly through a hope of being able soon to bring me relief. For the latter purpose he was constantly on the watch; but, in spite of the most constant vigilance, three days elapsed after the boat was cut adrift before any chance occurred. At length, on the night of the third day, there came on a heavy blow from the eastward, and all hands were called up to take in sail. During the confusion which ensued, he made his way below unobserved, and into the state-room. What was his grief and horror in discovering that the latter had been rendered a place of deposit for a variety of sea-stores and ship-furniture, and that several fathoms of old chain-cable, which had been stowed away beneath the companion-ladder, had been dragged thence to make room for a chest, and were now lying immediately upon the trap! To remove it without discovery was impossible, and he returned on deck as quickly as he could. As he came up, the mate seized him by the throat,

and demanding what he had been doing in the cabin, was about flinging him over the larboard bulwark, when his life was again preserved through the interference of Dirk Peters. Augustus was now put in handcuffs (of which there were several pairs on board), and his feet lashed tightly together. He was then taken into the steerage, and thrown into a lower berth next to the forecastle bulkheads, with the assurance that he should never put his foot on deck again "until the brig was no longer a brig." This was the expression of the cook, who threw him into the berth—it is hardly possible to say what precise meaning was intended by the phrase. The whole affair, however, proved the ultimate means of my relief, as will presently appear.

<center>CHAPTER V</center>

For some minutes after the cook had left the forecastle, Augustus abandoned himself to despair, never hoping to leave the berth alive. He now came to the resolution of acquainting the first of the men who should come down with my situation, thinking it better to let me take my chance with the mutineers than perish of thirst in the hold—for it had been ten days since I was first imprisoned, and my jug of water was not a plentiful supply even for four. As he was thinking on this subject, the idea came all at once into his head that it might be possible to communicate with me by way of the main hold. In any other circumstances, the difficulty and hazard of the undertaking would have prevented him from attempting it; but now he had, at all events, little prospect of life, and consequently little to lose; he bent his whole mind, therefore, upon the task.

His handcuffs were the first consideration. At first he saw no method of removing them, and feared that he should thus be baffled in the very outset; but upon a closer scrutiny he discovered that the irons could be slipped off and on at pleasure, with very little effort or inconvenience, merely by squeezing his hands through them, —this species of manacle being altogether ineffectual in confining young persons, in whom the smaller bones readily yield to pressure. He now untied his feet, and, leaving the cord in such a manner that it could easily

be readjusted in the event of any person's coming down, proceeded to examine the bulkhead where it joined the berth. The partition there was of soft pine board, an inch thick, and he saw that he should have little trouble in cutting his way through. A voice was now heard at the forecastle companion-way, and he had just time to put his right hand into its handcuff (the left had not been removed) and to draw the rope in a slipknot around his ankle, when Dirk Peters came below, followed by Tiger, who immediately leaped into the berth and lay down. The dog had been brought on board by Augustus, who knew my attachment to the animal, and thought it would give me pleasure to have him with me during the voyage. He went up to our house for him immediately after first taking me into the hold, but did not think of mentioning the circumstance upon his bringing the watch. Since the mutiny, Augustus had not seen him before his appearance with Dirk Peters, and had given him up for lost, supposing him to have been thrown overboard by some of the malignant villains belonging to the mate's gang. It appeared afterward that he had crawled into a hole beneath a whaleboat, from which, not having room to turn round, he could not extricate himself. Peters at last let him out, and, with a species of good feeling which my friend knew well how to appreciate, had now brought him to him in the forecastle as a companion, leaving at the same time some salt junk and potatoes, with a can of water; he then went on deck, promising to come down with something more to eat on the next day.

When he had gone, Augustus freed both hands from the manacles and unfastened his feet. He then turned down the head of the mattress on which he had been lying, and with his penknife (for the ruffians had not thought it worth while to search him) commenced cutting vigorously across one of the partition planks, as closely as possible to the floor of the berth. He chose to cut here, because, if suddenly interrupted, he would be able to conceal what had been done by letting the head of the mattress fall into its proper position. For the remainder of the day, however, no disturbance occurred, and by night he had completely divided the plank. It should here be observed that none of the crew occupied the forecastle as a sleeping-place, living altogether in the cabin since the mutiny, drinking the wines and feast-

ing on the sea-stores of Captain Barnard, and giving no
more heed than was absolutely necessary to the naviga-
tion of the brig. These circumstances proved fortunate
both for myself and Augustus; for, had matters been
otherwise, he would have found it impossible to reach
me. As it was, he proceeded with confidence in his de-
sign. It was near day-break, however, before he com-
pleted the second division of the board (which was
about a foot above the first cut), thus making an aper-
ture quite large enough to admit his passage through
with facility to the main orlop deck. Having got here, he
made his way with but little trouble to the lower main
hatch, although in so doing he had to scramble over
tiers of oil-casks piled nearly as high as the upper deck,
there being barely room enough left for his body. Upon
reaching the hatch he found that Tiger had followed him
below, squeezing between two rows of the casks. It was
now too late, however, to attempt getting to me before
dawn, as the chief difficulty lay in passing through the
close stowage in the lower hold. He therefore resolved
to return, and wait till the next night. With this design,
he proceeded to loosen the hatch, so that he might have
as little detention as possible when he should come again.
No sooner had he loosened it than Tiger sprang eagerly
to the small opening produced, snuffed for a moment,
and then uttered a long whine, scratching at the same
time, as if anxious to remove the covering with his paws.
There could be no doubt, from his behavior, that he was
aware of my being in the hold, and Augustus thought it
possible that he would be able to get to me if he put
him down. He now hit upon the expedient of sending the
note, as it was especially desirable that I should make
no attempt at forcing my way out, at least under exist-
ing circumstances, and there could be no certainty of
his getting to me himself on the morrow as he intended.
After-events proved how fortunate it was that the idea
occurred to him as it did; for, had it not been for the
receipt of the note, I should undoubtedly have fallen
upon some plan, however desperate, of alarming the
crew, and both our lives would most probably have
been sacrificed in consequence.

Having concluded to write, the difficulty was now to
procure the materials for so doing. An old toothpick
was soon made into a pen; and this by means of feel-

ing altogether, for the between-decks were as dark as
pitch. Paper enough was obtained from the back of a
letter—a duplicate of the forged letter from Mr. Ross.
This had been the original draught; but the handwriting
not being sufficiently well imitated, Augustus had writ-
ten another, thrusting the first, by good fortune, into his
coat-pocket, where it was now most opportunely dis-
covered. Ink alone was thus wanting, and a substitute
was immediately found for this by means of a slight in-
cision with the penknife on the back of a finger just
above the nail—a copious flow of blood ensuing, as
usual, from wounds in that vicinity. The note was now
written, as well as it could be in the dark and under
the circumstances. It briefly explained that a mutiny had
taken place; that Captain Barnard was set adrift; and
that I might expect immediate relief as far as provisions
were concerned, but must not venture upon making any
disturbance. It concluded with these words: *"I have
scrawled this with blood—your life depends upon lying
close."*

This slip of paper being tied upon the dog, he was now
put down the hatchway, and Augustus made the best
of his way back to the forecastle, where he found no
reason to believe that any of the crew had been in his
absence. To conceal the hole in the partition, he drove his
knife in just above it, and hung up a pea-jacket which he
found in the berth. His handcuffs were then replaced,
and also the rope around his ankles.

These arrangements were scarcely completed when
Dirk Peters came below, very drunk, but in excellent
humor, and bringing with him my friend's allowance of
provision for the day. This consisted of a dozen large Irish
potatoes roasted, and a pitcher of water. He sat for some
time on a chest by the berth, and talked freely about
the mate and the general concerns of the brig. His de-
meanor was exceedingly capricious, and even grotesque.
At one time Augustus was much alarmed by his odd con-
duct. At last, however, he went on deck, muttering a
promise to bring his prisoner a good dinner on the
morrow. During the day two of the crew (harpooners)
came down, accompanied by the cook, all three in nearly
the last stage of intoxication. Like Peters, they made no
scruple of talking unreservedly about their plans. It ap-
peared that they were much divided among themselves

as to their ultimate course, agreeing in no point, except the attack on the ship from the Cape Verd Islands, with which they were in hourly expectation of meeting. As far as could be ascertained, the mutiny had not been brought about altogether for the sake of booty; a private pique of the chief mate's against Captain Barnard having been the main instigation. There now seemed to be two principal factions among the crew—one headed by the mate, the other by the cook. The former party were for seizing the first suitable vessel which should present itself, and equipping it at some of the West India Islands for a piratical cruise. The latter division, however, which was the stronger, and included Dirk Peters among its partisans, were bent upon pursuing the course originally laid out for the brig into the South Pacific; there either to take whale, or act otherwise, as circumstances should suggest. The representations of Peters, who had frequently visited these regions, had great weight, apparently, with the mutineers, wavering, as they were, between half-engendered notions of profit and pleasure. He dwelt on the world of novelty and amusement to be found among the innumerable islands of the Pacific, on the perfect security and freedom from all restraint to be enjoyed, but, more particularly, on the deliciousness of the climate, on the abundant means of good living, and on the voluptuous beauty of the women. As yet, nothing had been absolutely determined upon; but the pictures of the hybrid line-manager were taking strong hold upon the ardent imaginations of the seamen, and there was every probability that his intentions would be finally carried into effect.

The three men went away in about an hour, and no one else entered the forecastle all day. Augustus lay quiet until nearly night. He then freed himself from the rope and irons, and prepared for his attempt. A bottle was found in one of the berths, and this he filled with water from the pitcher left by Peters, storing his pockets at the same time with cold potatoes. To his great joy he also came across a lantern, with a small piece of tallow candle in it. This he could light at any moment, as he had in his possession a box of phosphorus matches. When it was quite dark, he got through the hole in the bulkhead, having taken the precaution to arrange the bedclothes in the berth so as to convey the idea of a

person covered up. When through, he hung up the pea-jacket on his knife, as before, to conceal the aperture—this manœuvre being easily effected, as he did not re-adjust the piece of plank taken out until afterward. He was now on the main orlop deck, and proceeded to make his way, as before, between the upper deck and the oil-casks to the main hatchway. Having reached this, he lit the piece of candle, and descended, groping with ex-treme difficulty among the compact stowage of the hold. In a few moments he became alarmed at the insuffer-able stench and the closeness of the atmosphere. He could not think it possible that I had survived my con-finement for so long a period breathing so oppressive an air. He called my name repeatedly, but I made him no reply, and his apprehensions seemed thus to be con-firmed. The brig was rolling violently, and there was so much noise in consequence, that it was useless to listen for any weak sound, such as those of my breathing or snoring. He threw open the lantern, and held it as high as possible, whenever an opportunity occurred, in order that, by observing the light, I might, if alive, be aware that succor was approaching. Still nothing was heard from me, and the supposition of my death began to assume the character of certainty. He determined, nevertheless, to force a passage, if possible, to the box, and at least ascertain beyond a doubt the truth of his surmises. He pushed on for some time in a most pitiable state of anxiety, until, at length, he found the pathway utterly blocked up, and that there was no possibility of making any farther way by the course in which he had set out. Overcome now by his feelings, he threw himself among the lumber in despair, and wept like a child. It was at this period that he heard the crash occasioned by the bottle which I had thrown down. Fortunate, in-deed, was it that the incident occurred—for, upon this incident, trivial as it appears, the thread of my destiny depended. Many years elapsed, however, before I was aware of this fact. A natural shame and regret for his weakness and indecision prevented Augustus from con-fiding to me at once what a more intimate and unre-served communion afterward induced him to reveal. Upon finding his further progress in the hold impeded by obstacles which he could not overcome, he had re-solved to abandon his attempt at reaching me, and re-

turn at once to the forecastle. Before condemning him
entirely on this head, the harassing circumstances which
embarrassed him should be taken into consideration.
The night was fast wearing away, and his absence from
the forecastle might be discovered; and, indeed, would
necessarily be so, if he should fail to get back to the
berth by daybreak. His candle was expiring in the socket,
and there would be the greatest difficulty in retracing
his way to the hatchway in the dark. It must be allowed,
too, that he had every good reason to believe me dead;
in which event no benefit could result to me from his
reaching the box, and a world of danger would be en-
countered to no purpose by himself. He had repeatedly
called, and I had made him no answer. I had been now
eleven days and nights with no more water than that con-
tained in the jug which he had left with me—a supply
which it was not at all probable I had hoarded in the be-
ginning of my confinement, as I had every cause to ex-
pect a speedy release. The atmosphere of the hold, too,
must have appeared to him, coming from the com-
paratively open air of the steerage, of a nature absolutely
poisonous, and by far more intolerable than it had
seemed to me upon my first taking up my quarters in
the box—the hatchway at the time having been con-
stantly open for many months previous. Add to these
considerations that of the scene of bloodshed and terror
so lately witnessed by my friend; his confinement, priva-
tions, and narrow escapes from death, together with the
frail and equivocal tenure by which he still existed—
circumstances all so well calculated to prostrate every
energy of mind—and the reader will be easily brought,
as I have been, to regard his apparent falling off in
friendship and in faith with sentiments rather of sor-
row than of anger.

The crash of the bottle was distinctly heard, yet Augus-
tus was not sure that it proceeded from the hold. The
doubt, however, was sufficient inducement to persevere.
He clambered up nearly to the orlop deck by means of
the stowage, and then, watching for a lull in the pitch-
ings of the vessel, he called out to me in as loud a
tone as he could command, regardless, for the moment,
of being overheard by the crew. It will be remembered
that on this occasion the voice reached me, but I was so
entirely overcome by violent agitation as to be incapable

of reply. Confident, now, that his worst apprehensions
were well founded, he descended, with a view of getting
back to the forecastle without loss of time. In his haste
some small boxes were thrown down, the noise oc-
casioned by which I heard, as will be recollected. He had
made considerable progress on his return when the fall
of the knife again caused him to hesitate. He retraced
his steps immediately, and, clambering up the stowage
a second time, called out my name, loudly as before,
having watched for a lull. This time I found my voice to
answer. Overjoyed at discovering me to be still alive, he
now resolved to brave every difficulty and danger in
reaching me. Having extricated himself as quickly as pos-
sible from the labyrinth of lumber by which he was
hemmed in, he at length struck into an opening which
promised better, and finally, after a series of struggles,
arrived at the box in a state of utter exhaustion.

CHAPTER VI

THE leading particulars of this narration were all that
Augustus communicated to me while we remained near
the box. It was not until afterward that he entered fully
into all the details. He was apprehensive of being
missed, and I was wild with impatience to leave my de-
tested place of confinement. We resolved to make our
way at once to the hole in the bulkhead, near which I
was to remain for the present, while he went through to
reconnoitre. To leave Tiger in the box was what neither of
us could endure to think of; yet, how to act otherwise
was the question. He now seemed to be perfectly quiet,
and we could not even distinguish the sound of his
breathing upon applying our ears closely to the box. I
was convinced that he was dead, and determined to open
the door. We found him lying at full length, apparently
in a deep stupor, yet still alive. No time was to be lost,
yet I could not bring myself to abandon an animal who
had now been twice instrumental in saving my life, with-
out some attempt at preserving him. We therefore
dragged him along with us as well as we could, although
with the greatest difficulty and fatigue; Augustus, during
part of the time, being forced to clamber over the imped-
iments in our way with the huge dog in his arms—a

feat to which the feebleness of my frame rendered me totally inadequate. At length we succeeded in reaching the hole, when Augustus got through, and Tiger was pushed in afterward. All was found to be safe, and we did not fail to return sincere thanks to God for our deliverance from the imminent danger we had escaped. For the present, it was agreed that I should remain near the opening, through which my companion could readily supply me with part of his daily provision, and where I could have the advantages of breathing an atmosphere comparatively pure.

In explanation of some portions of this narrative, wherein I have spoken of the stowage of the brig, and which may appear ambiguous to some of my readers who may have seen a proper or regular stowage, I must here state that the manner in which this most important duty had been performed on board the Grampus was a most shameful piece of neglect on the part of Captain Barnard, who was by no means as careful or as experienced a seaman as the hazardous nature of the service on which he was employed would seem necessarily to demand. A proper stowage cannot be accomplished in a careless manner, and many most disastrous accidents, even within the limits of my own experience, have arisen from neglect or ignorance in this particular. Coasting vessels, in the frequent hurry and bustle attendant upon taking in or discharging cargo, are the most liable to mishap from the want of a proper attention to stowage. The great point is to allow no possibility of the cargo or ballast shifting position even in the most violent rollings of the vessel. With this end, great attention must be paid, not only to the bulk taken in, but to the nature of the bulk, and whether there be a full or only a partial cargo. In most kinds of freight the stowage is accomplished by means of a screw. Thus, in a load of tobacco or flour, the whole is screwed so tightly into the hold of the vessel that the barrels or hogsheads, upon discharging, are found to be completely flattened, and take some time to regain their original shape. This screwing, however, is resorted to principally with a view of obtaining more room in the hold; for in a *full* load of any such commodities as flour or tobacco, there can be no danger of any shifting whatever, at least none from which inconvenience can result. There have been instances, indeed,

where this method of screwing has resulted in the most lamentable consequences, arising from a cause altogether distinct from the danger attendant upon a shifting of cargo. A load of cotton, for example, tightly screwed while in certain conditions, has been known, through the expansion of its bulk, to rend a vessel asunder at sea. There can be no doubt, either, that the same result would ensue in the case of tobacco, while undergoing its usual course of fermentation, were it not for the interstices consequent upon the rotundity of the hogsheads.

It is when a partial cargo is received that danger is chiefly to be apprehended from shifting, and that precaution should be always taken to guard against such misfortune. Only those who have encountered a violent gale of wind, or rather who have experienced the rolling of a vessel in a sudden calm after the gale, can form an idea of the tremendous force of the plunges, and of the consequent terrible impetus given to all loose articles in the vessel. It is then that the necessity of a cautious stowage, when there is a partial cargo, becomes obvious. When lying-to (especially with a small head-sail), a vessel which is not properly modelled in the bows is frequently thrown upon her beam-ends; this occurring even every fifteen or twenty minutes upon an average, yet without any serious consequences resulting, *provided there be a proper stowage*. If this, however, has not been strictly attended to, in the first of these heavy lurches the whole of the cargo tumbles over to the side of the vessel which lies upon the water, and, being thus prevented from regaining her equilibrium, as she would otherwise necessarily do, she is certain to fill in a few seconds and go down. It is not too much to say that at least one half of the instances in which vessels have foundered in heavy gales at sea may be attributed to a shifting of cargo or of ballast.

When a partial cargo of any kind is taken on board, the whole, after being first stowed as compactly as may be, should be covered with a layer of stout shifting-boards, extending completely across the vessel. Upon these boards strong temporary stanchions should be erected, reaching to the timbers above, and thus securing every thing in its place. In cargoes consisting of grain, or any similar matter, additional precautions are requisite. A hold filled entirely with grain upon leaving port will be

found not more than three fourths full upon reaching its destination—this, too, although the freight, when measured bushel by bushel by the consignee, will overrun by a vast deal (on account of the swelling of the grain) the quantity consigned. This result is occasioned by *settling* during the voyage, and is the more perceptible in proportion to the roughness of the weather experienced. If grain loosely thrown in a vessel, then, is ever so well secured by shifting-boards and stanchions, it will be liable to shift in a long passage so greatly as to bring about the most distressing calamities. To prevent these, every method should be employed before leaving port to *settle* the cargo as much as possible; and for this there are many contrivances, among which may be mentioned the driving of wedges into the grain. Even after all this is done, and unusual pains taken to secure the shifting-boards, no seaman who knows what he is about will feel altogether secure in a gale of any violence with a cargo of grain on board, and least of all, with a partial cargo. Yet there are hundreds of our coasting vessels, and, it is likely, many more from the ports of Europe, which sail daily with partial cargoes, even of the most dangerous species, and without any precaution whatever. The wonder is that no more accidents occur than do actually happen. A lamentable instance of this heedlessness occurred to my knowledge in the case of Captain Joel Rice of the schooner Firefly, which sailed from Richmond, Virginia, to Madeira, with a cargo of corn, in the year 1825. The captain had gone many voyages without serious accident, although he was in the habit of paying no attention whatever to his stowage, more than to secure it in the ordinary manner. He had never before sailed with a cargo of grain, and on this occasion had the corn thrown on board loosely, when it did not much more than half fill the vessel. For the first portion of the voyage he met with nothing more than light breezes; but when within a day's sail of Madeira there came on a strong gale from the N.N.E. which forced him to lie-to. He brought the schooner to the wind under a double-reefed foresail alone, when she rode as well as any vessel could be expected to do, and shipped not a drop of water. Toward night the gale somewhat abated, and she rolled with more unsteadiness than before, but still did very well, until a heavy lurch threw her upon her beam-ends to starboard.

The corn was then heard to shift bodily, the force of the movement bursting open the main hatchway. The vessel went down like a shot. This happened within hail of a small sloop from Madeira, which picked up one of the crew (the only person saved), and which rode out the gale in perfect security, as indeed a jolly-boat might have done under proper management.

The stowage on board the Grampus was most clumsily done, if stowage that could be called which was little better than a promiscuous huddling together of oil-casks [1] and ship-furniture. I have already spoken of the condition of articles in the hold. On the orlop deck there was space enough for my body (as I have stated) between the oil-casks and the upper deck; a space was left open around the main hatchway; and several other large spaces were left in the stowage. Near the hole cut through the bulkhead by Augustus there was room enough for an entire cask, and in this space I found myself comfortably situated for the present.

By the time my friend had got safely into the berth, and readjusted his handcuffs and the rope, it was broad daylight. We had made a narrow escape indeed; for scarcely had he arranged all matters, when the mate came below with Dirk Peters and the cook. They talked for some time about the vessel from the Cape Verds, and seemed to be excessively anxious for her appearance. At length the cook came to the berth in which Augustus was lying, and seated himself in it near the head. I could see and hear every thing from my hiding-place, for the piece cut out had not been put back, and I was in momentary expectation that the negro would fall against the pea-jacket, which was hung up to conceal the aperture, in which case all would have been discovered, and our lives would, no doubt, have been instantly sacrificed. Our good fortune prevailed, however; and although he frequently touched it as the vessel rolled, he never pressed against it sufficiently to bring about a discovery. The bottom of the jacket had been carefully fastened to the bulkhead, so that the hole might not be seen by its swinging to one side. All this time Tiger was lying in the foot of the berth, and appeared to have recovered in some measure

[1] Whaling vessels are usually fitted with iron oil-tanks—why the Grampus was not I have never been able to ascertain.

his faculties, for I could see him occasionally open his eyes and draw a long breath.

After a few minutes the mate and cook went above, leaving Dirk Peters behind, who, as soon as they were gone, came and sat himself down in the place just occupied by the mate. He began to talk very sociably with Augustus, and we could now see that the greater part of his apparent intoxication, while the two others were with him, was a feint. He answered all my companion's questions with perfect freedom; told him that he had no doubt of his father's having been picked up, as there were no less than five sail in sight just before sundown on the day he was cut adrift; and used other language of a consolatory nature, which occasioned me no less surprise than pleasure. Indeed, I began to entertain hopes, that through the instrumentality of Peters we might be finally enabled to regain possession of the brig, and this idea I mentioned to Augustus as soon as I found an opportunity. He thought the matter possible, but urged the necessity of the greatest caution in making the attempt, as the conduct of the hybrid appeared to be instigated by the most arbitrary caprice alone; and, indeed, it was difficult to say if he was at any moment of sound mind. Peters went upon deck in about an hour, and did not return again until noon, when he brought Augustus a plentiful supply of junk beef and pudding. Of this, when we were left alone, I partook heartily, without returning through the hole. No one else came down into the forecastle during the day, and at night I got into Augustus' berth, where I slept soundly and sweetly until nearly daybreak, when he awakened me upon hearing a stir upon deck and I regained my hiding-place as quickly as possible. When the day was fully broke, we found that Tiger had recovered his strength almost entirely, and gave no indications of hydrophobia, drinking a little water that was offered him with great apparent eagerness. During the day he regained all his former vigor and appetite. His strange conduct had been brought on, no doubt, by the deleterious quality of the air of the hold, and had no connection with canine madness. I could not sufficiently rejoice that I had persisted in bringing him with me from the box. This day was the thirtieth of June, and the thirteenth since the Grampus made sail from Nantucket.

On the second of July the mate came below, drunk as usual, and in an excessively good-humor. He came to Augustus' berth, and, giving him a slap on the back, asked him if he thought he could behave himself if he let him loose, and whether he would promise not to be going into the cabin again. To this, of course, my friend answered in the affirmative, when the ruffian set him at liberty, after making him drink from a flask of rum which he drew from his coat-pocket. Both now went on deck, and I did not see Augustus for about three hours. He then came below with the good news that he had obtained permission to go about the brig as he pleased anywhere forward of the mainmast, and that he had been ordered to sleep, as usual, in the forecastle. He brought me, too, a good dinner, and a plentiful supply of water. The brig was still cruising for the vessel from the Cape Verds, and a sail was now in sight, which was thought to be the one in question. As the events of the ensuing eight days were of little importance, and had no direct bearing upon the main incidents of my narrative, I will here throw them into the form of a journal, as I do not wish to omit them altogether.

July 3d.—Augustus furnished me with three blankets, with which I contrived a comfortable bed in my hiding-place. No one came below, except my companion, during the day. Tiger took his station in the berth just by the aperture, and slept heavily, as if not yet entirely recovered from the effects of his sickness. Toward night a flaw of wind struck the brig before sail could be taken in, and very nearly capsized her. The puff died away immediately, however, and no damage was done beyond the splitting of the foretopsail. Dirk Peters treated Augustus all this day with great kindness, and entered into a long conversation with him respecting the Pacific Ocean, and the islands he had visited in that region. He asked him whether he would not like to go with the mutineers on a kind of exploring and pleasure voyage in those quarters, and said that the men were gradually coming over to the mate's views. To this Augustus thought it best to reply that he would be glad to go on such an adventure, since nothing better could be done, and that any thing was preferable to a piratical life.

July 4th.—The vessel in sight proved to be a small brig from Liverpool, and was allowed to pass unmolested.

Augustus spent most of his time on deck, with a view of obtaining all the information in his power respecting the intentions of the mutineers. They had frequent and violent quarrels among themselves, in one of which a harpooner, Jim Bonner, was thrown overboard. The party of the mate was gaining ground. Jim Bonner belonged to the cook's gang, of which Peters was a partisan.

July 5th.—About daybreak there came on a stiff breeze from the west, which at noon freshened into a gale, so that the brig could carry nothing more than her trysail and foresail. In taking in the foretopsail, Simms, one of the common hands, and belonging also to the cook's gang, fell overboard, being very much in liquor, and was drowned—no attempt being made to save him. The whole number of persons on board was now thirteen, to wit: Dirk Peters; Seymour, the black cook; —— Jones; —— Greely; Hartman Rogers; and William Allen, of the cook's party; the mate, whose name I never learned; Absalom Hicks; —— Wilson; John Hunt; and Richard Parker, of the mate's party;—besides Augustus and myself.

July 6th.—The gale lasted all this day, blowing in heavy squalls, accompanied with rain. The brig took in a good deal of water through her seams, and one of the pumps was kept continually going, Augustus being forced to take his turn. Just at twilight a large ship passed close by us, without having been discovered until within hail. The ship was supposed to be the one for which the mutineers were on the look-out. The mate hailed her, but the reply was drowned in the roaring of the gale. At eleven, a sea was shipped amidships, which tore away a great portion of the larboard bulwarks, and did some other slight damage. Toward morning the weather moderated, and at sunrise there was very little wind.

July 7th.—There was a heavy swell running all this day, during which the brig, being light, rolled excessively, and many articles broke loose in the hold, as I could hear distinctly from my hiding-place. I suffered a great deal from sea-sickness. Peters had a long conversation this day with Augustus, and told him that two of his gang, Greely and Allen, had gone over to the mate, and were resolved to turn pirates. He put several questions to Augustus which he did not then exactly understand. During a part of this evening the leak gained upon the vessel; and little could be done to remedy it, as it was occasioned

by the brig's straining, and taking in the water through
her seams. A sail was thrummed, and got under the bows,
which aided us in some measure, so that we began to
gain upon the leak.

July 8th.—A light breeze sprang up at sunrise from
the eastward, when the mate headed the brig to the south-
west, with the intention of making some of the West In-
dia islands, in pursuance of his piratical designs. No
opposition was made by Peters or the cook—at least
none in the hearing of Augustus. All idea of taking the
vessel from the Cape Verds was abandoned. The leak
was now easily kept under by one pump going every
three quarters of an hour. The sail was drawn from be-
neath the bows. Spoke two small schooners during the
day.

July 9th.—Fine weather. All hands employed in re-
pairing bulwarks. Peters had again a long conversation
with Augustus, and spoke more plainly than he had done
heretofore. He said nothing should induce him to come
into the mate's views, and even hinted his intention of
taking the brig out of his hands. He asked my friend if he
could depend upon his aid in such case, to which Au-
gustus said, "Yes," without hesitation. Peters then said he
would sound the others of his party upon the sub-
ject, and went away. During the remainder of the day
Augustus had no opportunity of speaking with him pri-
vately.

CHAPTER VII

JULY 10TH.—Spoke a brig from Rio, bound to Norfolk.
Weather hazy, with a light baffling wind from the east-
ward. To-day Hartman Rogers died, having been attacked
on the eighth with spasms after drinking a glass of grog.
This man was of the cook's party, and one upon whom
Peters placed his main reliance. He told Augustus that he
believed the mate had poisoned him, and that he ex-
pected, if he did not be on the lookout, his own turn
would come shortly. There were now only himself,
Jones, and the cook belonging to his own gang—on the
other side there were five. He had spoken to Jones about
taking the command from the mate; but the project hav-
ing been coolly received, he had been deterred from
pressing the matter any further, or from saying any thing

to the cook. It was well, as it happened, that he was so prudent, for in the afternoon the cook expressed his determination of siding with the mate, and went over formally to that party; while Jones took an opportunity of quarrelling with Peters, and hinted that he would let the mate know of the plan in agitation. There was now, evidently, no time to be lost, and Peters expressed his determination of attempting to take the vessel at all hazards, provided Augustus would lend him his aid. My friend at once assured him of his willingness to enter into any plan for that purpose, and, thinking the opportunity a favorable one, made known the fact of my being on board. At this the hybrid was not more astonished than delighted, as he had no reliance whatever upon Jones, whom he already considered as belonging to the party of the mate. They went below immediately, when Augustus called to me by name, and Peters and myself were soon made acquainted. It was agreed that we should attempt to retake the vessel upon the first good opportunity, leaving Jones altogether out of our councils. In the event of success, we were to run the brig into the first port that offered, and deliver her up. The desertion of his party had frustrated Peters' design of going into the Pacific—an adventure which could not be accomplished without a crew, and he depended upon either getting acquitted upon trial, on the score of insanity (which he solemnly averred had actuated him in lending his aid to the mutiny), or upon obtaining a pardon, if found guilty, through the representations of Augustus and myself. Our deliberations were interrupted for the present by the cry of, "All hands take in sail," and Peters and Augustus ran up on deck.

As usual, the crew were nearly all drunk; and, before sail could be properly taken in, a violent squall laid the brig on her beam-ends. By keeping her away, however, she righted, having shipped a good deal of water. Scarcely was every thing secure, when another squall took the vessel, and immediately afterward another— no damage being done. There was every appearance of a gale of wind, which, indeed, shortly came on, with great fury, from the northward and westward. All was made as snug as possible, and we laid-to, as usual, under a close-reefed foresail. As night drew on, the wind increased in violence, with a remarkably heavy sea. Peters now

came into the forecastle with Augustus, and we resumed
our deliberations.

We agreed that no opportunity could be more favor-
able than the present for carrying our design into effect,
as an attempt at such a moment would never be antici-
pated. As the brig was snugly laid-to, there would be no
necessity of manœuvring her until good weather, when,
if we succeeded in our attempt, we might liberate one, or
perhaps two of the men, to aid us in taking her into
port. The main difficulty was the great disproportion in
our forces. There were only three of us, and in the cabin
there were nine. All the arms on board, too, were in their
possession, with the exception of a pair of small pistols
which Peters had concealed about his person, and the
large seaman's knife which he always wore in the
waistband of his pantaloons. From certain indications,
too—such, for example, as there being no such thing as
an axe or a handspike lying in their customary places—
we began to fear that the mate had his suspicions, at
least in regard to Peters, and that he would let slip no
opportunity of getting rid of him. It was clear, indeed,
that what we should determine to do could not be done
too soon. Still the odds were too much against us to
allow of our proceeding without the greatest caution.

Peters proposed that he should go up on deck, and
enter into conversation with the watch (Allen), when he
would be able to throw him into the sea without trouble,
and without making any disturbance, by seizing a good
opportunity; that Augustus and myself should then come
up, and endeavor to provide ourselves with some kind of
weapons from the deck; and that we should then make a
rush together, and secure the companionway before any
opposition could be offered. I objected to this, because
I could not believe that the mate (who was a cunning fel-
low in all matters which did not affect his superstitious
prejudices) would suffer himself to be so easily en-
trapped. The very fact of there being a watch on deck
at all was sufficient proof that he was upon the alert—
it not being usual, except in vessels where discipline is
most rigidly enforced, to station a watch on deck when
a vessel is lying-to in a gale of wind. As I address my-
self principally, if not altogether, to persons who have
never been to sea, it may be as well to state the exact
condition of a vessel under such circumstances. Lying-

to, or, in sea-parlance, "laying-to," is a measure resorted to for various purposes, and effected in various manners. In moderate weather it is frequently done with a view of merely bringing the vessel to a stand-still, to wait for another vessel, or any similar object. If the vessel which lies-to is under full sail, the manœuvre is usually accomplished by throwing round some portion of her sails, so as to let the wind take them back, when she becomes stationary. But we are now speaking of lying-to in a gale of wind. This is done when the wind is ahead, and too violent to admit of carrying sail without danger of capsizing; and sometimes even when the wind is fair, but the sea too heavy for the vessel to be put before it. If a vessel be suffered to scud before the wind in a very heavy sea, much damage is usually done her by the shipping of water over her stern, and sometimes by the violent plunges she makes forward. This manœuvre, then, is seldom resorted to in such case, unless through necessity. When the vessel is in a leaky condition she is often put before the wind even in the heaviest seas; for, when lying-to, her seams are sure to be greatly opened by her violent straining, and it is not so much the case when scudding. Often, too, it becomes necessary to scud a vessel, either when the blast is so exceedingly furious as to tear in pieces the sail which is employed with a view of bringing her head to the wind, or when, through the false modeling of the frame or other causes, this main object cannot be effected.

Vessels in a gale of wind are laid-to in different manners, according to their peculiar construction. Some lie-to best under a foresail, and this, I believe, is the sail most usually employed. Large square-rigged vessels have sails for the express purpose, called storm-staysails. But the jib is occasionally employed by itself—sometimes the jib and foresail, or a double-reefed foresail, and not unfrequently the after-sails, are made use of. Foretopsails are very often found to answer the purpose better than any other species of sail. The Grampus was generally laid-to under a close-reefed foresail.

When a vessel is to be laid-to, her head is brought up to the wind just so nearly as to fill the sail under which she lies when hauled flat aft—that is, when brought diagonally across the vessel. This being done, the bows point within a few degrees of the direction from which the wind

issues, and the windward bow of course receives the shock of the waves. In this situation a good vessel will ride out a very heavy gale of wind without shipping a drop of water, and without any further attention being requisite on the part of the crew. The helm is usually lashed down, but this is altogether unnecessary (except on account of the noise it makes when loose), for the rudder has no effect upon the vessel when lying-to. Indeed, the helm had far better be left loose than lashed very fast, for the rudder is apt to be torn off by heavy seas if there be no room for the helm to play. As long as the sail holds, a well-modelled vessel will maintain her situation, and ride every sea, as if instinct with life and reason. If the violence of the wind, however, should tear the sail into pieces (a feat which it requires a perfect hurricane to accomplish under ordinary circumstances), there is then imminent danger. The vessel falls off from the wind, and, coming broadside to the sea, is completely at its mercy: the only recourse in this case is to put her quietly before the wind, letting her scud until some other sail can be set. Some vessels will lie-to under no sail whatever, but such are not to be trusted at sea.

But to return from this digression. It had never been customary with the mate to have any watch on deck when lying-to in a gale of wind, and the fact that he had now one, coupled with the circumstance of the missing axes and handspikes, fully convinced us that the crew were too well on the watch to be taken by surprise in the manner Peters had suggested. Something, however, was to be done, and that with as little delay as practicable, for there could be no doubt that a suspicion having been once entertained against Peters, he would be sacrificed upon the earliest occasion, and one would certainly be either found or made upon the breaking of the gale.

Augustus now suggested that if Peters could contrive to remove, under any pretext, the piece of chain-cable which lay over the trap in the stateroom, we might possibly be able to come upon them unawares by means of the hold; but a little reflection convinced us that the vessel rolled and pitched too violently for any attempt of that nature.

By good fortune I at length hit upon the idea of working upon the superstitious terrors and guilty conscience

of the mate. It will be remembered that one of the crew, Hartman Rogers, had died during the morning, having been attacked two days before with spasms after drinking some spirits and water. Peters had expressed to us his opinion that this man had been poisoned by the mate, and for this belief he had reasons, so he said, which were incontrovertible, but which he could not be prevailed upon to explain to us—this wayward refusal being only in keeping with other points of his singular character. But whether or not he had any better grounds for suspecting the mate than we had ourselves, we were easily led to fall in with his suspicion, and determined to act accordingly.

Rogers had died about eleven in the forenoon, in violent convulsions; and the corpse presented in a few minutes after death one of the most horrid and loathsome spectacles I ever remember to have seen. The stomach was swollen immensely, like that of a man who has been drowned and lain under water for many weeks. The hands were in the same condition, while the face was shrunken, shrivelled, and of a chalky whiteness, except where relieved by two or three glaring red blotches, like those occasioned by the erysipelas: one of these blotches extended diagonally across the face, completely covering up an eye as if with a band of red velvet. In this disgusting condition the body had been brought up from the cabin at noon to be thrown overboard, when the mate getting a glimpse of it (for he now saw it for the first time), and being either touched with remorse for his crime or struck with terror at so horrible a sight, ordered the men to sew the body up in its hammock, and allow it the usual rites of sea-burial. Having given these directions, he went below, as if to avoid any further sight of his victim. While preparations were making to obey his orders, the gale came on with great fury, and the design was abandoned for the present. The corpse, left to itself, was washed into the larboard scuppers, where it still lay at the time of which I speak, floundering about with the furious lurches of the brig.

Having arranged our plan, we set about putting it in execution as speedily as possible. Peters went upon deck, and, as he had anticipated, was immediately accosted by Allen, who appeared to be stationed more as a watch upon the forecastle than for any other pur-

pose. The fate of this villain, however, was speedily and silently decided; for Peters, approaching him in a careless manner, as if about to address him, seized him by the throat, and, before he could utter a single cry, tossed him over the bulwarks. He then called to us, and we came up. Our first precaution was to look about for something with which to arm ourselves, and in doing this we had to proceed with great care, for it was impossible to stand on deck an instant without holding fast, and violent seas broke over the vessel at every plunge forward. It was indispensable, too, that we should be quick in our operations, for every minute we expected the mate to be up to set the pumps going, as it was evident the brig must be taking in water very fast. After searching about for some time, we could find nothing more fit for our purpose than the two pump-handles, one of which Augustus took, and I the other. Having secured these, we stripped off the shirt of the corpse and dropped the body overboard. Peters and myself then went below, leaving Augustus to watch upon deck, where he took his station just where Allen had been placed, and with his back to the cabin companionway, so that, if any of the mate's gang should come up, he might suppose it was the watch.

As soon as I got below I commenced disguising myself so as to represent the corpse of Rogers. The shirt which we had taken from the body aided us very much, for it was of singular form and character, and easily recognizable—a kind of smock, which the deceased wore over his other clothing. It was a blue stockinet, with large white stripes running across. Having put this on, I proceeded to equip myself with a false stomach, in imitation of the horrible deformity of the swollen corpse. This was soon effected by means of stuffing with some bedclothes. I then gave the same appearance to my hands by drawing on a pair of white woollen mittens, and filling them in with any kind of rags that offered themselves. Peters then arranged my face, first rubbing it well over with white chalk, and afterward blotching it with blood, which he took from a cut in his finger. The streak across the eye was not forgotten, and presented a most shocking appearance.

CHAPTER VIII

As I viewed myself in a fragment of looking-glass which
hung up in the cabin, and by the dim light of a kind of
battle-lantern, I was so impressed with a sense of
vague awe at my appearance, and at the recollection of
the terrific reality which I was thus representing, that I
was seized with a violent tremor, and could scarcely
summon resolution to go on with my part. It was neces-
sary, however, to act with decision, and Peters and my-
self went upon deck.

We there found every thing safe, and, keeping close
to the bulwarks, the three of us crept to the cabin com-
panionway. It was only partially closed, precautions hav-
ing been taken to prevent its being suddenly pushed-to
from without, by means of placing billets of wood on the
upper step so as to interfere with the shutting. We
found no difficulty in getting a full view of the interior
of the cabin through the cracks where the hinges were
placed. It now proved to have been very fortunate for
us that we had not attempted to take them by surprise,
for they were evidently on the alert. Only one was asleep,
and he lying just at the foot of the companion-ladder,
with a musket by his side. The rest were seated on sev-
eral mattresses, which had been taken from the berths
and thrown on the floor. They were engaged in earnest
conversation; and although they had been carousing, as
appeared from two empty jugs, with some tin tumblers
which lay about, they were not as much intoxicated as
usual. All had knives, one or two of them pistols, and a
great many muskets were lying in a berth close at hand.

We listened to their conversation for some time before
we could make up our minds how to act, having as yet
resolved on nothing determinate, except that we would
attempt to paralyze their exertions, when we should at-
tack them, by means of the apparition of Rogers. They
were discussing their piratical plans, in which all we
could hear distinctly was, that they would unite with the
crew of a schooner Hornet, and, if possible, get the
schooner herself into their possession preparatory to
some attempt on a large scale, the particulars of which
could not be made out by either of us.

One of the men spoke of Peters, when the mate replied to him in a low voice which could not be distinguished, and afterward added more loudly, that "he could not understand his being so much forward with the captain's brat in the forecastle, and he thought the sooner both of them were overboard the better." To this no answer was made, but we could easily perceive that the hint was well received by the whole party, and more particularly by Jones. At this period I was excessively agitated, the more so as I could see that neither Augustus nor Peters could determine how to act. I made up my mind, however, to sell my life as dearly as possible, and not to suffer myself to be overcome by any feelings of trepidation.

The tremendous noise made by the roaring of the wind in the rigging, and the washing of the sea over the deck, prevented us from hearing what was said, except during momentary lulls. In one of these, we all distinctly heard the mate tell one of the men to "go forward, and order the d—d lubbers to come into the cabin," where he could have an eye upon them, for he wanted no such secret doings on board the brig. It was well for us that the pitching of the vessel at this moment was so violent as to prevent this order from being carried into instant execution. The cook got up from his mattress to go for us, when a tremendous lurch, which I thought would carry away the masts, threw him headlong against one of the larboard state-room doors, bursting it open, and creating a good deal of other confusion. Luckily, neither of our party was thrown from his position, and we had time to make a precipitate retreat to the forecastle, and arrange a hurried plan of action before the messenger made his appearance, or rather before he put his head out of the companion-hatch, for he did not come on deck. From this station he could not notice the absence of Allen, and he accordingly bawled out, as if to him, repeating the orders of the mate. Peters cried out, "Ay, ay," in a disguised voice, and the cook immediately went below, without entertaining a suspicion that all was not right.

My two companions now proceeded boldly aft and down into the cabin, Peters closing the door after him in the same manner he had found it. The mate received them with feigned cordiality, and told Augustus that, since he had behaved himself so well of late, he might

take up his quarters in the cabin and be one of them for the future. He then poured him out a tumbler half full of rum, and made him drink it. All this I saw and heard, for I followed my friends to the cabin as soon as the door was shut, and took up my old point of observation. I had brought with me the two pump-handles, one of which I secured near the companion-way, to be ready for use when required.

I now steadied myself as well as possible so as to have a good view of all that was passing within, and endeavored to nerve myself to the task of descending among the mutineers when Peters should make a signal to me, as agreed upon. Presently he contrived to turn the conversation upon the bloody deeds of the mutiny, and by degrees led the men to talk of the thousand superstitions which are so universally current among seamen. I could not make out all that was said, but I could plainly see the effects of the conversation in the countenances of those present. The mate was evidently much agitated and presently, when some one mentioned the terrific appearance of Rogers' corpse, I thought he was upon the point of swooning. Peters now asked him if he did not think it would be better to have the body thrown overboard at once as it was too horrible a sight to see it floundering about in the scuppers. At this the villain absolutely gasped for breath, and turned his head slowly round upon his companions, as if imploring some one to go up and perform the task. No one, however, stirred, and it was quite evident that the whole party were wound up to the highest pitch of nervous excitement. Peters now made me the signal. I immediately threw open the door of the companion-way, and, descending, without uttering a syllable, stood erect in the midst of the party.

The intense effect produced by this sudden apparition is not at all to be wondered at when the various circumstances are taken into consideration. Usually, in cases of a similar nature, there is left in the mind of the spectator some glimmering of doubt as to the reality of the vision before his eyes; a degree of hope, however feeble, that he is the victim of chicanery, and that the apparition is not actually a visitant from the old world of shadows. It is not too much to say that such remnants of doubt have been at the bottom of almost every such visitation, and that the appalling horror which has some-

times been brought about, is to be attributed, even in the
cases most in point, and where most suffering has been
experienced, more to a kind of anticipative horror, lest
the apparition *might possibly be* real, than to an unwav-
ering belief in its reality. But, in the present instance,
it will be seen immediately, that in the minds of the muti-
neers there was not even the shadow of a basis upon
which to rest a doubt that the apparition of Rogers
was indeed a revivification of his disgusting corpse, or
at least its spiritual image. The isolated situation of the
brig, with its entire inaccessibility on account of the gale,
confined the apparently possible means of deception with-
in such narrow and definite limits, that they must have
thought themselves enabled to survey them all at a
glance. They had now been at sea twenty-four days, with-
out holding more than a speaking communication with
any vessel whatever. The whole of the crew, too—at
least all whom they had the most remote reason for sus-
pecting to be on board—were assembled in the cabin,
with the exception of Allen, the watch; and his gigantic
stature (he was six feet six inches high) was too fa-
miliar in their eyes to permit the notion that he was the
apparition before them to enter their minds even for
an instant. Add to these considerations the awe-inspiring
nature of the tempest, and that of the conversation
brought about by Peters; the deep impression which the
loathsomeness of the actual corpse had made in the
morning upon the imaginations of the men; the excel-
lence of the imitation in my person, and the uncertain
and wavering light in which they beheld me, as the glare
of the cabin lantern, swinging violently to and fro, fell
dubiously and fitfully upon my figure, and there will be
no reason to wonder that the deception had even more
than the entire effect which we had anticipated. The
mate sprang up from the mattress on which he was lying,
and, without uttering a syllable, fell back, stone dead,
upon the cabin floor, and was hurled to the leeward like a
log by a heavy roll of the brig. Of the remaining seven,
there were but three who had at first any degree of pres-
ence of mind. The four others sat for some time rooted
apparently to the floor—the most pitiable objects of hor-
ror and utter despair my eyes ever encountered. The
only opposition we experienced at all was from the cook,
John Hunt, and Richard Parker; but they made but a

feeble and irresolute defence. The two former were shot
instantly by Peters, and I felled Parker with a blow on
the head from the pump-handle which I had brought with
me. In the mean time, Augustus seized one of the muskets
lying on the floor and shot another mutineer (———— Wil-
son) through the breast. There were now but three re-
maining; but by this time they had become aroused from
their lethargy, and perhaps began to see that a deception
had been practised upon them, for they fought with great
resolution and fury, and, but for the immense muscular
strength of Peters, might have ultimately got the better of
us. These three men were ———— Jones, ———— Greely, and
Absalom Hicks. Jones had thrown Augustus on the floor,
stabbed him in several places along the right arm, and
would no doubt have soon dispatched him (as neither
Peters nor myself could immediately get rid of our own
antagonists) had it not been for the timely aid of a friend,
upon whose assistance we, surely, had never depended.
This friend was no other than Tiger. With a low growl, he
bounded into the cabin, at a most critical moment for
Augustus, and, throwing himself upon Jones, pinned
him to the floor in an instant. My friend, however,
was now too much injured to render us any aid what-
ever, and I was so encumbered with my disguise that I
could do but little. The dog would not leave his hold
upon the throat of Jones—Peters, nevertheless, was
far more than a match for the two men who remained,
and would, no doubt, have dispatched them sooner, had
it not been for the narrow space in which he had to act,
and the tremendous lurches of the vessel. Presently he
was enabled to get hold of a heavy stool, several of
which lay about the floor. With this he beat out the brains
of Greely as he was in the act of discharging a musket
at me, and immediately afterward a roll of the brig
throwing him in contact with Hicks, he seized him by the
throat, and, by dint of sheer strength, strangled him in-
stantaneously. Thus, in far less time than I have taken to
tell it, we found ourselves masters of the brig.

The only person of our opponents who was left alive
was Richard Parker. This man, it will be remembered,
I had knocked down with a blow from the pump-handle
at the commencement of the attack. He now lay motion-
less by the door of the shattered state-room; but, upon
Peters touching him with his foot, he spoke, and en-

treated for mercy. His head was only slightly cut, and
otherwise he had received no injury, having been merely
stunned by the blow. He now got up, and, for the pres-
ent, we secured his hands behind his back. The dog was
still growling over Jones; but, upon examination, we
found him completely dead, the blood issuing in a stream
from a deep wound in the throat, inflicted, no doubt, by
the sharp teeth of the animal.

It was now about one o'clock in the morning, and
the wind was still blowing tremendously. The brig evi-
dently labored much more than usual, and it became ab-
solutely necessary that something should be done with a
view of easing her in some measure. At almost every roll
to leeward she shipped a sea, several of which came
partially down into the cabin during our scuffle, the
hatchway having been left open by myself when I de-
scended. The entire range of bulwarks to larboard had
been swept away, · as well as the caboose, together with
the jolly-boat from the counter. The creaking and work-
ing of the mainmast, too, gave indication that it was near-
ly sprung. To make room for more stowage in the after-
hold, the heel of this mast had been stepped between
decks (a very reprehensible practice, occasionally re-
sorted to by ignorant ship-builders), so that it was in im-
minent danger of working from its step. But, to crown all
our difficulties, we plumbed the well, and found no less
than seven feet of water.

Leaving the bodies of the crew lying in the cabin,
we got to work immediately at the pumps—Parker, of
course, being set at liberty to assist us in the labor. Au-
gustus' arm was bound up as well as we could effect it,
and he did what he could, but that was not much. How-
ever, we found that we could just manage to keep the
leak from gaining upon us by having one pump constant-
ly going. As there were only four of us, this was severe
labor; but we endeavored to keep up our spirits, and
looked anxiously for daybreak, when we hoped to
lighten the brig by cutting away the mainmast.

In this manner we passed a night of terrible anxiety
and fatigue, and, when the day at length broke, the gale
had neither abated in the least, nor were there any signs
of its abating. We now dragged the bodies on deck and
threw them overboard. Our next care was to get rid of
the mainmast. The necessary preparations having been

made, Peters cut away at the mast (having found axes in the cabin), while the rest of us stood by the stays and lanyards. As the brig gave a tremendous lee-lurch, the word was given to cut away the weather-lanyards, which being done, the whole mass of wood and rigging plunged into the sea, clear of the brig, and without doing any material injury. We now found that the vessel did not labor quite as much as before, but our situation was still exceedingly precarious, and, in spite of the utmost exertions, we could not gain upon the leak without the aid of both pumps. The little assistance which Augustus could render us was not really of any importance. To add to our distress, a heavy sea, striking the brig to the windward, threw her off several points from the wind, and, before she could regain her position, another broke completely over her, and hurled her full upon her beam-ends. The ballast now shifted in a mass to leeward (the stowage had been knocking about perfectly at random for some time), and for a few moments we thought nothing could save us from capsizing. Presently, however, we partially righted; but the ballast still retaining its place to larboard, we lay so much along that it was useless to think of working the pumps, which indeed we could not have done much longer in any case, as our hands were entirely raw with the excessive labor we had undergone, and were bleeding in the most horrible manner.

Contrary to Parker's advice, we now proceeded to cut away the foremast, and at length accomplished it after much difficulty, owing to the position in which we lay. In going overboard the wreck took with it the bowsprit, and left us a complete hulk.

So far we had had reason to rejoice in the escape of our long-boat, which had received no damage from any of the huge seas which had come on board. But we had not long to congratulate ourselves; for the foremast having gone, and, of course, the foresail with it, by which the brig had been steadied, every sea now made a complete breach over us, and in five minutes our deck was swept from stem to stern, the long-boat and starboard bulwarks torn off, and even the windlass shattered into fragments. It was, indeed, hardly possible for us to be in a more pitiable condition.

At noon there seemed to be some slight appearance

of the gale's abating, but in this we were sadly dis-
appointed, for it only lulled for a few minutes to blow
with redoubled fury. About four in the afternoon it was
utterly impossible to stand up against the violence of the
blast; and, as the night closed in upon us, I had not a
shadow of hope that the vessel would hold together
until morning.

By midnight we had settled very deep in the water,
which was now up to the orlop deck. The rudder went
soon afterward, the sea which tore it away lifting the
after-portion of the brig entirely from the water, against
which she thumped in her descent with such a concus-
sion as would be occasioned by going ashore. We had all
calculated that the rudder would hold its own to the
last, as it was unusually strong, being rigged as I have
never seen one rigged either before or since. Down its
main timber there ran a succession of stout iron hooks,
and others in the same manner down the stern-post.
Through these hooks there extended a very thick wrought-
iron rod, the rudder being thus held to the stern-post, and
swinging freely on the rod. The tremendous force of the
sea which tore it off may be estimated by the fact, that
the hooks in the stern-post, which ran entirely through
it, being clinched on the inside, were drawn every one
of them completely out of the solid wood.

We had scarcely time to draw breath after the vio-
lence of this shock, when one of the most tremendous
waves I had then ever known broke right on board of us,
sweeping the companion-way clear off, bursting in the
hatchways, and filling every inch of the vessel with water.

CHAPTER IX

LUCKILY, just before night, all four of us had lashed our-
selves firmly to the fragments of the windlass, lying in
this manner as flat upon the deck as possible. This pre-
caution alone saved us from destruction. As it was, we
were all more or less stunned by the immense weight of
water which tumbled upon us, and which did not roll
from above us until we were nearly exhausted. As
soon as I could recover breath, I called aloud to my
companions. Augustus alone replied, saying: "It is all
over with us, and may God have mercy upon our souls!"

By and by both the others were enabled to speak, when they exhorted us to take courage, as there was still hope; it being impossible, from the nature of the cargo, that the brig could go down, and there being every chance that the gale would blow over by the morning. These words inspired me with new life; for, strange as it may seem, although it was obvious that a vessel with a cargo of empty oil-casks would not sink, I had been hitherto so confused in mind as to have overlooked this consideration altogether; and the danger which I had for some time regarded as the most imminent was that of foundering. As hope revived within me, I made use of every opportunity to strengthen the lashings which held me to the remains of the windlass, and in this occupation I soon discovered that my companions were also busy. The night was as dark as it could possibly be, and the horrible shrieking din and confusion which surrounded us it is useless to attempt describing. Our deck lay level with the sea, or rather we were encircled with a towering ridge of foam, a portion of which swept over us every instant. It is not too much to say that our heads were not fairly out of the water more than one second in three. Although we lay close together, no one of us could see the other, or indeed, any portion of the brig itself, upon which we were so tempestuously hurled about. At intervals we called one to the other, thus endeavoring to keep alive hope, and render consolation and encouragement to such of us as stood most in need of it. The feeble condition of Augustus made him an object of solicitude with us all; and as, from the lacerated condition of his right arm, it must have been impossible for him to secure his lashings with any degree of firmness, we were in momentary expectation of finding that he had gone overboard—yet to render him aid was a thing altogether out of the question. Fortunately, his station was more secure than that of any of the rest of us; for the upper part of his body lying just beneath a portion of the shattered windlass, the seas, as they tumbled in upon him, were greatly broken in their violence. In any other situation than this (into which he had been accidentally thrown after having lashed himself in a very exposed spot) he must inevitably have perished before morning. Owing to the brig's lying so much along, we were all less liable to be washed off than otherwise

would have been the case. The heel, as I have before stated, was to larboard, about one half of the deck being constantly under water. The seas, therefore, which struck us to starboard were much broken by the vessel's side, only reaching us in fragments as we lay flat on our faces; while those which came from larboard, being what are called back-water seas, and obtaining little hold upon us on account of our posture, had not sufficient force to drag us from our fastenings.

In this frightful situation we lay until the day broke so as to show us more fully the horrors which surrounded us. The brig was a mere log, rolling about at the mercy of every wave; the gale was upon the increase, if any thing, blowing indeed a complete hurricane, and there appeared to us no earthly prospect of deliverance. For several hours we held on in silence, expecting every moment that our lashings would give way, that the remains of the windlass would go by the board, or that some of the huge seas, which roared in every direction around us and above us, would drive the hulk so far beneath the water that we should be drowned before it could regain the surface. By the mercy of God, however, we were preserved from these imminent dangers, and about midday were cheered by the light of the blessed sun. Shortly afterward we could perceive a sensible diminution in the force of the wind, when, now for the first time since the latter part of the evening before, Augustus spoke, asking Peters, who lay closest to him, if he thought there was any possibility of our being saved. As no reply was at first made to this question, we all concluded that the hybrid had been drowned where he lay; but presently, to our great joy, he spoke, although very feebly, saying that he was in great pain, being so cut by the tightness of his lashings across the stomach, that he must either find means of loosening them or perish, as it was impossible that he could endure his misery much longer. This occasioned us great distress, as it was altogether useless to think of aiding him in any manner while the sea continued washing over us as it did. We exhorted him to bear his sufferings with fortitude, and promised to seize the first opportunity which should offer itself to relieve him. He replied that it would soon be too late; that it would be all over with him before we could help him; and then, after moaning for

some minutes, lay silent, when we concluded that he had perished.

As the evening drew on, the sea had fallen so much that scarcely more than one wave broke over the hulk from windward in the course of five minutes, and the wind had abated a great deal, although still blowing a severe gale. I had not heard any of my companions speak for hours, and now called to Augustus. He replied, although very feebly, so that I could not distinguish what he said. I then spoke to Peters and to Parker, neither of whom returned any answer.

Shortly after this period I fell into a state of partial insensibility, during which the most pleasing images floated in my imagination; such as green trees, waving meadows of ripe grain, processions of dancing girls, troops of cavalry, and other phantasies. I now remembered that, in all which passed before my mind's eye, *motion* was a predominant idea. Thus, I never fancied any stationary object, such as a house, a mountain, or any thing of that kind; but windmills, ships, large birds, balloons, people on horseback, carriages driving furiously, and similar moving objects, presented themselves in endless succession. When I recovered from this state, the sun was, as near as I could guess, an hour high. I had the greatest difficulty in bringing to recollection the various circumstances connected with my situation, and for some time remained firmly convinced that I was still in the hold of the brig, near the box, and that the body of Parker was that of Tiger.

When I at length completely came to my senses, I found that the wind blew no more than a moderate breeze, and that the sea was comparatively calm; so much so that it only washed over the brig amidships. My left arm had broken loose from its lashings, and was much cut about the elbow; my right was entirely benumbed, and the hand and wrist swollen prodigiously by the pressure of the rope, which had worked from the shoulder downward. I was also in great pain from another rope which went about my waist, and had been drawn to an insufferable degree of tightness. Looking round upon my companions, I saw that Peters still lived, although a thick line was pulled so forcibly around his loins as to give him the appearance of being cut nearly in two; as I stirred, he made a feeble motion to me with

his hand, pointing to the rope. Augustus gave no indication of life whatever, and was bent nearly double across a splinter of the windlass. Parker spoke to me when he saw me moving, and asked me if I had not sufficient strength to release him from his situation, saying, that if I would summon up what spirits I could, and contrive to untie him, we might yet save our lives; but that otherwise, we must all perish. I told him to take courage, and I would endeavor to free him. Feeling in my pantaloons pocket, I got hold of my penknife, and, after several ineffectual attempts, at length succeeded in opening it. I then, with my left hand, managed to free my right from its fastenings, and afterward cut the other ropes which held me. Upon attempting, however, to move from my position, I found that my legs failed me altogether, and that I could not get up; neither could I move my right arm in any direction. Upon mentioning this to Parker, he advised me to lie quiet for a few minutes, holding on to the windlass with my left hand, so as to allow time for the blood to circulate. Doing this, the numbness presently began to die away so that I could move first one of my legs, and then the other, and shortly afterward I regained the partial use of my right arm. I now crawled with great caution toward Parker, without getting on my legs, and soon cut loose all the lashings about him, when, after a short delay, he also recovered the partial use of his limbs. We now lost no time in getting loose the rope from Peters. It had cut a deep gash through the waistband of his woollen pantaloons, and through two shirts, and made its way into his groin, from which the blood flowed out copiously as we removed the cordage. No sooner had we removed it, however, than he spoke, and seemed to experience instant relief, being able to move with much greater ease than either Parker or myself—this was no doubt owing to the discharge of blood.

We had little hopes that Augustus would recover, as he evinced no signs of life; but, upon getting to him, we discovered that he had merely swooned from loss of blood, the bandages we had placed around his wounded arm having been torn off by the water; none of the ropes which held him to the windlass were drawn sufficiently tight to occasion his death. Having relieved him from the fastenings, and got him clear of the broken

wood about the windlass, we secured him in a dry place to windward, with his head somewhat lower than his body, and all three of us busied ourselves in chafing his limbs. In about half an hour he came to himself, although it was not until the next morning that he gave signs of recognizing any of us, or had sufficient strength to speak. By the time we had thus got clear of our lashings it was quite dark, and it began to cloud up, so that we were again in the greatest agony lest it should come on to blow hard, in which event nothing could have saved us from perishing, exhausted as we were. By good fortune it continued very moderate during the night, the sea subsiding every minute, which gave us great hopes of ultimate preservation. A gentle breeze still blew from the N. W., but the weather was not at all cold. Augustus was lashed carefully to windward in such a manner as to prevent him from slipping overboard with the rolls of the vessel, as he was still too weak to hold on at all. For ourselves there was no such necessity. We sat close together, supporting each other with the aid of the broken ropes about the windlass, and devising methods of escape from our frightful situation. We derived much comfort from taking off our clothes and wringing the water from them. When we put them on after this, they felt remarkably warm and pleasant, and served to invigorate us in no little degree. We helped Augustus off with his, and wrung them for him, when he experienced the same comfort.

Our chief sufferings were now those of hunger and thirst, and when we looked forward to the means of relief in this respect, our hearts sunk within us, and we were induced to regret that we had escaped the less dreadful perils of the sea. We endeavored, however, to console ourselves with the hope of being speedily picked up by some vessel, and encouraged each other to bear with fortitude the evils that might happen.

The morning of the fourteenth at length dawned, and the weather still continued clear and pleasant, with a steady but very light breeze from the N. W. The sea was now quite smooth, and as, from some cause which we could not determine, the brig did not lie so much along as she had done before, the deck was comparatively dry, and we could move about with freedom. We had now been better than three entire days and nights with-

out either food or drink, and it became absolutely necessary that we should make an attempt to get up something from below. As the brig was completely full of water, we went to this work despondingly, and with but little expectation of being able to obtain any thing. We made a kind of drag by driving some nails which we broke out from the remains of the companion-hatch into two pieces of wood. Tying these across each other, and fastening them to the end of a rope, we threw them into the cabin, and dragged them to and fro, in the faint hope of being thus able to entangle some article which might be of use to us for food, or which might at least render us assistance in getting it. We spent the greater part of the morning in this labor without effect, fishing up nothing more than a few bedclothes, which were readily caught by the nails. Indeed, our contrivance was so very clumsy that any greater success was hardly to be anticipated.

We now tried the forecastle, but equally in vain, and were upon the brink of despair, when Peters proposed that we should fasten a rope to his body, and let him make an attempt to get up something by diving into the cabin. This proposition we hailed with all the delight which reviving hope could inspire. He proceeded immediately to strip off his clothes with the exception of his pantaloons; and a strong rope was then carefully fastened around his middle, being brought up over his shoulders in such a manner that there was no possibility of its slipping. The undertaking was one of great difficulty and danger; for, as we could hardly expect to find much, if any, provision in the cabin itself, it was necessary that the diver, after letting himself down, should make a turn to the right, and proceed under water a distance of ten or twelve feet, in a narrow passage, to the store-room, and return, without drawing breath.

Every thing being ready, Peters now descended into the cabin, going down the companion-ladder until the water reached his chin. He then plunged in, head first, turning to the right as he plunged, and endeavoring to make his way to the store-room. In this first attempt, however, he was altogether unsuccessful. In less than half a minute after his going down we felt the rope jerked violently (the signal we had agreed upon when he desired to be drawn up). We accordingly drew him up in-

stantly, but so incautiously as to bruise him badly against the ladder. He had brought nothing with him, and had been unable to penetrate more than a very little way into the passage, owing to the constant exertions he found it necessary to make in order to keep himself from floating up against the deck. Upon getting out he was very much exhausted, and had to rest full fifteen minutes before he could again venture to descend.

The second attempt met with even worse success; for he remained so long under water without giving the signal, that, becoming alarmed for his safety, we drew him out without it, and found that he was almost at the last gasp, having, as he said, repeatedly jerked at the rope without our feeling it. This was probably owing to a portion of it having become entangled in the balustrade at the foot of the ladder. This balustrade was, indeed, so much in the way, that we determined to remove it, if possible, before proceeding with our design. As we had no means of getting it away except by main force, we all descended into the water as far as we could on the ladder, and giving a pull against it with our united strength, succeeded in breaking it down.

The third attempt was equally unsuccessful with the two first, and it now became evident that nothing could be done in this manner without the aid of some weight with which the diver might steady himself, and keep to the floor of the cabin while making his search. For a long time we looked about in vain for something which might answer this purpose; but at length, to our great joy, we discovered one of the weather-forechains so loose that we had not the least difficulty in wrenching it off. Having fastened this securely to one of his ankles Peters now made his fourth descent into the cabin, and this time succeeded in making his way to the door of the steward's room. To his inexpressible grief, however, he found it locked, and was obliged to return without effecting an entrance, as, with the greatest exertion, he could remain under water not more, at the utmost extent, than a single minute. Our affairs now looked gloomy indeed, and neither Augustus nor myself could refrain from bursting into tears, as we thought of the host of difficulties which encompassed us, and the slight probability which existed of our finally making an escape. But this weakness was not of long duration. Throw-

ing ourselves on our knees to God, we implored His aid in the many dangers which beset us; and arose with renewed hope and vigor to think what could yet be done by mortal means toward accomplishing our deliverance.

<div align="center">CHAPTER X</div>

Shortly afterward an incident occurred which I am induced to look upon as more intensely productive of emotion, as far more replete with the extremes first of delight and then of horror, than even any of the thousand chances which afterward befell me in nine long years, crowded with events of the most startling and, in many cases, of the most unconceived and unconceivable character. We were lying on the deck near the companion-way, and debating the possibility of yet making our way into the store-room, when, looking toward Augustus, who lay fronting myself, I perceived that he had become all at once deadly pale, and that his lips were quivering in the most singular and unaccountable manner. Greatly alarmed, I spoke to him, but he made me no reply, and I was beginning to think that he was suddenly taken ill, when I took notice of his eyes, which were glaring apparently at some object behind me. I turned my head, and shall never forget the ecstatic joy which thrilled through every particle of my frame, when I perceived a large brig bearing down upon us, and not more than a couple of miles off. I sprung to my feet as if a musket bullet had suddenly struck me to the heart; and, stretching out my arms in the direction of the vessel, stood in this manner, motionless, and unable to articulate a syllable. Peters and Parker were equally affected, although in different ways. The former danced about the deck like a madman, uttering the most extravagant rodomontades, intermingled with howls and imprecations, while the latter burst into tears, and continued for many minutes weeping like a child.

The vessel in sight was a large hermaphrodite brig, of a Dutch build, and painted black, with a tawdry gilt figure-head. She had evidently seen a good deal of rough weather, and, we supposed, had suffered much in the gale which had proved so disastrous to ourselves; for her foretopmast was gone, and some of her starboard bul-

warks. When we first saw her, she was, as I have already said, about two miles off and to windward, bearing down upon us. The breeze was very gentle, and what astonished us chiefly was, that she had no other sails set than her foresail and mainsail, with a flying jib—of course she came down but slowly, and our impatience amounted nearly to phrensy. The awkward manner in which she steered, too, was remarked by all of us, even excited as we were. She yawed about so considerably, that once or twice we thought it impossible she could see us, or imagined that, having seen us, and discovered no person on board, she was about to tack and make off in another direction. Upon each of these occasions we screamed and shouted at the top of our voices, when the stranger would appear to change for a moment her intention, and again hold on toward us—this singular conduct being repeated two or three times, so that at last we could think of no other manner of accounting for it than by supposing the helmsman to be in liquor.

No person was seen upon her decks until she arrived within about a quarter of a mile of us. We then saw three seamen, whom by their dress we took to be Hollanders. Two of these were lying on some old sails near the forecastle, and the third, who appeared to be looking at us with great curiosity, was leaning over the starboard bow near the bowsprit. This last was a stout and tall man, with a very dark skin. He seemed by his manner to be encouraging us to have patience, nodding to us in a cheerful although rather odd way, and smiling constantly, so as to display a set of the most brilliantly white teeth. As his vessel drew nearer, we saw a red flannel cap which he had on fall from his head into the water; but of this he took little or no notice, continuing his odd smiles and gesticulations. I relate these things and circumstances minutely, and I relate them, it must be understood, precisely as they *appeared* to us.

The brig came on slowly, and now more steadily than before, and—I cannot speak calmly of this event—our hearts leaped up wildly within us, and we poured out our whole souls in shouts and thanksgiving to God for the complete, unexpected, and glorious deliverance that was so palpably at hand. Of a sudden, and all at once, there came wafted over the ocean from the strange vessel (which was now close upon us) a smell, a stench,

such as the whole world has no name for—no conception of—hellish—utterly suffocating—insufferable, inconceivable. I gasped for breath, and turning to my companions, perceived that they were paler than marble. But we had now no time left for question or surmise— the brig was within fifty feet of us, and it seemed to be her intention to run under our counter, that we might board her without putting out a boat. We rushed aft, when, suddenly, a wide yaw threw her off full five or six points from the course she had been running, and, as she passed under our stern at the distance of about twenty feet, we had a full view of her decks. Shall I ever forget the triple horror of that spectacle? Twenty-five or thirty human bodies, among whom were several females, lay scattered about between the counter and the galley in the last and most loathsome state of putrefaction. We plainly saw that not a soul lived in that fated vessel! Yet we could not help shouting to the dead for help! Yes, long and loudly did we beg, in the agony of the moment, that those silent and disgusting images would stay for us, would not abandon us to become like them, would receive us among their goodly company! We were raving with horror and despair—thoroughly mad through the anguish of our grievous disappointment.

As our first loud yell of terror broke forth, it was replied to by something, from near the bowsprit of the stranger, so closely resembling the scream of a human voice that the nicest ear might have been startled and deceived. At this instant another sudden yaw brought the region of the forecastle for a moment into view, and we beheld at once the origin of the sound. We saw the tall stout figure still leaning on the bulwark, and still nodding his head to and fro, but his face was now turned from us so that we could not behold it. His arms were extended over the rail, and the palms of his hands fell outward. His knees were lodged upon a stout rope, tightly stretched, and reaching from the heel of the bowsprit to a cathead. On his back, from which a portion of the shirt had been torn, leaving it bare, there sat a huge sea-gull, busily gorging itself with the horrible flesh, its bill and talons deep buried, and its white plumage spattered all over with blood. As the brig moved farther round so as to bring us close in view, the bird, with much apparent difficulty, drew out its crimsoned

head, and, after eying us for a moment as if stupefied, rose lazily from the body upon which it had been feasting, and, flying directly above our deck, hovered there a while with a portion of clotted and liver-like substance in its beak. The horrid morsel dropped at length with a sullen splash immediately at the feet of Parker. May God forgive me, but now, for the first time, there flashed through my mind a thought, a thought which I will not mention, and I felt myself making a step toward the ensanguined spot. I looked upward, and the eyes of Augustus met my own with a degree of intense and eager meaning which immediately brought me to my senses. I sprang forward quickly, and, with a deep shudder, threw the frightful thing into the sea.

The body from which it had been taken, resting as it did upon the rope, had been easily swayed to and fro by the exertions of the carnivorous bird, and it was this motion which had at first impressed us with the belief of its being alive. As the gull relieved it of its weight, it swung round and fell partially over, so that the face was fully discovered. Never, surely, was any object so terribly full of awe! The eyes were gone, and the whole flesh around the mouth, leaving the teeth utterly naked. This, then, was the smile which had cheered us on to hope! this the—but I forbear. The brig, as I have already told, passed under our stern, and made its way slowly but steadily to leeward. With her and her terrible crew went all our gay visions of deliverance and joy. Deliberately as she went by, we might possibly have found means of boarding her, had not our sudden disappointment, and the appalling nature of the discovery which accompanied it, laid entirely prostrate every active faculty of mind and body. We had seen and felt, but we could neither think nor act, until, alas! too late. How much our intellects had been weakened by this incident may be estimated by the fact, that when the vessel had proceeded so far that we could perceive no more than the half of her hull, the proposition was seriously entertained of attempting to overtake her by swimming!

I have, since this period, vainly endeavored to obtain some clew to the hideous uncertainty which enveloped the fate of the stranger. Her build and general appearance, as I have before stated, led us to the belief that she was a Dutch trader, and the dresses of the crew also

sustained this opinion. We might have easily seen the name upon her stern, and, indeed, taken other observations, which would have guided us in making out her character; but the intense excitement of the moment blinded us to everything of that nature. From the saffron-like hue of such of the corpses as were not entirely decayed, we concluded that the whole of her company had perished by the yellow fever, or some other virulent disease of the same fearful kind. If such were the case (and I know not what else to imagine), death, to judge from the positions of the bodies, must have come upon them in a manner awfully sudden and overwhelming—in a way totally distinct from that which generally characterizes even the most deadly pestilences with which mankind are acquainted. It is possible, indeed, that poison, accidentally introduced into some of their sea-stores, may have brought about the disaster; or that the eating some unknown venomous species of fish, or other marine animal, or oceanic bird, might have induced it—but it is utterly useless to form conjectures where all is involved, and will, no doubt, remain for ever involved, in the most appalling and unfathomable mystery.

CHAPTER XI

WE SPENT the remainder of the day in a condition of stupid lethargy, gazing after the retreating vessel until the darkness, hiding her from our sight, recalled us in some measure to our senses. The pangs of hunger and thirst then returned, absorbing all other cares and considerations. Nothing, however, could be done until the morning, and, securing ourselves as well as possible, we endeavored to snatch a little repose. In this I succeeded beyond my expectations, sleeping until my companions, who had not been so fortunate, aroused me at daybreak to renew our attempts at getting up provision from the hull.

It was now a dead calm, with the sea as smooth as I have ever known it—the weather warm and pleasant. The brig was out of sight. We commenced our operations by wrenching off, with some trouble, another of the forechains; and having fastened both to Peters' feet, he again made an endeavor to reach the door of the

store-room, thinking it possible that he might be able to force it open, provided he could get at it in sufficient time; and this he hoped to do, as the hulk lay much more steadily than before.

He succeeded very quickly in reaching the door, when, loosening one of the chains from his ankle, he made every exertion to force a passage with it, but in vain, the framework of the room being far stronger than was anticipated. He was quite exhausted with his long stay under water, and it became absolutely necessary that some other one of us should take his place. For this service Parker immediately volunteered; but, after making three ineffectual efforts, found that he could never even succeed in getting near the door. The condition of Augustus' wounded arm rendered it useless for him to attempt going down, as he would be unable to force the room open should he reach it, and it accordingly now devolved upon me to exert myself for our common deliverance.

Peters had left one of the chains in the passage, and I found, upon plunging in, that I had not sufficient balance to keep me firmly down. I determined, therefore, to attempt no more, in my first effort, than merely to recover the other chain. In groping along the floor of the passage for this, I felt a hard substance, which I immediately grasped, not having time to ascertain what it was, but returning and ascending instantly to the surface. The prize proved to be a bottle, and our joy may be conceived when I say that it was found to be full of port-wine. Giving thanks to God for this timely and cheering assistance, we immediately drew the cork with my pen-knife, and, each taking a moderate sup, felt the most indescribable comfort from the warmth, strength, and spirits with which it inspired us. We then carefully re-corked the bottle, and, by means of a handkerchief, swung it in such a manner that there was no possibility of its getting broken.

Having rested a while after this fortunate discovery, I again descended, and now recovered the chain, with which I instantly came up. I then fastened it on and went down for the third time, when I became fully satisfied that no exertions whatever, in that situation, would enable me to force open the door of the store-room. I therefore returned in despair.

There seemed now to be no longer any room for hope, and I could perceive in the countenances of my companions that they had made up their minds to perish. The wine had evidently produced in them a species of delirium, which, perhaps, I had been prevented from feeling by the immersion I had undergone since drinking it. They talked incoherently, and about matters unconnected with our condition, Peters repeatedly asking me questions about Nantucket. Augustus, too, I remember, approached me with a serious air, and requested me to lend him a pocket-comb, as his hair was full of fish-scales, and he wished to get them out before going on shore. Parker appeared somewhat less affected, and urged me to dive at random into the cabin, and bring up any article which might come to hand. To this I consented, and, in the first attempt, after staying under a full minute, brought up a small leather trunk belonging to Captain Barnard. This was immediately opened in the faint hope that it might contain something to eat or drink. We found nothing, however, except a box of razors and two linen shirts. I now went down again, and returned without any success. As my head came above water I heard a crash on deck, and, upon getting up, saw that my companions had ungratefully taken advantage of my absence to drink the remainder of the wine, having let the bottle fall in the endeavor to replace it before I saw them. I remonstrated with them on the heartlessness of their conduct, when Augustus burst into tears. The other two endeavored to laugh the matter off as a joke, but I hope never again to behold laughter of such a species: the distortion of countenance was absolutely frightful. Indeed, it was apparent that the stimulus, in the empty state of their stomachs, had taken instant and violent effect, and that they were all exceedingly intoxicated. With great difficulty I prevailed upon them to lie down, when they fell very soon into a heavy slumber, accompanied with loud stertorous breathing.

I now found myself, as it were, alone in the brig, and my reflections, to be sure, were of the most fearful and gloomy nature. No prospect offered itself to my view but a lingering death by famine, or, at the best, by being overwhelmed in the first gale which should spring up, for in our present exhausted condition we could have no hope of living through another.

The gnawing hunger which I now experienced was nearly insupportable, and I felt myself capable of going to any lengths in order to appease it. With my knife I cut off a small portion of the leather trunk, and endeavored to eat it, but found it utterly impossible to swallow a single morsel, although I fancied that some little alleviation of my suffering was obtained by chewing small pieces of it and spitting them out. Toward night my companions awoke, one by one, each in an indescribable state of weakness and horror, brought on by the wine, whose fumes had now evaporated. They shook as if with a violent ague, and uttered the most lamentable cries for water. Their condition affected me in the most lively degree, at the same time causing me to rejoice in the fortunate train of circumstances which had prevented me from indulging in the wine, and consequently from sharing their melancholy and most distressing sensations. Their conduct, however, gave me great uneasiness and alarm; for it was evident that, unless some favorable change took place, they could afford me no assistance in providing for our common safety. I had not yet abandoned all idea of being able to get up something from below; but the attempt could not possibly be resumed until some one of them was sufficiently master of himself to aid me by holding the end of the rope while I went down. Parker appeared to be somewhat more in possession of his senses than the others, and I endeavored, by every means in my power, to arouse him. Thinking that a plunge in the sea-water might have a beneficial effect, I contrived to fasten the end of a rope around his body, and then, leading him to the companionway (he remaining quite passive all the while), pushed him in, and immediately drew him out. I had good reason to congratulate myself upon having made this experiment; for he appeared much revived and invigorated, and, upon getting out, asked me, in a rational manner, why I had so served him. Having explained my object, he expressed himself indebted to me, and said that he felt greatly better from the immersion, afterward conversing sensibly upon our situation. We then resolved to treat Augustus and Peters in the same way, which we immediately did, when they both experienced much benefit from the shock. This idea of sudden immersion had been suggested to me by reading in some

medical work the good effect of the shower-bath in a case where the patient was suffering from *mania a potu*.

Finding that I could now trust my companions to hold the end of the rope, I again made three or four plunges into the cabin, although it was now quite dark, and a gentle but long swell from the northward rendered the hulk somewhat unsteady. In the course of these attempts I succeeded in bringing up two case-knives, a three-gallon jug—empty—and a blanket, but nothing which could serve us for food. I continued my efforts, after getting these articles, until I was completely exhausted, but brought up nothing else. During the night Parker and Peters occupied themselves by turns in the same manner; but nothing coming to hand, we now gave up this attempt in despair, concluding that we were exhausting ourselves in vain.

We passed the remainder of this night in a state of the most intense mental and bodily anguish that can possibly be imagined. The morning of the sixteenth at length dawned, and we looked eagerly around the horizon for relief, but to no purpose. The sea was still smooth, with only a long swell from the northward, as on yesterday. This was the sixth day since we had tasted either food or drink, with the exception of the bottle of port-wine, and it was clear that we could hold out but a very little while longer unless something could be obtained. I never saw before, nor wish to see again, human beings so utterly emaciated as Peters and Augustus. Had I met them on shore in their present condition I should not have had the slightest suspicion that I had ever beheld them. Their countenances were totally changed in character, so that I could not bring myself to believe them really the same individuals with whom I had been in company but a few days before. Parker, although sadly reduced, and so feeble that he could not raise his head from his bosom, was not so far gone as the other two. He suffered with great patience, making no complaint, and endeavoring to inspire us with hope in every manner he could devise. For myself, although at the commencement of the voyage I had been in bad health, and was at all times of a delicate constitution, I suffered less than any of us, being much less reduced in frame, and retaining my powers of mind in a surprising degree, while the rest were completely prostrated in intellect, and seemed

to be brought to a species of second childhood, generally simpering in their expressions, with idiotic smiles, and uttering the most absurd platitudes. At intervals, however, they would appear to revive suddenly, as if inspired all at once with a consciousness of their condition, when they would spring upon their feet in a momentary flash of vigor, and speak, for a short period, of their prospects, in a manner altogether rational, although full of the most intense despair. It is possible, however, that my companions may have entertained the same opinion of their own condition as I did of mine, and that I may have unwittingly been guilty of the same extravagances and imbecilities as themselves—this is a matter which cannot be determined.

About noon Parker declared that he saw land off the larboard quarter, and it was with the utmost difficulty I could restrain him from plunging into the sea with the view of swimming toward it. Peters and Augustus took little notice of what he said, being apparently wrapped up in moody contemplation. Upon looking in the direction pointed out, I could not perceive the faintest appearance of the shore—indeed, I was too well aware that we were far from any land to indulge in a hope of that nature. It was a long time, nevertheless, before I could convince Parker of his mistake. He then burst into a flood of tears, weeping like a child, with loud cries and sobs, for two or three hours, when, becoming exhausted, he fell asleep.

Peters and Augustus now made several ineffectual efforts to swallow portions of the leather. I advised them to chew it and spit it out; but they were too excessively debilitated to be able to follow my advice. I continued to chew pieces of it at intervals, and found some relief from so doing; my chief distress was for water, and I was only prevented from taking a draught from the sea by remembering the horrible consequences which thus have resulted to others who were similarly situated with ourselves.

The day wore on in this manner, when I suddenly discovered a sail to the eastward, and on our larboard bow. She appeared to be a large ship, and was coming nearly athwart us, being probably twelve or fifteen miles distant. None of my companions had as yet discovered

her, and I forebore to tell them of her for the present,
lest we might again be disappointed of relief. At length,
upon her getting nearer, I saw distinctly that she was
heading immediately for us, with her light sails filled. I
could now contain myself no longer, and pointed her
out to my fellow-sufferers. They immediately sprang to
their feet, again indulging in the most extravagant dem-
onstrations of joy, weeping, laughing in an idiotic man-
ner, jumping, stamping upon the deck, tearing their hair,
and praying and cursing by turns. I was so affected by
their conduct, as well as by what I now considered a
sure prospect of deliverance, that I could not refrain
from joining in with their madness, and gave way to the
impulses of my gratitude and ecstasy by lying and roll-
ing on the deck, clapping my hands, shouting, and other
similar acts, until I was suddenly called to my recollec-
tion, and once more to the extreme of human misery and
despair, by perceiving the ship all at once with her stern
fully presented toward us, and steering in a direction
nearly opposite to that in which I had at first perceived
her.

It was some time before I could induce my poor com-
panions to believe that this sad reverse in our prospects
had actually taken place. They replied to all my asser-
tions with a stare and a gesture implying that they were
not to be deceived by such misrepresentations. The con-
duct of Augustus most sensibly affected me. In spite of
all I could say or do to the contrary, he persisted in
saying that the ship was rapidly nearing us, and in mak-
ing preparations to go on board of her. Some sea-weed
floating by the brig, he maintained that it was the ship's
boat, and endeavored to throw himself upon it, howling
and shrieking in the most heart-rending manner, when
I forcibly restrained him from thus casting himself into
the sea.

Having become in some degree pacified, we continued
to watch the ship until we finally lost sight of her, the
weather becoming hazy, with a light breeze springing up.
As soon as she was entirely gone, Parker turned sud-
denly toward me with an expression of countenance
which made me shudder. There was about him an air
of self-possession which I had not noticed in him until
now, and before he opened his lips my heart told me

what he would say. He proposed, in a few words, that
one of us should die to preserve the existence of the
others.

CHAPTER XII

I HAD, for some time past, dwelt upon the prospect of
our being reduced to this last horrible extremity, and had
secretly made up my mind to suffer death in any shape
or under any circumstances rather than resort to such
a course. Nor was this resolution in any degree weak-
ened by the present intensity of hunger under which I
labored. The proposition had not been heard by either
Peters or Augustus. I therefore took Parker aside; and
mentally praying to God for power to dissuade him from
the horrible purpose he entertained, I expostulated with
him for a long time, and in the most supplicating man-
ner, begging him in the name of every thing which he
held sacred, and urging him by every species of argu-
ment which the extremity of the case suggested, to aban-
don the idea, and not to mention it to either of the other
two.

He heard all I said without attempting to controvert
any of my arguments, and I had begun to hope that he
would be prevailed upon to do as I desired. But when I
had ceased speaking, he said that he knew very well all
I had said was true, and that to resort to such a course
was the most horrible alternative which could enter
into the mind of man; but that he had now held out as
long as human nature could be sustained; that it was un-
necessary for all to perish, when, by the death of one, it
was possible, and even probable, that the rest might be
finally preserved; adding that I might save myself the
trouble of trying to turn him from his purpose, his mind
having been thoroughly made up on the subject even be-
fore the appearance of the ship, and that only her heav-
ing in sight had prevented him from mentioning his in-
tention at an earlier period.

I now begged him, if he would not be prevailed upon to
abandon his design, at least to defer it for another day,
when some vessel might come to our relief; again reit-
erating every argument I could devise, and which I
thought likely to have influence with one of his rough na-

ture. He said, in reply, that he had not spoken until
the very last possible moment, that he could exist no
longer without sustenance of some kind, and that there-
fore in another day his suggestion would be too late, as
regarded himself at least.

Finding that he was not to be moved by any thing I
could say in a mild tone, I now assumed a different de-
meanor, and told him that he must be aware I had suf-
fered less than any of us from our calamities; that my
health and strength, consequently, were at that moment
far better than his own, or than that either of Peters or
Augustus; in short, that I was in a condition to have my
own way by force if I found it necessary; and that if he
attempted in any manner to acquaint the others with his
bloody and cannibal designs, I would not hesitate to
throw him into the sea. Upon this he immediately seized
me by the throat, and drawing a knife, made several in-
effectual efforts to stab me in the stomach; an atrocity
which his excessive debility alone prevented him from ac-
complishing. In the meantime, being roused to a high
pitch of anger, I forced him to the vessel's side, with the
full intention of throwing him overboard. He was saved
from this fate, however, by the interference of Peters,
who now approached and separated us, asking the cause
of the disturbance. This Parker told before I could find
means in any manner to prevent him.

The effect of his words was even more terrible than
what I had anticipated. Both Augustus and Peters, who,
it seems, had long secretly entertained the same fearful
idea which Parker had been merely the first to broach,
joined with him in his design and insisted upon its imme-
diately being carried into effect. I had calculated that one
at least of the two former would be found still possessed
of sufficient strength of mind to side with myself in resist-
ing any attempt to execute so dreadful a purpose; and,
with the aid of either one of them, I had no fear of being
able to prevent its accomplishment. Being disappointed
in this expectation, it became absolutely necessary that
I should attend to my own safety, as a further resistance
on my part might possibly be considered by men in their
frightful condition a sufficient excuse for refusing me fair
play in the tragedy that I knew would speedily be enacted.

I now told them I was willing to submit to the proposal,
merely requesting a delay of about one hour, in order

that the fog which had gathered around us might have an opportunity of lifting, when it was possible that the ship we had seen might be again in sight. After great difficulty I obtained from them a promise to wait thus long; and, as I had anticipated (a breeze rapidly coming in), the fog lifted before the hour had expired, when, no vessel appearing in sight, we prepared to draw lots.

It is with extreme reluctance that I dwell upon the appalling scene which ensued; a scene which, with its minutest details, no after-events have been able to efface in the slightest degree from my memory, and whose stern recollection will embitter every future moment of my existence. Let me run over this portion of my narrative with as much haste as the nature of the events to be spoken of will permit. The only method we could devise for the terrific lottery, in which we were to take each a chance, was that of drawing straws. Small splinters of wood were made to answer our purpose, and it was agreed that I should be the holder. I retired to one end of the hulk, while my poor companions silently took up their station in the other with their backs turned toward me. The bitterest anxiety which I endured at any period of this fearful drama was while I occupied myself in the arrangement of the lots. There are few conditions into which man can possibly fall where he will not feel a deep interest in the preservation of his existence; an interest momentarily increasing with the frailness of the tenure by which that existence may be held. But now that the silent, definite, and stern nature of the business in which I was engaged (so different from the tumultuous dangers of the storm or the gradually approaching horrors of famine) allowed me to reflect on the few chances I had of escaping the most appalling of deaths —a death for the most appalling of purposes—every particle of that energy which had so long buoyed me up departed like feathers before the wind, leaving me a helpless prey to the most abject and pitiable terror. I could not, at first, even summon up sufficient strength to tear and fit together the small splinters of wood, my fingers absolutely refusing their office, and my knees knocking violently against each other. My mind ran over rapidly a thousand absurd projects by which to avoid becoming a partner in the awful speculation. I thought of falling on my knees to my companions, and entreating them to

let me escape this necessity; of suddenly rushing upon
them, and, by putting one of them to death, of rendering
the decision by lot useless—in short, of every thing but
of going through with the matter I had in hand. At last,
after wasting a long time in this imbecile conduct, I was
recalled to my senses by the voice of Parker, who urged
me to relieve them at once from the terrible anxiety they
were enduring. Even then I could not bring myself to ar-
range the splinters upon the spot, but thought over every
species of finesse by which I could trick some one of my
fellow-sufferers to draw the short straw, as it had been
agreed that whoever drew the shortest of four splinters
from my hand was to die for the preservation of the rest.
Before any one condemn me for this apparent heartless-
ness, let him be placed in a situation precisely similar to
my own.

At length delay was no longer possible, and, with a
heart almost bursting from my bosom, I advanced to the
region of the forecastle, where my companions were
awaiting me. I held out my hand with the splinters, and
Peters immediately drew. He was free—*his,* at least, was
not the shortest; and there was now another chance
against my escape. I summoned up all my strength, and
passed the lots to Augustus. He also drew immediately,
and he also was free; and now, whether I should live or
die, the chances were no more than precisely even. At
this moment all the fierceness of the tiger possessed my
bosom, and I felt toward my poor fellow-creature, Parker,
the most intense, the most diabolical hatred. But the feel-
ing did not last; and, at length, with a convulsive shudder
and closed eyes, I held out the two remaining splinters
toward him. It was full five minutes before he could sum-
mon resolution to draw, during which period of heart-
rending suspense I never once opened my eyes. Pres-
ently one of the two lots was quickly drawn from my
hand. The decision was then over, yet I knew not
whether it was for me or against me. No one spoke, and
still I dared not satisfy myself by looking at the splinter I
held. Peters at length took me by the hand, and I forced
myself to look up, when I immediately saw by the
countenance of Parker that I was safe, and that he it was
who had been doomed to suffer. Gasping for breath, I fell
senseless to the deck.

I recovered from my swoon in time to behold the con-

summation of the tragedy in the death of him who had been chiefly instrumental in bringing it about. He made no resistance whatever, and was stabbed in the back by Peters, when he fell instantly dead. I must not dwell upon the fearful repast which immediately ensued. Such things may be imagined, but words have no power to impress the mind with the exquisite horror of their reality. Let it suffice to say that, having in some measure appeased the raging thirst which consumed us by the blood of the victim, and having by common consent taken off the hands, feet, and head, throwing them together with the entrails, into the sea, we devoured the rest of the body, piecemeal, during the four ever memorable days of the seventeenth, eighteenth, nineteenth, and twentieth of the month.

On the nineteenth, there coming on a smart shower which lasted fifteen or twenty minutes, we contrived to catch some water by means of a sheet which had been fished up from the cabin by our drag just after the gale. The quantity we took in all did not amount to more than half a gallon; but even this scanty allowance supplied us with comparative strength and hope.

On the twenty-first we were again reduced to the last necessity. The weather still remained warm and pleasant, with occasional fogs and light breezes, most usually from N. to W.

On the twenty-second, as we were sitting close huddled together, gloomily revolving over our lamentable condition, there flashed through my mind all at once an idea which inspired me with a bright gleam of hope. I remembered that, when the foremast had been cut away, Peters, being in the windward chains, passed one of the axes into my hand, requesting me to put it, if possible, in a place of security, and that a few minutes before the last heavy sea struck the brig and filled her I had taken this axe into the forecastle and laid it in one of the larboard berths. I now thought it possible that, by getting at this axe, we might cut through the deck over the store-room, and thus readily supply ourselves with provisions.

When I communicated this project to my companions, they uttered a feeble shout of joy, and we all proceeded forthwith to the forecastle. The difficulty of descending here was greater than that of going down in the cabin, the opening being much smaller, for it will be remembered that the whole framework about the cabin companion-

hatch had been carried away, whereas the forecastle-way, being a simple hatch of only about three feet square, had remained uninjured. I did not hesitate, however, to attempt the descent; and a rope being fastened round my body as before, I plunged boldly in, feet foremost, made my way quickly to the berth, and at the first attempt brought up the axe. It was hailed with the most ecstatic joy and triumph, and the ease with which it had been obtained was regarded as an omen of our ultimate preservation.

We now commenced cutting at the deck with all the energy of rekindled hope, Peters and myself taking the axe by turns, Augustus' wounded arm not permitting him to aid us in any degree. As we were still so feeble as to be scarcely able to stand unsupported, and could consequently work but a minute or two without resting, it soon became evident that many long hours would be necessary to accomplish our task—that is, to cut an opening sufficiently large to admit of a free access to the store-room. This consideration, however, did not discourage us; and working all night by the light of the moon, we succeeded in effecting our purpose by daybreak on the morning of the twenty-third.

Peters now volunteered to go down; and, having made all arrangements as before, he descended, and soon returned bringing up with him a small jar, which, to our great joy, proved to be full of olives. Having shared these among us, and devoured them with the greatest avidity, we proceeded to let him down again. This time he succeeded beyond our utmost expectations, returning instantly with a large ham and a bottle of Madeira wine. Of the latter we each took a moderate sup, having learned by experience the pernicious consequences of indulging too freely. The ham, except about two pounds near the bone, was not in a condition to be eaten, having been entirely spoiled by the salt water. The sound part was divided among us. Peters and Augustus, not being able to restrain their appetite, swallowed theirs upon the instant; but I was more cautious, and ate but a small portion of mine, dreading the thirst which I knew would ensue. We now rested a while from our labors, which had been intolerably severe.

By noon, feeling somewhat strengthened and refreshed, we again renewed our attempt at getting up provision,

Peters and myself going down alternately, and always with more or less success, until sundown. During this interval we had the good fortune to bring up, altogether, four more small jars of olives, another ham, a carboy containing nearly three gallons of excellent Cape Madeira wine, and, what gave us still more delight, a small tortoise of the Gallipago breed, several of which had been taken on board by Captain Barnard, as the Grampus was leaving port, from the schooner Mary Pitts, just returned from a sealing voyage in the Pacific.

In a subsequent portion of this narrative I shall have frequent occasion to mention this species of tortoise. It is found principally, as most of my readers may know, in the group of islands called the Gallipagos, which, indeed, derive their name from the animal—the Spanish word Gallipago meaning a fresh-water terrapin. From the peculiarity of their shape and action they have been sometimes called the elephant tortoise. They are frequently found of an enormous size. I have myself seen several which would weigh from twelve to fifteen hundred pounds, although I do not remember that any navigator speaks of having seen them weighing more than eight hundred. Their appearance is singular, and even disgusting. Their steps are very slow, measured, and heavy, their bodies being carried about a foot from the ground. Their neck is long, and exceedingly slender; from eighteen inches to two feet is a very common length, and I killed one, where the distance from the shoulder to the extremity of the head was no less than three feet ten inches. The head has a striking resemblance to that of a serpent. They can exist without food for an almost incredible length of time, instances having been known where they have been thrown into the hold of a vessel and lain two years without nourishment of any kind—being as fat, and, in every respect, in as good order at the expiration of the time as when they were first put in. In one particular these extraordinary animals bear a resemblance to the dromedary, or camel of the desert. In a bag at the root of the neck they carry with them a constant supply of water. In some instances, upon killing them after a full year's deprivation of all nourishment, as much as three gallons of perfectly sweet and fresh water have been found in their bags. Their food is chiefly wild parsley and celery, with purslane, sea-kelp, and prickly-pears, upon which latter vegetable they thrive

wonderfully, a great quantity of it being usually found on
the hillsides near the shore wherever the animal itself is
discovered. They are excellent and highly nutritious food,
and have, no doubt, been the means of preserving the
lives of thousands of seamen employed in the whale-fish-
ery and other pursuits in the Pacific.

The one which we had the good fortune to bring up
from the store-room was not of a large size, weighing
probably sixty-five or seventy pounds. It was a female,
and in excellent condition, being exceedingly fat, and
having more than a quart of limpid and sweet water in
its bag. This was indeed a treasure; and, falling on our
knees with one accord, we returned fervent thanks to God
for so seasonable a relief.

We had great difficulty in getting the animal up through
the opening, as its struggles were fierce and its strength
prodigious. It was upon the point of making its escape
from Peters' grasp, and slipping back into the water, when
Augustus, throwing a rope with a slip-knot around its
throat, held it up in this manner until I jumped into the
hole by the side of Peters, and assisted him in lifting it
out.

The water we drew carefully from the bag into the jug,
which, it will be remembered, had been brought up before
from the cabin. Having done this, we broke off the neck
of a bottle so as to form, with the cork, a kind of glass,
holding not quite half a gill. We then each drank one of
these measures full, and resolved to limit ourselves to this
quantity per day as long as it should hold out.

During the last two or three days, the weather having
been dry and pleasant, the bedding we had obtained from
the cabin, as well as our clothing, had become thoroughly
dry, so that we passed this night (that of the twenty-
third) in comparative comfort, enjoying a tranquil repose,
after having supped plentifully on olives and ham, with a
small allowance of the wine. Being afraid of losing some
of our stores overboard during the night, in the event of
a breeze springing up, we secured them as well as possible
with cordage to the fragments of the windlass. Our tor-
toise, which we were anxious to preserve alive as long as
we could, we threw on its back, and otherwise carefully
fastened.

CHAPTER XIII

JULY 24TH.—This morning saw us wonderfully recruited in spirits and strength. Notwithstanding the perilous situation in which we were still placed, ignorant of our position, although certainly at a great distance from land, without more food than would last us for a fortnight even with great care, almost entirely without water, and floating about at the mercy of every wind and wave on the merest wreck in the world, still the infinitely more terrible distresses and dangers from which we had so lately and so providentially been delivered caused us to regard what we now endured as but little more than an ordinary evil—so strictly comparative is either good or ill.

At sunrise we were preparing to renew our attempts at getting up something from the store-room, when, a smart shower coming on, with some lightning, we turned our attention to the catching of water by means of the sheet we had used before for this purpose. We had no other means of collecting the rain than by holding the sheet spread out with one of the forechain-plates in the middle of it. The water, thus conducted to the centre, was drained through into our jug. We had nearly filled it in this manner, when, a heavy squall coming on from the northward, obliged us to desist, as the hulk began once more to roll so violently that we could no longer keep our feet. We now went forward, and, lashing ourselves securely to the remnant of the windlass as before, awaited the event with far more calmness than could have been anticipated or would have been imagined possible under the circumstances. At noon the wind had freshened into a two-reef breeze, and by night into a stiff gale, accompanied with a tremendously heavy swell. Experience having taught us, however, the best method of arranging our lashings, we weathered this dreary night in tolerable security, although thoroughly drenched at almost every instant by the sea, and in momentary dread of being washed off. Fortunately, the weather was so warm as to render the water rather grateful than otherwise.

July 25th.—This morning the gale had diminished to a mere ten-knot breeze, and the sea had gone down with it so considerably that we were able to keep ourselves dry

upon the deck. To our great grief, however, we found that
two jars of our olives, as well as the whole of our
ham, had been washed overboard, in spite of the careful
manner in which they had been fastened. We determined
not to kill the tortoise as yet, and contented ourselves
for the present with a breakfast on a few of the olives,
and a measure of water each, which latter we mixed, half
and half, with wine, finding great relief and strength
from the mixture, without the distressing intoxication
which had ensued upon drinking the port. The sea was
still far too rough for the renewal of our efforts at getting
up provision from the store-room. Several articles, of no
importance to us in our present situation, floated up
through the opening during the day, and were imme-
diately washed overboard. We also now observed that
the hulk lay more along than ever, so that we could not
stand an instant without lashing ourselves. On this ac-
count we passed a gloomy and uncomfortable day. At
noon the sun appeared to be nearly vertical, and we had
no doubt that we had been driven down by the long suc-
cession of northward and northwesterly winds into the
near vicinity of the equator. Toward evening saw sev-
eral sharks, and were somewhat alarmed by the audaci-
ous manner in which an enormously large one approached
us. At one time, a lurch throwing the deck very far be-
neath the water, the monster actually swam in upon us,
floundering for some moments just over the companion-
hatch, and striking Peters violently with his tail. A heavy
sea at length hurled him overboard, much to our relief.
In moderate weather we might have easily captured him.

July 26th.—This morning, the wind having greatly
abated, and the sea not being very rough, we determined
to renew our exertions in the store-room. After a great
deal of hard labor during the whole day, we found that
nothing further was to be expected from this quarter, the
partitions of the room having been stove during the night,
and its contents swept into the hold. This discovery, as
may be supposed, filled us with despair.

July 27th.—The sea nearly smooth, with a light wind,
and still from the northward and westward. The sun com-
ing out hotly in the afternoon, we occupied ourselves in
drying our clothes. Found great relief from thirst, and
much comfort otherwise, by bathing in the sea; in this,
however, we were forced to use great caution, being afraid

of sharks, several of which were seen swimming around the brig during the day.

July 28th.—Good weather still. The brig now began to lie along so alarmingly that we feared she would eventually roll bottom up. Prepared ourselves as well as we could for this emergency, lashing our tortoise, water-jug, and two remaining jars of olives as far as possible over to the windward, placing them outside the hull, below the main-chains. The sea very smooth all day, with little or no wind.

July 29th.—A continuance of the same weather. Augustus' wounded arm began to evince symptoms of mortification. He complained of drowsiness and excessive thirst, but no acute pain. Nothing could be done for his relief beyond rubbing his wounds with a little of the vinegar from the olives, and from this no benefit seemed to be experienced. We did every thing in our power for his comfort, and trebled his allowance of water.

July 30th.—An excessively hot day, with no wind. An enormous shark kept close by the hulk during the whole of the forenoon. We made several unsuccessful attempts to capture him by means of a noose. Augustus much worse, and evidently sinking as much from want of proper nourishment as from the effect of his wounds. He constantly prayed to be released from his sufferings, wishing for nothing but death. This evening we ate the last of our olives, and found the water in our jug so putrid that we could not swallow it at all without the addition of wine. Determined to kill our tortoise in the morning.

July 31st.—After a night of excessive anxiety and fatigue, owing to the position of the hulk, we set about killing and cutting up our tortoise. It proved to be much smaller than we had supposed, although in good condition—the whole meat about him not amounting to more than ten pounds. With a view of preserving a portion of this as long as possible, we cut it into fine pieces, and filled with them our three remaining olive-jars and the wine-bottle (all of which had been kept), pouring in afterward the vinegar from the olives. In this manner we put away about three pounds of the tortoise, intending not to touch it until we had consumed the rest. We concluded to restrict ourselves to about four ounces of the meat per day; the whole would thus last us thirteen days. A brisk shower, with severe thunder and lightning,

came on about dusk, but lasted so short a time that we only succeeded in catching about half a pint of water. The whole of this, by common consent, was given to Augustus, who now appeared to be in the last extremity. He drank the water from the sheet as we caught it (we holding it above him as he lay so as to let it run into his mouth), for we had now nothing left capable of holding water, unless we had chosen to empty out our wine from the carboy, or the stale water from the jug. Either of these expedients would have been resorted to had the shower lasted.

The sufferer seemed to derive but little benefit from the draught. His arm was completely black from the wrist to the shoulder, and his feet were like ice. We expected every moment to see him breathe his last. He was frightfully emaciated; so much so that, although he weighed a hundred and twenty-seven pounds upon his leaving Nantucket, he now did not weigh more than *forty or fifty at the farthest*. His eyes were sunk far in his head, being scarcely perceptible, and the skin of his cheeks hung so loosely as to prevent his masticating any food, or even swallowing any liquid, without great difficulty.

August 1st.—A continuance of the same calm weather, with an oppressively hot sun. Suffered exceedingly from thirst, the water in the jug being absolutely putrid and swarming with vermin. We contrived, nevertheless, to swallow a portion of it by mixing it with wine; our thirst, however, was but little abated. We found more relief by bathing in the sea, but could not avail ourselves of this expedient except at long intervals, on account of the continual presence of sharks. We now saw clearly that Augustus could not be saved—that he was evidently dying. We could do nothing to relieve his sufferings, which appeared to be great. About twelve o'clock he expired in strong convulsions, and without having spoken for several hours. His death filled us with the most gloomy forebodings, and had so great an effect upon our spirits that we sat motionless by the corpse during the whole day, and never addressed each other except in a whisper. It was not until some time after dark that we took courage to get up and throw the body overboard. It was then loathsome beyond expression, and so far decayed that, as Peters attempted to lift it, an en-

tire leg came off in his grasp. As the mass of putrefaction slipped over the vessel's side into the water, the glare of phosphoric light with which it was surrounded plainly discovered to us seven or eight large sharks, the clashing of whose horrible teeth, as their prey was torn to pieces among them, might have been heard at the distance of a mile. We shrunk within ourselves in the extremity of horror at the sound.

August 2d.—The same fearfully calm and hot weather. The dawn found us in a state of pitiable dejection as well as bodily exhaustion. The water in the jug was now absolutely useless, being a thick gelatinous mass—nothing but frightful-looking worms mingled with slime. We threw it out, and washed the jug well in the sea, afterward pouring a little vinegar in it from our bottles of pickled tortoise. Our thirst could now scarcely be endured, and we tried in vain to relieve it by wine, which seemed only to add fuel to the flame, and excited us to a high degree of intoxication. We afterward endeavored to relieve our sufferings by mixing the wine with sea-water; but this instantly brought about the most violent retchings, so that we never again attempted it. During the whole day we anxiously sought an opportunity of bathing, but to no purpose; for the hulk was now entirely besieged on all sides with sharks—no doubt the identical monsters who had devoured our poor companion on the evening before, and who were in momentary expectation of another similar feast. This circumstance occasioned us the most bitter regret, and filled us with the most depressing and melancholy forebodings. We had experienced indescribable relief in bathing, and to have this resource cut off in so frightful a manner was more than we could bear. Nor, indeed, were we altogether free from the apprehension of immediate danger, for the least slip or false movement would have thrown us at once within reach of those voracious fish, who frequently thrust themselves directly upon us, swimming up to leeward. No shouts or exertions on our part seemed to alarm them. Even when one of the largest was struck with an axe by Peters and much wounded, he persisted in his attempts to push in where we were. A cloud came up at dusk, but, to our extreme anguish, passed over without discharging itself. It is quite impossible to conceive our sufferings from thirst at this

period. We passed a sleepless night, both on this ac-
count and through dread of the sharks.

August 3d.—No prospect of relief, and the brig lying
still more and more along, so that now we could not
maintain a footing upon deck at all. Busied ourselves in
securing our wine and tortoise-meat, so that we might
not lose them in the event of our rolling over. Got out
two stout spikes from the forechains, and, by means
of the axe, drove them into the hull to windward within
a couple of feet of the water; this not being very far
from the keel, as we were nearly upon our beam-ends.
To these spikes we now lashed our provisions, as being
more secure than their former position beneath the
chains. Suffered great agony from thirst during the whole
day—no chance of bathing on account of the sharks,
which never left us for a moment. Found it impossible
to sleep.

August 4th.—A little before daybreak we perceived
that the hulk was heeling over, and aroused ourselves to
prevent being thrown off by the movement. At first the
roll was slow and gradual, and we contrived to clamber
over to windward very well, having taken the precaution
to leave ropes hanging from the spikes we had driven in
for the provision. But we had not calculated sufficiently
upon the acceleration of the impetus; for, presently the
heel became too violent to allow of our keeping pace
with it; and, before either of us knew what was to hap-
pen, we found ourselves hurled furiously into the sea,
and struggling several fathoms beneath the surface, with
the huge hull immediately above us.

In going under the water I had been obliged to let go
my hold upon the rope; and finding that I was com-
pletely beneath the vessel, and my strength nearly ex-
hausted, I scarcely made a struggle for life, and re-
signed myself, in a few seconds, to die. But here again I
was deceived, not having taken into consideration the
natural rebound of the hull to windward. The whirl of the
water upward, which the vessel occasioned in rolling
partially back, brought me to the surface still more
violently than I had been plunged beneath. Upon coming
up I found myself about twenty yards from the hulk, as
near as I could judge. She was lying keel up, rocking
furiously from side to side, and the sea in all directions
around was much agitated, and full of strong whirlpools.

I could see nothing of Peters. An oil-cask was floating within a few feet of me, and various other articles from the brig were scattered about.

My principal terror was now on account of the sharks, which I knew to be in my vicinity. In order to deter these, if possible, from approaching me, I splashed the water vigorously with both hands and feet as I swam toward the hulk, creating a body of foam. I have no doubt that to this expedient, simple as it was, I was indebted for my preservation; for the sea all round the brig, just before her rolling over, was so crowded with these monsters, that I must have been, and really was, in actual contact with some of them during my progress. By great good fortune, however, I reached the side of the vessel in safety, although so utterly weakened by the violent exertion I had used that I should never have been able to get upon it but for the timely assistance of Peters, who, now, to my great joy, made his appearance (having scrambled up to the keel from the opposite side of the hull), and threw me the end of a rope—one of those which had been attached to the spikes.

Having barely escaped this danger, our attention was now directed to the dreadful imminency of another— that of absolute starvation. Our whole stock of provision had been swept overboard in spite of all our care in securing it; and seeing no longer the remotest possibility of obtaining more, we gave way both of us to despair, weeping aloud like children, and neither of us attempting to offer consolation to the other. Such weakness can scarcely be conceived, and to those who have never been similarly situated will, no doubt, appear unnatural; but it must be remembered that our intellects were so entirely disordered by the long course of privation and terror to which we had been subjected, that we could not justly be considered, at that period, in the light of rational beings. In subsequent perils, nearly as great, if not greater, I bore up with fortitude against all the evils of my situation, and Peters, it will be seen, evinced a stoical philosophy nearly as incredible as his present childlike supineness and imbecility—the mental condition made the difference.

The overturning of the brig, even with the consequent loss of the wine and turtle, would not, in fact, have rendered our situation more deplorable than before, ex-

cept for the disappearance of the bedclothes by which
we had been hitherto enabled to catch rain-water, and
of the jug in which we had kept it when caught; for we
found the whole bottom, from within two or three feet of
the bends as far as the keel, together with the keel it-
self, *thickly covered with large barnacles, which proved
to be excellent and highly nutritious food*. Thus, in two
important respects, the accident we had so greatly
dreaded proved a benefit rather than an injury; it had
opened to us a supply of provisions which we could not
have exhausted, using it moderately, in a month; and it
had greatly contributed to our comfort as regards posi-
tion, we being much more at our ease, and in infinitely
less danger, than before.

The difficulty, however, of now obtaining water blinded
us to all the benefits of the change in our condition.
That we might be ready to avail ourselves, as far as pos-
sible, of any shower which might fall, we took off our
shirts, to make use of them as we had of the sheets—
not hoping, of course, to get more in this way, even
under the most favorable circumstances, than half a
gill at a time. No signs of a cloud appeared during the
day, and the agonies of our thirst were nearly intolerable.
At night, Peters obtained about an hour's disturbed
sleep, but my intense sufferings would not permit me to
close my eyes for a single moment.

August 5th.—To-day, a gentle breeze springing up
carried us through a vast quantity of sea-weed, among
which we were so fortunate as to find eleven small
crabs, which afforded us several delicious meals. Their
shells being quite soft, we ate them entire, and found
that they irritated our thirst far less than the barnacles.
Seeing no trace of sharks among the sea-weed, we also
ventured to bathe, and remained in the water for four
or five hours, during which we experienced a very sen-
sible diminution of our thirst. Were greatly refreshed,
and spent the night somewhat more comfortably than
before, both of us snatching a little sleep.

August 6th.—This day we were blessed by a brisk
and continual rain, lasting from about noon until after
dark. Bitterly did we now regret the loss of our jug and
carboy; for, in spite of the little means we had of catch-
ing the water, we might have filled one, if not both of
them. As it was, we contrived to satisfy the cravings of

thirst by suffering the shirts to become saturated, and
then wringing them so as to let the grateful fluid trickle
into our mouths. In this occupation we passed the entire
day.

August 7th.—Just at daybreak we both at the same
instant descried a sail to the eastward, and *evidently
coming toward us!* We hailed the glorious sight with a
long, although feeble shout of rapture; and began in-
stantly to make every signal in our power, by flaring the
shirts in the air, leaping as high as our weak condition
would permit, and even by hallooing with all the strength
of our lungs, although the vessel could not have been
less than fifteen miles distant. However, she still con-
tinued to near our hulk, and we felt that, if she but held
her present course, she must eventually come so close
as to perceive us. In about an hour after we first discov-
ered her, we could clearly see the people on her decks.
She was a long, low, and rakish-looking topsail schooner,
with a black ball in her foretopsail, and had, apparently,
a full crew. We now became alarmed, for we could
hardly imagine it possible that she did not observe us,
and were apprehensive that she meant to leave us to per-
ish as we were—an act of fiendish barbarity, which,
however incredible it may appear, has been repeatedly
perpetrated at sea, under circumstances very nearly
similar, and by beings who were regarded as belonging
to the human species.[1] In this instance, however, by

[1] The case of the brig Polly, of Boston, is one so much in point,
and her fate, in many respects, so remarkably similar to our
own, that I cannot forbear alluding to it here. This vessel, of
one hundred and thirty tons burden, sailed from Boston, with a
cargo of lumber and provisions, for Santa Croix, on the 12th of
December, 1811, under the command of Captain Casneau. There
were eight souls on board besides the captain—the mate, four
seamen, and the cook, together with a Mr. Hunt, and a negro
girl belonging to him. On the fifteenth, having cleared the shoal
of Georges, she sprung a leak in a gale of wind from the
southeast, and was finally capsized; but, the masts going by the
board, she afterward righted. They remained in this situation,
without fire, and with very little provision, for the period of *one
hundred and ninety-one days* (from December the fifteenth to
June the twentieth), when Captain Casneau and Samuel Badger,
the only survivors, were taken off the wreck by the Fame, of Hull,
Captain Featherstone, bound home from Rio Janeiro. When
picked up, they were in latitude 28° N., longitude 13° W.,
having drifted above two thousand miles! On the ninth of July

the mercy of God, we were destined to be most happily deceived; for, presently we were aware of a sudden commotion on the deck of the stranger, who immediately afterward ran up a British flag, and, hauling her wind, bore up directly upon us. In half an hour more we found ourselves in her cabin. She proved to be the Jane Guy, of Liverpool, Captain Guy, bound on a sealing and trading voyage to the South Seas and Pacific.

CHAPTER XIV

THE Jane Guy was a fine-looking topsail schooner of a hundred and eighty tons burden. She was unusually sharp in the bows, and on a wind, in moderate weather, the fastest sailer I have ever seen. Her qualities, however, as a rough sea-boat, were not so good, and her draught of water was by far too great for the trade to which she was destined. For this peculiar service, a larger vessel, and one of a light proportionate draught, is desirable—say a vessel of from three hundred to three hundred and fifty tons. She should be bark-rigged, and in other respects of a different construction from the usual South Sea ships. It is absolutely necessary that she should be well armed. She should have, say ten or twelve twelve-pound carronades, and two or three long twelves, with brass blunderbusses, and water-tight arm-chests for each top. Her anchors and cables should be of far greater strength than is required for any other species of trade, and, above all, her crew should be numerous and efficient—not less, for such a vessel as I have described, than fifty or sixty able-bodied men. The Jane Guy had a crew of thirty-five, all able seamen, besides the captain and mate, but she was not altogether as well

the Fame fell in with the brig Dromeo, Captain Perkins, who landed the two sufferers in Kennebeck. The narrative from which we gather these details ends in the following words:

"It is natural to inquire how they could float such a vast distance, upon the most frequented part of the Atlantic, and not be discovered all this time. *They were passed by more than a dozen sail, one of which came so nigh them that they could distinctly see the people on deck and on the rigging looking at them; but, to the inexpressible disappointment of the starving and freezing men, they stifled the dictates of compassion, hoisted sail, and cruelly abandoned them to their fate.*"

armed or otherwise equipped, as a navigator acquainted with the difficulties and dangers of the trade could have desired.

Capain Guy was a gentleman of great urbanity of manner, and of considerable experience in the southern traffic, to which he had devoted the greater portion of his life. He was deficient, however, in energy, and, consequently, in that spirit of enterprise which is here so absolutely requisite. He was part owner of the vessel in which he sailed, and was invested with discretionary powers to cruise in the South Seas for any cargo which might come most readily to hand. He had on board, as usual in such voyages, beads, looking-glasses, tinderworks, axes, hatchets, saws, adzes, planes, chisels, gouges, gimlets, files, spoke-shaves, rasps, hammers, nails, knives, scissors, razors, needles, thread, crockeryware, calico, trinkets, and other similar articles.

The schooner sailed from Liverpool on the tenth of July, crossed the tropic of Cancer on the twenty-fifth, in longitude twenty degrees west, and reached Sal, one of the Cape Verd islands, on the twenty-ninth, where she took in salt and other necessaries for the voyage. On the third of August, she left the Cape Verds and steered southwest, stretching over toward the coast of Brazil, so as to cross the equator between the meridians of twenty-eight and thirty degrees west longitude. This is the course usually taken by vessels bound from Europe to the Cape of Good Hope, or by that route to the East Indies. By proceeding thus they avoid the calms and strong contrary currents which continually prevail on the coast of Guinea, while, in the end, it is found to be the shortest track, as westerly winds are never wanting afterward by which to reach the Cape. It was Captain Guy's intention to make his first stoppage at Kerguelen's Land—I hardly know for what reason. On the day we were picked up the schooner was off Cape St. Roque, in longitude thirty-one degrees west; so that, when found, we had drifted probably, from north to south, *not less than five-and-twenty degrees!*

On board the Jane Guy we were treated with all the kindness our distressed situation demanded. In about a fortnight, during which time we continued steering to the southeast, with gentle breezes and fine weather both Peters and myself recovered entirely from the effects of

our late privation and dreadful suffering, and we began
to remember what had passed rather as a frightful
dream from which we had been happily awakened, than
as events which had taken place in sober and naked
reality. I have since found that this species of partial
oblivion is usually brought about by sudden transition,
whether from joy to sorrow or from sorrow to joy—
the degree of forgetfulness being proportioned to the
degree of difference in the exchange. Thus, in my own
case, I now feel it impossible to realize the full extent
of the misery which I endured during the days spent
upon the hulk. The incidents are remembered, but not
the feelings which the incidents elicited at the time of
their occurrence. I only know, that when they did oc-
cur, I *then* thought human nature could sustain nothing
more of agony.

We continued our voyage for some weeks without
any incidents of greater moment than the occasional
meeting with whaling-ships, and more frequently with
the black or right whale, so called in contradistinction
to the spermaceti. These, however, were chiefly found
south of the twenty-fifth parallel. On the sixteenth of
September, being in the vicinity of the Cape of Good Hope,
the schooner encountered her first gale of any violence
since leaving Liverpool. In this neighborhood, but more
frequently to the south and east of the promontory
(we were to the westward), navigators have often to
contend with storms from the northward, which rage
with great fury. They always bring with them a heavy
sea, and one of their most dangerous features is the in-
stantaneous chopping round of the wind, an occurrence
almost certain to take place during the greatest force of
the gale. A perfect hurricane will be blowing at one
moment from the northward or northeast, and in the
next not a breath of wind will be felt in that direction,
while from the southwest it will come out all at once
with a violence almost inconceivable. A bright spot to
the southward is the sure forerunner of the change, and
vessels are thus enabled to take the proper precautions.

It was about six in the morning when the blow came on
with a white squall, and, as usual, from the northward.
By eight it had increased very much, and brought down
upon us one of the most tremendous seas I had then
ever beheld. Every thing had been made as snug as pos-

sible, but the schooner labored excessively, and gave
evidence of her bad qualities as a sea-boat, pitching her
forecastle under at every plunge, and with the greatest
difficulty struggling up from one wave before she was
buried in another. Just before sunset the bright spot
for which we had been on the look-out made its appear-
ance in the southwest, and in an hour afterward we
perceived the little head-sail we carried flapping listlessly
against the mast. In two minutes more, in spite of every
preparation, we were hurled on our beam-ends, as if
by magic, and a perfect wilderness of foam made a
clear breach over us as we lay. The blow from the south-
west, however, luckily proved to be nothing more than a
squall, and we had the good fortune to right the vessel
without the loss of a spar. A heavy cross sea gave us
great trouble for a few hours after this, but toward
morning we found ourselves in nearly as good condition
as before the gale. Captain Guy considered that he had
made an escape little less than miraculous.

On the thirteenth of October we came in sight of
Prince Edward Island, in latitude 46° 53′ S., longitude
37° 46′ E. Two days afterward we found ourselves
near Possession Island, and presently passed the islands
of Crozet, in latitude 42° 59′ S., longitude 48° E. On
the eighteenth we made Kerguelen's or Desolation Is-
land, in the Southern Indian Ocean, and came to anchor
in Christmas Harbor, having four fathoms of water.

This island, or rather group of islands, bears southeast
from the Cape of Good Hope, and is distant therefrom
nearly eight hundred leagues. It was first discovered in
1772, by the Baron de Kergulen, or Kerguelen, a
Frenchman, who, thinking the land to form a portion
of an extensive southern continent, carried home in-
formation to that effect, which produced much excite-
ment at the time. The government, taking the matter up,
sent the baron back in the following year for the pur-
pose of giving his new discovery a critical examination,
when the mistake was discovered. In 1777, Captain Cook
fell in with the same group, and gave to the principal
one the name of Desolation Island, a title which it cer-
tainly well deserves. Upon approaching the land, how-
ever, the navigator might be induced to suppose other-
wise, as the sides of most of the hills, from September
to March, are clothed with very brilliant verdure. This

deceitful appearance is caused by a small plant resembling saxifrage, which is abundant, growing in large patches on a species of crumbling moss. Besides this plant there is scarcely a sign of vegetation on the island, if we except some coarse rank grass near the harbor, some lichen, and a shrub which bears resemblance to a cabbage shooting into seed, and which has a bitter and acrid taste.

The face of the country is hilly, although none of the hills can be called lofty. Their tops are perpetually covered with snow. There are several harbors, of which Christmas Harbor is the most convenient. It is the first to be met with on the northeast side of the island after passing Cape François, which forms the northern shore, and, by its peculiar shape, serves to distinguish the harbor. Its projecting point terminates in a high rock, through which is a large hole, forming a natural arch. The entrance is in latitude 48° 40' S., longitude 69° 6' E. Passing in here, good anchorage may be found under the shelter of several small islands, which form a sufficient protection from all easterly winds. Proceeding on eastwardly from this anchorage you come to Wasp Bay, at the head of the harbor. This is a small basin, completely landlocked, into which you can go with four fathoms, and find anchorage in from ten to three, hard clay bottom. A ship might lie here with her best bower ahead all the year round without risk. To the westward, at the head of Wasp Bay, is a small stream of excellent water, easily procured.

Some seal of the fur and hair species are still to be found on Kerguelen Island, and sea-elephants abound. The feathered tribes are discovered in great numbers. Penguins are very plentiful, and of these there are four different kinds. The royal penguin, so called from its size and beautiful plumage, is the largest. The upper part of the body is usually gray, sometimes of a lilac tint; the under portion of the purest white imaginable. The head is of a glossy and most brilliant black, the feet also. The chief beauty of the plumage, however, consists in two broad stripes of a gold color, which pass along from the head to the breast. The bill is long, and either pink or bright scarlet. These birds walk erect, with a stately carriage. They carry their heads high with their wings drooping like two arms, and, as their tails project from their body in a line with the legs, the resemblance to a

human figure is very striking, and would be apt to deceive the spectator at a casual glance or in the gloom of the evening. The royal penguins which we met with on Kerguelen Land were rather larger than a goose. The other kinds are the macaroni, the jackass, and the rookery penguin. These are much smaller, less beautiful in plumage, and different in other respects.

Besides the penguin many other birds are here to be found, among which may be mentioned sea-hens, blue peterels, teal, ducks, Port Egmont hens, shags, Cape pigeons, the nelly, sea-swallows, terns, sea-gulls, Mother Carey's chickens, Mother Carey's geese, or the great peterel, and, lastly, the albatross.

The great peterel is as large as the common albatross, and is carnivorous. It is frequently called the break-bones, or osprey peterel. They are not at all shy, and, when properly cooked, are palatable food. In flying they sometimes sail very close to the surface of the water, with the wings expanded, without appearing to move them in the least degree, or make any exertion with them whatever.

The albatross is one of the largest and fiercest of the South Sea birds. It is of the gull species, and takes its prey on the wing, never coming on land except for the purpose of breeding. Between this bird and the penguin the most singular friendship exists. Their nests are constructed with great uniformity upon a plan concerted between the two species—that of the albatross being placed in the centre of a little square formed by the nests of four penguins. Navigators have agreed in calling an assemblage of such encampments *a rookery*. These rookeries have been often described, but as my readers may not all have seen these descriptions, and as I shall have occasion hereafter to speak of the penguin and albatross, it will not be amiss to say something here of their mode of building and living.

When the season for incubation arrives, the birds assemble in vast numbers, and for some days appear to be deliberating upon the proper course to be pursued. At length they proceed to action. A level piece of ground is selected, of suitable extent, usually comprising three or four acres, and situated as near the sea as possible, being still beyond its reach. The spot is chosen with reference to its evenness of surface, and that is preferred which is the least encumbered with stones. This matter

being arranged, the birds proceed, with one accord, and actuated apparently by one mind, to trace out, with mathematical accuracy, either a square or other parallelogram, as may best suit the nature of the ground, and of just sufficient size to accommodate easily all the birds assembled, and no more—in this particular seeming determined upon preventing the access of future stragglers who have not participated in the labor of the encampment. One side of the place thus marked out runs parallel with the water's edge, and is left open for ingress or egress.

Having defined the limits of the rookery, the colony now begin to clear it of every species of rubbish, picking up stone by stone, and carrying them outside of the lines, and close by them, so as to form a wall on the three inland sides. Just within this wall a perfectly level and smooth walk is formed, from six to eight feet wide, and extending around the encampment—thus serving the purpose of a general promenade.

The next process is to partition out the whole area into small squares exactly equal in size. This is done by forming narrow paths, very smooth, and crossing each other at right angles throughout the entire extent of the rookery. At each intersection of these paths the nest of an albatross is constructed, and a penguin's nest in the centre of each square—thus every penguin is surrounded by four albatrosses, and each albatross by a like number of penguins. The penguin's nest consists of a hole in the earth, very shallow, being only just of sufficient depth to keep her single egg from rolling. The albatross is somewhat less simple in her arrangements, erecting a hillock about a foot high and two in diameter. This is made of earth, sea-weed, and shells. On its summit she builds her nest.

The birds take especial care never to leave their nests unoccupied for an instant during the period of incubation, or, indeed, until the young progeny are sufficiently strong to take care of themselves. While the male is absent at sea in search of food, the female remains on duty, and it is only upon the return of her partner that she ventures abroad. The eggs are never left uncovered at all—while one bird leaves the nest the other nestling in by its side. This precaution is rendered necessary by the thievish propensities prevalent in the rookery, the inhab-

itants making no scruple to purloin each other's eggs at every good opportunity.

Although there are some rookeries in which the penguin and albatross are the sole population, yet in most of them a variety of oceanic birds are to be met with, enjoying all the privileges of citizenship, and scattering their nests here and there, wherever they can find room, never interfering, however, with the stations of the larger species. The appearance of such encampments, when seen from a distance, is exceedingly singular. The whole atmosphere just above the settlement is darkened with the immense number of the albatross (mingled with the smaller tribes) which are continually hovering over it, either going to the ocean or returning home. At the same time a crowd of penguins are to be observed, some passing to and fro in the narrow alleys, and some marching with the military strut so peculiar to them, around the general promenade-ground which encircles the rookery. In short, survey it as we will, nothing can be more astonishing than the spirit of reflection evinced by these feathered beings, and nothing surely can be better calculated to elicit reflection in every well-regulated human intellect.

On the morning after our arrival in Christmas Harbor the chief mate, Mr. Patterson, took the boats, and (although it was somewhat early in the season) went in search of seal, leaving the captain and a young relation of his on a point of barren land to the westward, they having some business, whose nature I could not ascertain, to transact in the interior of the island. Captain Guy took with him a bottle, in which was a sealed letter, and made his way from the point on which he was set on shore toward one of the highest peaks in the place. It is probable that his design was to leave the letter on that height for some vessel which he expected to come after him. As soon as we lost sight of him we proceeded (Peters and myself being in the mate's boat) on our cruise around the coast, looking for seal. In this business we were occupied about three weeks, examining with great care every nook and corner, not only of Kerguelen Land, but of the several small islands in the vicinity. Our labors, however, were not crowned with any important success. We saw a great many fur seal, but they were exceedingly shy, and with the greatest exertions, we could only procure

three hundred and fifty skins in all. Sea-elephants were
abundant, especially on the western coast of the main-
land, but of these we killed only twenty, and this with
great difficulty. On the smaller islands we discovered a
good many of the hair seal, but did not molest them. We
returned to the schooner on the eleventh, where we found
Captain Guy and his nephew, who gave a very bad ac-
count of the interior, representing it as one of the most
dreary and utterly barren countries in the world. They
had remained two nights on the island, owing to some
misunderstanding, on the part of the second mate, in re-
gard to the sending a jolly-boat from the schooner to take
them off.

CHAPTER XV

ON THE twelfth we made sail from Christmas Harbor, re-
tracing our way to the westward, and leaving Marion's
Island, one of Crozet's group, on the larboard. We after-
ward passed Prince Edward Island, leaving it also on our
left; then, steering more to the northward, made, in fifteen
days, the islands of Tristan da Cunha, in latitude 37°
8′ S., longitude 12° 8′ W.

This group, now so well known, and which consists of
three circular islands, was first discovered by the Portu-
guese, and was visited afterward by the Dutch in 1643,
and by the French in 1767. The three islands together
form a triangle, and are distant from each other about ten
miles, there being fine open passages between. The land
in all of them is very high, especially in Tristan da Cunha,
properly so called. This is the largest of the group, being
fifteen miles in circumference, and so elevated that it
can be seen in clear weather at the distance of eighty or
ninety miles. A part of the land toward the north rises
more than a thousand feet perpendicularly from the sea.
A table-land at this height extends back nearly to the
centre of the island, and from this table-land arises a
lofty cone like that of Teneriffe. The lower half of this
cone is clothed with trees of good size, but the upper
region is barren rock, usually hidden among the clouds,
and covered with snow during the greater part of the year.
There are no shoals or other dangers about the island,
the shores being remarkably bold and the water deep.

On the northwestern coast is a bay, with a beach of black sand, where a landing with boats can be easily effected, provided there be a southerly wind. Plenty of excellent water may here be readily procured; also cod and other fish may be taken with hook and line.

The next island in point of size, and the most westwardly of the group, is that called the Inaccessible. Its precise situation is 37° 17′ S. latitude, longitude 12° 24′ W. It is seven or eight miles in circumference, and on all sides presents a forbidding and precipitous aspect. Its top is perfectly flat, and the whole region is sterile, nothing growing upon it except a few stunted shrubs.

Nightingale Island, the smallest and most southerly, is in latitude 37° 26′ S., longitude 12° 12′ W. Off its southern extremity is a high ledge of rocky islets; a few also of a similar appearance are seen to the northeast. The ground is irregular and sterile, and a deep valley partially separates it.

The shores of these islands abound, in the proper season, with sea-lions, sea-elephants, the hair and fur seal, together with a great variety of oceanic birds. Whales are also plentiful in their vicinity. Owing to the ease with which these various animals were here formerly taken, the group has been much visited since its discovery. The Dutch and French frequented it at a very early period. In 1790, Captain Patten, of the ship Industry, of Philadelphia, made Tristan da Cunha, where he remained seven months (from August, 1790, to April, 1791) for the purpose of collecting seal-skins. In this time he gathered no less than five thousand six hundred, and says that he would have had no difficulty in loading a large ship with oil in three weeks. Upon his arrival he found no quadrupeds, with the exception of a few wild goats; the island now abounds with all our most valuable domestic animals, which have been introduced by subsequent navigators.

I believe it was not long after Captain Patten's visit that Captain Colquhoun, of the American brig Betsey, touched at the largest of the islands for the purpose of refreshment. He planted onions, potatoes, cabbages, and a great many other vegetables, an abundance of all which is now to be met with.

In 1811, a Captain Haywood, in the Nereus, visited Tristan. He found there three Americans, who were re-

siding upon the island to prepare seal-skins and oil. One
of these men was named Jonathan Lambert, and he called
himself the sovereign of the country. He had cleared and
cultivated about sixty acres of land, and turned his at-
tention to raising the coffee-plant and sugar-cane, with
which he had been furnished by the American Minister at
Rio de Janeiro. This settlement, however, was finally aban-
doned, and in 1817 the islands were taken possession of
by the British Government, who sent a detachment for
that purpose from the Cape of Good Hope. They did not,
however, retain them long; but, upon the evacuation of
the country as a British possession, two or three English
families took up their residence there independently of the
Government. On the twenty-fifth of March, 1824, the Ber-
wick, Captain Jeffrey, from London to Van Diemen's
Land, arrived at the place, where they found an English-
man of the name of Glass, formerly a corporal in the
British artillery. He claimed to be supreme governor of
the islands, and had under his control twenty-one men
and three women. He gave a very favorable account of
the salubrity of the climate and of the productiveness of
the soil. The population occupied themselves chiefly in
collecting seal-skins and sea-elephant oil, with which they
traded to the Cape of Good Hope, Glass owning a small
schooner. At the period of our arrival the governor was
still a resident, but his little community had multiplied,
there being fifty-six persons upon Tristan, besides a small-
er settlement of seven on Nightingale Island. We had no
difficulty in procuring almost every kind of refreshment
which we required—sheep, hogs, bullocks, rabbits, poul-
try, goats, fish in great variety, and vegetables were
abundant. Having come to anchor close in with the large
island, in eighteen fathoms, we took all we wanted on
board very conveniently. Captain Guy also purchased of
Glass five hundred seal-skins and some ivory. We re-
mained here a week, during which the prevailing winds
were from the northward and westward, and the weather
somewhat hazy. On the fifth of November we made sail
to the southward and westward, with the intention of hav-
ing a thorough search for a group of islands called the
Auroras, respecting whose existence a great diversity of
opinion has existed.

These islands are said to have been discovered as early
as 1762, by the commander of the ship Aurora. In 1790,

Captain Manuel de Oyarudo, in the ship Princess, belonging to the Royal Philippine Company, sailed, as he asserts, directly among them. In 1794, the Spanish corvette Atrevida went with the determination of ascertaining their precise situation, and, in a paper published by the Royal Hydrographical Society of Madrid in the year 1809, the following language is used respecting this expedition: "The corvette Atrevida practised, in their immediate vicinity, from the twenty-first to the twenty-seventh of January, all the necessary observations, and measured by chronometers the difference of longitude between these islands and the port of Soledad in the Manilas. The islands are three; they are very nearly in the same meridian; the centre one is rather low, and the other two may be seen at nine leagues' distance." The observations made on board the Atrevida give the following results as the precise situation of each island. The most northern is in latitude 52° 37' 24" S., longitude 47° 43' 15" W.; the middle one in latitude 53° 2' 40" S., longitude 47° 55' 15" W.; and the most southern in latitude 53° 15' 22" S., longitude 47° 57' 15" W.

On the twenty-seventh of January 1820, Captain James Weddel, of the British navy, sailed from Staten Land also in search of the Auroras. He reports that, having made the most diligent search and passed not only immediately over the spots indicated by the commander of the Atrevida, but in every direction throughout the vicinity of these spots, he could discover no indication of land. These conflicting statements have induced other navigators to look out for the islands; and, strange to say, while some have sailed through every inch of sea where they are supposed to lie without finding them, there have been not a few who declare positively that they have seen them; and even been close in with their shores. It was Captain Guy's intention to make every exertion within his power to settle the question so oddly in dispute.[1]

We kept on our course, between the south and west, with variable weather, until the twentieth of the month, when we found ourselves on the debated ground,

[1] Among the vessels which at various times have professed to meet with the Auroras may be mentioned the ship San Miguel, in 1769; the ship Aurora, in 1774; the brig Pearl, in 1779; and the ship Dolores, in 1790. They all agree in giving the mean latitude fifty-three degrees south.

being in latitude 53° 15′ S., longitude 47° 58′ W.
—that is to say, very nearly upon the spot indicated as the
situation of the most southern of the group. Not perceiv-
ing any sign of land, we continued to the westward in the
parallel of fifty-three degrees south, as far as the meridian
of fifty degrees west. We then stood to the north as far
as the parallel of fifty-two degrees south, when we turned
to the eastward, and kept our parallel by double alti-
tudes, morning and evening, and meridian altitudes of the
planets and moon. Having thus gone eastwardly to the
meridian of the western coast of Georgia, we kept that
meridian until we were in the latitude from which we set
out. We then took diagonal courses throughout the en-
tire extent of sea circumscribed, keeping a look-out con-
stantly at the masthead, and repeating our examination
with the greatest care for a period of three weeks, during
which the weather was remarkably pleasant and fair, with
no haze whatsoever. Of course we were thoroughly satis-
fied that, whatever islands might have existed in this vi-
cinity at any former period, no vestige of them remained
at the present day. Since my return home I find that the
same ground was traced over, with equal care, in 1822,
by Captain Johnson, of the American schooner Henry,
and by Captain Morrell, in the American schooner Wasp
—in both cases with the same result as in our own.

CHAPTER XVI

IT HAD been Captain Guy's original intention, after sat-
isfying himself about the Auroras, to proceed through
the Strait of Magellan, and up along the western coast
of Patagonia; but information received at Tristan da
Cunha induced him to steer to the southward, in the
hope of falling in with some small islands said to lie
about the parallel of 60° S., longitude 41° 20′ W.
In the event of his not discovering these lands, he de-
signed, should the season prove favorable, to push on
toward the pole. Accordingly, on the twelfth of Decem-
ber, we made sail in that direction. On the eighteenth
we found ourselves about the station indicated by
Glass, and cruised for three days in that neighborhood
without finding any traces of the islands he had men-
tioned. On the twenty-first, the weather being unusually

pl:asant, we again made sail to the southward, with the resolution of penetrating in that course as far as possible. Before entering upon this portion of my narrative, it may be as well, for the information of those readers who have paid little attention to the progress of discovery in these regions, to give some brief account of the very few attempts at reaching the southern pole which have hitherto been made.

That of Captain Cook was the first of which we have any distinct account. In 1772 he sailed to the south in the Resolution, accompanied by Lieutenant Furneaux in the Adventure. In December he found himself as far as the fifty-eighth parallel of south latitude, and in longitude 26° 57′ E. Here he met with narrow fields of ice, about eight or ten inches thick, and running northeast and southeast. This ice was in large cakes, and usually it was packed so closely that the vessel had great difficulty in forcing a passage. At this period Captain Cook supposed, from the vast number of birds to be seen, and from other indications, that he was in the near vicinity of land. He kept on to the southward, the weather being exceedingly cold, until he reached the sixty-fourth parallel, in longitude 38° 14′ E. Here he had mild weather, with gentle breezes, for five days, the thermometer being at thirty-six. In January, 1773, the vessels crossed the Antarctic circle, but did not succeed in penetrating much farther; for, upon reaching latitude 67° 15′, they found all farther progress impeded by an immense body of ice, extending all along the southern horizon as far as the eye could reach. This ice was of every variety—and some large floes of it, miles in extent, formed a compact mass, rising eighteen or twenty feet above the water. It being late in the season, and no hope entertained of rounding these obstructions, Captain Cook now reluctantly turned to the northward.

In the November following he renewed his search in the Antarctic. In latitude 59° 40′ he met with a strong current setting to the southward. In December, when the vessels were in latitude 67° 31′, longitude 142° 54′ W., the cold was excessive, with heavy gales and fog. Here also birds were abundant; the albatross, the penguin, and the peterel especially. In latitude 70° 23′ some large islands of ice were encountered, and shortly afterward the clouds to the southward were observed to

be of a snowy whiteness, indicating the vicinity of field ice. In latitude 71° 10′, longitude 106° 54′ W., the navigators were stopped, as before, by an immense frozen expanse, which filled the whole area of the southern horizon. The northern edge of this expanse was ragged and broken, so firmly wedged together as to be utterly impassable, and extending about a mile to the southward. Behind it the frozen surface was comparatively smooth for some distance, until terminated in the extreme background by gigantic ranges of ice-mountains, the one towering above the other. Captain Cook concluded that this vast field reached the southern pole or was joined to a continent. Mr. J. N. Reynolds, whose great exertions and perseverance have at length succeeded in getting set on foot a national expedition, partly for the purpose of exploring these regions, thus speaks of the attempt of the Resolution: "We are not surprised that Captain Cook was unable to go beyond 71° 10′, but we are astonished that he did attain that point on the meridian of 106° 54′ west longitude. Palmer's Land lies south of the Shetland, latitude sixty-four degrees, and tends to the southward and westward farther than any navigator has yet penetrated. Cook was standing for this land when his progress was arrested by the ice; which, we apprehend, must always be the case in that point, and so early in the season as the sixth of January—and we should not be surprised if a portion of the icy mountains described was attached to the main body of Palmer's Land, or to some other portions of land lying farther to the southward and westward."

In 1803, Captains Kreutzenstern and Lisiausky were dispatched by Alexander of Russia for the purpose of circumnavigating the globe. In endeavoring to get south, they made no farther than 59° 58′, in longitude 70° 15′ W. They here met with strong current setting eastwardly. Whales were abundant, but they saw no ice. In regard to this voyage, Mr. Reynolds observes that, if Kreutzenstern had arrived where he did earlier in the season, he must have encountered ice—it was March when he reached the latitude specified. The winds, prevailing, as they do, from the southward and westward, had carried the floes, aided by currents, into that icy region bounded on the north by Georgia, east by Sand-

wich Land and the South Orkneys, and west by the South Shetland islands.

In 1822, Captain James Weddel, of the British navy, with two very small vessels, penetrated farther to the south than any previous navigator, and this too, without encountering extraordinary difficulties. He states that although he was frequently hemmed in by ice *before* reaching the seventy-second parallel, yet, upon attaining it, not a particle was to be discovered, and that, upon arriving at the latitude of 74° 15′, no fields, and only three islands of ice were visible. It is somewhat remarkable that, although vast flocks of birds were seen, and other usual indications of land, and although, south of the Shetlands, unknown coasts were observed from the mast-head tending southwardly, Weddel discourages the idea of land existing in the polar regions of the south.

On the 11th of January, 1823, Captain Benjamin Morrell, of the American schooner Wasp, sailed from Kerguelen's Land with a view of penetrating as far south as possible. On the first of February he found himself in latitude 64° 52′ S., longitude 118° 27′ E. The following passage is extracted from his journal of that date: "The wind soon freshened to an eleven-knot breeze, and we embraced this opportunity of making to the west; being however convinced that the farther we went south beyond latitude sixty-four degrees, the less ice was to be apprehended, we steered a little to the southward, until we crossed the Antarctic circle, and were in latitude 69° 15′ E. In this latitude there was *no field ice,* and very few ice islands in sight."

Under the date of March fourteenth I find also this entry: "The sea was now entirely free of field ice, and there were not more than a dozen ice islands in sight. At the same time the temperature of the air and water was at least thirteen degrees higher (more mild) than we had ever found it between the parallels of sixty and sixty-two south. We were now at latitude 70° 14′ S., and the temperature of the air was forty-seven, and that of the water forty-four. In this situation I found the variation to be 14° 27′ easterly, per azimuth. * * * I have several times passed within the Antarctic circle, on different meridians, and have uniformly found the temperature, both of the air and water, to become more

and more mild the farther I advanced beyond the sixty-fifth degree of south latitude, and that the variation decreases in the some proportion. While north of this latitude, say between sixty and sixty-five south, we frequently had great difficulty in finding a passage for the vessel between the immense and almost innumerable ice islands, some of which were from one to two miles in circumference, and more than five hundred feet above the surface of the water."

Being nearly destitute of fuel and water, and without proper instruments, it being also late in the season, Captain Morrell was now obliged to put back, without attempting any farther progress to the westward, although an entirely open sea lay before him. He expresses the opinion that had not these overruling considerations obliged him to retreat, he could have penetrated, if not to the pole itself, at least to the eighty-fifth parallel. I have given his ideas respecting these matters somewhat at length, that the reader may have an opportunity of seeing how far they were borne out by my own subsequent experience.

In 1831, Captain Briscoe, in the employ of the Messieurs Enderby, whale-ship owners of London, sailed in the brig Lively for the South Seas, accompanied by the cutter Tula. On the twenty-eighth of February, being in latitude 66° 30′ S., longitude 47° 13′ E., he descried land, and "clearly discovered through the snow the black peaks of a range of mountains running E. S. E." He remained in this neighborhood during the whole of the following month, but was unable to approach the coast nearer than within ten leagues, owing to the boisterous state of the weather. Finding it impossible to make further discovery during this season, he returned northward to winter in Van Diemen's Land.

In the beginning of 1832 he again proceeded southwardly, and on the fourth of February land was seen to the southeast in latitude 67° 15′, longitude 69° 29′ W. This was soon found to be an island near the headland of the country he had first discovered. On the twenty-first of the month he succeeded in landing on the latter, and took possession of it in the name of William IV, calling it Adelaide's Island, in honor of the English queen. These particulars being made known to the Royal Geographical Society of London, the conclusion was drawn

by that body "that there is a continuous tract of land extending from 47° 30′ E. to 69° 29′ W. longitude, running the parallel of from sixty-six to sixty-seven degrees south latitude." In respect to this conclusion Mr. Reynolds observes: "In the correctness of it we by no means concur; nor do the discoveries of Briscoe warrant any such inference. It was within these limits that Weddel proceeded south on a meridian to the east of Georgia, Sandwich Land, and the South Orkney and Shetland islands." My own experience will be found to testify most directly to the falsity of the conclusion arrived at by the society.

These are the principal attempts which have been made at penetrating to a high southern latitude, and it will now be seen that there remained, previous to the voyage of the Jane, nearly three hundred degrees of longitude in which the Antarctic circle had not been crossed at all. Of course a wide field lay before us for discovery, and it was with feelings of most intense interest that I heard Captain Guy express his resolution of pushing boldly to the southward.

CHAPTER XVII

WE KEPT our course southwardly for four days after giving up the search for Glass' islands, without meeting with any ice at all. On the twenty-sixth, at noon, we were in latitude 63° 23′ S., longitude 41° 25′ W. We now saw several large ice islands, and a floe of field ice, not however, of any great extent. The winds generally blew from the southeast, or the northeast, but were very light. Whenever we had a westerly wind, which was seldom, it was invariably attended with a rain squall. Every day we had more or less snow. The thermometer, on the twenty-seventh stood at thirty-five.

January 1, 1828.—This day we found ourselves completely hemmed in by the ice, and our prospects looked cheerless indeed. A strong gale blew, during the whole forenoon, from the northeast, and drove large cakes of the drift against the rudder and counter with such violence that we all trembled for the consequences. Toward evening, the gale still blowing with fury, a large field in front separated, and we were enabled, by carrying a

press of sail, to force a passage through the smaller flakes into some open water beyond. As we approached this space we took in sail by degrees, and having at length got clear, lay-to under a single-reefed foresail.

January 2d.—We had now tolerably pleasant weather. At noon we found ourselves in latitude 69° 10' S., longitude 42° 20' W., having crossed the Antarctic circle. Very little ice was to be seen to the southward, although large fields of it lay behind us. This day we rigged some sounding gear, using a large iron pot capable of holding twenty gallons, and a line of two hundred fathoms. We found the current setting to the north, about a quarter of a mile per hour. The temperature of the air was now about thirty-three. Here we found the variation to be 14° 28' easterly, per azimuth.

January 5th.—We had still held on to the southward without any very great impediments. On this morning, however, being in latitude 73° 15' S., longitude 42° 10' W., we were again brought to a stand by an immense expanse of firm ice. We saw, nevertheless, much open water to the southward, and felt no doubt of being able to reach it eventually. Standing to the eastward along the edge of the floe, we at length came to a passage of about a mile in width, through which we warped our way by sundown. The sea in which we now were was thickly covered with ice islands, but had no field ice, and we pushed on boldy as before. The cold did not seem to increase, although we had snow very frequently, and now and then hail squalls of great violence. Immense flocks of the albatross flew over the schooner this day, going from southeast to northwest.

January 7th.—The sea still remained pretty well open, so that we had no difficulty in holding on our course. To the westward we saw some icebergs of incredible size, and in the afternoon passed very near one whose summit could not have been less than four hundred fathoms from the surface of the ocean. Its girth was probably, at the base, three quarters of a league, and several streams of water were running from crevices in its sides. We remained in sight of this island two days, and then only lost it in a fog.

January 10th.—Early this morning we had the misfortune to lose a man overboard. He was an American, named Peter Vredenburgh, a native of New York, and was

one of the most valuable hands on board the schooner. In going over the bows his foot slipped, and he fell between two cakes of ice, never rising again. At noon of this day we were in latitude 78° 30′, longitude 40° 15′ W. The cold was now excessive, and we had hail squalls continually from the northward and eastward. In this direction also we saw several more immense icebergs, and the whole horizon to the eastward appeared to be blocked up with field ice, rising in tiers, one mass above the other. Some driftwood floated by during the evening, and a great quantity of birds flew over, among which were nellies, peterels, albatrosses, and a large bird of a brilliant blue plumage. The variation here, per azimuth, was less than it had been previously to our passing the Antarctic circle.

January 12th.—Our passage to the south again looked doubtful, as nothing was to be seen in the direction of the pole but one apparently limitless floe, backed by absolute mountains of ragged ice, one precipice of which arose frowningly above the other. We stood to the westward until the fourteenth, in the hope of finding an entrance.

January 14th.—This morning we reached the western extremity of the field which had impeded us, and, weathering it, came to an open sea, without a particle of ice. Upon sounding with two hundred fathoms, we here found a current setting southwardly at the rate of half a mile per hour. The temperature of the air was forty-seven, that of the water thirty-four. We now sailed to the southward without meeting any interruption of moment until the sixteenth, when, at noon, we were in latitude 81° 21′, longitude 42° W. We here again sounded, and found a current setting still southwardly, and at the rate of three quarters of a mile per hour. The variation per azimuth had diminished, and the temperature of the air was mild and pleasant, the thermometer being as high as fifty-one. At this period not a particle of ice was to be discovered. All hands on board now felt certain of attaining the pole.

January 17th.—This day was full of incidents. Innumerable flights of birds flew over us from the southward, and several were shot from the deck; one of them, a species of pelican, proved to be excellent eating. About midday a small floe of ice was seen from the mast-

head off the larboard bow, and upon it there appeared
to be some large animal. As the weather was good and
nearly calm, Captain Guy ordered out two of the boats
to see what it was. Dirk Peters and myself accompanied
the mate in the larger boat. Upon coming up with the
floe, we perceived that it was in possession of a gigantic
creature of the race of the Arctic bear, but far exceeding
in size the largest of these animals. Being well armed,
we made no scruple of attacking it at once. Several
shots were fired in quick succession, the most of which
took effect, apparently, in the head and body. Nothing
discouraged, however, the monster threw himself from
the ice, and swam, with open jaws, to the boat in which
were Peters and myself. Owing to the confusion which
ensued among us at this unexpected turn of the adven-
ture, no person was ready immediately with a second
shot, and the bear had actually succeeded in getting half
his vast bulk across our gunwale, and seizing one of the
men by the small of his back, before any efficient means
were taken to repel him. In this extremity nothing but the
promptness and agility of Peters saved us from destruc-
tion. Leaping upon the back of the huge beast, he
plunged the blade of a knife behind the neck, reaching the
spinal marrow at a blow. The brute tumbled into the
sea lifeless, and without a struggle, rolling over Peters
as he fell. The latter soon recovered himself, and a rope
being thrown him, he secured the carcass before entering
the boat. We then returned in triumph to the schooner,
towing our trophy behind us. This bear, upon admeasure-
ment, proved to be full fifteen feet in his greatest length.
His wool was perfectly white, and very coarse, curling
tightly. The eyes were of a blood red, and larger than those
of the Arctic bear; the snout also more rounded, rather
resembling the snout of the bull-dog. The meat was ten-
der, but excessively rank and fishy, although the men
devoured it with avidity, and declared it excellent eat-
ing.

Scarcely had we got our prize alongside, when the
man at the mast-head gave the joyful shout of "land on
the starboard bow!" All hands were now upon the alert,
and, a breeze springing up very opportunely from the
northward and eastward, we were soon close in with the
coast. It proved to be a low rocky islet, of about a league
in circumference, and altogether destitute of vegetation,

if we except a species of prickly-pear. In approaching it from the northward, a singular ledge of rock is seen projecting into the sea, and bearing a strong resemblance to corded bales of cotton. Around this ledge to the westward is a small bay, at the bottom of which our boats effected a convenient landing.

It did not take us long to explore every portion of the island, but, with one exception, we found nothing worthy of our observation. In the southern extremity, we picked up near the shore, half buried in a pile of loose stones, a piece of wood, which seemed to have formed the prow of a canoe. There had been evidently some attempt at carving upon it, and Captain Guy fancied that he made out the figure of a tortoise, but the resemblance did not strike me very forcibly. Besides this prow, if such it were, we found no other token that any living creature had ever been here before. Around the coast we discovered occasional small floes of ice—but these were very few. The exact situation of this islet (to which Captain Guy gave the name of Bennet's Isle, in honor of his partner in the ownership of the schooner) is 82° 50′ S. latitude, 42° 20′ W. longitude.

We had now advanced to the southward more than eight degrees farther than any previous navigators, and the sea still lay perfectly open before us. We found, too, that the variation uniformly decreased as we proceeded, and, what was still more surprising, that the temperature of the air, and latterly of the water, became milder. The weather might even be called pleasant, and we had a steady but very gentle breeze always from some northern point of the compass. The sky was usually clear, with now and then a slight appearance of thin vapor in the southern horizon—this, however, was invariably of brief duration. Two difficulties alone presented themselves to our view; we were getting short of fuel, and symptoms of scurvy had occurred among several of the crew. These considerations began to impress upon Captain Guy the necessity of returning, and he spoke of it frequently. For my own part, confident as I was of soon arriving at land of some description upon the course we were pursuing, and having every reason to believe, from present appearances, that we should not find it the sterile soil met with in the higher Arctic latitudes, I warmly pressed upon him the expediency of persevering,

at least for a few days longer, in the direction we were now holding. So tempting an opportunity of solving the great problem in regard to an Antarctic continent had never yet been afforded to man, and I confess that I felt myself bursting with indignation at the timid and ill-timed suggestions of our commander. I believe, indeed, that what I could not refrain from saying to him on this head had the effect of inducing him to push on. While, therefore, I cannot but lament the most unfortunate and bloody events which immediately arose from my advice, I must still be allowed to feel some degree of gratification at having been instrumental, however remotely, in opening to the eye of science one of the most intensely exciting secrets which has ever engrossed its attention.

CHAPTER XVIII

JANUARY 18TH.—This morning[1] we continued to the southward, with the same pleasant weather as before. The sea was entirely smooth, the air tolerably warm and from the northeast, the temperature of the water fifty-three. We now again got our sounding-gear in order, and, with a hundred and fifty fathoms of line, found the current setting toward the pole at the rate of a mile an hour. This constant tendency to the southward, both in the wind and current, caused some degree of speculation, and even of alarm, in different quarters of the schooner, and I saw distinctly that no little impression had been made upon the mind of Captain Guy. He was exceedingly sensitive to ridicule, however, and I finally succeeded in laughing him out of his apprehensions. The variation was now very trivial. In the course of the day we saw several large whales of the right species, and

[1] The terms *morning* and *evening*, which I have made use of to avoid confusion in my narrative, as far as possible, must not, of course, be taken in their ordinary sense. For a long time past we had had no night at all, the daylight being continual. The dates throughout are according to nautical time, and the bearings must be understood as per compass. I would also remark, in this place, that I cannot, in the first portion of what is here written, pretend to strict accuracy in respect to dates, or latitudes and longitudes, having kept no regular journal until after the period of which this first portion treats. In many instances I have relied altogether upon memory.

innumerable flights of the albatross passed over the vessel. We also picked up a bush, full of red berries, like those of the hawthorn, and the carcass of a singular-looking land-animal. It was three feet in length, and but six inches in height, with four very short legs, the feet armed with long claws of a brilliant scarlet, and resembling coral in substance. The body was covered with a straight silky hair, perfectly white. The tail was peaked like that of a rat, and about a foot and a half long. The head resembled a cat's with the exception of the ears— these were flopped like the ears of a dog. The *teeth* were of the same brilliant scarlet as the claws.

January 19th.—To-day, being in latitude 83° 20', longitude 43° 5' W. (the sea being of an extraordinarily dark color), we again saw land from the mast-head, and, upon a closer scrutiny, found it to be one of a group of very large islands. The shore was precipitous, and the interior seemed to be well wooded, a circumstance which occasioned us great joy. In about four hours from our first discovering the land we came to anchor in ten fathoms, sandy bottom, a league from the coast, as a high surf, with strong ripples here and there, rendered a nearer approach of doubtful expediency. The two largest boats were now ordered out, and a party, well armed (among whom were Peters and myself), proceeded to look for an opening in the reef which appeared to encircle the islands. After searching about for some time, we discovered an inlet, which we were entering, when we saw four large canoes put off from the shore, filled with men who seemed to be well armed. We waited for them to come up, and, as they moved with great rapidity, they were soon within hail. Captain Guy now held up a white handkerchief on the blade of an oar, when the strangers made a full stop, and commenced a loud jabbering all at once, intermingled with occasional shouts, in which we could distinguish the word *Anamoo-moo!* and *Lama-Lama!* They continued this for at least half an hour, during which we had a good opportunity of observing their appearance.

In the four canoes, which might have been fifty feet long and five broad, there were a hundred and ten savages in all. They were about the ordinary stature of Europeans, but of a more muscular and brawny frame. Their complexion a jet black, with thick and long woolly hair.

They were clothed in skins of an unknown black animal, shaggy and silky, and made to fit the body with some degree of skill, the hair being inside, except where turned out about the neck, wrists, and ankles. Their arms consisted principally of clubs, of a dark, and apparently very heavy wood. Some spears, however, were observed among them, headed with flint, and a few slings. The bottoms of the canoes were full of black stones about the size of a large egg.

When they had concluded their harangue (for it was clear they intended their jabbering for such), one of them who seemed to be the chief stood up in the prow of his canoe, and made signs for us to bring our boats alongside of him. This hint we pretended not to understand, thinking it the wiser plan to maintain, if possible, the interval between us, as their number more than quadrupled our own. Finding this to be the case, the chief ordered the three other canoes to hold back, while he advanced toward us with his own. As soon as he came up with us he leaped on board the largest of our boats, and seated himself by the side of Captain Guy, pointing at the same time to the schooner, and repeating the words *Anamoo-moo!* and *Lama-Lama!* We now put back to the vessel, the four canoes following at a little distance.

Upon getting alongside, the chief evinced symptoms of extreme surprise and delight, clapping his hands, slapping his thighs and breast, and laughing obstreperously. His followers behind joined in his merriment, and for some minutes the din was so excessive as to be absolutely deafening. Quiet being at length restored, Captain Guy ordered the boats to be hoisted up, as a necessary precaution, and gave the chief (whose name we soon found to be *Too-wit*) to understand that we could admit no more than twenty of his men on deck at one time. With this arrangement he appeared perfectly satisfied, and gave some directions to the canoes, when one of them approached, the rest remaining about fifty yards off. Twenty of the savages now got on board, and proceeded to ramble over every part of the deck, and scramble about among the rigging, making themselves much at home, and examining every article with great inquisitiveness.

It was quite evident that they had never before seen any of the white race—from whose complexion, indeed, they appeared to recoil. They believed the Jane to be a

living creature, and seemed to be afraid of hurting it with the points of their spears, carefully turning them up. Our crew were much amused with the conduct of Too-wit in one instance. The cook was splitting some wood near the galley, and, by accident, struck his axe into the deck, making a gash of considerable depth. The chief immediately ran up, and pushing the cook on one side rather roughly, commenced a half whine, half howl, strongly indicative of sympathy in what he considered the sufferings of the schooner, patting and smoothing the gash with his hand, and washing it from a bucket of sea-water which stood by. This was a degree of ignorance for which we were not prepared, and for my part I could not help thinking some of it affected.

When the visitors had satisfied, as well as they could, their curiosity in regard to our upper works, they were admitted below, when their amazement exceeded all bounds. Their astonishment now appeared to be far too deep for words, for they roamed about in silence, broken only by low ejaculations. The arms afforded them much food for speculation, and they were suffered to handle and examine them at leisure. I do not believe that they had the least suspicion of their actual use, but rather took them for idols, seeing the care we had of them, and the attention with which we watched their movements while handling them. At the great guns their wonder was redoubled. They approached them with every mark of the profoundest reverence and awe, but forbore to examine them minutely. There were two large mirrors in the cabin, and here was the acme of their amazement. Too-wit was the first to approach them, and he had got in the middle of the cabin, with his face to one and his back to the other, before he fairly perceived them. Upon raising his eyes and seeing his reflected self in the glass, I thought the savage would go mad; but, upon turning short round to make a retreat, and beholding himself a second time in the opposite direction, I was afraid he would expire upon the spot. No persuasion could prevail upon him to take another look; but, throwing himself upon the floor, with his face buried in his hands, he remained thus until we were obliged to drag him upon deck.

The whole of the savages were admitted on board in this manner, twenty at a time, Too-wit being suffered to remain during the entire period. We saw no disposition to

thievery among them, nor did we miss a single article after
their departure. Throughout the whole of their visit they
evinced the most friendly manner. There were, however
some points in their demeanor which we found it impos-
sible to understand; for example, we could not get them
to approach several very harmless objects—such as the
schooner's sails, an egg, an open book, or a pan of flour.
We endeavored to ascertain if they had among them
any articles which might be turned to account in the way
of traffic, but found great difficulty in being compre-
hended. We made out, nevertheless, what greatly aston-
ished us, that the islands abounded in the large tortoise
of the Gallipagos, one of which we saw in the canoe of
Too-wit. We saw also some *biche de mer* in the hands of
one of the savages, who was greedily devouring it in its
natural state. These anomalies—for they were such when
considered in regard to the latitude—induced Captain
Guy to wish for a thorough investigation of the coun-
try, in the hope of making a profitable speculation in his
discovery. For my own part, anxious as I was to know
something more of these islands, I was still more ear-
nestly bent on prosecuting the voyage to the southward
without delay. We had now fine weather, but there was
no telling how long it would last; and being already in the
eighty-fourth parallel, with an open sea before us, a cur-
rent setting strongly to the southward, and the wind fair,
I could not listen with any patience to a proposition of
stopping longer than was absolutely necessary for the
health of the crew and the taking on board a proper
supply of fuel and fresh provisions. I represented to the
captain that we might easily make this group on our re-
turn, and winter here in the event of being blocked up
by the ice. He at length came into my views (for in some
way, hardly known to myself, I had acquired much in-
fluence over him), and it was finally resolved that, even in
the event of our finding *biche de mer,* we should only stay
here a week to recruit, and then push on to the south-
ward while we might. Accordingly we made every neces-
sary preparation, and, under the guidance of Too-wit, got
the Jane through the reef in safety, coming to anchor
about a mile from the shore, in an excellent bay, com-
pletely landlocked, on the southeastern coast of the main
island, and in ten fathoms of water, black sandy bottom.
At the head of this bay there were three fine springs

(we were told) of good water, and we saw abundance of wood in the vicinity. The four canoes followed us in, keeping, however, at a respectful distance. Too-wit himself remained on board, and, upon dropping our anchor, invited us to accompany him on shore, and visit his village in the interior. To this Captain Guy consented; and ten savages being left on board as hostages, a party of us, twelve in all, got in readiness to attend the chief. We took care to be well armed, yet without evincing any distrust. The schooner had her guns run out, her boarding-nettings up, and every other proper precaution was taken to guard against surprise. Directions were left with the chief mate to admit no person on board during our absence, and, in the event of our not appearing in twelve hours, to send the cutter, with a swivel, around the island in search of us.

At every step we took inland the conviction forced itself upon us that we were in a country differing essentially from any hitherto visited by civilized men. We saw nothing with which we had been formerly conversant. The trees resembled no growth of either the torrid, the temperate, or the northern frigid zones, and were altogether unlike those of the lower southern latitudes we had already traversed. The very rocks were novel in their mass, their color, and their stratification; and the streams themselves, utterly incredible as it may appear, had so little in common with those of other climates, that we were scrupulous of tasting them, and, indeed, had difficulty in bringing ourselves to believe that their qualities were purely those of nature. At a small brook which crossed our path (the first we had reached) Too-wit and his attendants halted to drink. On account of the singular character of the water, we refused to taste it, supposing it to be polluted; and it was not until some time afterward we came to understand that such was the appearance of the streams throughout the whole group. I am at a loss to give a distinct idea of the nature of this liquid, and cannot do so without many words. Although it flowed with rapidity in all declivities where common water would do so, yet never, except when falling in a cascade, had it the customary appearance of *limpidity*. It was, nevertheless, in point of fact, as perfectly limpid as any limestone water in existence, the difference being only in appearance. At first sight, and especially in cases where little

declivity was found, it bore resemblance, as regards consistency, to a thick infusion of gum arabic in common water. But this was only the least remarkable of its extraordinary qualities. It was *not* colorless, nor was it of any one uniform color—presenting to the eye, as it flowed, every possible shade of purple, like the hues of a changeable silk. This variation in shade was produced in a manner which excited as profound astonishment in the minds of our party as the mirror had done in the case of Too-wit. Upon collecting a basinful, and allowing it to settle thoroughly, we perceived that the whole mass of liquid was made up of a number of distinct veins, each of a distinct hue; that these veins did not commingle; and that their cohesion was perfect in regard to their own particles among themselves, and imperfect in regard to neighboring veins. Upon passing the blade of a knife athwart the veins, the water closed over it immediately, as with us, and also, in withdrawing it, all traces of the passage of the knife were instantly obliterated. If, however, the blade was passed down accurately between the two veins, a perfect separation was effected, which the power of cohesion did not immediately rectify. The phenomena of this water formed the first definite link in that vast chain of apparent miracles with which I was destined to be at length encircled.

CHAPTER XIX

WE WERE nearly three hours in reaching the village, it being more than nine miles in the interior, and the path lying through a rugged country. As we passed along, the party of Too-wit (the whole hundred and ten savages of the canoes) was momentarily strengthened by smaller detachments, of from two to six or seven, which joined us, as if by accident, at different turns of the road. There appeared so much of system in this that I could not help feeling distrust, and I spoke to Captain Guy of my apprehensions. It was now too late, however, to recede, and we concluded that our best security lay in evincing a perfect confidence in the good faith of Too-wit. We accordingly went on, keeping a wary eye upon the manœuvres of the savages, and not permitting them to divide our numbers

by pushing in between. In this way, passing through a precipitous ravine, we at length reached what we were told was the only collection of habitations upon the island. As we came in sight of them, the chief set up a shout, and frequently repeated the word *Klock-klock,* which we supposed to be the name of the village, or perhaps the generic name for villages.

The dwellings were of the most miserable description imaginable, and, unlike those of even the lowest of the savage races with which mankind are acquainted, were of no uniform plan. Some of them (and these we found belonged to the *Wampoos* or *Yampoos,* the great men of the land) consisted of a tree cut down at about four feet from the root, with a large black skin thrown over it, and hanging in loose folds upon the ground. Under this the savage nestled. Others were formed by means of rough limbs of trees, with the withered foliage upon them, made to recline, at an angle of forty-five degrees, against a bank of clay, heaped up, without regular form, to the height of five or six feet. Others, again, were mere holes dug in the earth perpendicularly, and covered over with similar branches, these being removed when the tenant was about to enter, and pulled on again when he had entered. A few were built among the forked limbs of trees as they stood, the upper limbs being partially cut through, so as to bend over upon the lower, thus forming thicker shelter from the weather. The greater number, however, consisted of small shallow caverns, apparently scratched in the face of a precipitous ledge of dark stone, resembling fuller's earth, with which three sides of the village were bounded. At the door of each of these primitive caverns was a small rock, which the tenant carefully placed before the entrance upon leaving his residence, for what purpose I could not ascertain, as the stone itself was never of sufficient size to close up more than a third of the opening.

This village, if it were worthy of the name, lay in a valley of some depth, and could only be approached from the southward, the precipitous ledge of which I have already spoken cutting off all access in other directions. Through the middle of the valley ran a brawling stream of the same magical-looking water which has been described. We saw several strange animals about the dwell-

ings, all appearing to be thoroughly domesticated. The largest of these creatures resembled our common hog in the structure of the body and snout; the tail, however, was bushy, and the legs slender as those of the antelope. Its motion was exceedingly awkward and indecisive, and we never saw it attempt to run. We noticed also several animals very similar in appearance, but of a greater length of body, and covered with a black wool. There were a great variety of tame fowls running about, and these seemed to constitute the chief food of the natives. To our astonishment we saw black albatross among these birds in a state of entire domestication, going to sea periodically for food, but always returning to the village as a home, and using the southern shore in the vicinity as a place of incubation. There they were joined by their friends the pelicans as usual, but these latter never followed them to the dwellings of the savages. Among the other kinds of tame fowls were ducks, differing very little from the canvas-back of our own country, black gannets, and a large bird not unlike the buzzard in appearance, but not carnivorous. Of fish there seemed to be a great abundance. We saw, during our visit, a quantity of dried salmon, rock cod, blue dolphins, mackerel, blackfish, skate, conger eels, elephant-fish, mullets, soles, parrot-fish, leather-jackets, gurnards, hake, flounders, paracutas, and innumerable other varieties. We noticed, too, that most of them were similar to the fish about the group of the Lord Auckland islands, in a latitude as low as fifty-one degrees south. The Gallipago tortoise was also very plentiful. We saw but few wild animals, and none of a large size, or of a species with which we were familiar. One or two serpents of a formidable aspect crossed our path, but the natives paid them little attention, and we concluded that they were not venomous.

As we approached the village with Too-wit and his party, a vast crowd of the people rushed out to meet us, with loud shouts, among which we could only distinguish the everlasting *Anamoo-moo!* and *Lama-Lama!* We were much surprised at perceiving that, with one or two exceptions, these new comers were entirely naked, the skins being used only by the men of the canoes. All the weapons of the country seemed also to be in the possession of the latter, for there was no appearance of any

among the villagers. There were a great many women and
children, the former not altogether wanting in what
might be termed personal beauty. They were straight,
tall, and well formed, with a grace and freedom of car-
riage not to be found in civilized society. Their lips, how-
ever, like those of the men, were thick and clumsy, so
that, even when laughing, the teeth were never disclosed.
Their hair was of a finer texture than that of the males.
Among these naked villagers there might have been ten
or twelve who were clothed, like the party of Too-wit,
in dresses of black skin, and armed with lances and heavy
clubs. These appeared to have great influence among
the rest, and were always addressed by the title *Wampoo*.
These, too, were the tenants of the black skin palaces.
That of Too-wit was situated in the centre of the village,
and was much larger and somewhat better constructed
than others of its kind. The tree which formed its sup-
port was cut off at a distance of twelve feet or there-
about from the root, and there were several branches
left just below the cut, these serving to extend the cover-
ing, and in this way prevent its flapping about the trunk.
The covering, too, which consisted of four very large
skins fastened together with wooden skewers, was se-
cured at the bottom with pegs driven through it and into
the ground. The floor was strewed with a quantity of dry
leaves by way of carpet.

To this hut we were conducted with great solemnity,
and as many of the natives crowded in after us as pos-
sible. Too-wit seated himself on the leaves, and made
signs that we should follow his example. This we did,
and presently found ourselves in a situation peculiarly
uncomfortable, if not indeed critical. We were on the
ground, twelve in number, with the savages, as many as
forty, sitting on their hams so closely around us that,
if any disturbance had arisen, we should have found it
impossible to make use of our arms, or indeed to have
risen on our feet. The pressure was not only inside the
tent, but outside, where probably was every individual on
the whole island, the crowd being prevented from
trampling us to death only by the incessant exertions
and vociferations of Too-wit. Our chief security lay,
however, in the presence of Tooo-wit himself among us,
and we resolved to stick by him closely, as the best

chance of extricating ourselves from the dilemma, sacri-
ficing him immediately upon the first appearance of
hostile design.

After some trouble a certain degree of quiet was re-
stored, when the chief addressed us in a speech of great
length, and very nearly resembling the one delivered in
the canoes, with the exception that the *Anamoo-moos!*
were now somewhat more strenuously insisted upon than
the *Lama-Lamas!* We listened in profound silence until
the conclusion of his harangue, when Captain Guy re-
plied by assuring the chief of his eternal friendship and
good-will, concluding what he had to say by a present of
several strings of blue beads and a knife. At the former
the monarch, much to our surprise, turned up his nose
with some expression of contempt; but the knife gave him
the most unlimited satisfaction, and he immediately or-
dered dinner. This was handed into the tent over the heads
of the attendants, and consisted of the palpitating en-
trails of a species of unknown animal, probably one of the
slim-legged hogs which we had observed in our approach
to the village. Seeing us at a loss how to proceed, he
began, by way of setting us an example, to devour yard
after yard of the enticing food, until we could positively
stand it no longer, and evinced such manifest symptoms
of rebellion of stomach as inspired his majesty with a
degree of astonishment only inferior to that brought
about by the looking-glasses. We declined, however,
partaking of the delicacies before us, and endeavored to
make him understand that we had no appetite whatever,
having just finished a hearty *déjeuner.*

When the monarch had made an end of his meal, we
commenced a series of cross-questioning in every ingen-
ious manner we could devise, with a view of discovering
what were the chief productions of the country, and
whether any of them might be turned to profit. At length
he seemed to have some idea of our meaning, and offered
to accompany us to a part of the coast where he assured
us the *biche de mer* (pointing to a specimen of that
animal) was to be found in great abundance. We were
glad of this early opportunity of escaping from the op-
pression of the crowd, and signified our eagerness to
proceed. We now left the tent, and, accompanied by
the whole population of the village, followed the chief

to the southeastern extremity of the island, not far from the bay where our vessel lay at anchor. We waited here for about an hour, until the four canoes were brought round by some of the savages to our station. The whole of our party then getting into one of them, we were paddled along the edge of the reef before mentioned, and of another still farther out, where we saw a far greater quantity of *biche de mer* than the oldest seaman among us had ever seen in those groups of the lower altitudes most celebrated for this article of commerce. We stayed near these reefs only long enough to satisfy ourselves that we could easily load a dozen vessels with the animal if necessary, when we were taken alongside the schooner, and parted with Too-wit, after obtaining from him a promise that he would bring us, in the course of twenty-four hours, as many of the canvasback ducks and Gallipago tortoises as his canoes would hold. In the whole of this adventure we saw nothing in the demeanor of the natives calculated to create suspicion, with the single exception of the systematic manner in which their party was strengthened during our route from the schooner to the village.

CHAPTER XX

THE chief was as good as his word, and we were soon plentifully supplied with fresh provisions. We found the tortoises as fine as we had ever seen, and the ducks surpassed our best species of wild fowl, being exceedingly tender, juicy, and well-flavored. Besides these, the savages brought us, upon our making them comprehend our wishes, a vast quantity of brown celery and scurvy-grass, with a canoe-load of fresh fish and some dried. The celery was a treat indeed, and the scurvy-grass proved of incalculable benefit in restoring those of our men who had shown symptoms of disease. In a very short time we had not a single person on the sick-list. We had also plenty of other kinds of fresh provisions, among which may be mentioned a species of shell-fish resembling the mussel in shape, but with the taste of an oyster. Shrimps, too, and prawns were abundant, and albatross and other birds' eggs with dark shells. We

took in, too, a plentiful stock of the flesh of the hog which
I have mentioned before. Most of the men found it a
palatable food, but I thought it fishy and otherwise dis-
agreeable. In return for these good things we presented
the natives with blue beads, brass trinkets, nails, knives,
and pieces of red cloth, they being fully delighted in the
exchange. We established a regular market on shore,
just under the guns of the schooner, where our barter-
ings were carried on with every appearance of good
faith, and a degree of order which their conduct at the
village of *Klock-klock* had not led us to expect from the
savages.

Matters went on thus very amicably for several days,
during which parties of the natives were frequently on
board the schooner, and parties of our men frequently
on shore, making long excursions into the interior, and
receiving no molestation whatever. Finding the ease with
which the vessel might be loaded with *biche de mer,*
owing to the friendly disposition of the islanders, and the
readiness with which they would render us assistance in
collecting it, Captain Guy resolved to enter into negotia-
tion with Too-wit for the erection of suitable houses in
which to cure the article, and for the services of himself
and tribe in gathering as much as possible, while he him-
self took advantage of the fine weather to prosecute his
voyage to the southward. Upon mentioning this project
to the chief he seemed very willing to enter into an
agreement. A bargain was accordingly struck, perfectly
satisfactory to both parties, by which it was arranged
that, after making the necessary preparations, such as
laying off the proper grounds, erecting a portion of the
buildings, and doing some other work in which the whole
of our crew would be required, the schooner should
proceed on her route, leaving three of her men on the
island to superintend the fulfilment of the project, and
instruct the natives in drying the *biche de mer.* In regard
to terms, these were made to depend upon the exertions
of the savages in our absence. They were to receive a
stipulated quantity of blue beads, knives, red cloth, and
so forth, for every certain number of piculs of the
biche de mer which should be ready on our return.

A description of the nature of this important article of
commerce, and the method of preparing it, may prove of

some interest to my readers, and I can find no more suitable place than this for introducing an account of it. The following comprehensive notice of the substance is taken from a modern history of a voyage to the South Seas:

"It is that *mollusca* from the Indian Seas which is known to commerce by the French name *bouche de mer* (a nice morsel from the sea). If I am not much mistaken, the celebrated Cuvier calls it *gasteropoda pulmonifera*. It is abundantly gathered in the coasts of the Pacific islands, and gathered especially for the Chinese market, where it commands a great price, perhaps as much as their much-talked-of edible birds' nests, which are probably made up of the gelatinous matter picked up by a species of swallow from the body of these molluscæ. They have no shell, no legs, nor any prominent part, except an *absorbing* and an *excretory,* opposite organs; but, by their elastic wings, like caterpillars or worms, they creep in shallow waters, in which, when low, they can be seen by a kind of swallow, the sharp bill of which, inserted in the soft animal, draws a gummy and filamentous substance, which, by drying, can be wrought into the solid walls of their nest. Hence the name of *gasteropoda pulmonifera.*

"This mollusca is oblong, and of different sizes, from three to eighteen inches in length; and I have seen a few that were not less than two feet long. They were nearly round, a little flattish on one side, which lies next to the bottom of the sea; and they are from one to eight inches thick. They crawl up into shallow water at particular seasons of the year, probably for the purpose of gendering, as we often find them in pairs. It is when the sun has the most power on the water, rendering it tepid, that they approach the shore; and they often go up into places so shallow that, on the tide's receding, they are left dry, exposed to the heat of the sun. But they do not bring forth their young in shallow water, as we never see any of their progeny, and the full-grown ones are always observed coming in from deep water. They feed principally on that class of zoöphites which produce the coral.

"The *biche de mer* is generally taken in three or four feet of water; after which they are brought on shore, and split at one end with a knife, the incision being one inch

or more, according to the size of the mollusca. Through this opening the entrails are forced out by pressure, and they are much like those of any other small tenant of the deep. The article is then washed, and afterward boiled to a certain degree, which must not be too much or too little. They are then buried in the ground for four hours, then boiled again for a short time, after which they are dried, either by the fire or the sun. Those cured by the sun are worth the most; but where one picul (133⅓ lbs.) can be cured that way, I can cure thirty piculs by the fire. When once properly cured, they can be kept in a dry place for two or three years without any risk; but they should be examined once in every few months, say four times a year, to see if any dampness is likely to affect them.

"The Chinese, as before stated, consider *biche de mer* a very great luxury, believing that it wonderfully strengthens and nourishes the system, and renews the exhausted system of the immoderate voluptuary. The first quality commands a high price in Canton, being worth ninety dollars a picul; the second quality, seventy-five dollars; the third, fifty dollars; the fourth, thirty dollars; the fifth, twenty dollars; the sixth, twelve dollars; the seventh, eight dollars; and the eighth, four dollars; small cargoes, however, will often bring more in Manila, Singapore, and Batavia."

An agreement having been thus entered into, we proceeded immediately to land every thing necessary for preparing the buildings and clearing the ground. A large flat space near the eastern shore of the bay was selected, where there was plenty of both wood and water, and within a convenient distance of the principal reefs on which the *biche de mer* was to be procured. We now all set to work in good earnest, and soon, to the great astonishment of the savages, had felled a sufficient number of trees for our purpose, getting them quickly in order for the framework of the houses, which in two or three days were so far under way that we could safely trust the rest of the work to the three men whom we intended to leave behind. These were John Carson, Alfred Harris,—— Peterson (all natives of London, I believe), who volunteered their services in this respect.

By the last of the month we had every thing in readi-

iness for departure. We had agreed, however, to pay a
formal visit of leave-taking to the village, and Too-wit
insisted so pertinaciously upon our keeping the promise,
that we did not think it advisable to run the risk of
offending him by a final refusal. I believe that not one of
us had at this time the slightest suspicion of the good
faith of the savages. They had uniformly behaved with
the greatest decorum, aiding us with alacrity in our
work, offering us their commodities, frequently without
price, and never, in any instance, pilfering a single arti-
cle, although the high value they set upon the goods we
had with us was evident by the extravagant demonstra-
tions of joy always manifested upon our making them a
present. The women especially were most obliging in every
respect, and, upon the whole, we should have been the
most suspicious of human beings had we entertained a
single thought of perfidy on the part of a people who
treated us so well. A very short while sufficed to prove
that this apparent kindness of disposition was only the
result of a deeply laid plan for our destruction, and that
the islanders for whom we entertained such inordinate
feelings of esteem, were among the most barbarous,
subtle, and blood-thirsty wretches that ever contami-
nated the face of the globe.

It was on the first of February that we went on shore
for the purpose of visiting the village. Although, as said
before, we entertained not the slightest suspicion, still
no proper precaution was neglected. Six men were left
in the schooner, with instructions to permit none of the
savages to approach the vessel during our absence, under
any pretence whatever, and to remain constantly on
deck. The boarding-nettings were up, the guns double-
shotted with grape and canister, and the swivels loaded
with canisters of musket-balls. She lay, with her anchor
apeak, about a mile from the shore, and no canoe could
approach her in any direction without being distinctly
seen and exposed to the full fire of our swivels immedi-
ately.

The six men being left on board, our shore-party con-
sisted of thirty-two persons in all. We were armed to the
teeth, having with us muskets, pistols, and cutlasses; be-
sides, each had a long kind of seaman's knife, some-
what resembling the bowie knife now so much used

throughout our western and southern country. A hundred
of the black-skin warriors met us at the landing for the
purpose of accompanying us on our way. We noticed,
however, with some surprise, that they were now entirely
without arms; and, upon questioning Too-wit in relation
to this circumstance, he merely answered that *Mattee
non we pa pa si*—meaning that there was no need of
arms where all were brothers. We took this in good part,
and proceeded.

We had passed the spring and rivulet of which I before
spoke, and were now entering upon a narrow gorge
leading through the chain of soapstone hills among
which the village was situated. This gorge was very rocky
and uneven, so much so that it was with no little diffi-
culty we scrambled through it on our first visit to Klock-
klock. The whole length of the ravine might have been
a mile and a half, or probably two miles. It wound in
every possible direction through the hills (having appar-
ently formed, at some remote period, the bed of a tor-
rent), in no instance proceeding more than twenty yards
without an abrupt turn. The sides of this dell would have
averaged, I am sure, seventy or eighty feet in perpendic-
ular altitude throughout the whole of their extent, and
in some portions they arose to an astonishing height,
overshadowing the pass so completely that but little of
the light of day could penetrate. The general width was
about forty feet, and occasionally it diminished so as not
to allow the passage of more than five or six persons
abreast. In short, there could be no place in the world
better adapted for the consummation of an ambuscade,
and it was no more than natural that we should look
carefully to our arms as we entered upon it. When I now
think of our egregious folly, the chief subject of astonish-
ment seems to be, that we should have ever ventured,
under any circumstances, so completely into the power
of unknown savages as to permit them to march both be-
fore and behind us in our progress through this ravine.
Yet such was the order we blindly took up, trusting fool-
ishly to the force of our party, the unarmed condition of
Too-wit and his men, the certain efficacy of our fire-
arms (whose effect was yet a secret to the natives), and,
more than all, to the long-sustained pretension of friend-
ship kept up by these infamous wretches. Five or six of

them went on before, as if to lead the way, ostentatiously busying themselves in removing the larger stones and rubbish from the path. Next came our own party. We walked closely together, taking care only to prevent separation. Behind followed the main body of the savages, observing unusual order and decorum.

Dirk Peters, a man named Wilson Allen, and myself were on the right of our companions, examining, as we went along, the singular stratification of the precipice which overhung us. A fissure in the soft rock attracted our attention. It was about wide enough for one person to enter without squeezing, and extended back into the hill some eighteen or twenty feet in a straight course, sloping afterward to the left. The height of the opening, as far as we could see into it from the main gorge, was perhaps sixty or seventy feet. There were one or two stunted shrubs growing from the crevices, bearing a species of filbert which I felt some curiosity to examine, and pushed in briskly for that purpose, gathering five or six of the nuts at a grasp, and then hastily retreating. As I turned, I found that Peters and Allen had followed me. I desired them to go back, as there was not room for two persons to pass, saying they should have some of my nuts. They accordingly turned, and were scrambling back, Allen being close to the mouth of the fissure, when I was suddenly aware of a concussion resembling nothing I had ever before experienced, and which impressed me with a vague conception, if indeed I then thought of any thing, that the whole foundations of the solid globe were suddenly rent asunder, and that the day of universal dissolution was at hand.

CHAPTER XXI

As soon as I could collect my scattered senses, I found myself nearly suffocated, and grovelling in utter darkness among a quantity of loose earth, which was also falling upon me heavily in every direction, threatening to bury me entirely. Horribly alarmed at this idea, I struggled to gain my feet, and at last succeeded. I then remained motionless for some moments, endeavoring to conceive what had happened to me, and where I was.

Presently I heard a deep groan just at my ear, and afterward the smothered voice of Peters calling to me for aid in the name of God. I scrambled one or two paces forward, when I fell directly over the head and shoulders of my companion, who, I soon discovered, was buried in a loose mass of earth as far as his middle, and struggling desperately to free himself from the pressure. I tore the dirt from around him with all the energy I could command, and at length succeeded in getting him out.

As soon as we sufficiently recovered from our fright and surprise to be capable of conversing rationally, we both came to the conclusion that the walls of the fissure in which we had ventured had, by some convulsion of nature, or probably from their own weight, caved in overhead, and that we were consequently lost for ever, being thus entombed alive. For a long time we gave up supinely to the most intense agony and despair, such as cannot be adequately imagined by those who have never been in a similar position. I firmly believe that no incident ever occurring in the course of human events is more adapted to inspire the supremeness of mental and bodily distress than a case like our own, of living inhumation. The blackness of darkness which envelops the victim, the terrific oppression of lungs, the stifling fumes from the damp earth, unite with the ghastly considerations that we are beyond the remotest confines of hope, and that such is the allotted portion of *the dead*, to carry into the human heart a degree of appalling awe and horror not to be tolerated—never to be conceived.

At length Peters proposed that we should endeavor to ascertain precisely the extent of our calamity, and grope about our prison; it being barely possible, he observed, that some opening might yet be left us for escape. I caught eagerly at this hope, and, arousing myself to exertion, attempted to force my way through the loose earth. Hardly had I advanced a single step before a glimmer of light became perceptible, enough to convince me that, at all events, we should not immediately perish for want of air. We now took some degree of heart, and encouraged each other to hope for the best. Having scrambled over a bank of rubbish which impeded our farther progress in the direction of the light, we found less difficulty in advancing and also experienced some re-

lief from the excessive oppression of lungs which had
tormented us. Presently we were enabled to obtain a
glimpse of the objects around, and discovered that we
were near the extremity of the straight portion of the
fissure, where it made a turn to the left. A few struggles
more, and we reached the bend, when, to our inexpres-
sible joy, there appeared a long seam or crack extending
upward a vast distance, generally at an angle of about
forty-five degrees, although sometimes much more pre-
cipitous. We could not see through the whole extent of
this opening; but, as a good deal of light came down it,
we had little doubt of finding at the top of it (if we could
by any means reach the top) a clear passage into the
open air.

I now called to mind that three of us had entered the
fissure from the main gorge, and that our companion,
Allen, was still missing; we determined at once to re-
trace our steps and look for him. After a long search,
and much danger from the farther caving in of the earth
above us, Peters at length cried out to me that he had
hold of our companion's foot, and that his whole body
was deeply buried beneath the rubbish beyond the possi-
bility of extricating him. I soon found that what he said
was too true, and that, of course, life had been long ex-
tinct. With sorrowful hearts, therefore, we left the corpse
to its fate, and again made our way to the bend.

The breadth of the seam was barely sufficient to admit
us, and, after one or two ineffectual efforts at getting
up, we began once more to despair. I have before said
that the chain of hills through which ran the main gorge
was composed of a species of soft rock resembling soap-
stone. The sides of the cleft we were now attempting to
ascend were of the same material, and so excessively
slippery, being wet, that we could get but little foot-
hold upon them even in their least precipitous parts;
in some places, where the ascent was nearly perpendicu-
lar, the difficulty was, of course, much aggravated; and,
indeed, for some time we thought insurmountable. We
took courage, however, from despair; and what, by dint
of cutting steps in the soft stone with our bowie knives,
and swinging at the risk of our lives, to small projecting
points of a harder species of slaty rock which now and
then protruded from the general mass, we at length

reached a natural platform, from which was perceptible a patch of blue sky, at the extremity of a thickly-wooded ravine. Looking back now, with somewhat more leisure, at the passage through which we had thus far proceeded, we clearly saw from the appearance of its sides, that it was of late formation, and we concluded that the concussion, whatever it was, which had so unexpectedly overwhelmed us, had also, at the same moment, laid open this path for escape. Being quite exhausted with exertion, and, indeed, so weak that we were scarcely able to stand or articulate, Peters now proposed that we should endeavor to bring our companions to the rescue by firing the pistols which still remained in our girdles—the muskets as well as cutlasses had been lost among the loose earth at the bottom of the chasm. Subsequent events proved that, had we fired, we should have sorely repented it, but luckily a half suspicion of foul play had by this time arisen in my mind, and we forebore to let the savages know of our whereabouts.

After having reposed for about an hour, we pushed on slowly up the ravine, and had gone no great way before we heard a succession of tremendous yells. At length we reached what might be called the surface of the ground; for our path hitherto, since leaving the platform, had lain beneath an archway of high rock and foliage, at a vast distance overhead. With great caution we stole to a narrow opening, through which we had a clear sight of the surrounding country, when the whole dreadful secret of the concussion broke upon us in one moment and at one view.

The spot from which we looked was not far from the summit of the highest peak in the range of the soapstone hills. The gorge in which our party of thirty-two had entered ran within fifty feet to the left of us. But, for at least one hundred yards, the channel or bed of this gorge was entirely filled up with the chaotic ruins of more than a million tons of earth and stone that had been artificially tumbled within it. The means by which the vast mass had been precipitated were not more simple than evident, for sure traces of the murderous work were yet remaining. In several spots along the top of the eastern side of the gorge (we were now on the western) might be seen stakes of wood driven into the

earth. In these spots the earth had not given way; but throughout the whole extent of the face of the precipice from which the mass *had* fallen, it was clear, from marks left in the soil resembling those made by the drill of the rock-blaster, that stakes similar to those we saw standing had been inserted, at not more than a yard apart, for the length of perhaps three hundred feet, and ranging at about ten feet back from the edge of the gulf. Strong cords of grape vine were attached to the stakes still remaining on the hill, and it was evident that such cords had also been attached to each of the other stakes. I have already spoken of the singular stratification of these soapstone hills; and the description just given of the narrow and deep fissure through which we effected our escape from inhumation will afford a further conception of its nature. This was such that almost every natural convulsion would be sure to split the soil into perpendicular layers or ridges running parallel with one another; and a very moderate exertion of art would be sufficient for effecting the same purpose. Of this stratification the savages had availed themselves to accomplish their treacherous ends. There can be no doubt that, by the continuous line of stakes, a partial rupture of the soil had been brought about, probably to the depth of one or two feet, when, by means of a savage pulling at the end of each of the cords (these cords being attached to the tops of the stakes, and extending back from the edge of the cliff), a vast leverage power was obtained, capable of hurling the whole face of the hill, upon a given signal, into the bosom of the abyss below. The fate of our poor companions was no longer a matter of uncertainty. We alone had escaped from the tempest of that overwhelming destruction. We were the only living white men upon the island.

CHAPTER XXII

OUR situation, as it now appeared, was scarcely less dreadful than when we had conceived ourselves entombed forever. We saw before us no prospect but that of being put to death by the savages, or of dragging out a miserable existence in captivity among them. We

might, to be sure, conceal ourselves for a time from their observation among the fastnesses of the hills, and, as a final resort, in the chasm from which we had just issued; but we must either perish in the long polar winter through cold and famine, or be ultimately discovered in our efforts to obtain relief.

The whole country around us seemed to be swarming with savages, crowds of whom, we now perceived, had come over from the islands to the southward on flat rafts, doubtless with a view of lending their aid in the capture and plunder of the Jane. The vessel still lay calmly at anchor in the bay, those on board being apparently quite unconscious of any danger awaiting them. How we longed at that moment to be with them! either to aid in effecting their escape, or to perish with them in attempting a defence. We saw no chance even of warning them of their danger without bringing immediate destruction upon our own heads, with but a remote hope of benefit to them. A pistol fired might suffice to apprise them that something wrong had occurred; but the report could not possibly inform them that their only prospect of safety lay in getting out of the harbor forthwith—it could not tell them that no principles of honor now bound them to remain, that their companions were no longer among the living. Upon hearing the discharge they could not be more thoroughly prepared to meet the foe, who were now getting ready to attack, than they already were, and always had been. No good, therefore, and infinite harm, would result from our firing, and, after mature deliberation, we forbore.

Our next thought was to attempt to rush toward the vessel, to seize one of the four canoes which lay at the head of the bay, and endeavor to force a passage on board. But the utter impossibility of succeeding in this desperate task soon became evident. The country, as I said before, was literally swarming with the natives, skulking among the bushes and recesses of the hills, so as not to be observed from the schooner. In our immediate vicinity especially, and blockading the sole path by which we could hope to attain the shore at the proper point, were stationed the whole party of the black-skin warriors, with Too-wit at their head, and apparently only waiting for some re-enforcement to commence his onset

upon the Jane. The canoes, too, which lay at the head of the bay, were manned with savages, unarmed, it is true, but who undoubtedly had arms within reach. We were forced, therefore, however unwillingly, to remain in our place of concealment, mere spectators of the conflict which presently ensued.

In about half an hour we saw some sixty or seventy rafts, or flat-boats, with outriggers, filled with savages, and coming round the southern bight of the harbor. They appeared to have no arms except short clubs, and stones which lay in the bottom of the rafts. Immediately afterward another detachment, still larger, approached in an opposite direction, and with similar weapons. The four canoes, too, were now quickly filled with natives, starting up from the bushes at the head of the bay, and put off swiftly to join the other parties. Thus, in less time than I have taken to tell it, and as if by magic, the Jane saw herself surrounded by an immense multitude of desperadoes evidently bent upon capturing her at all hazards.

That they would succeed in so doing could not be doubted for an instant. The six men left in the vessel, however resolutely they might engage in her defence, were altogether unequal to the proper management of the guns, or in any manner to sustain a contest at such odds. I could hardly imagine that they would make resistance at all, but in this was deceived; for presently I saw them get springs upon the cable, and bring the vessel's starboard broadside to bear upon the canoes, which by this time were within pistol range, the rafts being nearly a quarter of a mile to windward. Owing to some cause unknown, but most probably to the agitation of our poor friends at seeing themselves in so hopeless a situation, the discharge was an entire failure. Not a canoe was hit or a single savage injured, the shots striking short and *ricochetting* over their heads. The only effect produced upon them was astonishment at the unexpected report and smoke, which was so excessive that for some moments I almost thought they would abandon their design entirely, and return to the shore. And this they would most likely have done had our men followed up their broadside by a discharge of small-arms, in which, as the canoes were now so near at hand, they could not have failed in doing some execution, sufficient, at least,

to deter this party from a farther advance, until they could have given the rafts also a broadside. But, in place of this, they left the canoe party to recover from their panic, and, by looking about them, to see that no injury had been sustained, while they flew to the larboard to get ready for the rafts.

The discharge to larboard produced the most terrible effect. The star and double-headed shot of the large guns cut seven or eight of the rafts completely asunder, and killed, perhaps, thirty or forty of the savages outright, while a hundred of them, at least, were thrown into the water, the most of them dreadfully wounded. The remainder, frightened out of their senses, commenced at once a precipitate retreat, not even waiting to pick up their maimed companions, who were swimming about in every direction, screaming and yelling for aid. This great success, however, came too late for the salvation of our devoted people. The canoe party were already on board the schooner to the number of more than a hundred and fifty, the most of them having succeeded in scrambling up the chains and over the boarding-nettings even before the matches had been applied to the larboard guns. Nothing now could withstand their brute rage. Our men were borne down at once, overwhelmed, trodden under foot, and absolutely torn to pieces in an instant.

Seeing this, the savages on the rafts got the better of their fears, and came up in shoals to the plunder. In five minutes the Jane was a pitiable scene indeed of havoc and tumultuous outrage. The decks were split open and ripped up; the cordage, sails, and every thing movable on deck demolished as if by magic; while, by dint of pushing at the stern, towing with the canoes, and hauling at the sides, as they swam in thousands around the vessel, the wretches finally forced her on shore (the cable having been slipped), and delivered her over to the good offices of Too-wit, who, during the whole of the engagement, had maintained, like a skilful general, his post of security and reconnoissance among the hills, but, now that the victory was completed to his satisfaction, condescended to scamper down with his warriors of the black skin, and become a partaker in the spoils.

Too-wit's descent left us at liberty to quit our hiding-

place and reconnoitre the hill in the vicinity of the chasm. At about fifty yards from the mouth of it we saw a small spring of water, at which we slaked the burning thirst that now consumed us. Not far from the spring we discovered several of the filbert-bushes which I mentioned before. Upon tasting the nuts we found them palatable, and very nearly resembling in flavor the common English filbert. We collected our hats full immediately, deposited them within the ravine, and returned for more. While we were busily employed in gathering these, a rustling in the bushes alarmed us, and we were upon the point of stealing back to our covert, when a large black bird of the bittern species strugglingly and slowly arose above the shrubs. I was so much startled that I could do nothing, but Peters had sufficient presence of mind to run up to it before it could make its escape, and seize it by the neck. Its struggles and screams were tremendous, and we had thoughts of letting it go, lest the noise should alarm some of the savages who might be still lurking in the neighborhood. A stab with a bowie knife, however, at length brought it to the ground, and we dragged it into the ravine, congratulating ourselves that, at all events, we had thus obtained a supply of food enough to last us for a week.

We now went out again to look about us, and ventured a considerable distance down the southern declivity of the hill, but met with nothing else which could serve us for food. We therefore collected a quantity of dry wood and returned, seeing one or two large parties of the natives on their way to the village, laden with the plunder of the vessel, and who, we were apprehensive, might discover us in passing beneath the hill.

Our next care was to render our place of concealment as secure as possible, and with this object, we arranged some brushwood over the aperture which I have before spoken of as the one through which we saw the patch of blue sky, on reaching the platform from the interior of the chasm. We left only a very small opening, just wide enough to admit of our seeing the bay, without the risk of being discovered from below. Having done this, we congratulated ourselves upon the security of the position; for we were now completely excluded from observation, as long as we chose to remain within the

ravine itself, and not venture out upon the hill. We could perceive no traces of the savages having ever been within this hollow; but, indeed, when we came to reflect upon the probability that the fissure through which we attained it had been only just now created by the fall of the cliff opposite, and that no other way of attaining it could be perceived, we were not so much rejoiced at the thought of being secure from molestation as fearful lest there should be absolutely no means left us for descent. We resolved to explore the summit of the hill thoroughly, when a good opportunity should offer. In the meantime we watched the motions of the savages through our loophole.

They had already made a complete wreck of the vessel, and were now preparing to set her on fire. In a little while we saw the smoke ascending in huge volumes from her main hatchway, and, shortly afterward, a dense mass of flame burst up from the forecastle. The rigging, masts, and what remained of the sails caught immediately, and the fire spread rapidly along the decks. Still a great many of the savages retained their stations about her, hammering with large stones, axes, and cannon-balls at the bolts and other iron and copper work. On the beach, and in canoes and rafts, there were not less, altogether, in the immediate vicinity of the schooner, than ten thousand natives, besides the shoals of them who, laden with booty, were making their way inland and over to the neighboring islands. We now anticipated a catastrophe, and were not disappointed. First of all there came a smart shock (which we felt as distinctly where we were as if we had been slightly galvanized), but unattended with any visible signs of an explosion. The savages were evidently startled, and paused for an instant from their labors and yellings. They were upon the point of recommencing, when suddenly a mass of smoke puffed up from the decks, resembling a black and heavy thunder-cloud—then, as if from its bowels, arose a tall stream of vivid fire to the height, apparently, of a quarter of a mile—then there came a sudden circular expansion of the flame—then the whole atmosphere was magically crowded, in a single instant, with a wild chaos of wood, and metal, and human limbs—and, lastly, came the concussion in its fullest fury, which hurled us impetuously

from our feet, while the hills echoed and re-echoed the tumult, and a dense shower of the minutest fragments of the ruins tumbled headlong in every direction around us.

The havoc among the savages far exceeded our utmost expectation, and they had now, indeed, reaped the full and perfect fruits of their treachery. Perhaps a thousand perished by the explosion, while at least an equal number were desperately mangled. The whole surface of the bay was literally strewn with the struggling and drowning wretches, and on shore matters were even worse. They seemed utterly appalled by the suddenness and completeness of their discomfiture, and made no efforts at assisting one another. At length we observed a total change in their demeanor. From absolute stupor, they appeared to be, all at once, aroused to the highest pitch of excitement, and rushed wildly about, going to and from a certain point on the beach, with the strangest expressions of mingled horror, rage, and intense curiosity depicted on their countenances, and shouting, at the top of their voices, *"Tekeli-li! Tekeli-li!"*

Presently we saw a large body go off into the hills, whence they returned in a short time, carrying stakes of wood. These they brought to the station where the crowd was the thickest, which now separated so as to afford us a view of the object of all this excitement. We perceived something white lying upon the ground, but could not immediately make out what it was. At length we saw that it was the carcass of the strange animal with the scarlet teeth and claws which the schooner had picked up at sea on the eighteenth of January. Captain Guy had had the body preserved for the purpose of stuffing the skin and taking it to England. I remember he had given some directions about it just before our making the island, and it had been brought into the cabin and stowed away in one of the lockers. It had now been thrown on shore by the explosion; but why it had occasioned so much concern among the savages was more than we could comprehend. Although they crowded around the carcass at a little distance, none of them seemed willing to approach it closely. By and by the men with the stakes drove them in a circle around it, and, no sooner was this arrangement completed, than

the whole of the vast assemblage rushed into the interior
of the island, with loud screams of *"Tekeli-li! Tekeli-li!"*

CHAPTER XXIII

DURING the six or seven days immediately following we
remained in our hiding-place upon the hill, going out
only occasionally, and then with the greatest precaution,
for water and filberts. We had made a kind of pent-
house on the platform, furnishing it with a bed of dry
leaves, and placing in it three large flat stones, which
served us for both fireplace and table. We kindled a fire
without difficulty by rubbing two pieces of dry wood
together, the one soft, the other hard. The bird we had
taken in such good season proved excellent eating, al-
though somewhat tough. It was not an oceanic fowl, but
a species of bittern, with jet black and grizzly plumage,
and diminutive wings in proportion to its bulk. We after-
ward saw three of the same kind in the vicinity of the
ravine, apparently seeking for the one we had captured;
but, as they never alighted, we had no opportunity of
catching them.

As long as this fowl lasted we suffered nothing from
our situation, but it was now entirely consumed, and it
became absolutely necessary that we should look out for
provision. The filberts would not satisfy the cravings of
hunger, afflicting us, too, with severe gripings of the
bowels, and, if freely indulged in, with violent headache.
We had seen several large tortoises near the sea-shore
to the eastward of the hill, and perceived they might be
easily taken, if we could get at them without the observa-
tion of the natives. It was resolved, therefore, to make an
attempt at descending.

We commenced by going down the southern declivity,
which seemed to offer the fewest difficulties, but had not
proceeded a hundred yards before (as we had anticipated
from appearances on the hilltop) our progress was en-
tirely arrested by a branch of the gorge in which our
companions had perished. We now passed along the edge
of this for about a quarter of a mile, when we were
again stopped by a precipice of immense depth, and,
not being able to make our way along the brink of it,
we were forced to retrace our steps by the main ravine.

We now pushed over to the eastward, but with precisely similar fortune. After an hour's scramble, at the risk of breaking our necks, we discovered that we had merely descended into a vast pit of black granite, with fine dust at the bottom, and whence the only egress was by the rugged path in which we had come down. Toiling again up this path, we now tried the northern edge of the hill. Here we were obliged to use the greatest possible caution in our manœuvres, as the least indiscretion would expose us to the full view of the savages in the village. We crawled along, therefore, on our hands and knees, and, occasionally, were even forced to throw ourselves at full length, dragging our bodies along by means of the shrubbery. In this careful manner we had proceeded but a little way, when we arrived at a chasm far deeper than any we had yet seen, and leading directly into the main gorge. Thus our fears were fully confirmed, and we found ourselves cut off entirely from access to the world below. Thoroughly exhausted by our exertions, we made the best of our way back to the platform, and, throwing ourselves upon the bed of leaves, slept sweetly and soundly for some hours.

For several days after this fruitless search we were occupied in exploring every part of the summit of the hill, in order to inform ourselves of its actual resources. We found that it would afford us no food, with the exception of the unwholesome filberts, and a rank species of scurvy-grass, which grew in a little patch of not more than four rods square, and would be soon exhausted. On the fifteenth of February, as near as I can remember, there was not a blade of this left, and the nuts were growing scarce; our situation, therefore, could hardly be more lamentable.[1] On the sixteenth we again went round the walls of our prison, in hope of finding some avenue of escape; but to no purpose. We also descended the chasm in which we had been overwhelmed, with the faint expectation of discovering, through this channel, some opening to the main ravine. Here, too, we were disappointed, although we found and brought up with us a musket.

On the seventeenth we set out with the determination

[1] This day was rendered remarkable by our observing in the south several huge wreaths of the grayish vapor I have before spoken of.

of examining more thoroughly the chasm of black granite into which we had made our way in the first search. We remembered that one of the fissures in the sides of this pit had been but partially looked into, and we were anxious to explore it, although with no expectation of discovering here any opening.

We found no great difficulty in reaching the bottom of the hollow as before, and were now sufficiently calm to survey it with some attention. It was, indeed, one of the most singular-looking places imaginable, and we could scarcely bring ourselves to believe it altogether the work of nature. The pit, from its eastern to its western extremity, was about five hundred yards in length, when all its windings were threaded; the distance from east to west in a straight line not being more (I should suppose, having no means of accurate examination) than forty or fifty yards. Upon first descending into the chasm—that is to say, for a hundred feet downward from the summit of the hill, the sides of the abyss bore little resemblance to each other, and, apparently, had at no time been connected, the one surface being of the soapstone, and the other of marl, granulated with some metallic matter. The average breadth or interval between the two cliffs was probably here sixty feet, but there seemed to be no regularity of formation. Passing down, however, beyond the limit spoken of, the interval rapidly contracted, and the sides began to run parallel, although, for some distance farther, they were still dissimilar in their material and form of surface. Upon arriving within fifty feet of the bottom, a perfect regularity commenced. The sides were now entirely uniform in substance, in color, and in lateral direction, the material being a very black and shining granite, and the distance between the two sides, at all points, facing each other, exactly twenty yards. The precise formation of the chasm will be best understood by means of a delineation taken upon the spot; for I had luckily with me a pocket-book and pencil, which I preserved with great care through a long series of subsequent adventure, and to which I am indebted for memoranda of many subjects which would otherwise have been crowded from my remembrance.

This figure (see fig. 1) gives the general outlines of the chasm, without the minor cavities in the sides, of which

FIG. 1.

there were several, each cavity having a corresponding protuberance opposite. The bottom of the gulf was covered to the depth of three or four inches with a powder almost impalpable, beneath which we found a continuation of the black granite. To the right, at the lower extremity, will be noticed the appearance of a small opening; this is the fissure alluded to above, and to examine which more minutely than before was the object of our second visit. We now pushed into it with vigor, cutting away a quantity of brambles which impeded us, and removing a vast heap of sharp flints somewhat resembling arrow-heads in shape. We were encouraged to persevere, however, by perceiving some little

FIG. 2

light proceeding from the farther end. We at length squeezed our way for about thirty feet, and found that the aperture was a low and regularly formed arch, having a bottom of the same impalpable powder as that in the main chasm. A strong light now broke upon us, and, turning a short bend, we found ourselves in another lofty chamber, similar to the one we had left in every respect but longitudinal in form. Its general figure is here given. (See fig. 2.)

The total length of this chasm, commencing at the opening *a* and proceeding round the curve *b* to the extremity *d,* is five hundred and fifty yards. At *c* we discovered a small aperture similar to the one through which we had issued from the other chasm, and this was choked up in the same manner with brambles and a quantity of the white arrow-head flints. We forced our way through it, finding it about forty feet long, and emerged into a third chasm. This, too, was precisely like the first, except in its longitudinal shape, which was thus. (See fig. 3.)

We found the entire length of the third chasm three hundred and twenty yards. At the point *a* was an opening

FIG. 3 FIG. 5

about six feet wide, and extending fifteen feet into the rock, where it terminated in a bed of marl, there being no other chasm beyond, as we had expected. We were about leaving this fissure, into which very little light was admitted, when Peters called my attention to a range of singular-looking indentures in the surface of the marl forming the termination of the *cul-de-sac*. With a very slight exertion of the imagination, the left, or most northern of these indentures might have been taken for the intentional, although rude, representation of a human figure standing erect, with out-stretched arm. The rest of them bore also some little resemblance to

alphabetical characters, and Peters was willing, at all events, to adopt the idle opinion that they were really such. I convinced him of his error, finally, by directing his attention to the floor of the fissure, where, among the powder, we picked up, piece by piece, several large flakes of the marl, which had evidently been broken off by some convulsion from the surface where the indentures were found, and which had projecting points exactly fitting the indentures; thus proving them to have been the work of nature. Fig. 4 presents an accurate copy of the whole.

FIG. 4

After satisfying ourselves that these singular caverns afforded us no means of escape from our prison, we made our way back, dejected and dispirited, to the summit of the hill. Nothing worth mentioning occurred during the next twenty-four hours, except that, in examining the ground to the eastward of the third chasm, we found two triangular holes of great depth, and also with black granite sides. Into these holes we did not think it worth while to attempt descending, as they had the appearance of mere natural wells, without outlet. They were each about twenty yards in circumference, and their shape, as well as relative position in regard to the third chasm, is shown in figure 5, page 358.

CHAPTER XXIV

ON THE twentieth of the month, finding it altogether impossible to subsist any longer upon the filberts, the use of which occasioned us the most excruciating torment, we resolved to make a desperate attempt at descending

the southern declivity of the hill. The face of the precipice was here of the softest species of soapstone, although nearly perpendicular throughout its whole extent (a depth of a hundred and fifty feet at the least), and in many places even overarching. After a long search we discovered a narrow ledge about twenty feet below the brink of the gulf; upon this Peters contrived to leap, with what assistance I could render him by means of our pocket-handkerchiefs tied together. With somewhat more difficulty I also got down; and we then saw the possibility of descending the whole way by the process in which we had clambered up from the chasm when we had been buried by the fall of the hill—that is, by cutting steps in the face of the soapstone with our knives. The extreme hazard of the attempt can scarcely be conceived; but, as there was no other resource, we determined to undertake it.

Upon the ledge where we stood there grew some filbert-bushes; and to one of these we made fast an end of our rope of handkerchiefs. The other end being tied round Peters' waist, I lowered him down over the edge of the precipice until the handkerchiefs were stretched tight. He now proceeded to dig a deep hole in the soapstone (as far in as eight or ten iches), sloping away the rock above to the height of a foot, or thereabout, so as to allow of his driving, with the butt of a pistol, a tolerably strong peg into the levelled surface. I then drew him up for about four feet, when he made a hole similar to the one below, driving in a peg as before, and having thus a resting-place for both feet and hands. I now unfastened the handkerchiefs from the bush, throwing him the end, which he tied to the peg in the uppermost hole, letting himself down gently to a station about three feet lower than he had yet been—that is, to the full extent of the handkerchiefs. Here he dug another hole, and drove another peg. He then drew himself up, so as to rest his feet in the hole just cut, taking hold with his hands upon the peg in the one above. It was now necessary to untie the handkerchiefs from the topmost peg, with the view of fastening them to the second; and here he found that an error had been committed in cutting the holes at so great a distance apart. However, after one or two unsuccessful and dangerous attempts at

reaching the knot (having to hold on with his left hand
while he labored to undo the fastening with his right),
he at length cut the string, leaving six inches of it affixed
to the peg. Tying the handkerchiefs now to the second
peg, he descended to a station below the third, taking
care not to go too far down. By these means (means
which I should never have conceived of myself, and for
which we were indebted altogether to Peters' ingenuity
and resolution) my companion finally succeeded, with the
occasional aid of projections in the cliff, in reaching the
bottom without accident.

It was some time before I could summon sufficient
resolution to follow him; but I did at length attempt it.
Peters had taken off his shirt before descending, and
this, with my own, formed the rope necessary for the
adventure. After throwing down the musket found in the
chasm, I fastened this rope to the bushes, and let myself
down rapidly, striving, by the vigor of my movements, to
banish the trepidation which I could overcome in no other
manner. This answered sufficiently well for the first four
or five steps; but presently I found my imagination grow-
ing terribly excited by thoughts of the vast depths yet to
be descended, and the precarious nature of the pegs and
soapstone holes which were my only support. It was in
vain I endeavored to banish these reflections, and to
keep my eyes steadily bent upon the flat surface of the
cliff before me. The more earnestly I struggled *not to
think,* the more intensely vivid became my conceptions,
and the more horribly distinct. At length arrived that
crisis of fancy, so fearful in all similar cases, the crisis
in which we begin to anticipate the feelings with which
we *shall* fall—to picture to ourselves the sickness, and
dizziness, and the last struggle, and the half swoon, and
the final bitterness of the rushing and headlong descent.
And now I found these fancies creating their own real-
ities, and all imagined horrors crowding upon me in
fact. I felt my knees strike violently together, while my
fingers were gradually but certainly relaxing their grasp.
There was a ringing in my ears, and I said, "This is my
knell of death!" And now I was consumed with the
irrepressible desire of looking below. I could not, I
would not, confine my glances to the cliff; and, with a
wild, indefinable emotion, half of horror, half of a re-

lieved oppression, I threw my vision far down into the
abyss. For one moment my fingers clutched convulsive-
ly upon their hold, while, with the movement, the faintest
possible idea of ultimate escape wandered, like a shadow,
through my mind—in the next my whole soul was pre-
vaded with a *longing to fall*; a desire, a yearning, a pas-
sion utterly uncontrollable. I let go at once my grasp
upon the peg, and, turning half round from the precipice,
remained tottering for an instant against its naked face.
But now there came a spinning of the brain; a shrill-
sounding and phantom voice screamed within my ears;
a dusky, fiendish, and filmy figure stood immediately
beneath me; and, sighing, I sunk down with a bursting
heart, and plunged within its arms.

I had swooned, and Peters had caught me as I fell.
He had observed my proceedings from his station at the
bottom of the cliff; and perceiving my imminent danger,
had endeavored to inspire me with courage by every
suggestion he could devise; although my confusion of
mind had been so great as to prevent my hearing what
he said, or being conscious that he had even spoken to
me at all. At length, seeing me totter, he hastened to
ascend to my rescue, and arrived just in time for my
preservation. Had I fallen with my full weight, the rope
of linen would inevitably have snapped, and I should have
been precipitated into the abyss; as it was, he contrived
to let me down gently, so as to remain suspended with-
out danger until animation returned. This was in about
fifteen minutes. On recovery, my trepidation had en-
tirely vanished; I felt a new being, and, with some little
further aid from my companion, reached the bottom also
in safety.

We now found ourselves not far from the ravine
which had proved the tomb of our friends, and to the
southward of the spot where the hill had fallen. The
place was one of singular wildness, and its aspect brought
to my mind the descriptions given by travellers of those
dreary regions marking the site of degraded Babylon.
Not to speak of the ruins of the disruptured cliff, which
formed a chaotic barrier in the vista to the northward,
the surface of the ground in every other direction was
strewn with huge tumuli, apparently the wreck of some
gigantic structures of art; although, in detail, no sem-

blance of art could be detected. Scoria were abundant, and large shapeless blocks of the black granite, intermingled with others of marl,[1] and both granulated with metal. Of vegetation there were no traces whatsoever throughout the whole of the desolate area within sight. Several immense scorpions were seen, and various reptiles not elsewhere to be found in the high latitudes.

As food was our most immediate object, we resolved to make our way to the sea-coast, distant not more than half a mile, with a view of catching turtle, several of which we had observed from our place of concealment on the hill. We had proceeded some hundred yards, threading our route cautiously between the huge rocks and tumuli, when, upon turning a corner, five savages sprung upon us from a small cavern, felling Peters to the ground with a blow from a club. As he fell the whole party rushed upon him to secure their victim, leaving me time to recover from my astonishment. I still had the musket, but the barrel had received so much injury in being thrown from the precipice that I cast it aside as useless, preferring to trust my pistols, which had been carefully preserved in order. With these I advanced upon the assailants, firing one after the other in quick succession. Two savages fell, and one, who was in the act of thrusting a spear into Peters, sprung to his feet without accomplishing his purpose. My companion being thus released, we had no further difficulty. He had his pistols also, but prudently declined using them, confiding in his great personal strength, which far exceeded that of any person I have ever known. Seizing a club from one of the savages who had fallen, he dashed out the brains of the three who remained, killing each instantaneously with a single blow of the weapon, and leaving us completely masters of the field.

So rapidly had these events passed, that we could scarcely believe in their reality, and were standing over the bodies of the dead in a species of stupid contemplation, when we were brought to recollection by the sound of shouts in the distance. It was clear that the savages had been alarmed by the firing, and that we had little

[1] The marl was also black; indeed, we noticed no light-colored substances of any kind upon the island.

chance of avoiding discovery. To regain the cliff, it would
be necessary to proceed in the direction of the shouts;
and even should we succeed in arriving at its base, we
should never be able to ascend it without being seen.
Our situation was one of the greatest peril, and we were
hesitating in which path to commence a flight, when one
of the savages whem I had shot, and supposed dead,
sprang briskly to his feet, and attempted to make his
escape. We overtook him, however, before he had ad-
vanced many paces, and were about to put him to death,
when Peters suggested that we might derive some benefit
from forcing him to accompany us in our attempt to
escape. We therefore dragged him with us, making him
understand that we would shoot him if he offered resis-
tance. In a few minutes he was perfectly submissive, and
ran by our sides as we pushed in among the rocks, mak-
ing for the seashore.

So far, the irregularities of the ground we had been
traversing hid the sea, except at intervals, from our
sight, and, when we first had it fairly in view, it was, per-
haps, two hundred yards distant. As we emerged into
the open beach we saw, to our great dismay, an im-
mense crowd of the natives pouring from the village, and
from all visible quarters of the island, making toward us
with gesticulations of extreme fury, and howling like
wild beasts. We were upon the point of turning upon our
steps, and trying to secure a retreat among the fastnesses
of the rougher ground, when I discovered the bows of two
canoes projecting from behind a large rock which ran
out into the water. Toward these we now ran with all
speed, and, reaching them, found them unguarded, and
without any other freight than three of the large Galli-
pago turtles and the usual supply of paddles for sixty
rowers. We instantly took possession of one of them, and,
forcing our captive on board, pushed out to sea with
all the strength we could command.

We had not made, however, more than fifty yards
from the shore before we became sufficiently calm to
perceive the great oversight of which we had been guilty
in leaving the other canoe in the power of the savages,
who, by this time, were not more than twice as far
from the beach as ourselves, and were rapidly advancing
to the pursuit. No time was now to be lost. Our hope was,

at best, a forlorn one, but we had none other. It was very doubtful whether, with the utmost exertion, we could get back in time to anticipate them in taking possession of the canoe; but yet there was a chance that we could. We might save ourselves if we succeeded, while not to make the attempt was to resign ourselves to inevitable butchery.

The canoe was modelled with the bow and stern alike, and, in place of turning it around, we merely changed our position in paddling. As soon as the savages perceived this they redoubled their yells, as well as their speed, and approached with inconceivable rapidity. We pulled, however, with all the energy of desperation, and arrived at the contested point before more than one of the natives had attained it. This man paid dearly for his superior agility, Peters shooting him through the head with a pistol as he approached the shore. The foremost among the rest of his party were probably some twenty or thirty paces distant as we seized upon the canoe. We at first endeavored to pull her into the deep water, beyond the reach of the savages, but, finding her too firmly aground, and there being no time to spare, Peters, with one or two heavy strokes from the butt of the musket, succeeded in dashing out a large portion of the bow and of one side. We then pushed off. Two of the natives by this time had got hold of our boat, obstinately refusing to let go, until we were forced to dispatch them with our knives. We were now clear off, and making great way out to sea. The main body of the savages, upon reaching the broken canoe, set up the most tremendous yell of rage and disappointment conceivable. In truth, from every thing I could see of these wretches, they appeared to be the most wicked, hypocritical, vindictive, bloodthirsty, and altogether fiendish race of men upon the face of the globe. It is clear we should have had no mercy had we fallen into their hands. They made a mad attempt at following us in the fractured canoe, but, finding it useless, again vented their rage in a series of hideous vociferations, and rushed up into the hills.

We were thus relieved from immediate danger, but our situation was still sufficiently gloomy. We knew that four canoes of the kind we had were at one time in the

possession of the savages, and were not aware of the
fact (afterward ascertained from our captive) that two
of these had been blown to pieces in the explosion of
the Jane Guy. We calculated, therefore, upon being yet
pursued, as soon as our enemies could get round to the
bay (distant about three miles) where the boats were
usually laid up. Fearing this, we made every exertion to
leave the island behind us, and went rapidly through the
water, forcing the prisoner to take a paddle. In about
half an hour, when we had gained, probably, five or six
miles to the southward, a large fleet of the flat-bottomed
canoes or rafts were seen to emerge from the bay evi-
dently with the design of pursuit. Presently they put
back, despairing to overtake us.

CHAPTER XXV

We now found ourselves in the wide and desolate Ant-
arctic Ocean, in a latitude exceeding eighty-four degrees,
in a frail canoe, and with no provision but the three
turtles. The long polar winter, too, could not be consid-
ered as far distant, and it became necessary that we
should deliberate well upon the course to be pursued.
There were six or seven islands in sight belonging to the
same group, and distant from each other about five or
six leagues; but upon neither of these had we any inten-
tion to venture. In coming from the northward in the
Jane Guy we had been gradually leaving behind us the
severest regions of ice—this, however little it may be in
accordance with the generally received notions respect-
ing the Antarctic, was a fact experience would not per-
mit us to deny. To attempt, therefore, getting back would
be folly—especially at so late a period of the season.
Only one course seemed to be left open for hope. We re-
solved to steer boldly to the southward, where there
was at least a probability of discovering other lands, and
more than a probability of finding a still milder climate.

So far we had found the Antarctic, like the Arctic
Ocean, peculiarly free from violent storms or immod-
erately rough water; but our canoe was, at best, of frail
structure, although large, and we set busily to work with
a view of rendering her as safe as the limited means in

our possession would admit. The body of the boat was
of no better material than bark—the bark of a tree un-
known. The ribs were of a tough osier, well adapted to
the purpose for which it was used. We had fifty feet
room from stem to stern, from four to six in breadth, and
in depth throughout four feet and a half—the boats
thus differing vastly in shape from those of any other
inhabitants of the Southern Ocean with whom civilized
nations are acquainted. We never did believe them the
workmanship of the ignorant islanders who owned them;
and some days after this period discovered, by question-
ing our captive, that they were in fact made by the na-
tives of a group to the southwest of the country where we
found them, having fallen accidentally into the hands
of our barbarians. What we could do for the security of
our boat was very little indeed. Several wide rents were
discovered near both ends, and these we contrived to
patch up with pieces of woollen jacket. With the help of
the superfluous paddles, of which there were a great
many, we erected a kind of framework about the bow, so
as to break the force of any seas which might threaten
to fill us in that quarter. We also set up two paddle-
blades for masts, placing them opposite each other, one
by each gunwale, thus saving the necessity of a yard. To
these masts we attached a sail made of our shirts—
doing this with some difficulty, as here we could get no
assistance from our prisoner whatever, although he had
been willing enough to labor in all the other operations.
The sight of the linen seemed to affect him in a very
singular manner. He could not be prevailed upon to
touch it or go near it, shuddering when we attempted to
force him, and shrieking out, *"Tekeli-li!"*

Having completed our arrangements in regard to the
security of the canoe, we now set sail to the south-south-
east for the present, with the view of weathering the
most southerly of the group in sight. This being done,
we turned the bow full to the southward. The weather
could by no means be considered disagreeable. We had
a prevailing and very gentle wind from the northward,
a smooth sea, and continual daylight. No ice whatever
was to be seen; *nor did I ever see one particle of this
after leaving the parallel of Bennet's Islet.* Indeed, the
temperature of the water was here far too warm for its

existence in any quantity. Having killed the largest of our
tortoises, and obtained from him not only food but a
copious supply of water, we continued on our course,
without any incident of moment, for perhaps seven or
eight days, during which period we must have proceeded
a vast distance to the southward, as the wind blew con-
stantly with us, and a very strong current set continually
in the direction we were pursuing.

 March 1st.[1]—Many unusual phenomena now indi-
cated that we were entering upon a region of novelty and
wonder. A high range of light gray vapor appeared con-
stantly in the southern horizon, flaring up occasionally
in lofty streaks, now darting from east to west, now from
west to east, and again presenting a level and uniform
summit—in short, having all the wild variations of the
Aurora Borealis. The average height of this vapor, as
apparent from our station, was about twenty-five de-
grees. The temperature of the sea seemed to be increas-
ing momentarily, and there was a very perceptible altera-
tion in its color.

 March 2d.—To-day by repeated questioning of our
captive, we came to the knowledge of many particulars
in regard to the island of the massacre, its inhabitants,
and customs—but with these how can I *now* detain the
reader? I may say, however, that we learned there were
eight islands in the group—that they were governed by
a common king, named *Tsalemon* or *Psalemoun,* who
resided in one of the smallest of the islands; that the
black skins forming the dress of the warriors came from
an animal of huge size to be found only in a valley near
the court of the king—that the inhabitants of the group
fabricated no other boats than the flat-bottomed rafts;
the four canoes being all of the kind in their possession,
and these having been obtained, by mere accident, from
some large island in the southwest—that his own name
was Nu-Nu—that he had no knowledge of Bennet's Islet
—and that the appellation of the island he had left was
Tsalal. The commencement of the words *Tsalemon* and
Tsalal was given with a prolonged hissing sound, which

[1] For obvious reasons I cannot pretend to strict accuracy in
these dates. They are given principally with a view to perspicuity
of narration, and as set down in my pencil memorandum.

we found it impossible to imitate, even after repeated endeavors, and which was precisely the same with the note of the black bittern we had eaten up on the summit of the hill.

March 3d.—The heat of the water was now truly remarkable, and in color was undergoing a rapid change, being no longer transparent, but of a milky consistency and hue. In our immediate vicinity it was usually smooth, never so rough as to endanger the canoe—but we were frequently surprised at perceiving, to our right and left, at different distances, sudden and extensive agitations of the surface—these, we at length noticed, were always preceded by wild flickerings in the region of the vapor to the southward.

March 4th.—To-day, with the view of widening our sail, the breeze from the northward dying away perceptibly, I took from my coat-pocket a white handkerchief. Nu-Nu was seated at my elbow, and the linen accidentally flaring in his face, he became violently affected with convulsions. These were succeeded by drowsiness and stupor, and low murmurings of *"Tekeli-li! Tekeli-li!"*

March 5th.—The wind had entirely ceased, but it was evident that we were still hurrying on to the southward, under the influence of a powerful current. And now, indeed, it would seem reasonable that we should experience some alarm at the turn events were taking—but we felt none. The countenance of Peters indicated nothing of this nature, although it wore at times an expression I could not fathom. The polar winter appeared to be coming on—but coming without its terrors. I felt a *numbness* of body and mind—a dreaminess of sensation—but this was all.

March 6th.—The gray vapor had now arisen many more degrees above the horizon, and was gradually losing its grayness of tint. The heat of the water was extreme, even unpleasant to the touch, and its milky hue was more evident than ever. To-day a violent agitation of the water occurred very close to the canoe. It was attended, as usual, with a wild flaring up of the vapor at its summit, and a momentary division at its base. A fine white powder, resembling ashes—but certainly not such —fell over the canoe and over a large surface of the water, as the flickering died away among the vapor and

the commotion subsided in the sea. Nu-Nu now threw himself on his face in the bottom of the boat, and no persuasions could induce him to arise.

March 7th.—This day we questioned Nu-Nu concerning the motives of his countrymen in destroying our companions; but he appeared to be too utterly overcome by terror to afford us any rational reply. He still obstinately lay in the bottom of the boat; and, upon our reiterating the questions as to the motive, made use only of idiotic gesticulations, such as raising with his forefinger the upper lip, and displaying the teeth which lay beneath it. These were black. We had never before seen the teeth of an inhabitant of Tsalal.

March 8th.—To-day there floated by us one of the white animals whose appearance upon the beach at Tsalal had occasioned so wild a commotion among the savages. I would have picked it up, but there came over me a sudden listlessness, and I forbore. The heat of the water still increased, and the hand could no longer be endured within it. Peters spoke little, and I knew not what to think of his apathy. Nu-Nu breathed, and no more.

March 9th.—The whole ashy material fell now continually around us, and in vast quantities. The range of vapor to the southward had arisen prodigiously in the horizon, and began to assume more distinctness of form. I can liken it to nothing but a limitless cataract, rolling silently into the sea from some immense and far-distant rampart in the heaven. The gigantic curtain ranged along the whole extent of the southern horizon. It emitted no sound.

March 21st.—A sullen darkness now hovered above us —but from out the milky depths of the ocean a luminous glare arose, and stole up along the bulwarks of the boat. We were nearly overwhelmed by the white ashy shower which settled upon us and upon the canoe, but melted into the water as it fell. The summit of the cataract was utterly lost in the dimness and the distance. Yet we were evidently approaching it with a hideous velocity. At intervals there were visible in it wide, yawning, but momentary rents, and from out these rents, within which was a chaos of flitting and indistinct images, there came rushing and mighty, but soundless winds, tearing up the enkindled ocean in their course.

March 22d.—The darkness had materially increased, relieved only by the glare of the water thrown back from the white curtain before us. Many gigantic and pallidly white birds flew continuously now from beyond the veil, and their scream was the eternal *Tekeli-li!* as they retreated from our vision. Hereupon Nu-Nu stirred in the bottom of the boat; but upon touching him, we found his spirit departed. And now we rushed into the embraces of the cataract, where a chasm threw itself open to receive us. But there arose in our pathway a shrouded human figure, very far larger in its proportions than any dweller among men. And the hue of the skin of the figure was of the perfect whiteness of the snow.

NOTE

THE circumstances connected with the late sudden and distressing death of Mr. Pym are already well known to the public through the medium of the daily press. It is feared that the few remaining chapters which were to have completed his narrative, and which were retained by him, while the above were in type, for the purpose of revision, have been irrecoverably lost through the accident by which he perished himself. This, however, may prove not to be the case, and the papers, if ultimately found, will be given to the public.

No means have been left untried to remedy the deficiency. The gentleman whose name is mentioned in the preface, and who, from the statement there made, might be supposed able to fill the vacuum, has declined the task—this, for satisfactory reasons connected with the general inaccuracy of the details afforded him, and his disbelief in the entire truth of the latter portions of the narration. Peters, from whom some information might be expected, is still alive, and a resident of Illinois, but cannot be met with at present. He may hereafter be found, and will, no doubt, afford material for a conclusion of Mr. Pym's account.

The loss of two or three final chapters (for there were but two or three) is the more deeply to be regretted, as, it cannot be doubted, they contained matter relative to the Pole itself, or at least to regions in its very near proximity; and as, too, the statements of the author in relation to these regions may shortly be verified or contradicted by means of the governmental expedition now preparing for the Southern Ocean.

On one point in the narrative some remarks may well be offered; and it would afford the writer of this appendix much pleasure if what he may here observe should have a tendency to throw credit, in any degree, upon the very singular pages now published. We allude to the chasms found in the island of

Tsalal, and to the whole of the figures upon pages 357, 358, 359.

Mr. Pym has given the figures of the chasms without comment, and speaks decidedly of the *indentures* found at the extremity of the most easterly of these chasms as having but a fanciful resemblance to alphabetical characters, and, in short, as being positively *not such*. This assertion is made in a manner so simple, and sustained by a species of demonstration so conclusive (viz., the fitting of the projections of the fragments found among the dust into the indentures upon the wall), that we are forced to believe the writer in earnest; and no reasonable reader should suppose otherwise. But as the facts in relation to *all* the figures are most singular (especially when taken in connection with statements made in the body of the narrative), it may be as well to say a word or two concerning them all—this, too, the more especially as the facts in question have, beyond doubt, escaped the attention of Mr. Poe.

Figure 1, then, figure 2, figure 3, and figure 5, when conjoined with one another in the precise order which the chasms themselves presented, and when deprived of the small lateral branches or arches (which, it will be remembered, served only as a means of communication between the main chambers, and were of totally distinct character), constitute an Ethiopian verbal root—the root ⟨ A ⟩ "To be shady,"—whence all the inflections of shadow or darkness.

In regard to the "left or most northwardly" of the indentures in figure 4, it is more than probable that the opinion of Peters was correct, and that the hieroglyphical appearance was really the work of art, and intended as the representation of a human form. The delineation is before the reader, and he may, or may not, perceive the resemblance suggested; but the rest of the indentures afford strong confirmation of Peters' idea. The upper range is evidently the Arabic verbal root ⟨ ⟩ "To be white," whence all the inflections of brilliancy and whiteness. The lower range is not so immediately perspicuous. The characters are somewhat broken and disjointed; nevertheless, it cannot be doubted that, in their perfect state, they formed the full Egyptian word Π & Ψ Ψ Φ Η Ϲ , "The region of the south." It should be observed that these interpretations confirm the opinion of Peters in regard to the "most northwardly" of the figures. The arm is outstretched toward the south.

Conclusions such as these open a wide field for speculation and exciting conjecture. They should be regarded, perhaps, in connection with some of the most faintly-detailed incidents of the narrative; although in no visible manner is this chain of connection complete. Tekeli-li! was the cry of the affrighted natives of Tsalal upon discovering the carcass of the *white* animal picked up at sea. This also was the shuddering exclamation of the captive Tsalalian upon encountering the *white* materials in possession of Mr. Pym. This also was the shriek of the swift-flying, *white*, and gigantic birds which issued from the vapory

white curtain of the South. Nothing *white* was to be found at Tsalal, and nothing otherwise in the subsequent voyage to the region beyond. It is not impossible that "Tsalal," the appellation of the island of the chasms, may be found, upon minute philological scrutiny, to betray either some alliance with the chasms themselves, or some reference to the Ethiopian characters so mysteriously written in their windings.

"I have graven it within the hills and my vengeance upon the dust within the rock."

come a writer, juvenilia up to 1931 or so ... clearly to
have a strong flavor of Poe; since then, Hemingway,
Sartre, or Eliot shows most clearly ... all of us who are
ble should have read. Now, but none of us has ever rol

Afterword

One of the extraordinary things about Poe is that in our own country he has been most popular with the young. Many a boy or girl, on reading him, has wanted to become a writer. Juvenilia up to 1920 or so were likely to have a strong flavor of Poe; since then, Hemingway, Salinger, or Eliot shows most clearly. All of us who are old enough have used Poe, but none of us has ever got to be a better writer—a manager of words—by that use. On the other hand, great writers in France—Baudelaire, Rimbaud, Mallarmé, Valéry—made out of Poe a great figure and, indeed, a master craftsman, whom it is very difficult for us to recognize in his own language. This difficulty bothers T. S. Eliot in his essay "From Poe to Valéry," and it is another version of this difficulty that seems to have led Allen Tate to write his two deeply grasping essays, "The Angelic Imagination," and "Our Cousin, Mr. Poe"—an essay which he ends with this sentence: "He is so close to me that I am sometimes tempted to enter the mists of pre-American genealogy to find out whether he may not actually be my cousin."

Those who feel this temptation should go to Mr. Tate; they will see how genuine his temptation is and out of how near a reality it springs: the reality of the "undead" within us and the worse reality of the condition of the individual who sits in the place of God. My own speculations wish to look into a different dark corner. Children and young would-be writers read Poe with excitement, French poets find Poe a master—Valéry even finding "Eureka" genuine metaphysics. But we also find (in Eliot's words) that "If we examine his work in detail, we seem to find in it nothing but slipshod writing, puerile thinking unsupported by wide reading or profound scholarship, haphazard experiments in various

types of writing, chiefly under pressure of financial need, without perfection in any detail."

Eliot suggests that we must look at Poe's work as a whole, but that would not explain the excitement of the child or the admiration of the French. Children read one thing at a time perhaps even more than the rest of us, and the French poets named above are not thought to have loved slipshod writing or puerile thinking. Where then is the force in Poe that will explain the extremes of his active reputation? Let us say to begin with that Poe gives us a chance at a make-believe world and that he seems also to be about the business of remaking the world within his own scope if not quite in his own image, thus satisfying what children and French Symbolists are supposed to be up to. The important thing to say at once is that this force seems to operate as nearly as possible without regard to the language. At his best, like Blake on vision, his force works through, not with, the language. At his more ordinary levels, his force gains nothing and sometimes loses a good deal because of the language in which he deploys it. The words do not matter much but what does matter would not be there without them. It is rather like reading a love letter during a crisis in the affair; it would be meaningless to anyone but yourself, for it is only you who can know, however dubiously, the meaning that passes through the words without touching them. You must know ahead of time and also find afterwards the charge of force. Such letters can be very shattering, and so can be some of the tales and poems of Poe. Both raise make-believe to inclusive action and both require a world that cannot exist unless we create it.

Here we have vast resources. Mr. Tate, in his essay about "Our Cousin, Mr. Poe," remembers what he read as a child, and how he had so much to meet it with. I read Poe in Cambridge, Massachusetts, rather than in whatever part of the South Mr. Tate was a fourteen-year-old boy, and found different things to put into such tales as greatly struck me—say "The Cask of Amontillado" and "The Fall of the House of Usher." I thought then the cask might be found in the walled-up tunnel under Christ Church parish house, which Washington was supposed to have had ready for escape from the British, or if not there then in the secret passages

thought still to lurk in Warren House. Right now, I think it might be found under the lower church at Assisi. But I also remember the hysterical laughter which I gave to Poe's joke about Masons, for I had two uncles of that order, one diffident, the other diligent, and it seemed to me the diffident one, a doctor with black lustrous eyes and fierce mustaches, might play the mason with one of his patients as the Lord of Montresor did with Fortunato—for how did I know what either my uncle or I myself might do next?

"The Fall of the House of Usher" concerned more the force of the external world which might give way—on Cambridge Street between Quincy and Sumner Road —and we all fall into the gap. For the House of Usher was for us a square blank gray house, with shutters mainly drawn, and with a deeply recessed portico and an invisible colorless door. No one lived in it—though it was large enough for a great family and great entertainments—except a man to whom the owners had lent it and whom we identified with Roderick. The Lady Madeline was dubiously within; this we knew, for all the dubious signs were about, especially on gray or wintry days and at dusk. The resident emerged or disappeared within, as it seemed to us, without aid of the door, yet the door seemed just to have clanged. He was a dandy, as Roderick was, and our mothers warned us away from him. Later on I learned that he had one probable thing in common with Roderick, which was heraldry; but at the time he was an Usher throughout our expectant selves, and there was no night storm in which the house did not dilapidate in our hearts. As the narrator says of the "disordered fancy" of Roderick Usher, so it was with us. "The idea had assumed a more daring character, and trespassed, under certain conditions, upon the kingdom of disorganization." There the tarn was greedy to receive us along with the Ushers and their house.

"The Pit and the Pendulum" was more private. Neither the outer world nor any of my relatives had anything to do with it, and if the Inquisitor and his agents were in any way responsible it was in the role of the Holy Ghost of immediate evil. This sort of thing cannot be anywhere but in one's created self, and in the farce of horror that oneself knows. I think of the rats in the dungeon who had the formal job of chewing loose the vic-

tim's bandage which held him under the descending strokes of the pendulum. "Forth from the well they hurried in fresh troops. They clung to the wood—they overran it, and leaped in hundreds upon my person. The measured movement of the pendulum disturbed them not at all. Avoiding its strokes, they busied themselves with the anointed bandage. They pressed—they swarmed upon me in ever accumulating heaps. They writhed upon my throat; their cold lips sought my own; I was half stifled by their thronging pressure; disgust, for which the world has no name, swelled my bosom, and chilled, with a heavy clamminess, my heart." He was, of course, gnawed free, to find himself "in the grasp of the Inquisition." That bit about the cold lips of the rats is possible only in the self-welling farce of nightmare; and it is to this farce that Poe applied his method. He made a clear form out of nightmare, farce of spirit, and melodrama.

"The Pit and the Pendulum" will do as an archetype for the form, and if the reader wants another, where more of what we generally think of as the person is engaged, I suggest "William Wilson." There the identical twin of the self pursues the self, is slain, and slays the self. "I could have fancied that I myself was speaking," says the narrator. We are all familiar with our consciences pursuing us, and some of us know that there is a chance that our better selves might catch up with us —or even with just our behavior. William Wilson catches up with himself, and it is himself speaking, and a new form of the unforgivable sin has been discovered—new precisely because it is one's own. I remember how easily, at thirteen or fourteen, I could identify myself with both the William Wilsons—Eton, Oxford, riches, cheating at cards, Italian seductions, and all. I was as near them as Poe. I also remember, at the same age, running after dark as hard as I could and hearing in the pelt of my feet the avenging monster of my pursuing self; and here no doubt Poe and I were on the same footing.

It is easy and apt to say that all this is romanticism, obscurantism, symbolism, and, if you like, a retreat from humanity into an ideal realm where as much as possible of the human is left out. Yvor Winters, Leslie Fiedler, and D. H. Lawrence have in their different polemics said this very well. The Lady Madeline, or Lig-

eia, or Berenice will not do as a heroine or as a solvent
for passion, only as a fetish or a kind of taboo of the
self—something to stand for, or something to prevent,
the self, as the self commonly exists between the wind
and weather of daily life. There is a puerility about all
our visions of paradise, even the hellish ones; but there
is an attractive force in such visions which seems to be
only the greater because of their puerility, and in certain
moods of groundless anxiety or even of ordinary sloth
there are no visions we would rather see than these.
They have the advantage of giving the sense of extremity
and the sense of mystery (what people loosely call the
"mystical") without any initial cost beyond a surrender
to spontaneity. Illusions always seem free. Poe provides
us the near thing to such illusions and such visions in
forms which we can readily make our own without any
serious commitment precisely because Poe never made
them much *his* own, and never had in him, one thinks,
the capacity to make a commitment at all; he had no
grasp of the particular.

It is the particularity the reader brings that fills out
the form, whether as children out of their hereditary ac-
tive natures—so near the mistakes of their ancestors
—or as permanent adolescents. There is hardly anyone
who has not enough of the adolescent in him to appre-
hend as heroic the sentiments as the opening of "The
Assignation," and they will be very little devalued if we
call them the sentiments of the Byronic man. "Ill-fated
and mysterious man!—bewildered in the brilliancy of
thine own imagination, and fallen in the flames of thine
own youth!" And so on. Which of us has not the au-
thority in him to lend particularity to "The Assignation"
for the length of the tale? Who is not this hero? or if a
woman, who is not the Marchesa Aphrodite? The scene
is Venice, which was Poe's Venice because he did not
know it, and which is our Venice because we do not
know it: we can do anything we like with it so long as
we keep within the gothic and romantic frame. All that
counts when Poe's gondolier loses his single oar is the
idea of oarlessness. Nothing matters in Poe but the frame
of suasion. The authority is ours—almost the authorship
—which is not true of many writers we greatly admire,
but it is handy to have authors like Poe because we

can always feel equal to them. We do as much work as
they do.

I have been talking of the reaction to Poe which has to
do with his popularity, and now ask again how it was
that Baudelaire made him a great writer. Was it not
that Baudelaire wrote down his reaction and gave it, in
his French, the authority, the genuineness, to which it
never pretended in English, both in his actual transla-
tions and in his critical expansions? As readers we
make personal translations. Baudelaire made a permanent
and public translation, the difference being between his
sensibility and ours, and between Poe's command of Eng-
lish and Baudelaire's command of French. Poe provided
the opportunity, and Baudelaire provided the authority.
It is almost as if Poe were part of Baudelaire's juvenilia.
But it is also, and more important, as if Baudelaire could
see in a foreign language imperfectly understood not
only what was imperfectly present but could supply in
his translation what had never been there at all. He
made solid Poe's loose provision of opportunity. The
Italian *traduttore, traditore* for once does not apply.
The translation, rather, transfigures. This is a matter
worth much discussion since it touches on how it is that
all authors, to the degree that they command their lan-
guage with style, translate from one mode of thought to
another, in every act of writing, and perhaps more so
when they work in their native rather than a foreign
language. It is worth reflecting, too, that Baudelaire and
his successors down to Valéry got from Poe a leading
idea: that neither the intellect nor the language of a
writer need be committed to the understanding or the
use of the society which he intends to re-create or at
least to change. The French Symbolists made Poe into a
sacred book, and the original contents being thin and
frustrate, the gospel disappears more rapidly than usual
into the theology—but still affects their tone and bent.
There is something of Poe in the structure of culture that
contains the fusion of the senses and the purity of poe-
try, symbolism, and existentialism, the Ivory Tower and
the Ivory Cellar. Whether this concerns the substantive
nature of French culture I leave it to the French, and
their enemies, to say.*

* The reader may find an excessive account of the damage
Poe did to the French, and ourselves, in Mario Praz' *The Romantic
Agony*, or, for an earlier work, Max Nordau's *Degeneration*. But
these are the works of enemies who saw no fun.

If one wishes to withdraw from these high considerations, one can say that it was Poe who invited us in for an entertainment where our weaknesses became tottering strengths and our quaverings gasping cries—and that it was Baudelaire who closed the door of commitment, of seriousness, upon him and us. It is like the spirit of perverseness in "The Black Cat," the ventriloquy in "Thou Art the Man," the great ape in "The Murders in the Rue Morgue," or the blackness of the vegetation in "The Narrative of A. Gordon Pym"—they are all out of this world and do not touch it, or us, unless we invite them to do so. They are, so to speak, only reflections of a method in the results of which we believe only so long as we know they are impossible—like the ski tracks on both sides of the tree in Charles Addams' *New Yorker* cartoon of twenty years ago, or like Poe himself in "The Man that Was Used Up." It is partly the method of spiritual farce and partly the method of ratiocination and partly a lapse of humanity. Poe knew this, and something extra. F. O. Matthiessen makes a quotation I have not located. "Poe," he says, "once commented on his tales of ratiocination that 'people think them more ingenious than they are—on account of their method and *air* of method.'" Every reader will choose for himself what value to set on method and on the air of method as aspects of what was called above the frame of suasion. On the whole it is better to worry about method and the air of method—control and pretense of control—than it is to worry about the sort of thing that Walter Pater could say of Coleridge, from whom Poe got so much and whom, in a lesser way, he resembles (the difference being that Coleridge put more meaning into his words than most people and Poe put less). "More than Childe Harold, more than Werther, more than René himself, Coleridge, by what he did, what he was, and what he failed to do, represents that inexhaustible discontent, languor, and homesickness, that endless regret, the chords of which ring all through our modern literature." I do not mean that Pater would have written just this of Poe, but it does quite sufficiently for what people like Pater thought about Poe through the end of the first World War. I prefer either the French transfiguration or method and air of method.

Nevertheless all these points of view apply well enough

to Poe, and no doubt many more (as for example the view that the power in Poe is in his manipulation of the great archetypes of the human psyche in action) would apply with greater immediacy. But I do not think we want much immediacy for Poe; we want barriers and remedies: we do not want to enact what we see and we do want to be able to explain away, to disinfect, what we do see. We cannot be between sleep and waking all day. Perhaps Henry James was right when he complained of the unrelieved prodigies in most treatments of the supernatural. "Intrinsic values they have none—as we feel for instance in such a matter as the would-be portentous climax of Edgar Poe's 'Arthur Gordon Pym,' where the indispensable history is absent, where the phenomena evoked, the moving accidents, coming straight, as I say, are immediate and flat, and the attempt is all at the horrific in itself. The result is that, to my sense, the climax fails—fails because it stops short for want of connexions, There *are* no connexions; not only, I mean, in the sense of further statement, but of our own further relation to the elements, which hang in the void." James is perhaps right, yet Poe is nearer ordinary reality in "Pym" than in any of his stories except, perhaps, "Diddling." (In that story the possible edges into the impossible; in most others it is the impossible that trespasses.) "Pym" is based on and indeed includes a great deal of documentary material, and there are potential and virtual connections up to the very end, when a farce of nightmare descends, and we are left to grasp what shadows we will.

What shadows we will. But it is a maelstrom into which we shall never be wholly swept, for the most extreme addict is swept only into illusion. While we read, as while Poe composed, but not while he wrote, we have the habit of thinking the obscure richer than the clear, the recondite better than the known, the glamour better than the grammar, other reason better than our own, superstition better than religion, the inhuman better than the known human: just as we all have a permanent fear of being buried alive, and so would wish to destroy all of ourselves that could be injured walled up. These are barbarous games to which we are all prone, and the proneness shows in much of the literature which we

make popular but which does not reassure us: the liter-
ature which deals with our discontent with every prac-
ticed or practicable debauchery; the fruitless search for
the unseemly; the anxiety for the spiritual substitute for
physical failure; above all the foreknowledge, more a
fear than a knowledge, of the constant intruder, whom
Poe called the spirit of perverseness. One should almost
give the appropriate passage from "The Black Cat" in
Baudelaire's French, since he set great store by it and
quoted it separately; but we are not bound to the French
tradition. "And then came, as if to my final and irrevo-
cable overthrow, the spirit of PERVERSENESS. Of this spirit
philosophy takes no account. Yet I am not more sure
that my soul lives, than I am that perverseness is one of
the primitive impulses of the human heart—one of the
indivisible primary faculties, or sentiments, which give
direction to the character of Man. Who has not, a hun-
dred times, found himself committing a vile or a stupid
action, for no other reason than because he knows he
should *not*. Have we not a perpetual inclination, in the
teeth of our best judgment, to violate that which is *Law*,
merely because we understand it to be such? This spirit
of perverseness, I say, came to be my final overthrow. It
was this unfathomable longing of the soul *to vex itself*—
to offer violence to its own nature—to do wrong for the
wrong's sake only—that urged me to continue and final-
ly to consummate the injury I had inflicted upon the un-
offending brute." As it happened, the speaker only
hanged the cat from which he had already gouged one
eye; the sort of thing which one became acquainted
with in other children at the age of eight and in under-
graduates at eighteen or twenty. But what underlay or
overtopped it at other and ultimate ages, whatever ages
we like to call adult, was the subject of Poe's discourse
all his shortened life. We have a part in that.

 —R. P. BLACKMUR

SELECTED BIBLIOGRAPHY

WORKS BY EDGAR ALLAN POE

Tamerlane and Other Poems, 1827 Poems
Al Araf, Tamerlane, and Minor Poems, 1829 Poems
Poems: Second Edition, 1831 Poems
The Narrative of Arthur Gordon Pym, 1838 Novel
Tales of the Grotesque and Arabesque, 1840 Stories
Tales, 1845 Stories
The Raven and Other Poems, 1845 Poems
Eureka: A Prose Poem, 1848 Prose

BIOGRAPHY AND CRITICISM

Bonaparte, Marie. *The Life and Works of Edgar Allan Poe: A Psycho-Analytic Interpretation*. Foreword by Sigmund Freud. Trans. John Rodker. London: Imago, 1949.

Hoffman, Daniel. *Poe Poe Poe Poe Poe Poe Poe*. Garden City, N.Y.: Doubleday, 1972.

Jacobs, Robert D. *Poe: Journalist and Critic*. Baton Rouge: Louisiana State Univ. Press, 1969.

Krutch, Joseph Wood. *Edgar Allan Poe: A Study in Genius*. New York: Knopf, 1926.

Levin, Harry. *The Power of Blackness; Hawthorne, Poe, Melville*. New York: Knopf, 1958.

Miller, Perry. *The Raven and the Whale: The War of Words and Wits in the Era of Poe and Melville*. New York: Harcourt, Brace, 1956.

Porte, Joel. *The Romance in America*. Middletown, Connecticut: Wesleyan Univ. Press, 1969.

Quinn, Patrick F. *The French Face of Edgar Allan Poe*. Carbondale: Southern Illinois Univ. Press, 1957.

Rans, Geoffrey. *Edgar Allan Poe*. Edinburgh: Oliver and Boyd, 1965.

Regan, Robert. *Poe: A Collection of Critical Essays*. Englewood Cliffs, N.J.: Prentice-Hall, 1967.

Stovall, Floyd. *Edgar Poe the Poet: Essays New and Old on the Man and His Work*. Charlottesville: Univ. Press of Virginia, 1969.

Thompson, G. R. *Poe's Fiction: Romantic Irony in the Gothic Tales*. Madison: Univ. of Wisconsin Press, 1973.

Wagenknecht, Edward. *Edgar Allan Poe: The Man Behind the Legend*. New York: Oxford Univ. Press, 1963.

Wilson, Edmund. "Poe at Home and Abroad," In his *The Shores of Light*. New York: Farrar, Straus and Young, 1952, pp. 179–190.